image® comics presents

SKULL KICKERS

INFINITE ICONS of the ENDLESS EPIC

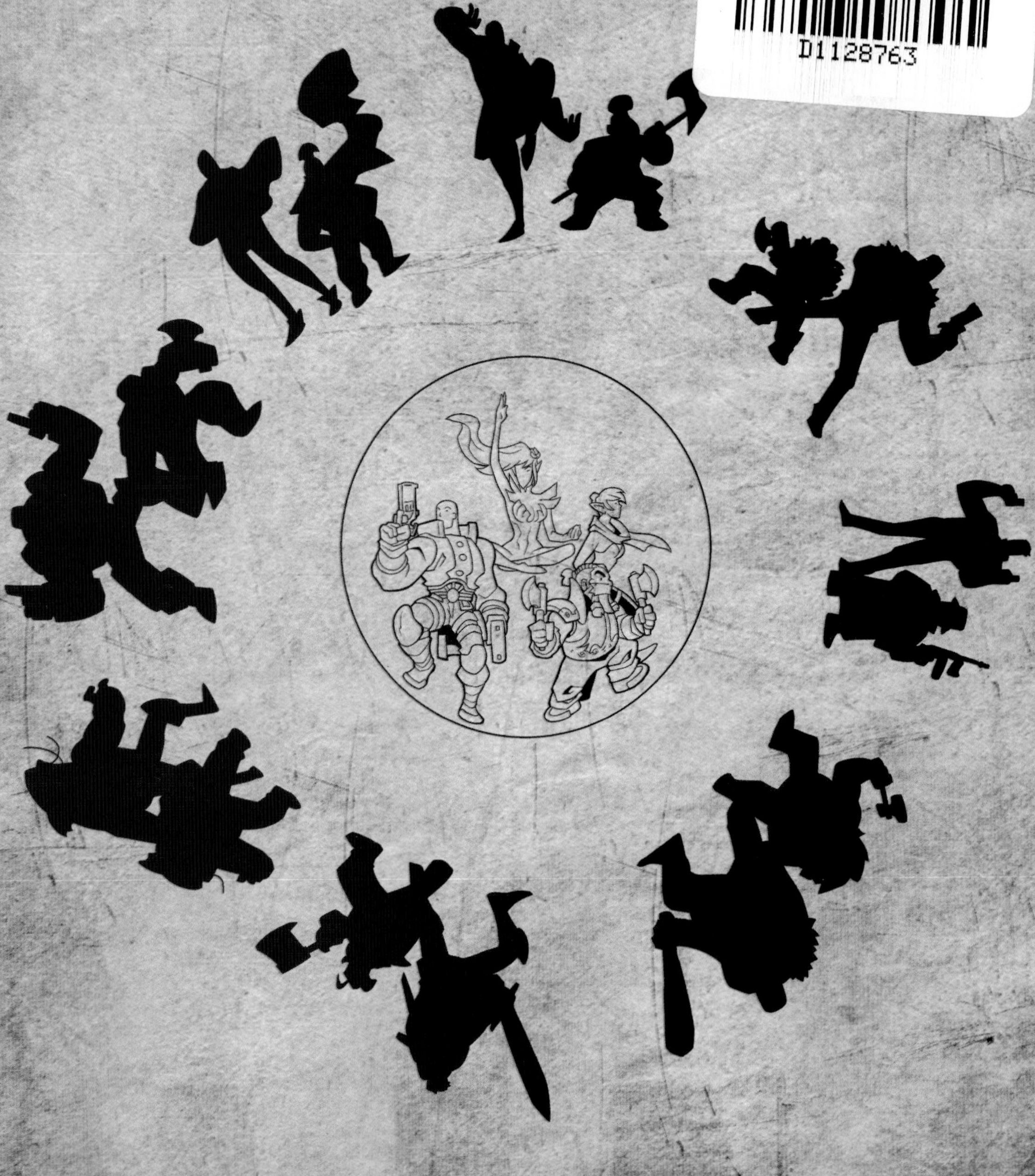

IMAGE COMICS, INC.
Robert Kirkman – Chief Operating Officer
Erik Larsen – Chief Financial Officer
Todd McFarlane – President
Marc Silvestri – Chief Executive Officer
Jim Valentino – Vice-President

Eric Stephenson – Publisher
Corey Murphy – Director of Sales
Jeremy Sullivan – Director of Digital Sales
Kat Salazar – Director of PR & Marketing
Emily Miller – Director of Operations
Branwyn Bigglestone – Senior Accounts Manager
Sarah Mello – Accounts Manager
Drew Gill – Art Director
Jonathan Chan – Production Manager
Meredith Wallace – Print Manager
Randy Okamura – Marketing Production Designer
David Brothers – Branding Manager
Ally Power – Content Manager
Addison Duke – Production Artist
Vincent Kukua – Production Artist
Sasha Head – Production Artist
Tricia Ramos – Production Artist
Emilio Bautista – Sales Assistant
Chloe Ramos-Peterson – Administrative Assistant
IMAGECOMICS.COM

SKULLKICKERS VOLUME 6
ISBN: 978-1-63215-343-2
First Printing

Published by Image Comics, Inc. Office of publication: 2001 Center St., 6th Floor, Berkeley, California 94704.

International Rights Representative:
foreignlicensing@imagecomics.com

PRINTED IN THE U.S.A. For information regarding the CPSIA on this printed material call: 203-595-3636 and provide reference # RICH – 633517.

Special Thanks
YOU! YES, YOU! THE PERSON OR CREATURE READING THIS RIGHT NOW! YOU'RE SPECIAL!

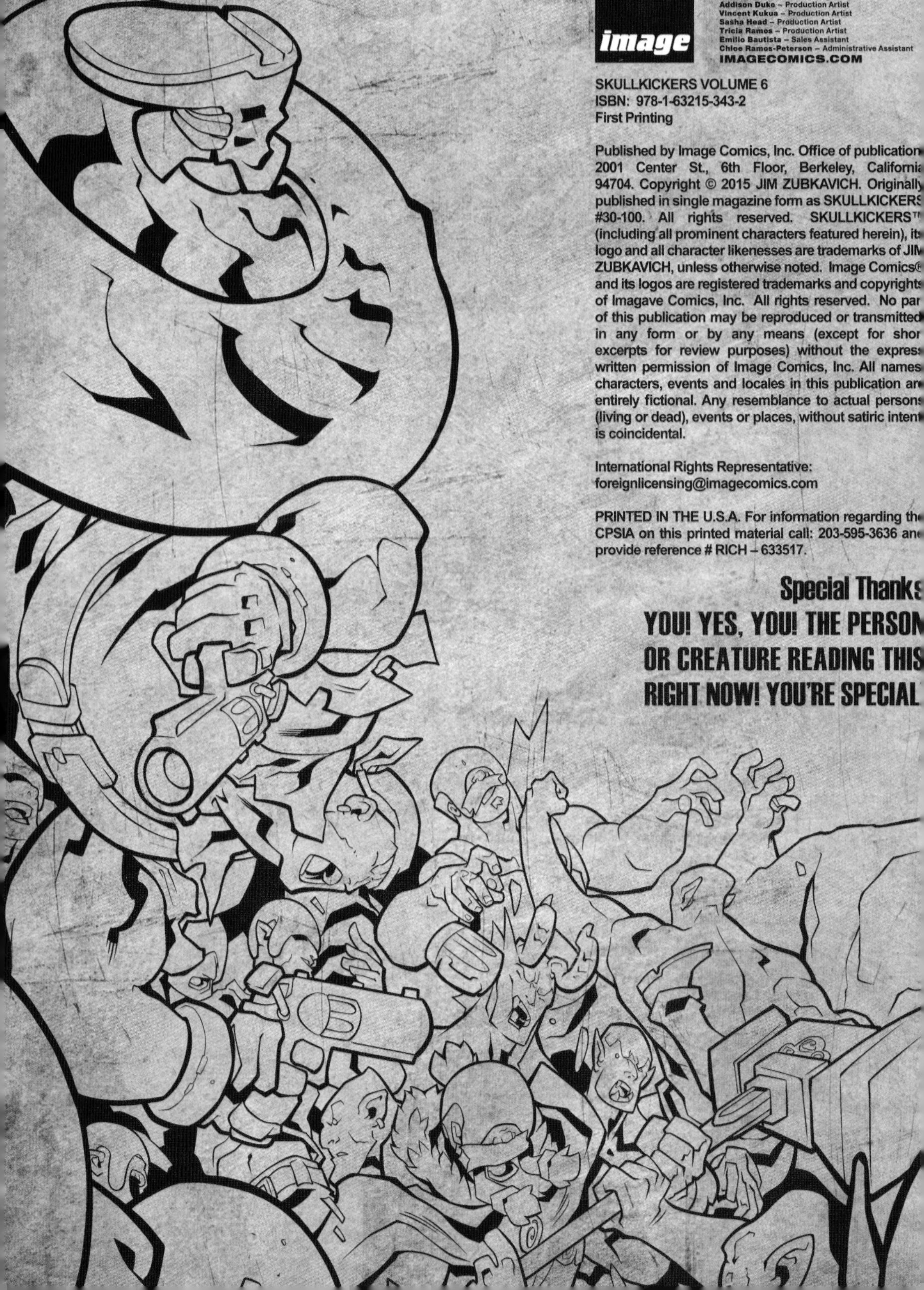

Writer
JIM ZUB

Pencils
EDWIN HUANG

Inks
EDWIN HUANG
KEVIN RAGANIT

Colors
MISTY COATS
ROSS A. CAMPBELL

Color Flatting
LUDWIG OLIMBA

Lettering
MARSHALL DILLON

"Tavern Tales" Writers
WILL HINDMARCH
JIM ZUB

"Tavern Tales" Artists
JEFF "CHAMBA" CRUZ
ROYCE "FOORAY" SOUTHERLAND

Issue Covers
JEFF "CHAMBA" CRUZ
JAMES GHIO
ESPEN GRUNDETJERN
EDWIN HUANG
CHRIS STEVENS

Trade Cover
ESPEN GRUNDETJERN
EDWIN HUANG

Graphic Design
JIM ZUB

Skullkickers Logo
STEVEN FINCH

Skullkickers
Created by
JIM ZUB
CHRIS STEVENS

Tales of the Mighty Red Box

I was there when Jim opened the **Dungeon & Dragons** red box and created his first character. Jim was 8 years old and wanted to "do cool things." I, as his 12 year old brother, was his Dungeon Master.

Of course, at that age, we didn't really understand the rules so much. We hadn't read Conan, Tolkien, or other fantasy novels, so a lot of the tropes weren't known to us. A tabletop RPG was more like a Choose Your Own Adventure story with no limits in the number of choices or pages to turn to. We made stuff up (like 'Dwelflings' – the child of a Dwarf, Elf, and Halfling, of course) and laughed at the crazy things that happened based on ridiculous dice rolls. It was a great way for two brothers to spend a large amount of time together without fighting.

Every waking moment seemed to be a chance to play. We'd spend hours at our parent's cottage diving into D&D sessions, exploring the next dungeon, defeating the next monster, and retrieving the next treasure. Characters would grow, learn, and become stronger.

I still remember many of Jim's characters. The early iterations of Rolf would be quite recognizable to readers of this fine comic. He was a headstrong dwarf more focused on treasure and loot than anything else. The Village of Hommlet never recovered from Rolf's rampage, and neither did the haunted house in the Sinister Secret of Saltmarsh. Victory Lion's adventures battling against the Slavers' Stockade was epic to us. There was also Erin Ruby Strongbow, whose graceful skill with a sword matched her witty repartee as she faced the dangers of the Vampire Lord Strahd in Castle Ravenloft.

If you've ever had a chance to sit down and chat with Jim, you'd know what I mean when I say he has the 'gift of gab.' Many of the character interactions in our games challenged my ability to keep up with him (and stay in character). He played each role to the hilt and would often make me laugh so hard that I'd choke on whatever I was eating at the time.

We played for years, and then Jim went off and gamed with his high school friends (with Taxthalmus appearing as a major demonic villain in those campaigns) as I headed off to university. Our gaming paths crossed again years later when we both played Malkavians in the Toronto Masquerade LARP. There I saw a grown-up Jim come into his own, playing a role with gusto and creating a lot of frantic fun for everyone around him. One of Jim's greatest strengths is his ability to stay positive and have fun. He involves others, keeps people entertained, and creates memorable moments. After all, isn't that what life's supposed to be about?

In a similar vein, Jim put together the Skullkickers creative team with Edwin Huang, Misty Coats, and Marshall Dillon like a tightly knit gaming group and now they've built something equally memorable on the comic page. In this age of instant internet gratification and multimedia extravaganza, they've managed to make a story that's drawn acclaim from critics and captivated thousands of readers.

I must say I've been privileged. For longer than most, I've had the opportunity to watch Jim and his team grow and become true storytellers. Storytellers who greatly surpass my ability as they create something that entertains so many people. Storytellers who continue to grow and will share many more stories in the future.

In your hands is the final volume of this epic tale. So, let's get going. I've been looking forward to it longer than anyone else. Let's enjoy it together!

—Joe Zubkavich
   The Original Zub-DM
   April 2015

TAVERN TALES THROUGH TIME

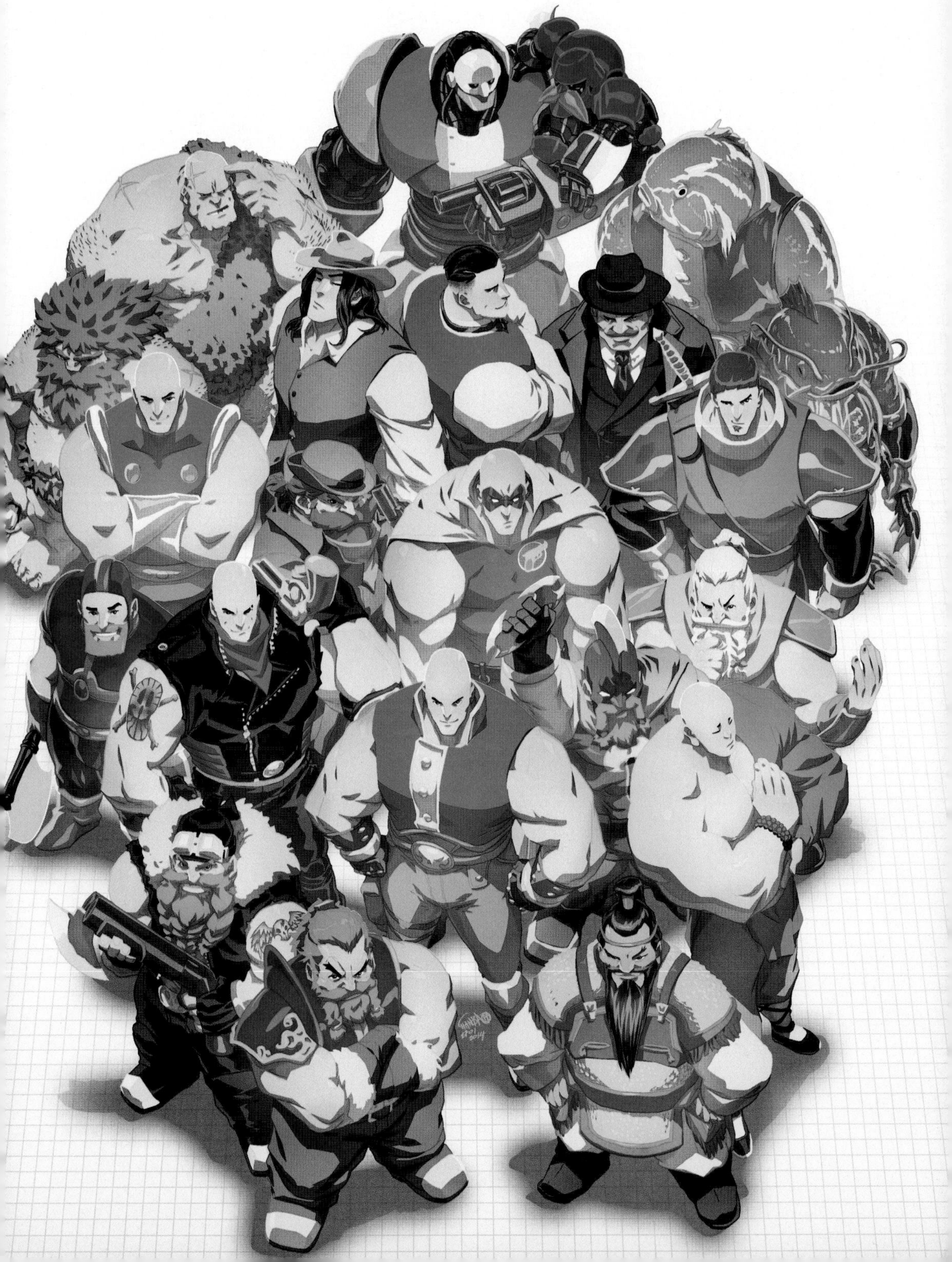

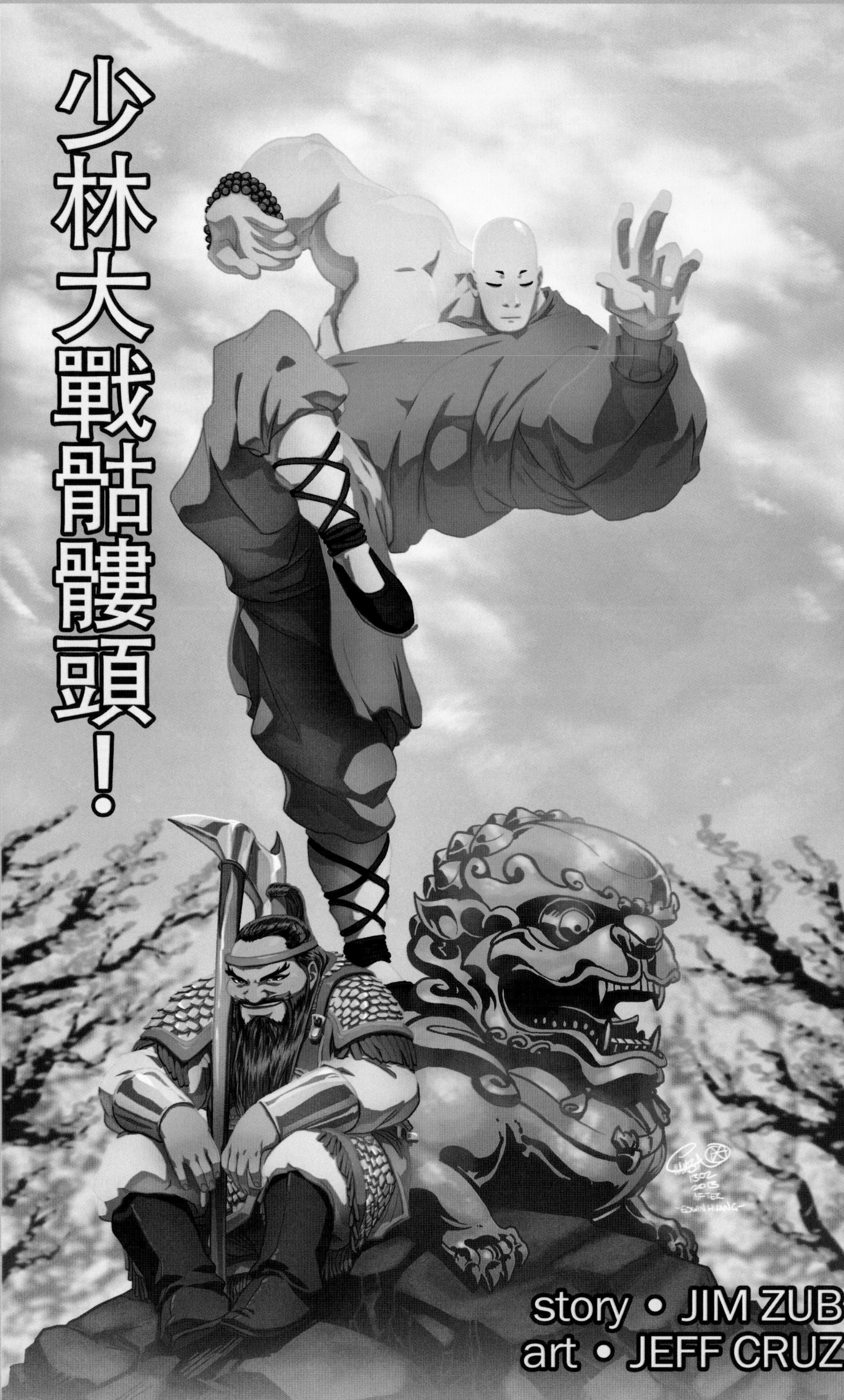
少林大戰骷髏頭！
story • JIM ZUB
art • JEFF CRUZ

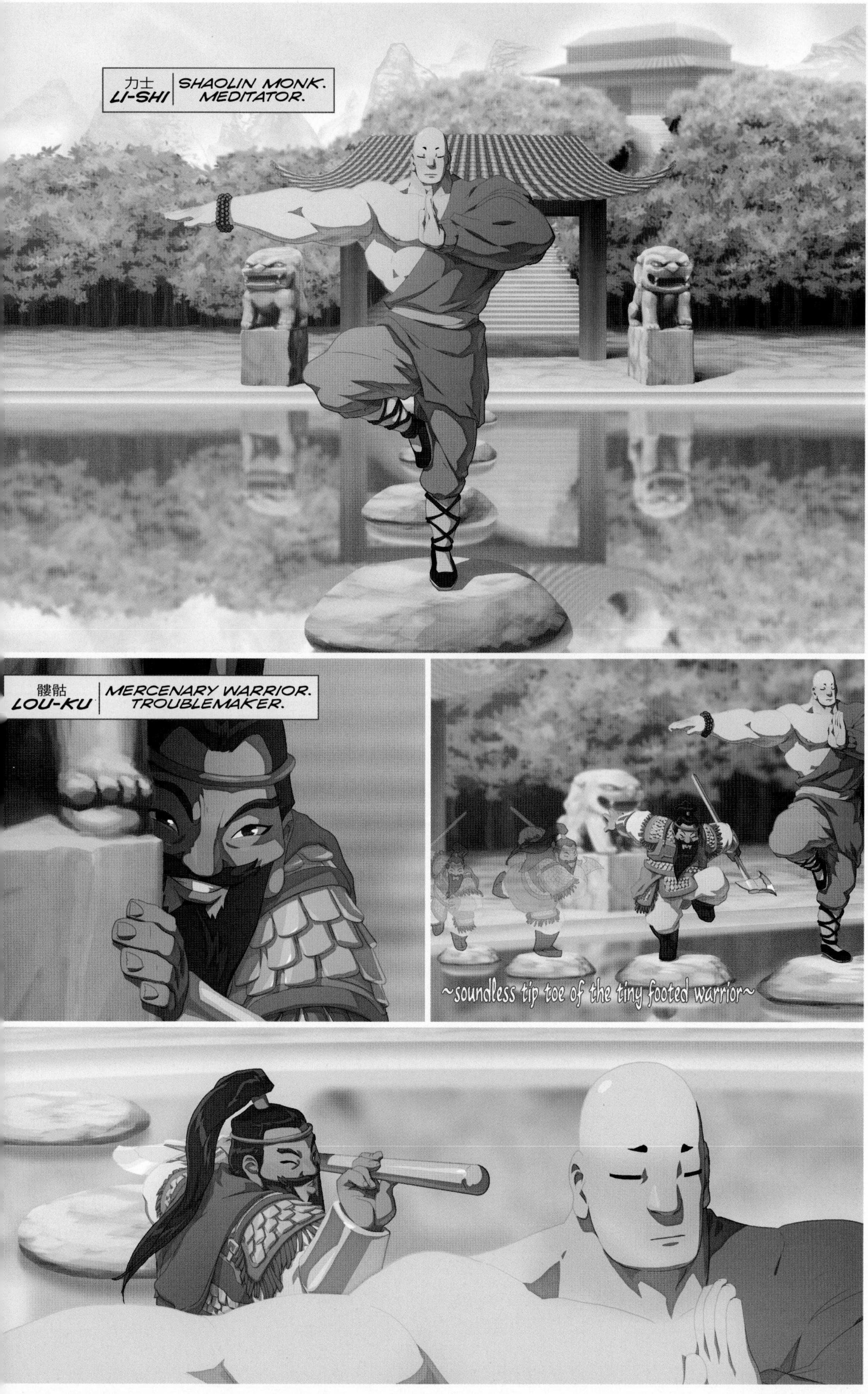
力士
LI-SHI
SHAOLIN MONK.
MEDITATOR.
髏骷
LOU-KU
MERCENARY WARRIOR.
TROUBLEMAKER.
~soundless tip toe of the tiny footed warrior~

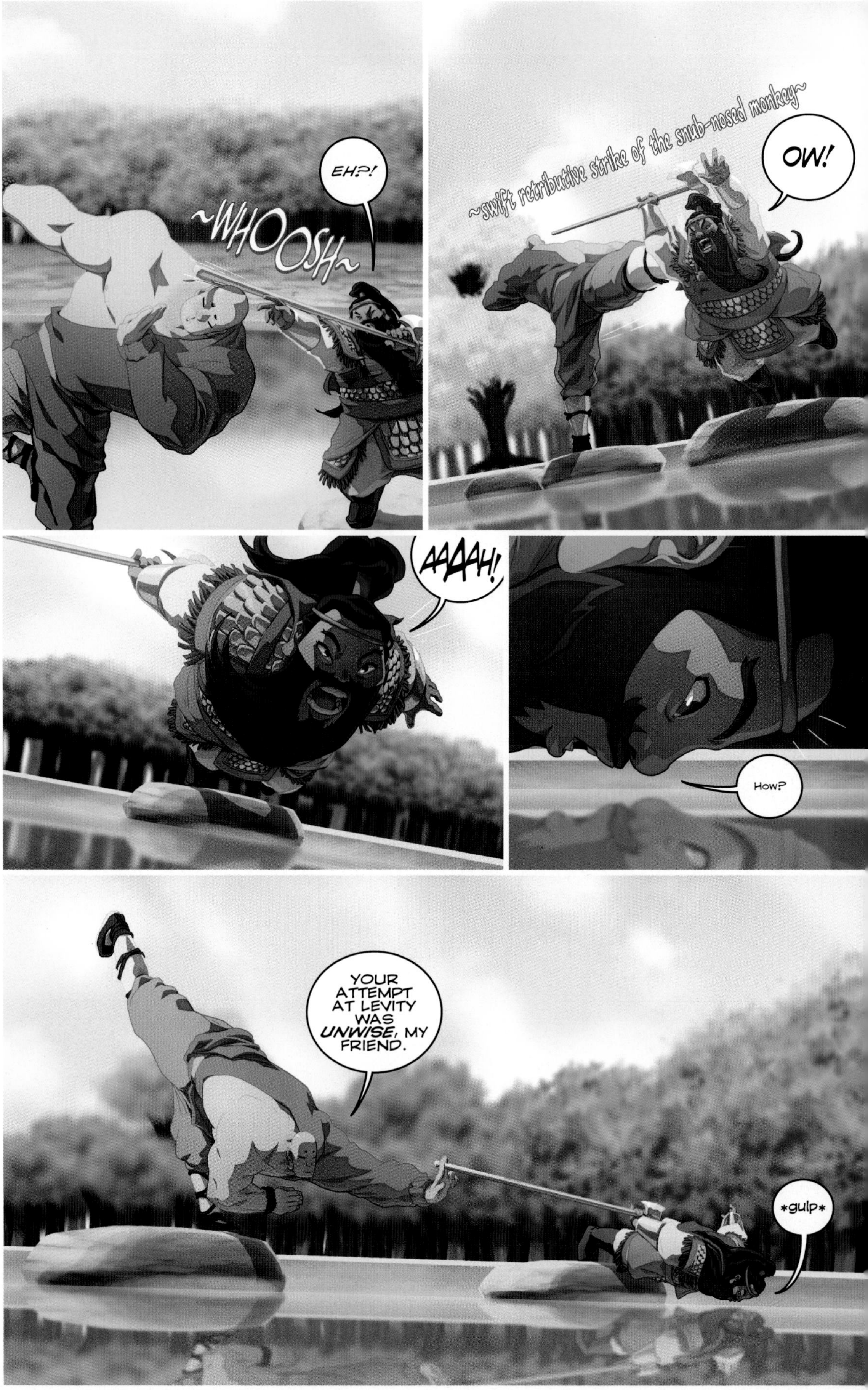
EH?!
~WHOOSH~
~swift retributive strike of the snub-nosed monkey~
OW!
AAAAH!
HOW?
YOUR ATTEMPT AT LEVITY WAS *UNWISE*, MY FRIEND.
gulp

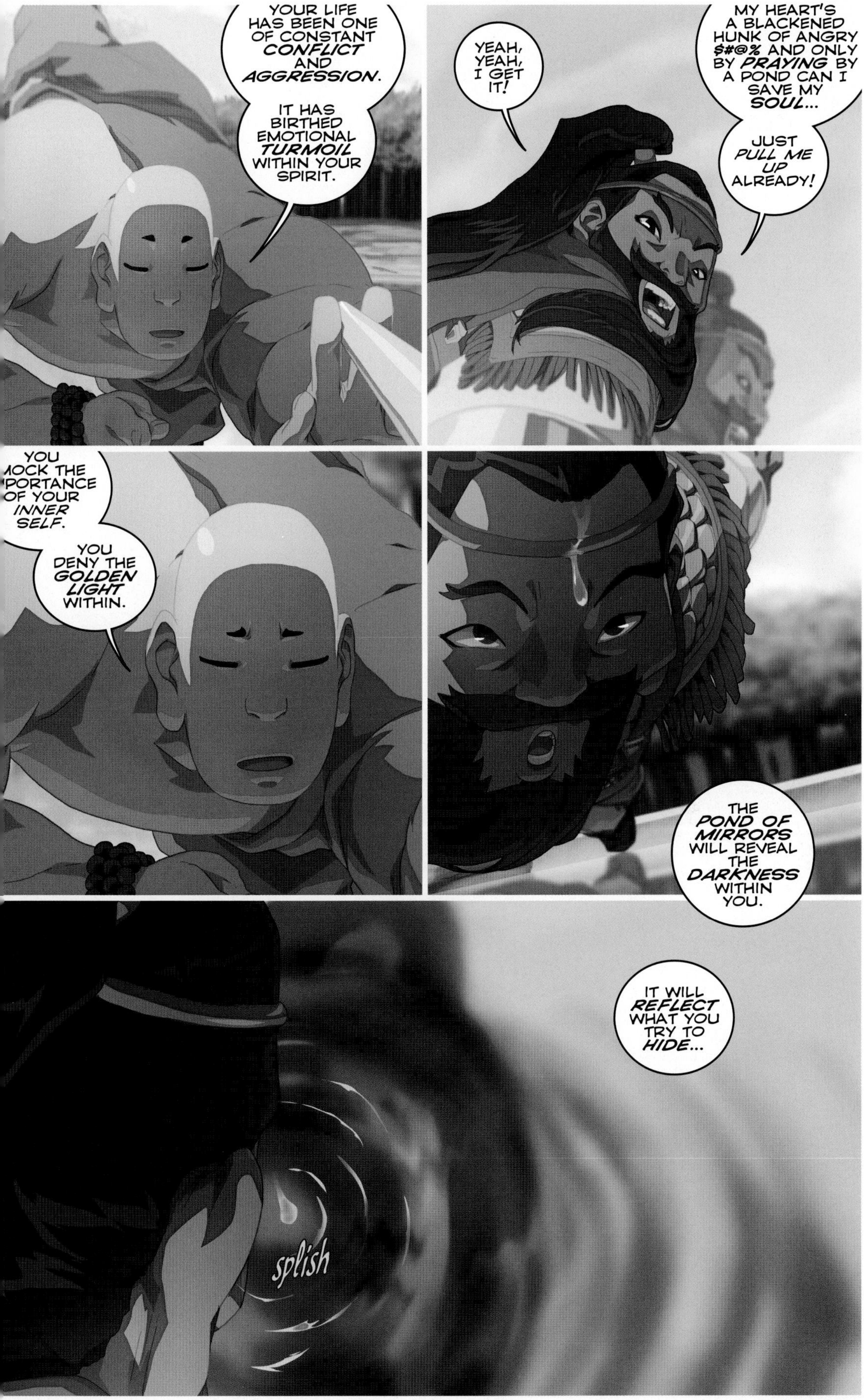

YOUR LIFE HAS BEEN ONE OF CONSTANT CONFLICT AND AGGRESSION.
IT HAS BIRTHED EMOTIONAL TURMOIL WITHIN YOUR SPIRIT.
YEAH, YEAH, I GET IT!
MY HEART'S A BLACKENED HUNK OF ANGRY $#@% AND ONLY BY PRAYING BY A POND CAN I SAVE MY SOUL...
JUST PULL ME UP ALREADY!
YOU MOCK THE IMPORTANCE OF YOUR INNER SELF.
YOU DENY THE GOLDEN LIGHT WITHIN.
THE POND OF MIRRORS WILL REVEAL THE DARKNESS WITHIN YOU.
IT WILL REFLECT WHAT YOU TRY TO HIDE...
splish

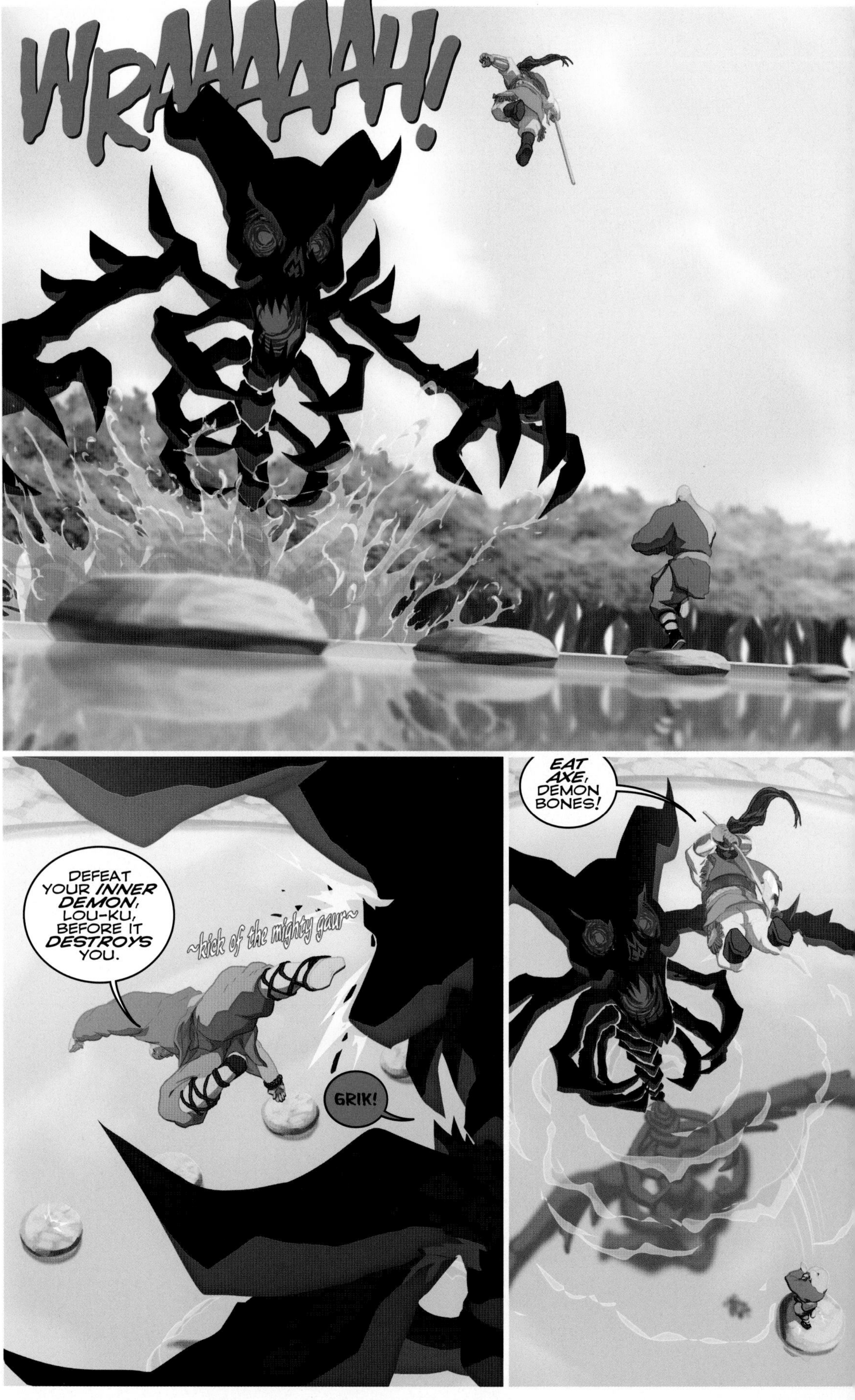
WRAAAAAH!
DEFEAT YOUR INNER DEMON, LOU-KU, BEFORE IT DESTROYS YOU.
~kick of the mighty gaur~
GRIK!
EAT AXE, DEMON BONES!

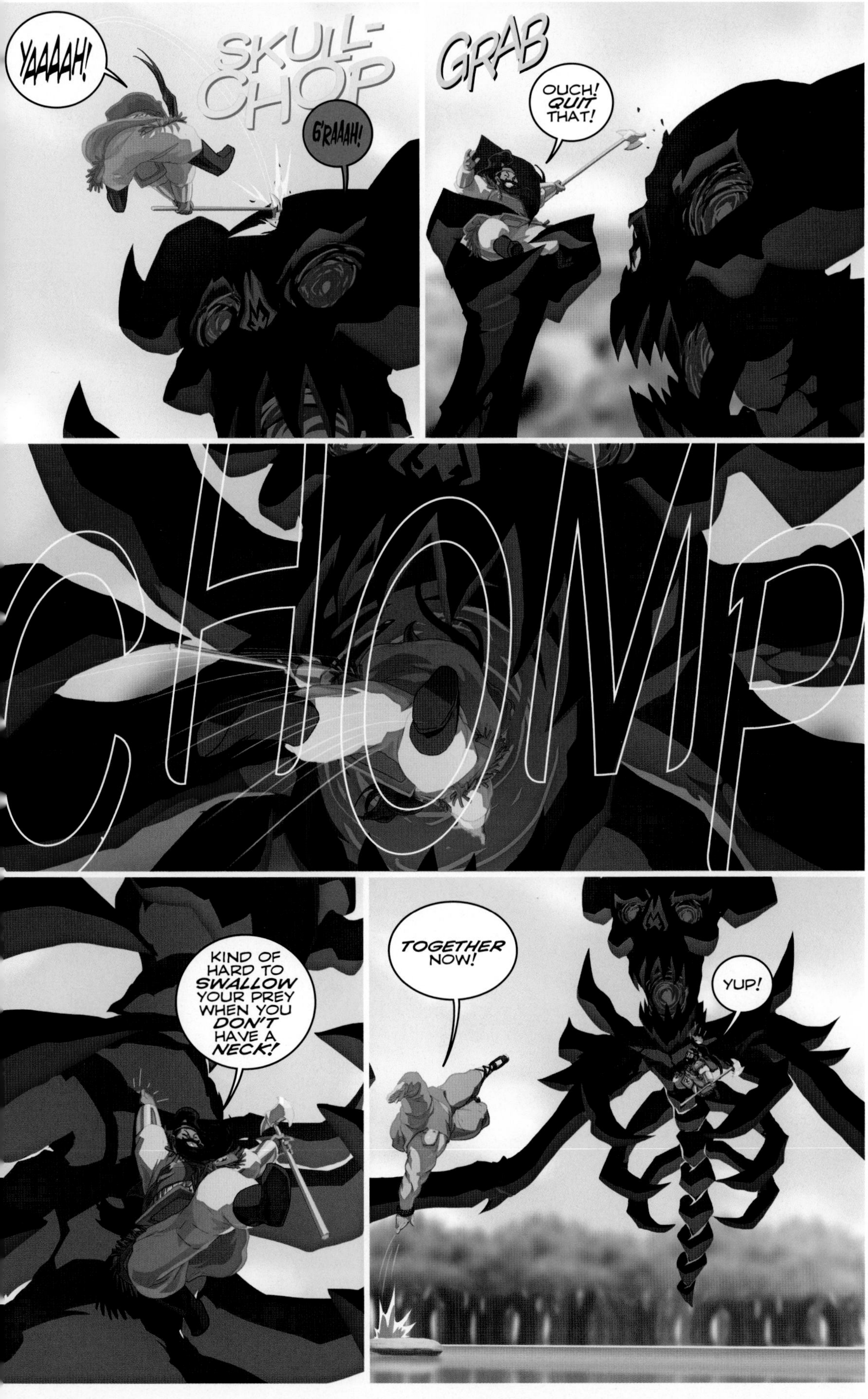
YAAAAH!
SKULL-CHOP
G'RAAAH!
GRAB
OUCH! QUIT THAT!
CHOMP
KIND OF HARD TO SWALLOW YOUR PREY WHEN YOU DON'T HAVE A NECK!
TOGETHER NOW!
YUP!

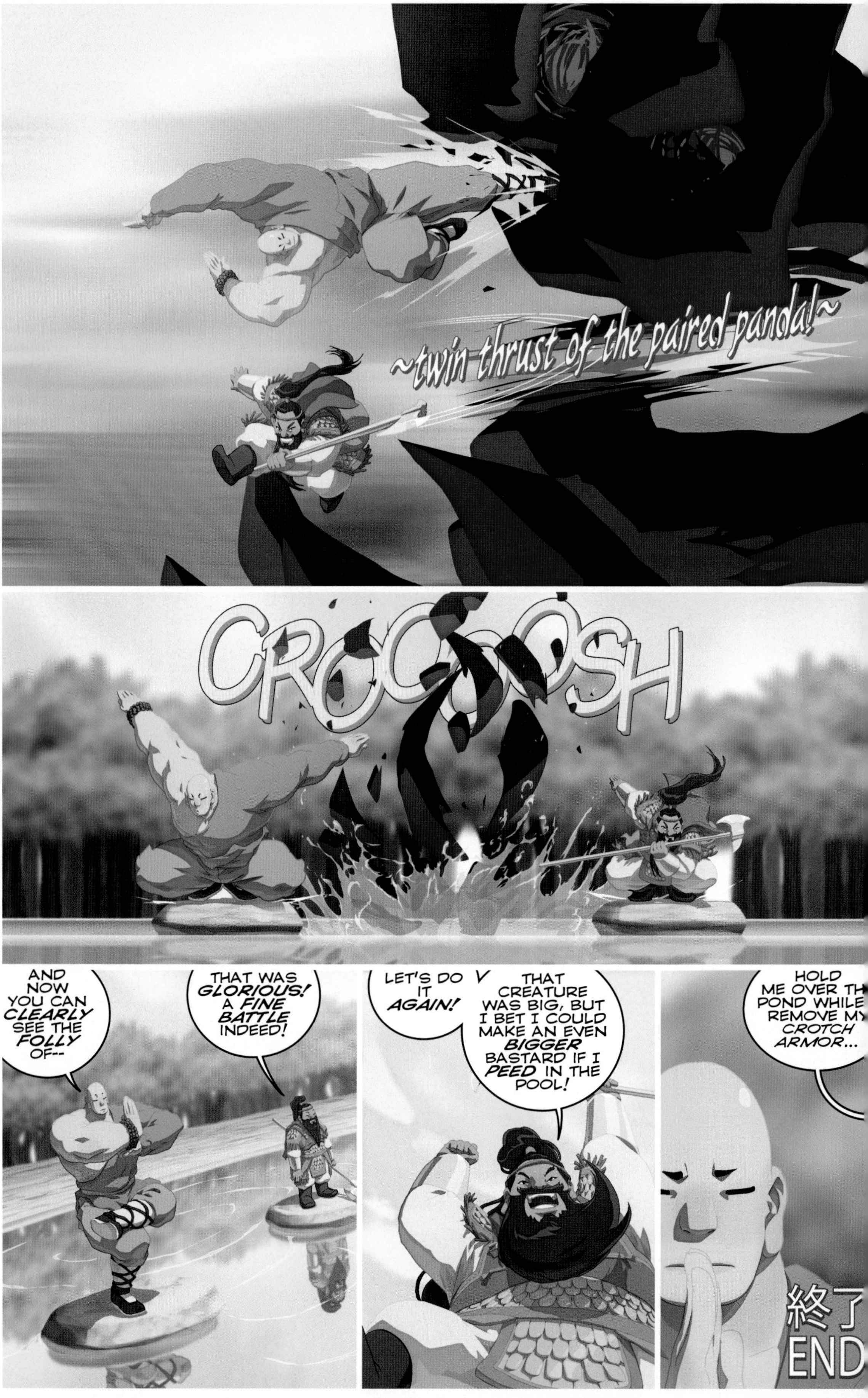
~twin thrust of the paired panda!~
CROOOSH
AND NOW YOU CAN CLEARLY SEE THE FOLLY OF--
THAT WAS GLORIOUS! A FINE BATTLE INDEED!
LET'S DO IT AGAIN!
THAT CREATURE WAS BIG, BUT I BET I COULD MAKE AN EVEN BIGGER BASTARD IF I PEED IN THE POOL!
HOLD ME OVER THE POND WHILE I REMOVE MY CROTCH ARMOR...
終了
END

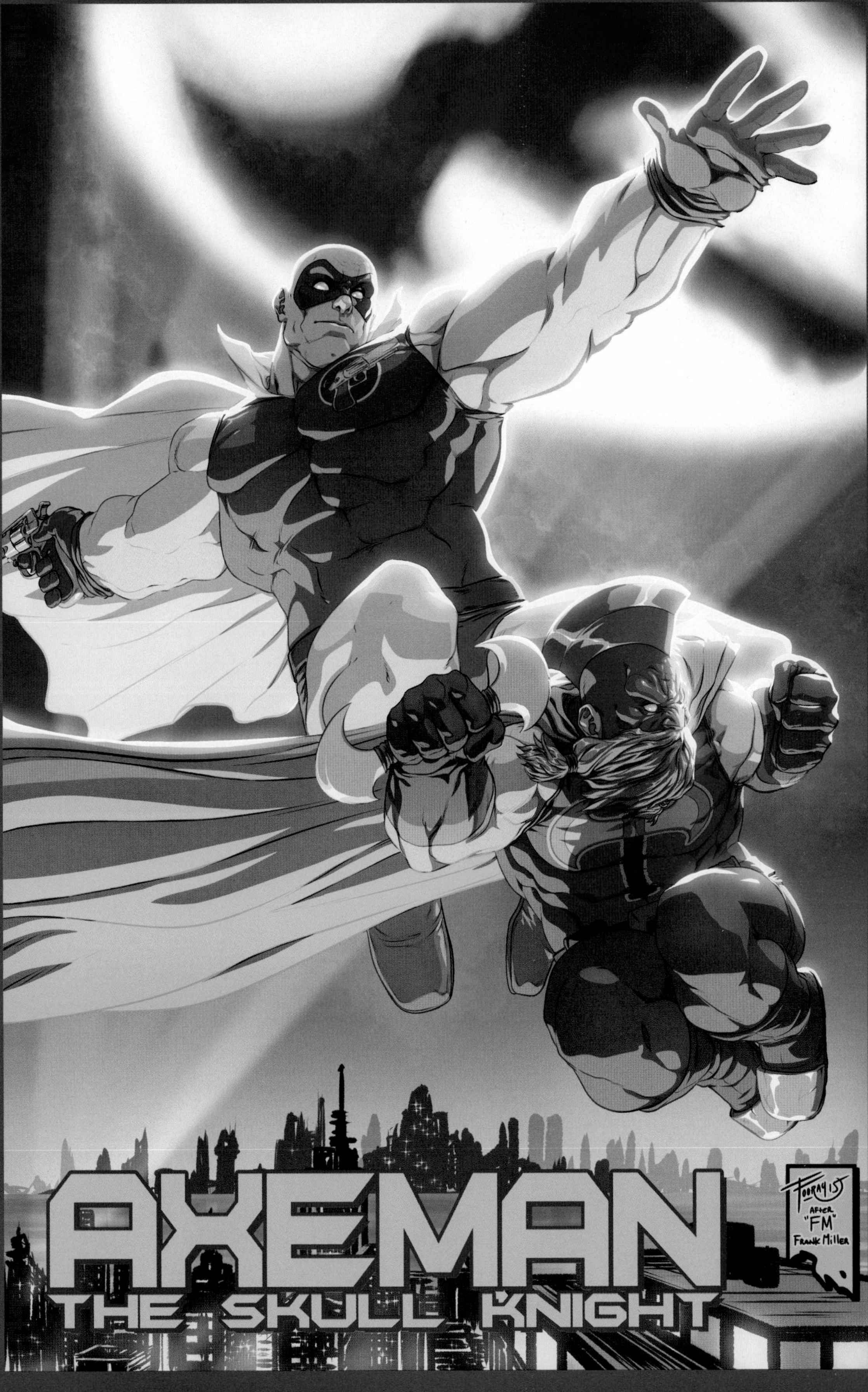
AXEMAN
THE SKULL KNIGHT
Fooray '15
AFTER
"FM"
Frank Miller

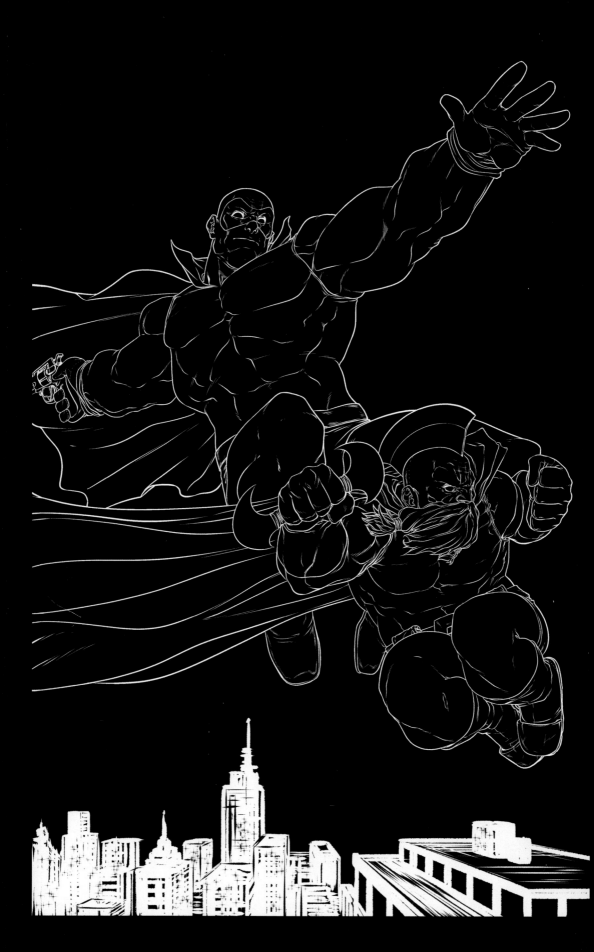

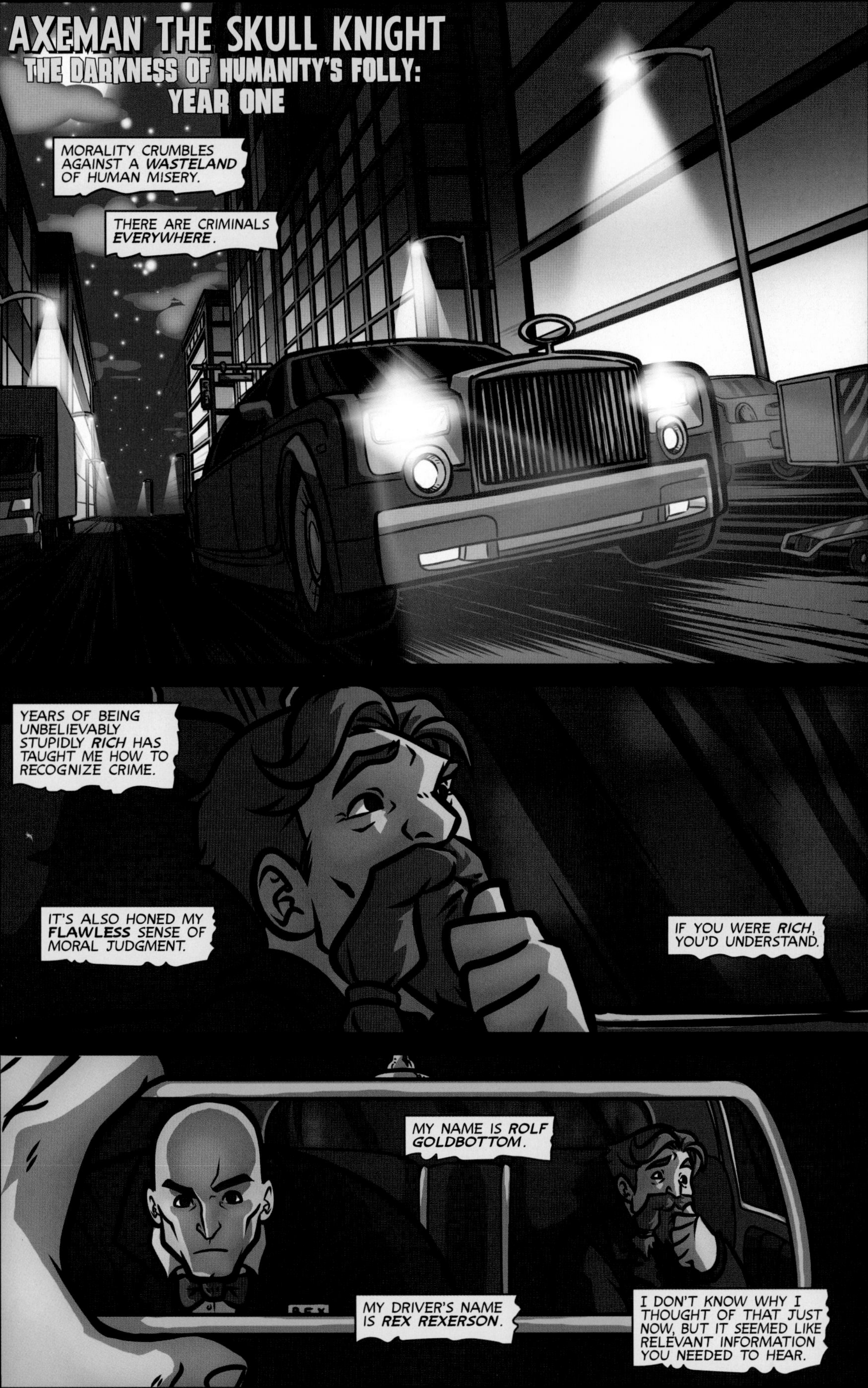
AXEMAN THE SKULL KNIGHT
THE DARKNESS OF HUMANITY'S FOLLY: YEAR ONE
MORALITY CRUMBLES AGAINST A WASTELAND OF HUMAN MISERY.
THERE ARE CRIMINALS EVERYWHERE.
YEARS OF BEING UNBELIEVABLY STUPIDLY RICH HAS TAUGHT ME HOW TO RECOGNIZE CRIME.
IT'S ALSO HONED MY FLAWLESS SENSE OF MORAL JUDGMENT.
IF YOU WERE RICH, YOU'D UNDERSTAND.
MY NAME IS ROLF GOLDBOTTOM.
MY DRIVER'S NAME IS REX REXERSON.
I DON'T KNOW WHY I THOUGHT OF THAT JUST NOW, BUT IT SEEMED LIKE RELEVANT INFORMATION YOU NEEDED TO HEAR.

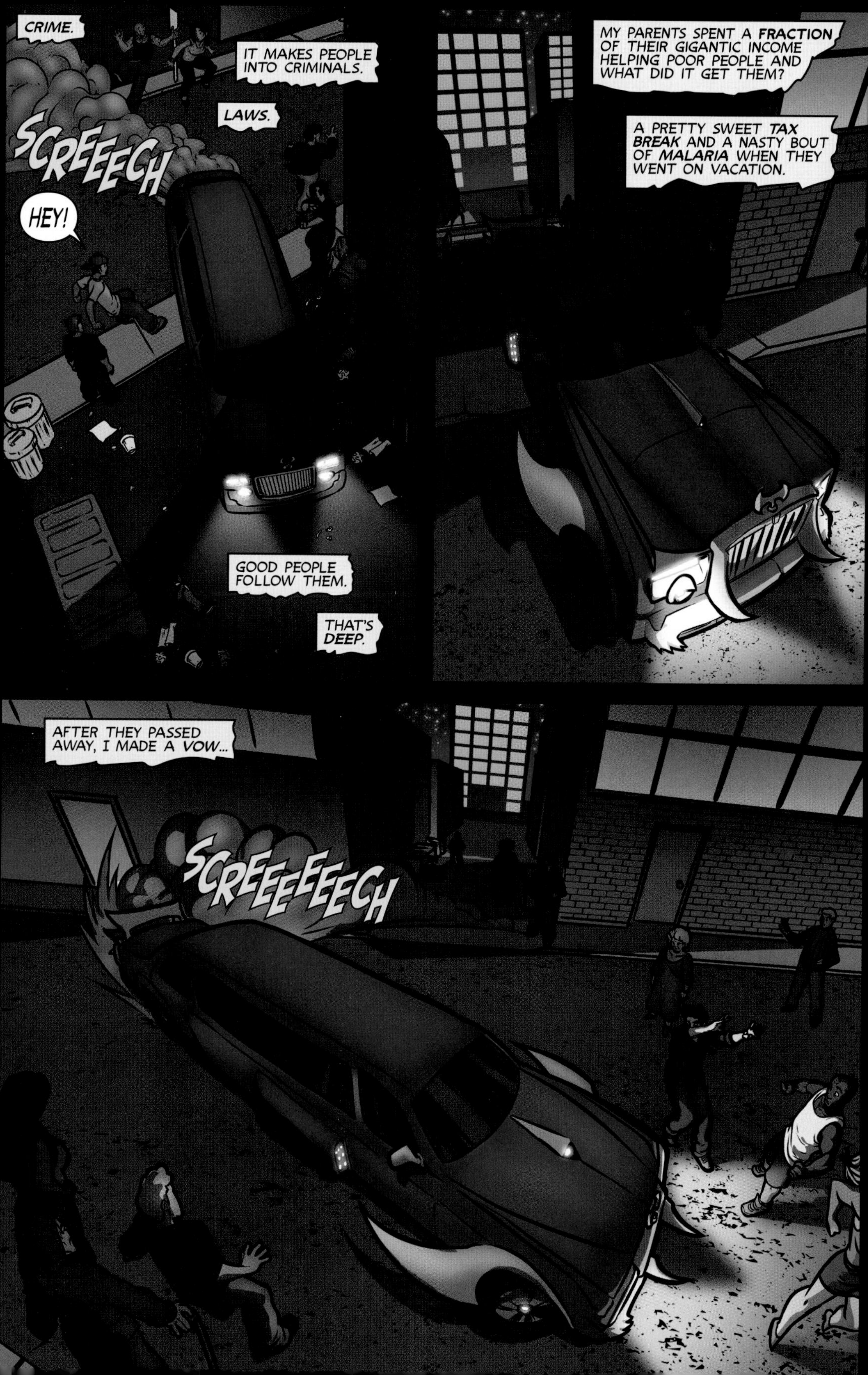
CRIME.
IT MAKES PEOPLE INTO CRIMINALS.
LAWS.
SCREEECH
HEY!
GOOD PEOPLE FOLLOW THEM.
THAT'S DEEP.
MY PARENTS SPENT A FRACTION OF THEIR GIGANTIC INCOME HELPING POOR PEOPLE AND WHAT DID IT GET THEM?
A PRETTY SWEET TAX BREAK AND A NASTY BOUT OF MALARIA WHEN THEY WENT ON VACATION.
AFTER THEY PASSED AWAY, I MADE A VOW...
SCREEEEEEECH

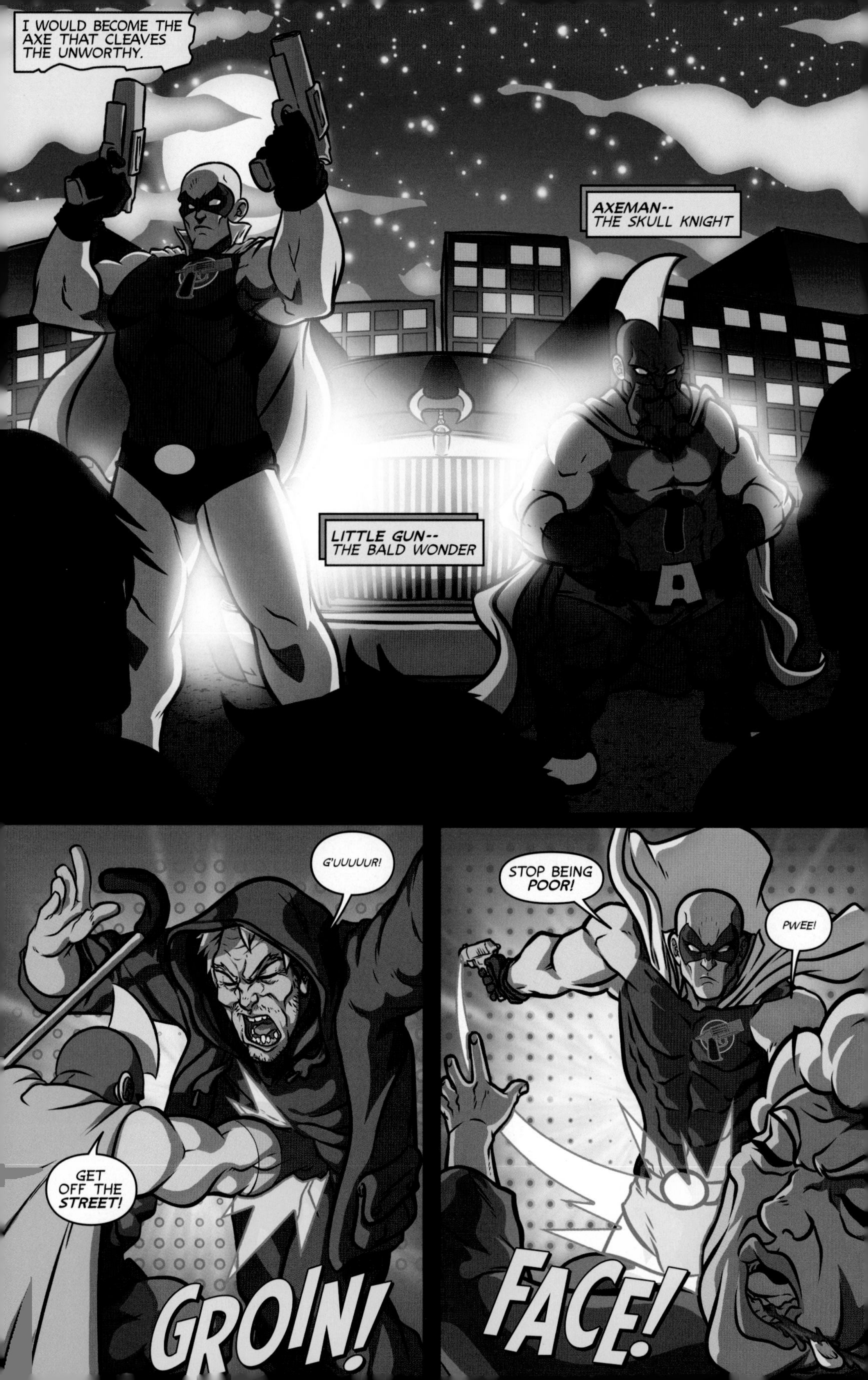
I WOULD BECOME THE AXE THAT CLEAVES THE UNWORTHY.
AXEMAN-- THE SKULL KNIGHT
LITTLE GUN-- THE BALD WONDER
G'UUUUUR!
GET OFF THE STREET!
GROIN!
STOP BEING POOR!
PWEE!
FACE!

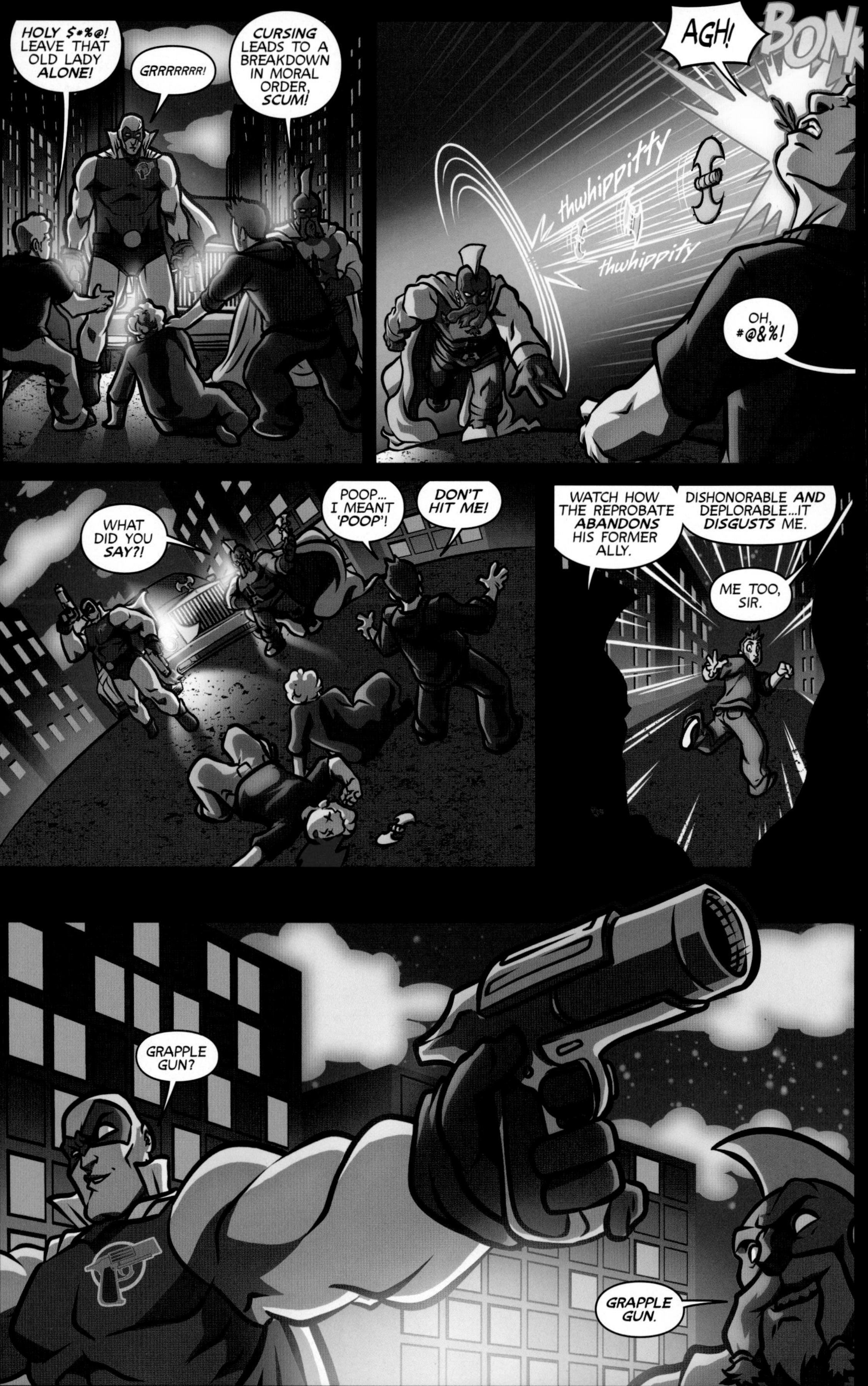
HOLY $*%@! LEAVE THAT OLD LADY ALONE!
GRRRRRRR!
CURSING LEADS TO A BREAKDOWN IN MORAL ORDER, SCUM!
AGH!
BONK
thwhippitty
thwhippity
OH, #@&%!
WHAT DID YOU SAY?!
POOP... I MEANT 'POOP'!
DON'T HIT ME!
WATCH HOW THE REPROBATE ABANDONS HIS FORMER ALLY.
DISHONORABLE AND DEPLORABLE...IT DISGUSTS ME.
ME TOO, SIR.
GRAPPLE GUN?
GRAPPLE GUN.

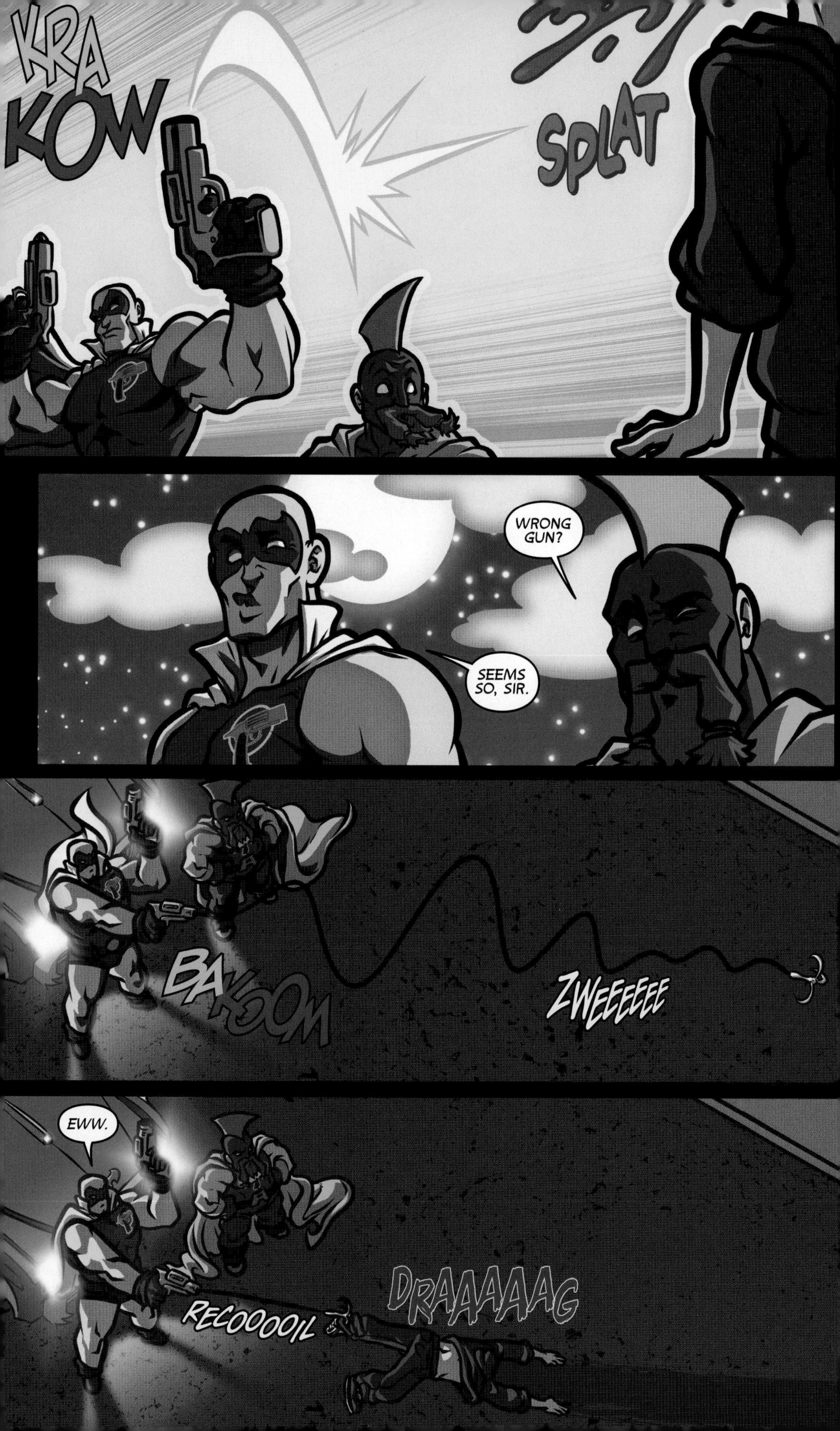
KRA
KOW
SPLAT
WRONG GUN?
SEEMS SO, SIR.
BAKOOM
ZWEEEEEE
EWW.
RECOOOOIL
DRAAAAAG

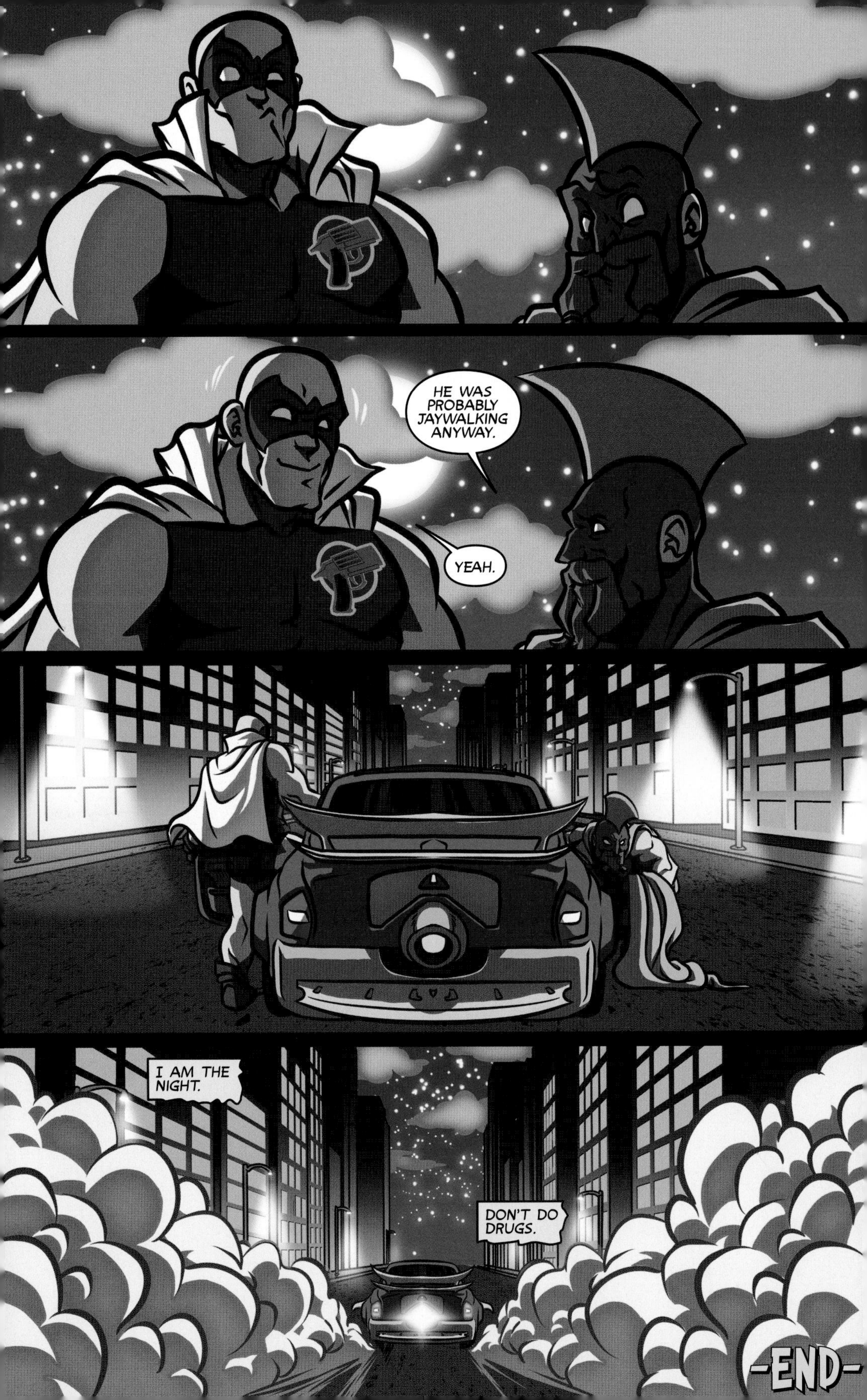
HE WAS PROBABLY JAYWALKING ANYWAY.
YEAH.
I AM THE NIGHT.
DON'T DO DRUGS.
-END-

The Sky Countess of Jupiter

A TALE OF SPACE-FARING HIGH ADVENTURE

BY WILL HINDMARCH, JEFF CRUZ, AND MARSHALL DILLON

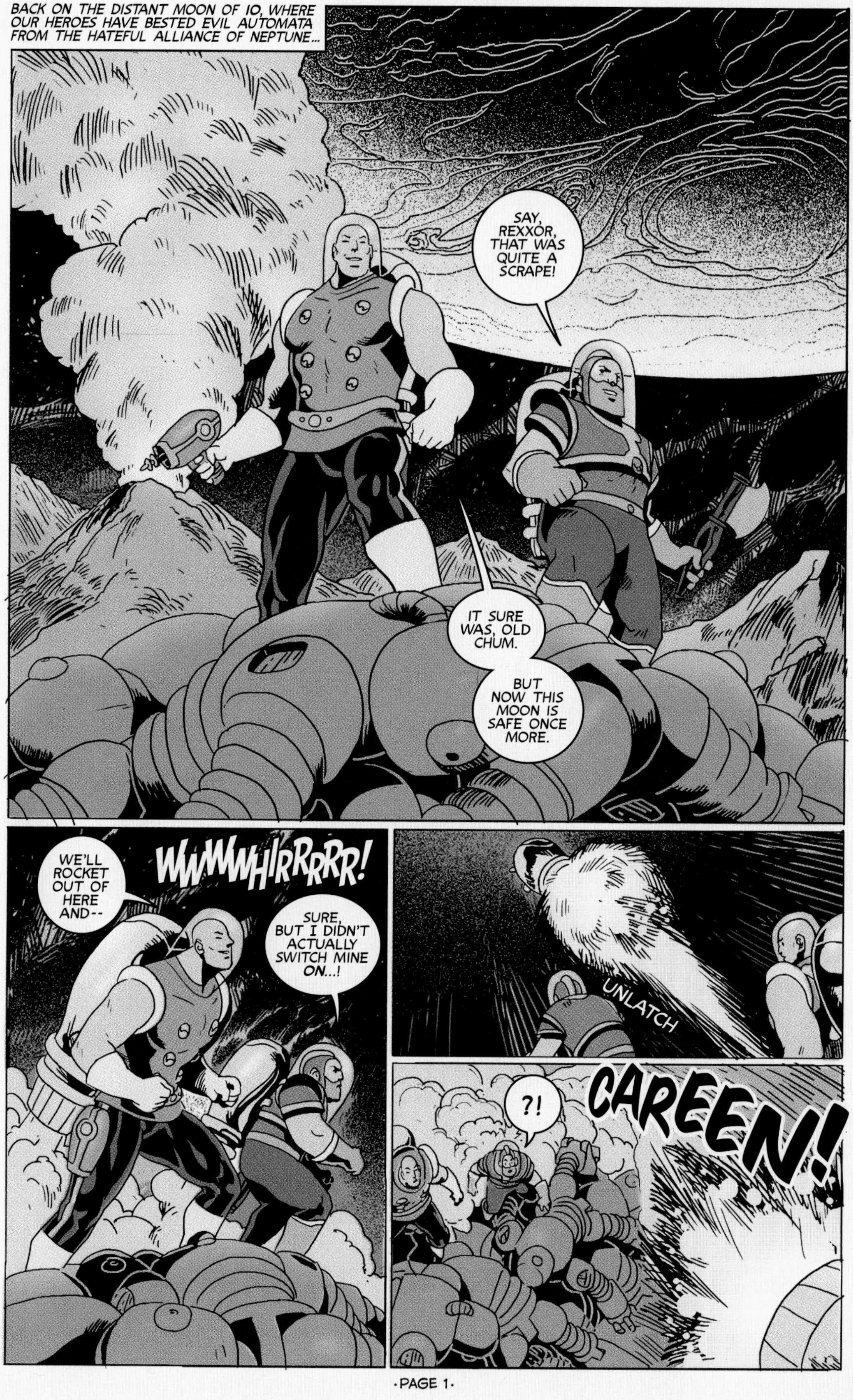
BACK ON THE DISTANT MOON OF IO, WHERE OUR HEROES HAVE BESTED EVIL AUTOMATA FROM THE HATEFUL ALLIANCE OF NEPTUNE...
SAY, REXXOR, THAT WAS QUITE A SCRAPE!
IT SURE WAS, OLD CHUM.
BUT NOW THIS MOON IS SAFE ONCE MORE.
WE'LL ROCKET OUT OF HERE AND--
WWWWHIRRRRR!
SURE, BUT I DIDN'T ACTUALLY SWITCH MINE ON...!
UNLATCH
?!
CAREEN!

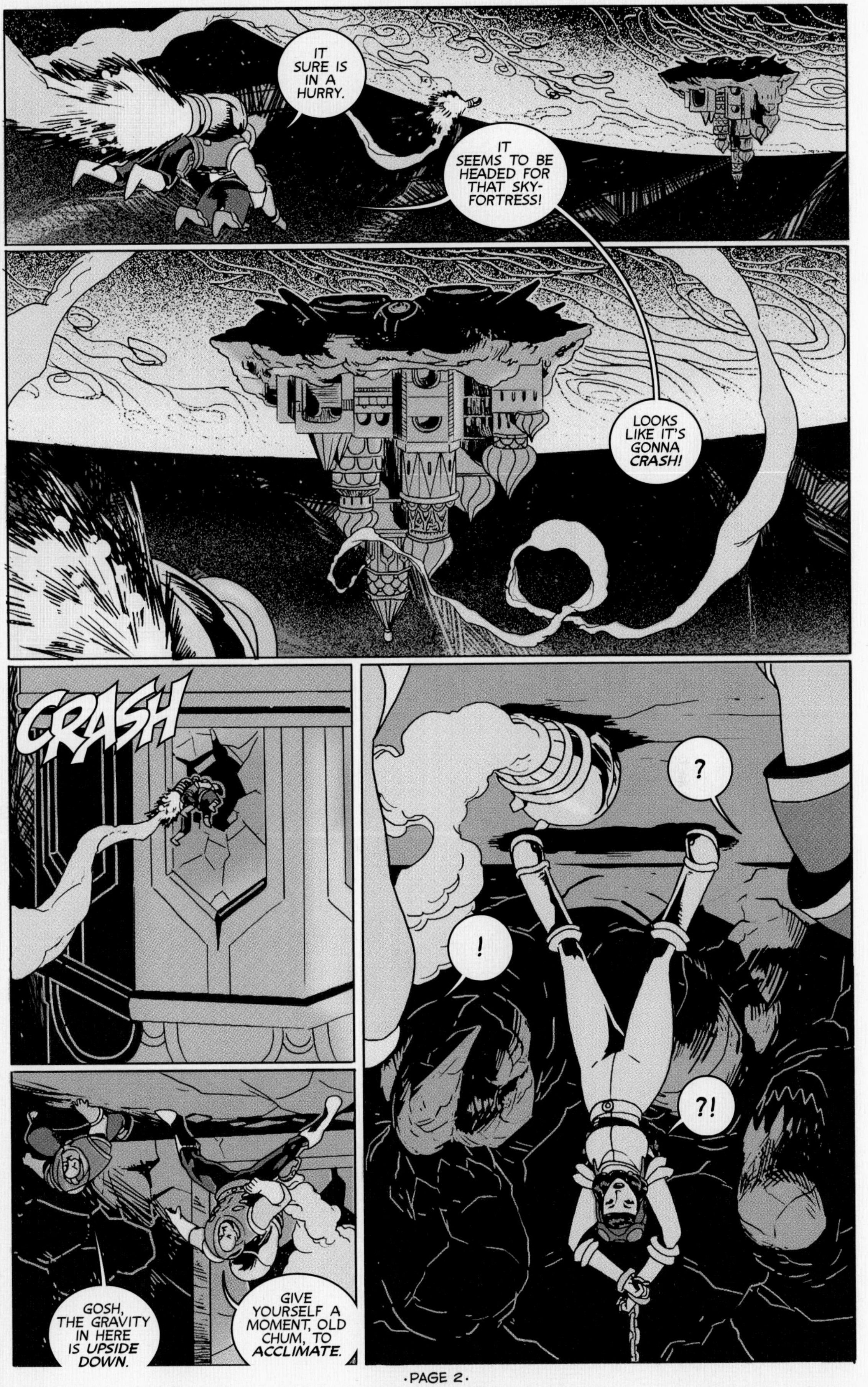
IT SURE IS IN A HURRY.
IT SEEMS TO BE HEADED FOR THAT SKY-FORTRESS!
LOOKS LIKE IT'S GONNA CRASH!
CRASH
?
!
?!
GOSH, THE GRAVITY IN HERE IS UPSIDE DOWN.
GIVE YOURSELF A MOMENT, OLD CHUM, TO ACCLIMATE.

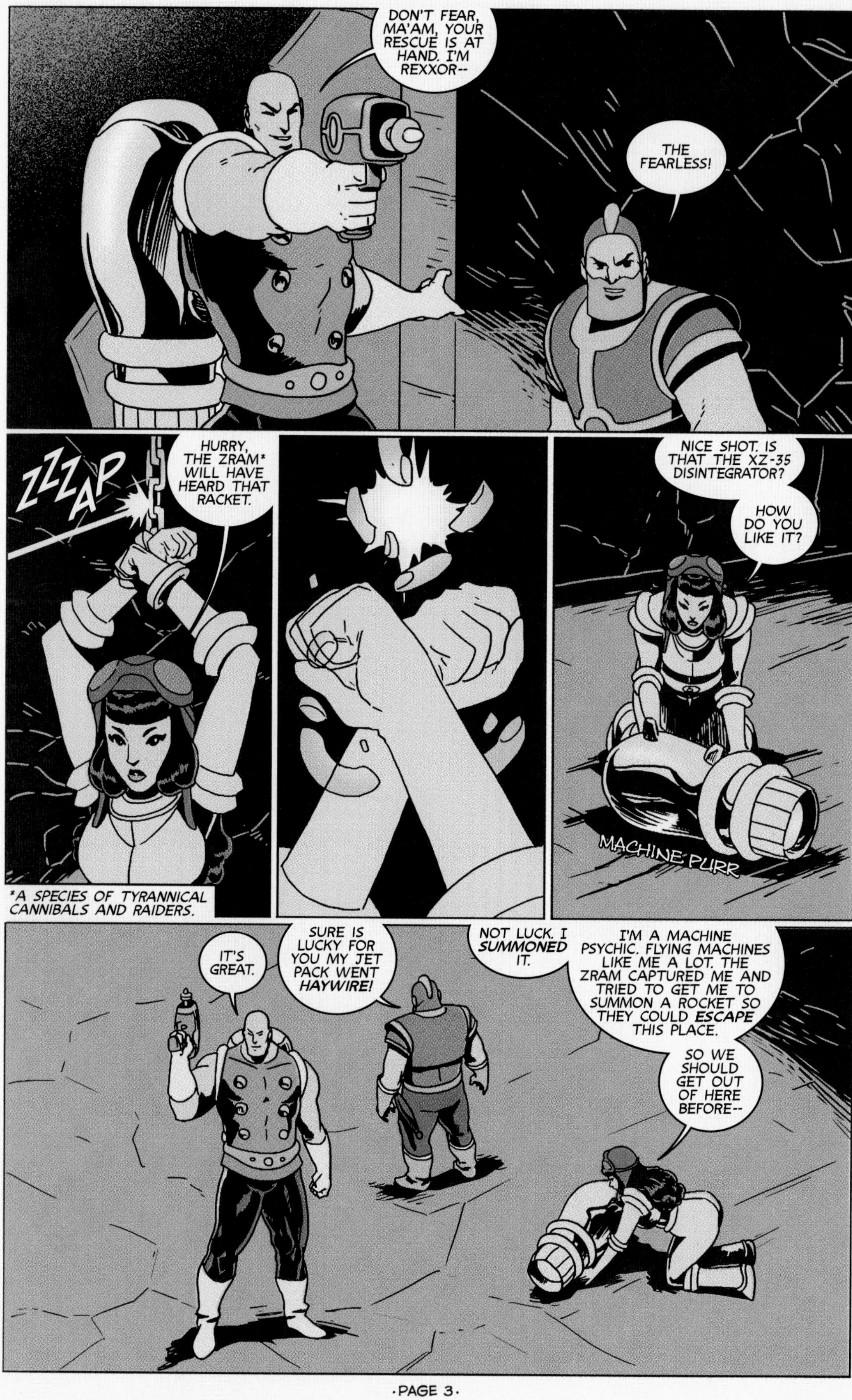
DON'T FEAR, MA'AM, YOUR RESCUE IS AT HAND. I'M REXXOR--
THE FEARLESS!
ZZZAP
HURRY, THE ZRAM* WILL HAVE HEARD THAT RACKET.
*A SPECIES OF TYRANNICAL CANNIBALS AND RAIDERS.
NICE SHOT. IS THAT THE XZ-35 DISINTEGRATOR?
HOW DO YOU LIKE IT?
MACHINE PURR
IT'S GREAT.
SURE IS LUCKY FOR YOU MY JET PACK WENT HAYWIRE!
NOT LUCK. I SUMMONED IT.
I'M A MACHINE PSYCHIC. FLYING MACHINES LIKE ME A LOT. THE ZRAM CAPTURED ME AND TRIED TO GET ME TO SUMMON A ROCKET SO THEY COULD ESCAPE THIS PLACE.
SO WE SHOULD GET OUT OF HERE BEFORE--

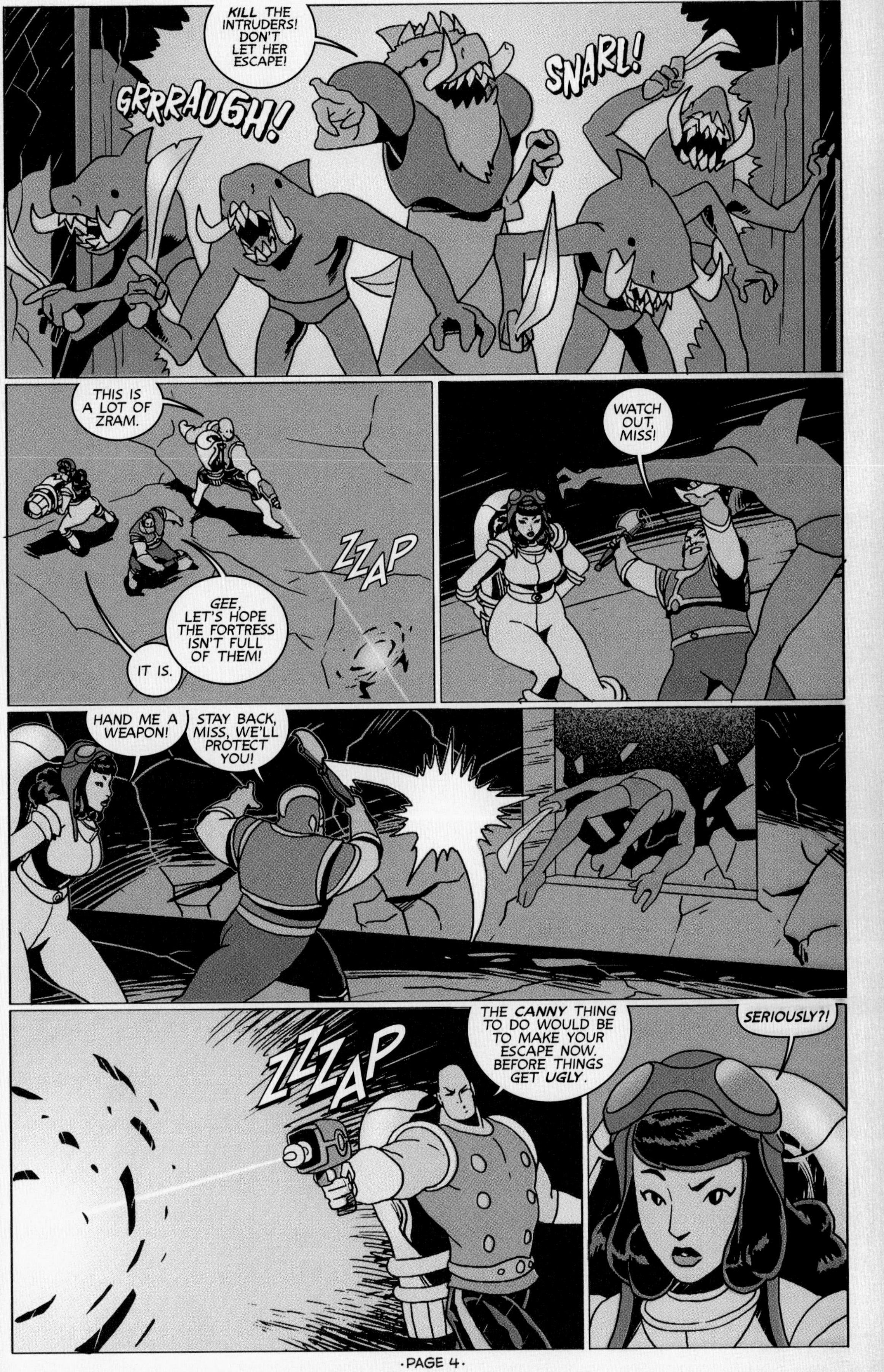
KILL THE INTRUDERS! DON'T LET HER ESCAPE!
GRRRAUGH!
SNARL!
THIS IS A LOT OF ZRAM.
ZZAP
GEE, LET'S HOPE THE FORTRESS ISN'T FULL OF THEM!
IT IS.
WATCH OUT, MISS!
HAND ME A WEAPON!
STAY BACK, MISS, WE'LL PROTECT YOU!
ZZZAP
THE CANNY THING TO DO WOULD BE TO MAKE YOUR ESCAPE NOW. BEFORE THINGS GET UGLY.
SERIOUSLY?!

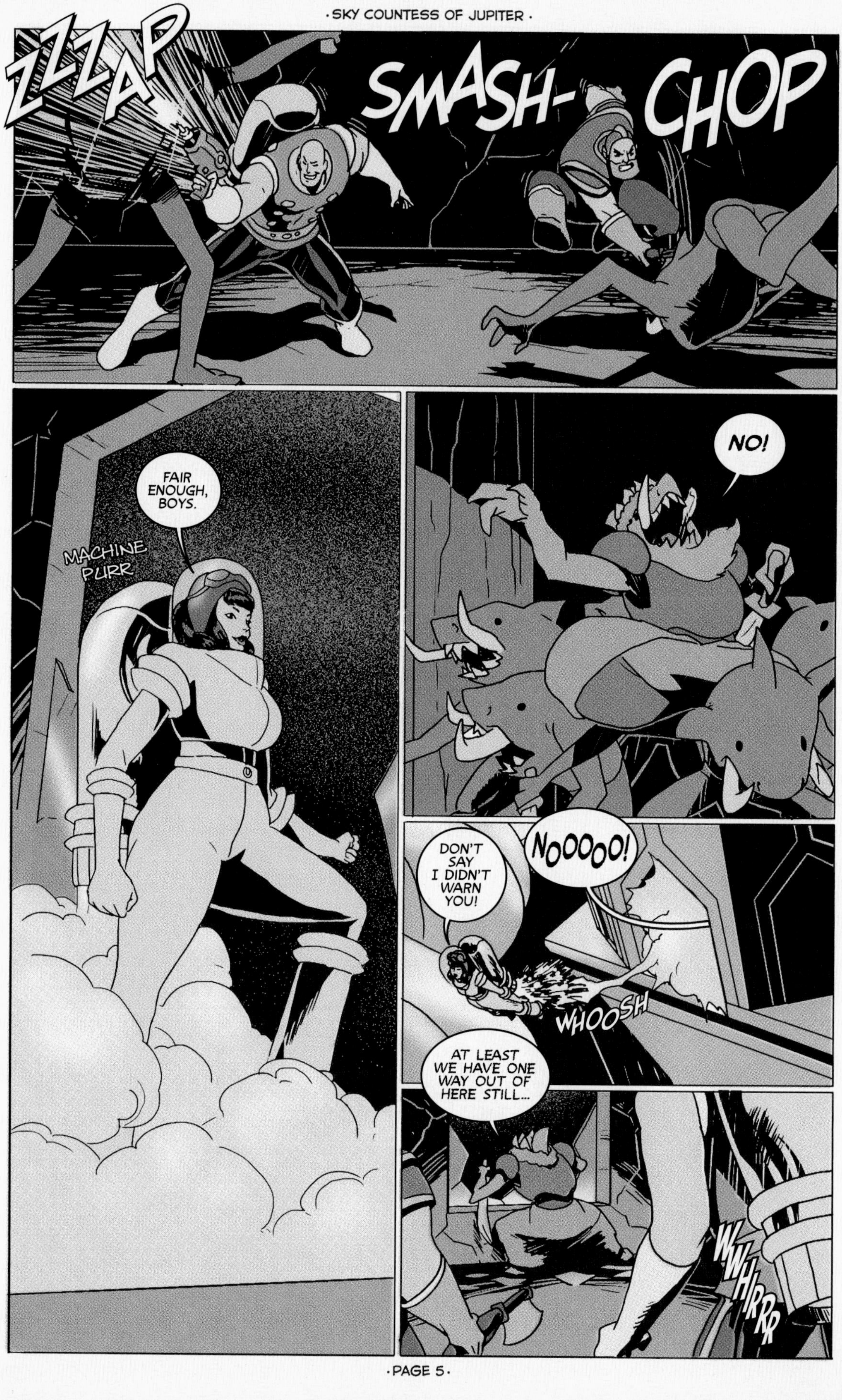
ZZZAP
SMASH-
CHOP
FAIR ENOUGH, BOYS.
MACHINE PURR
NO!
DON'T SAY I DIDN'T WARN YOU!
NOOOOO!
WHOOSH
AT LEAST WE HAVE ONE WAY OUT OF HERE STILL...
WWHIRRR

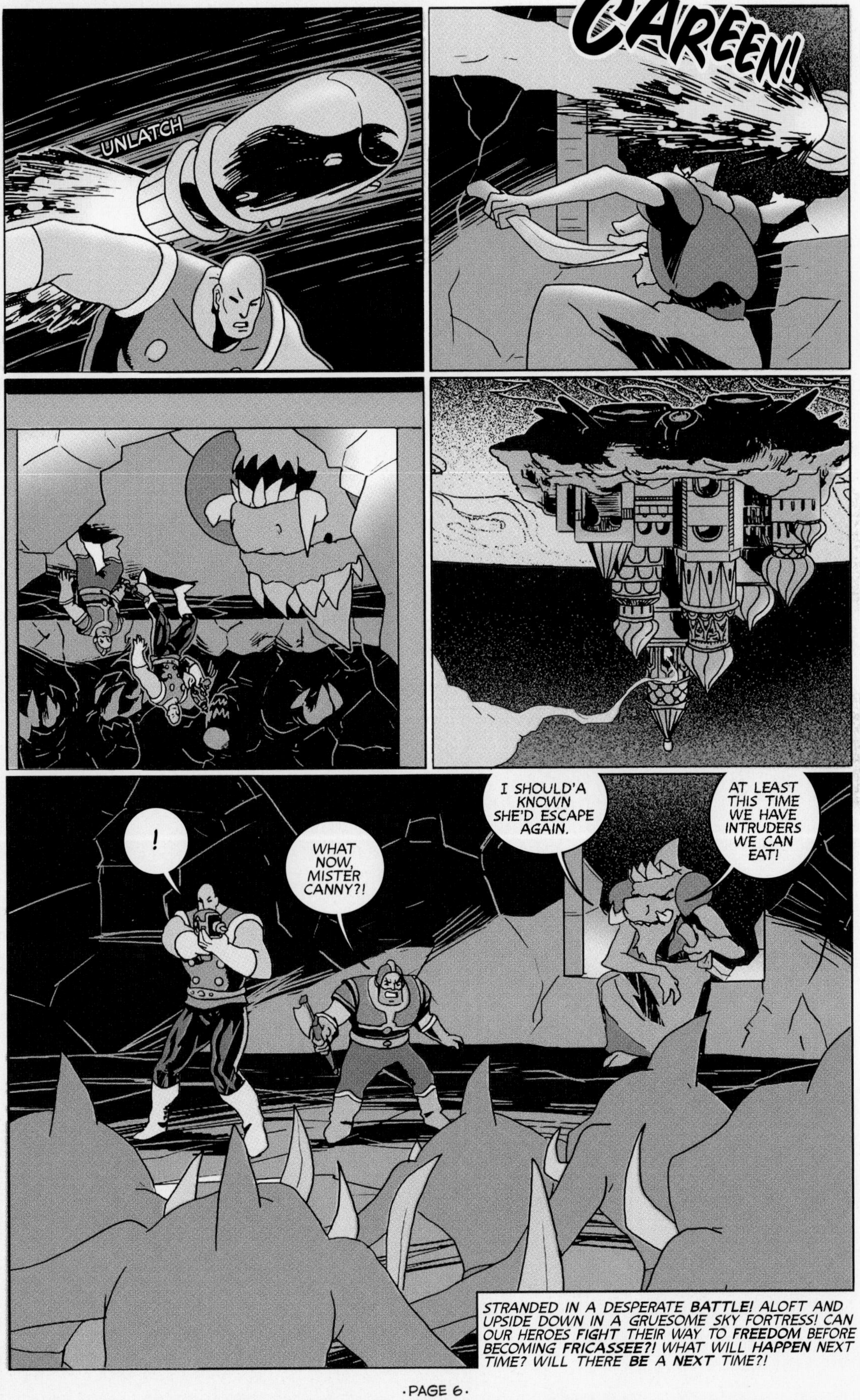
UNLATCH
CAREEN!
!
WHAT NOW, MISTER CANNY?!
I SHOULD'A KNOWN SHE'D ESCAPE AGAIN.
AT LEAST THIS TIME WE HAVE INTRUDERS WE CAN EAT!
STRANDED IN A DESPERATE BATTLE! ALOFT AND UPSIDE DOWN IN A GRUESOME SKY FORTRESS! CAN OUR HEROES FIGHT THEIR WAY TO FREEDOM BEFORE BECOMING FRICASSEE?! WHAT WILL HAPPEN NEXT TIME? WILL THERE BE A NEXT TIME?!

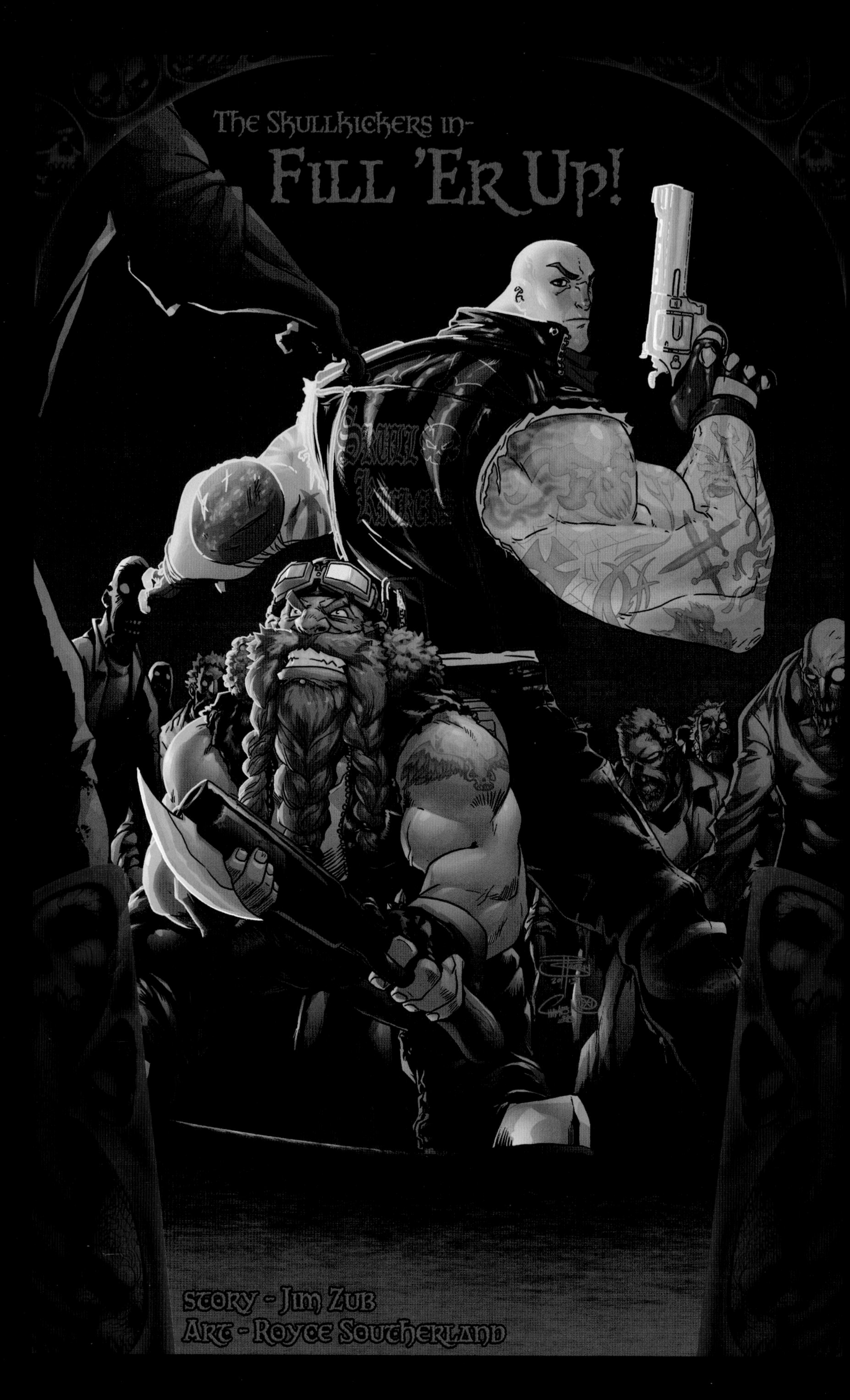
The Skullkickers in-
FILL 'ER UP!
STORY - JIM ZUB
ART - ROYCE SOUTHERLAND

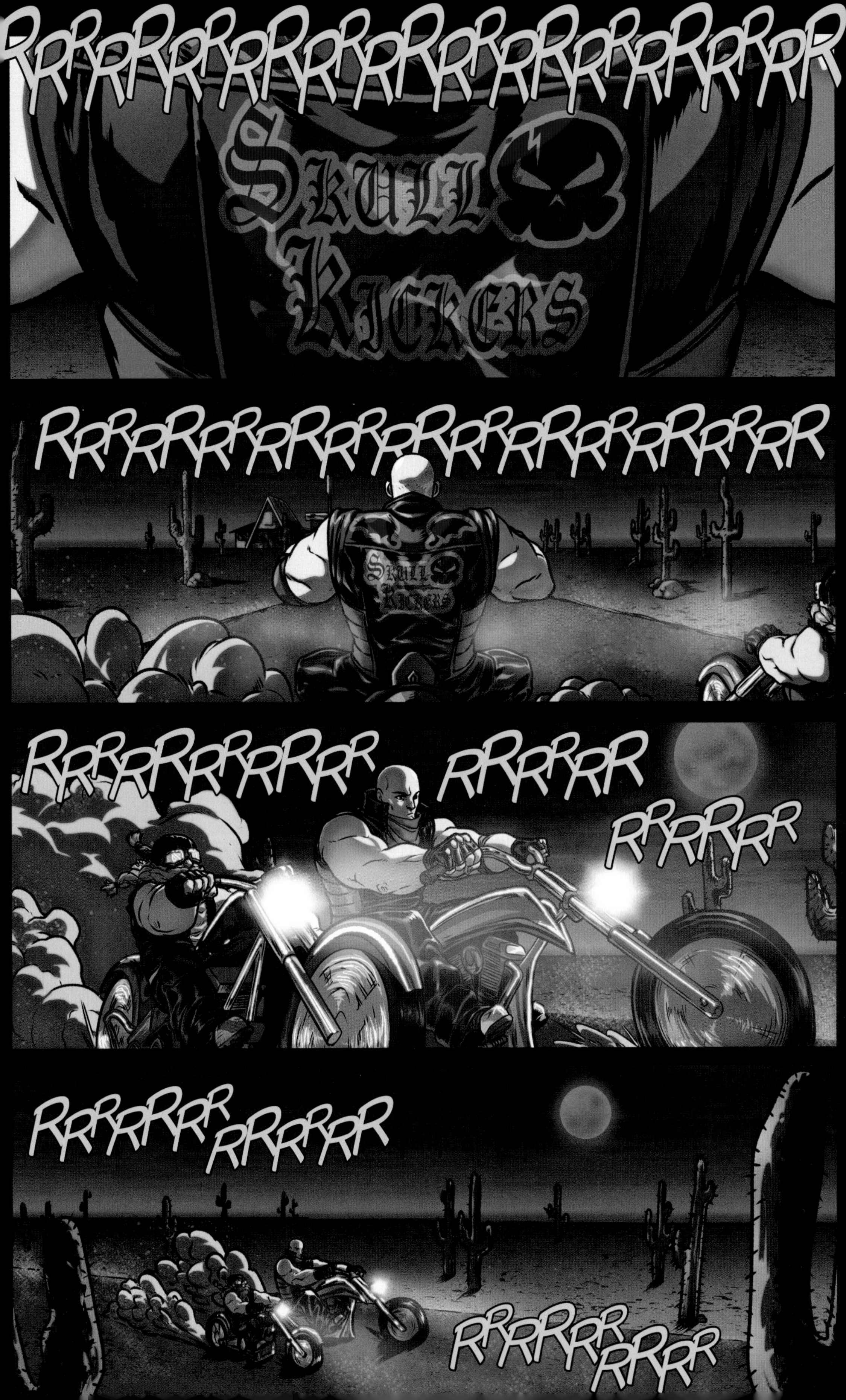

RRRRRRRRRRRRRRRRRRRRRRR
SKULL KICKERS
RRRRRRRRRRRRRRRRRRRRRR
SKULL KICKERS
RRRRRRRRRRRR
RRRRRR
RRRRRR
RRRRRRR
RRRRRRR
RRRRRR
RRRRR

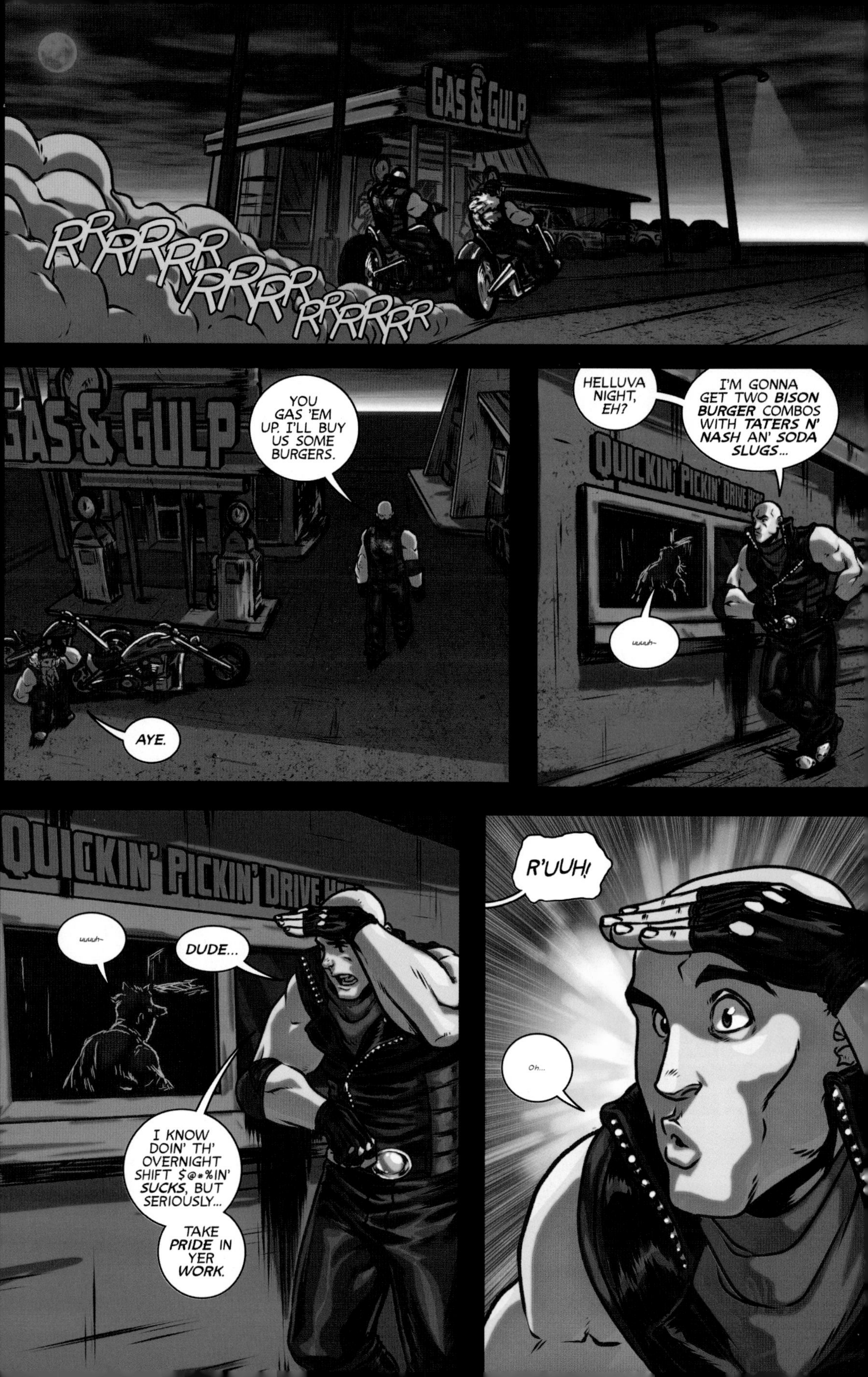
GAS & GULP
RRRRRRR RRRRRR RRRRRR
GAS & GULP
YOU GAS 'EM UP. I'LL BUY US SOME BURGERS.
AYE.
HELLUVA NIGHT, EH?
I'M GONNA GET TWO BISON BURGER COMBOS WITH TATERS N' NASH AN' SODA SLUGS...
QUICKIN' PICKIN' DRIVE HERE
uuuuh~
QUICKIN' PICKIN' DRIVE HE
uuuuh~
DUDE...
I KNOW DOIN' TH' OVERNIGHT SHIFT $@#%IN' SUCKS, BUT SERIOUSLY...
TAKE PRIDE IN YER WORK.
R'UUH!
Oh...

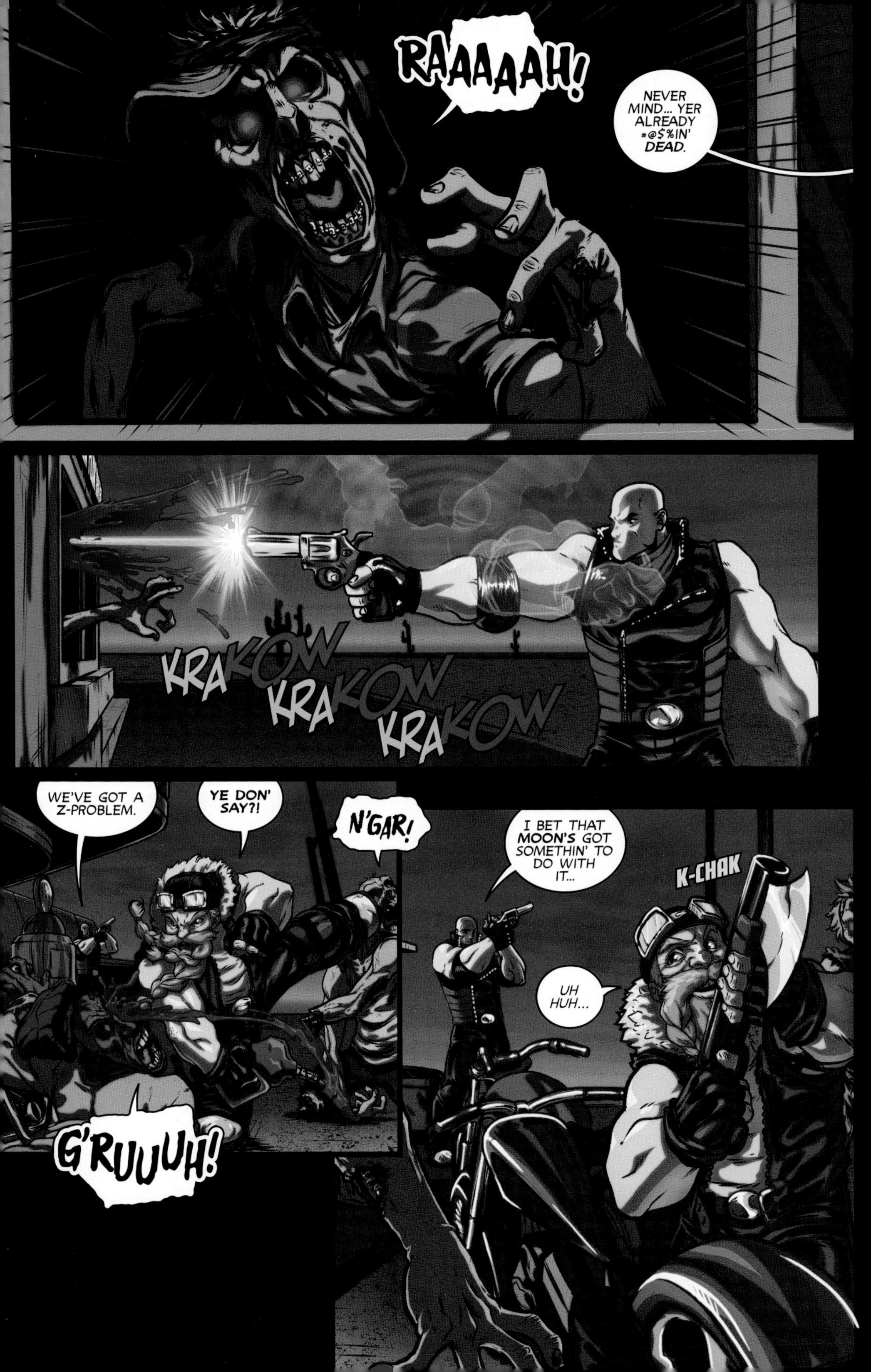
RAAAAAH!
NEVER MIND... YER ALREADY #@$%IN' DEAD.
KRAKOW KRAKOW KRAKOW
WE'VE GOT A Z-PROBLEM.
YE DON' SAY?!
N'GAR!
G'RUUUH!
I BET THAT MOON'S GOT SOMETHIN' TO DO WITH IT...
K-CHAK
UH HUH...

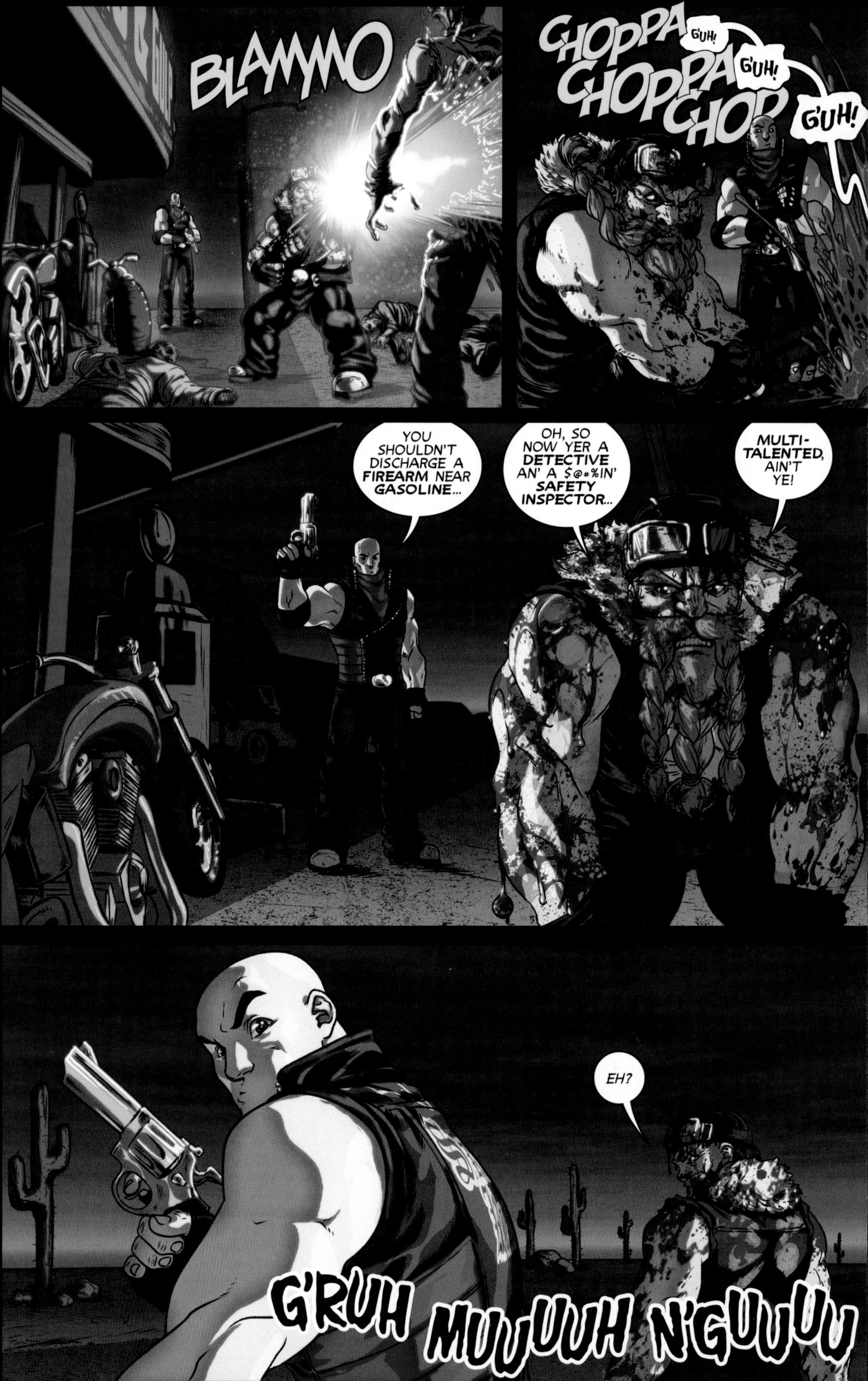
BLAMMO
CHOPPA CHOPPA CHOPPA CHOP
G'UH!
G'UH!
G'UH!
YOU SHOULDN'T DISCHARGE A FIREARM NEAR GASOLINE...
OH, SO NOW YER A DETECTIVE AN' A $@#%IN' SAFETY INSPECTOR...
MULTI-TALENTED, AIN'T YE!
EH?
G'RUH MUUUUH N'GUUUU

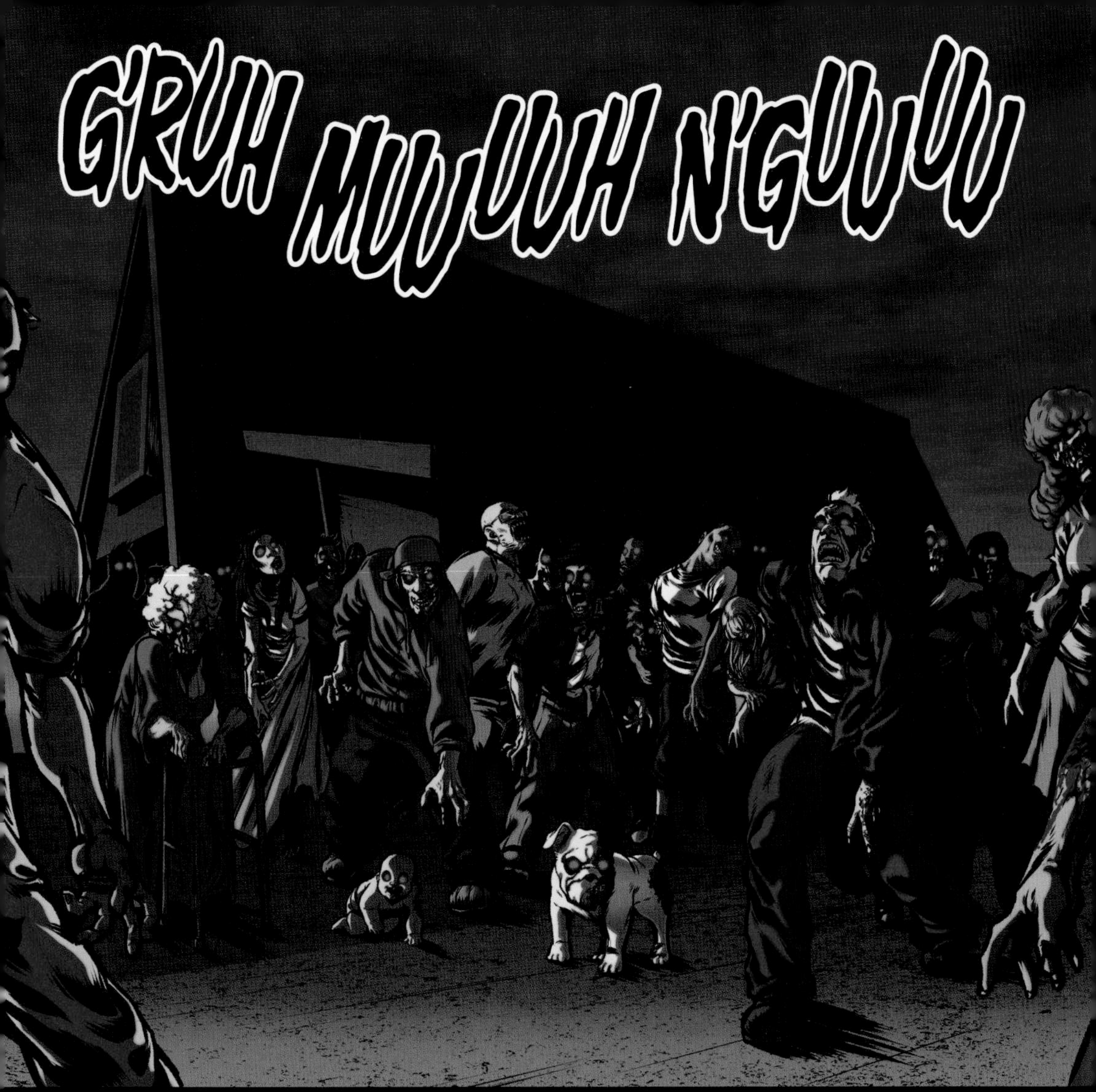
G'RUH MUUUUH N'GUUUU

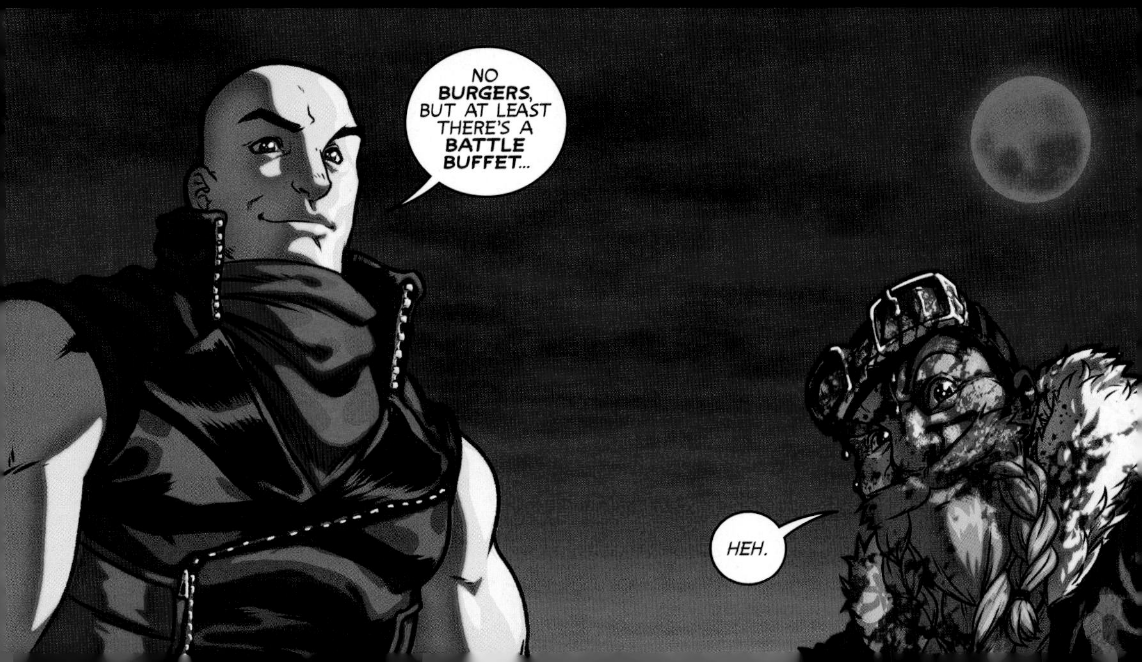
NO BURGERS, BUT AT LEAST THERE'S A BATTLE BUFFET...
HEH.

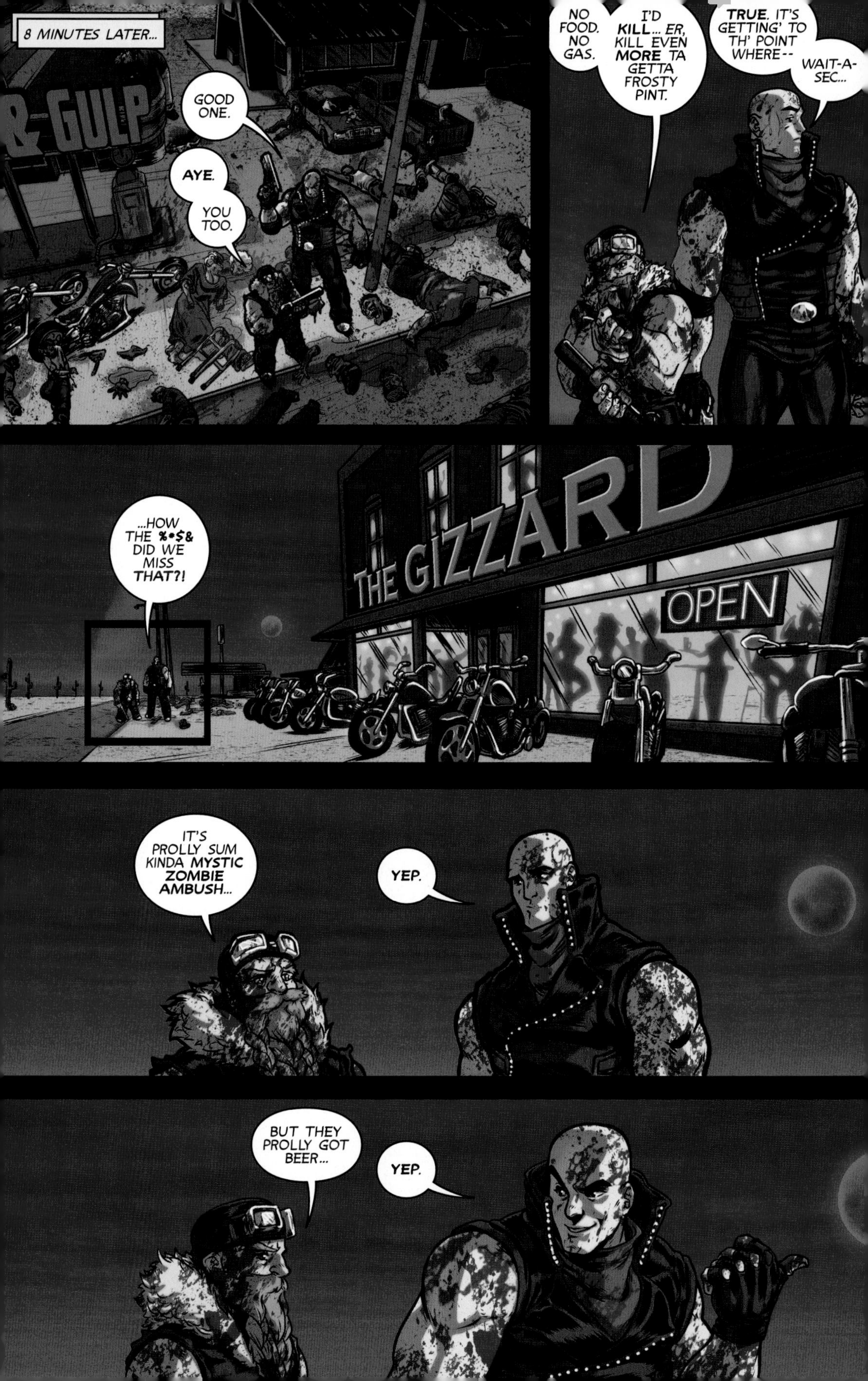
8 MINUTES LATER...
& GULP
GOOD ONE.
AYE.
YOU TOO.
NO FOOD. NO GAS.
I'D KILL... ER, KILL EVEN MORE TA GETTA FROSTY PINT.
TRUE. IT'S GETTING' TO TH' POINT WHERE--
WAIT-A-SEC...
...HOW THE %*$& DID WE MISS THAT?!
THE GIZZARD
OPEN
IT'S PROLLY SUM KINDA MYSTIC ZOMBIE AMBUSH...
YEP.
BUT THEY PROLLY GOT BEER...
YEP.

CHAPTER ONE

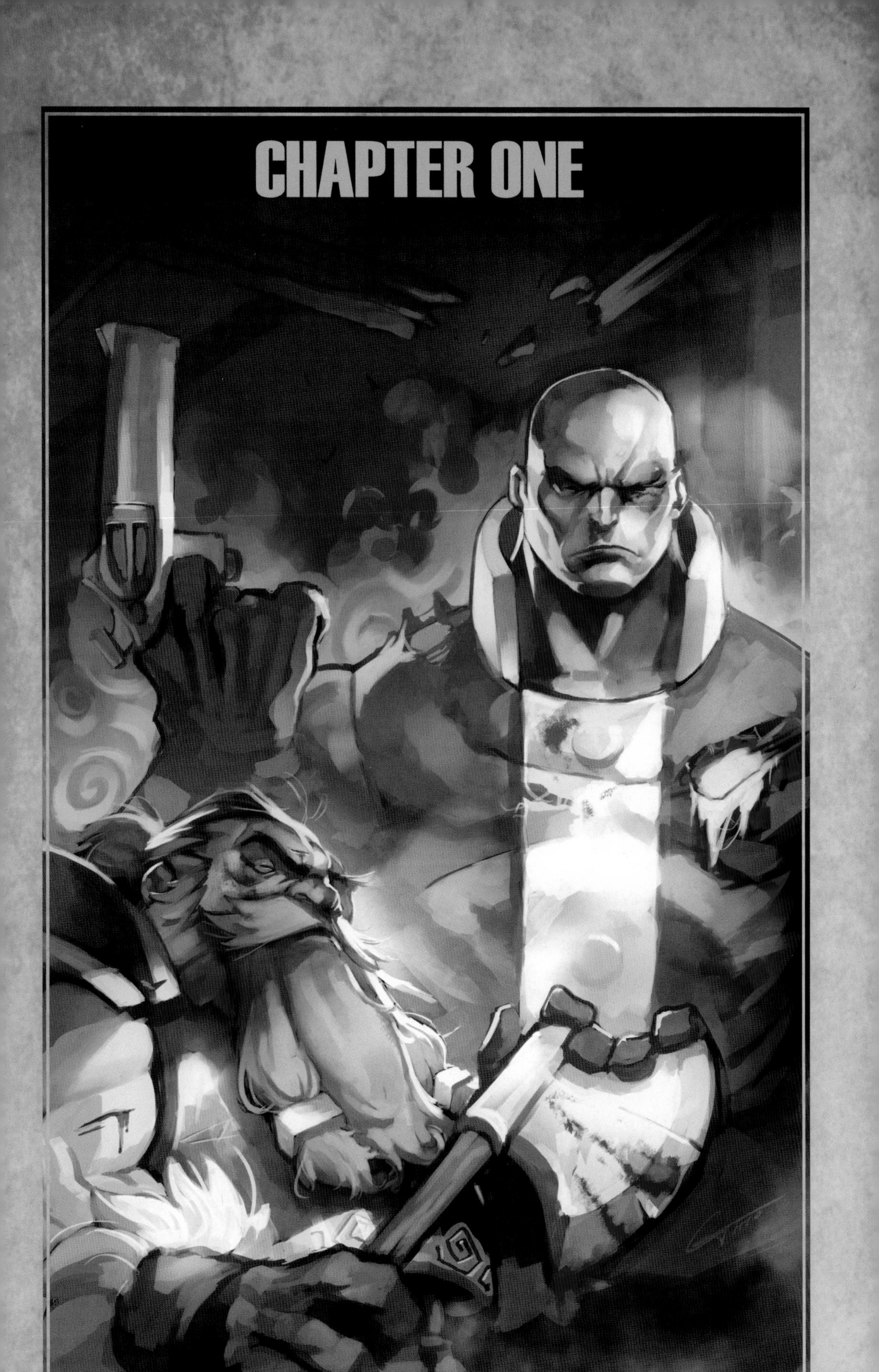

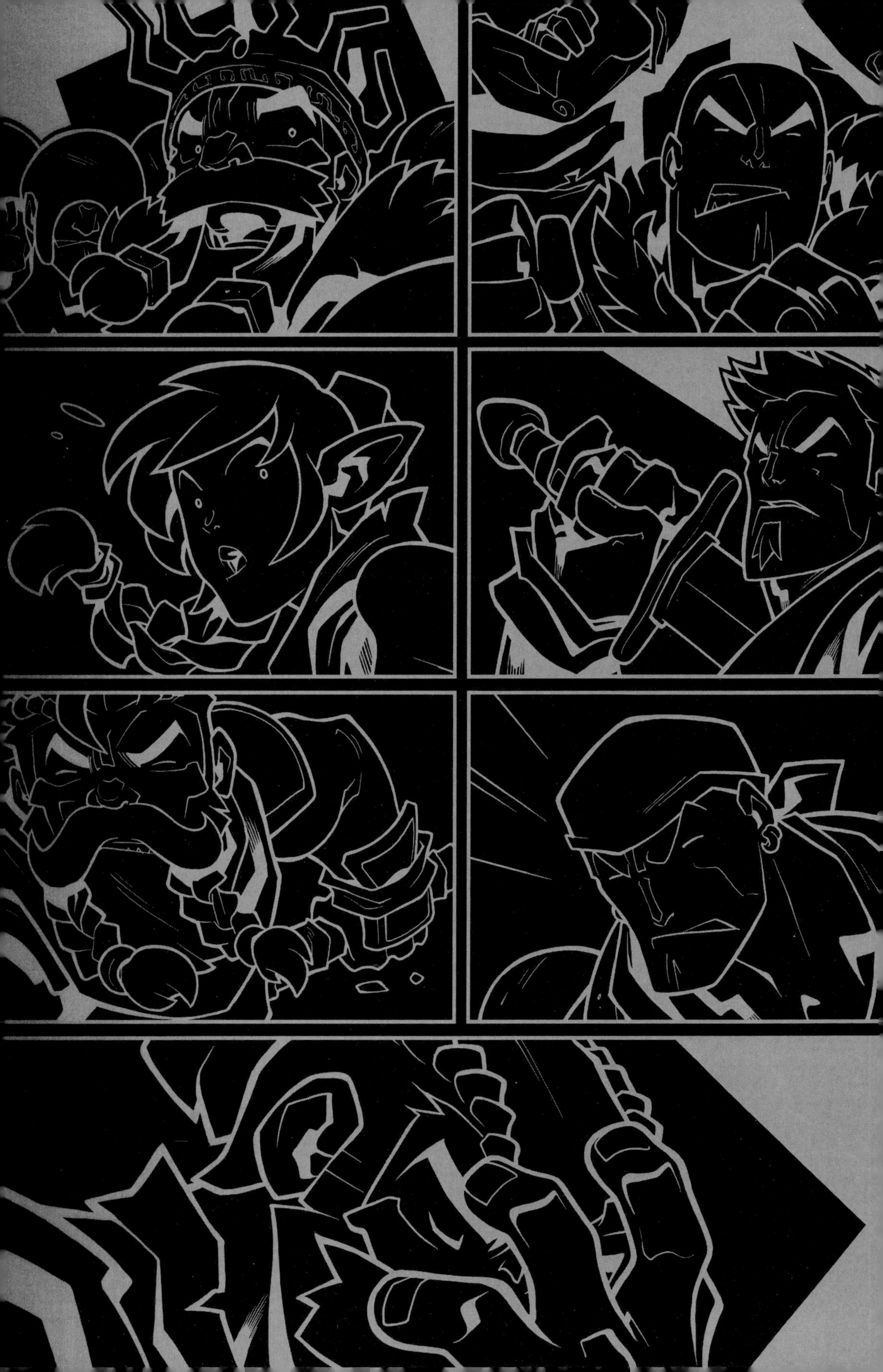

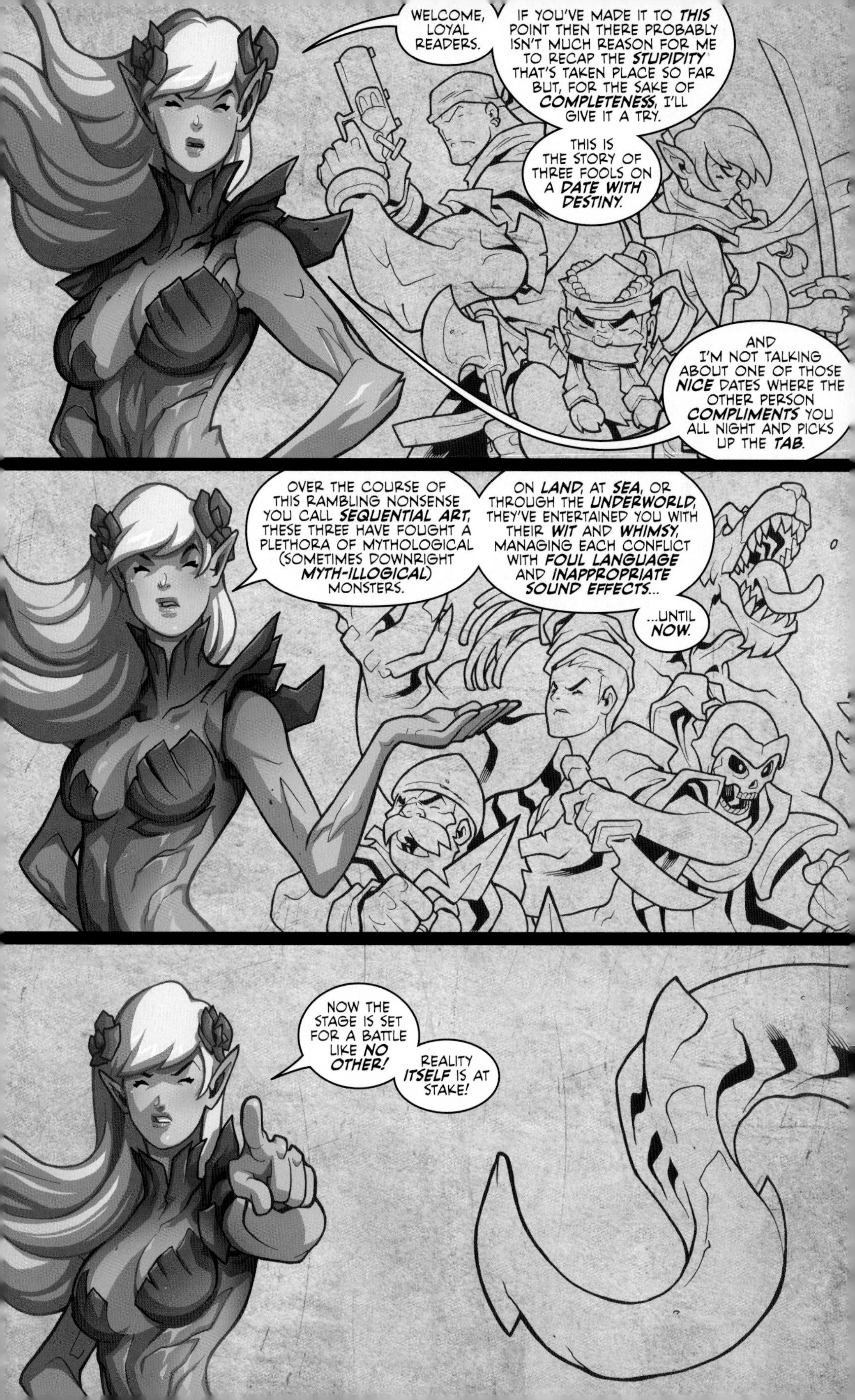
WELCOME, LOYAL READERS.
IF YOU'VE MADE IT TO THIS POINT THEN THERE PROBABLY ISN'T MUCH REASON FOR ME TO RECAP THE STUPIDITY THAT'S TAKEN PLACE SO FAR BUT, FOR THE SAKE OF COMPLETENESS, I'LL GIVE IT A TRY.
THIS IS THE STORY OF THREE FOOLS ON A DATE WITH DESTINY.
AND I'M NOT TALKING ABOUT ONE OF THOSE NICE DATES WHERE THE OTHER PERSON COMPLIMENTS YOU ALL NIGHT AND PICKS UP THE TAB.
OVER THE COURSE OF THIS RAMBLING NONSENSE YOU CALL SEQUENTIAL ART, THESE THREE HAVE FOUGHT A PLETHORA OF MYTHOLOGICAL (SOMETIMES DOWNRIGHT MYTH-ILLOGICAL) MONSTERS.
ON LAND, AT SEA, OR THROUGH THE UNDERWORLD, THEY'VE ENTERTAINED YOU WITH THEIR WIT AND WHIMSY, MANAGING EACH CONFLICT WITH FOUL LANGUAGE AND INAPPROPRIATE SOUND EFFECTS...
...UNTIL NOW.
NOW THE STAGE IS SET FOR A BATTLE LIKE NO OTHER!
REALITY ITSELF IS AT STAKE!

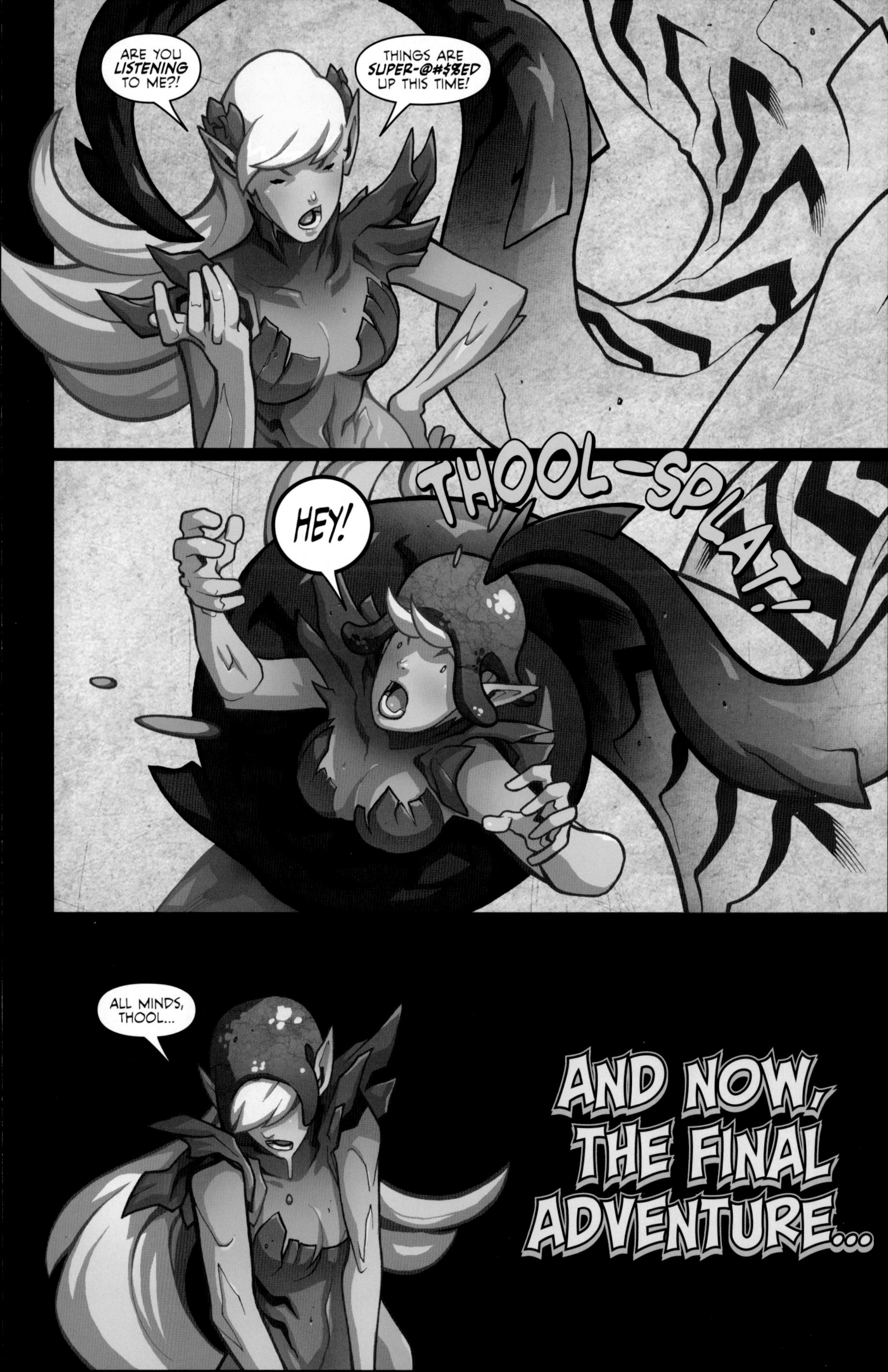

ARE YOU LISTENING TO ME?!
THINGS ARE SUPER-@#$%ED UP THIS TIME!
THOOL-SPLAT!!
HEY!
ALL MINDS, THOOL...
AND NOW, THE FINAL ADVENTURE...

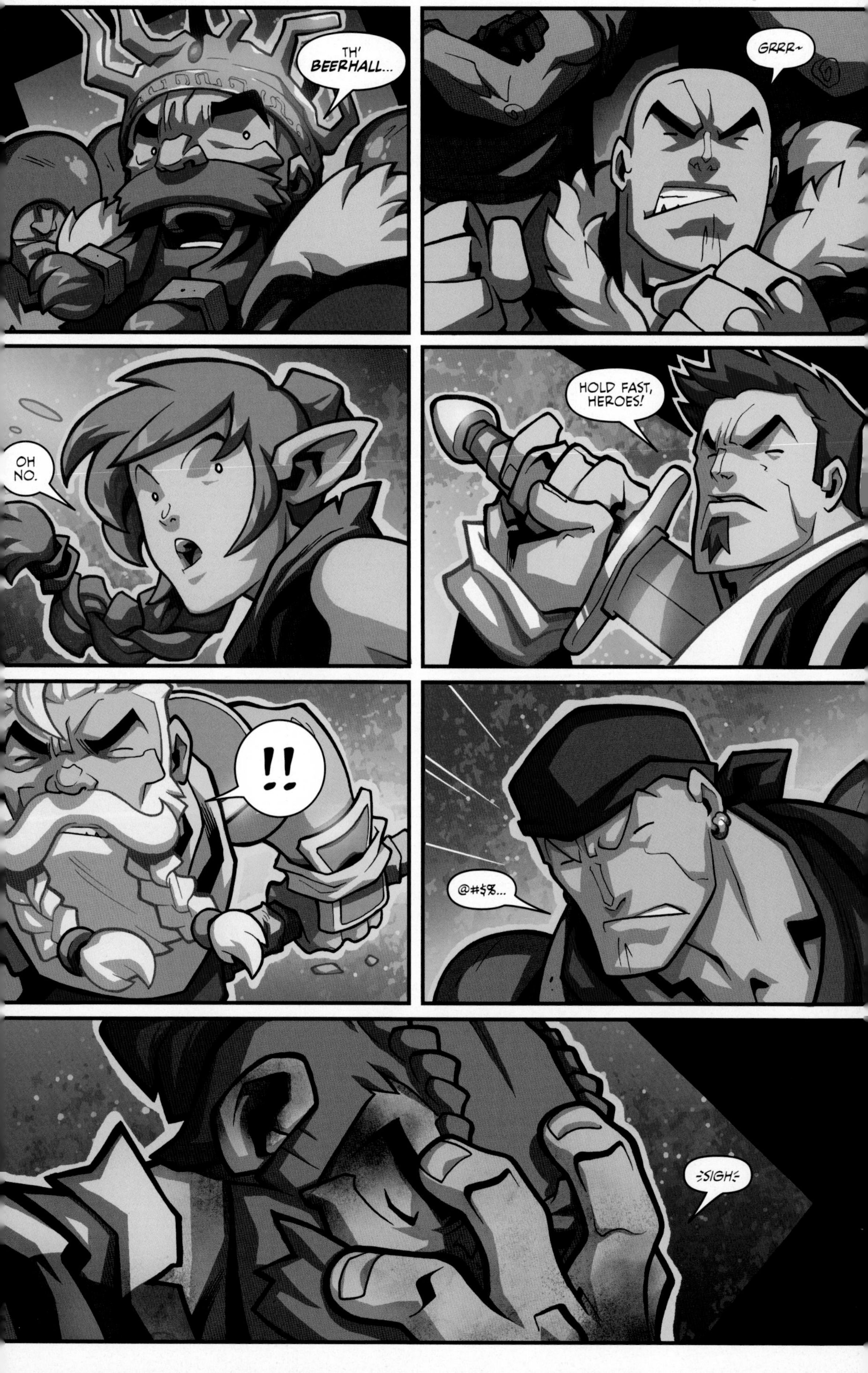
TH' BEERHALL...
GRRR~
OH NO.
HOLD FAST, HEROES!
!!
@#$%...
SIGH

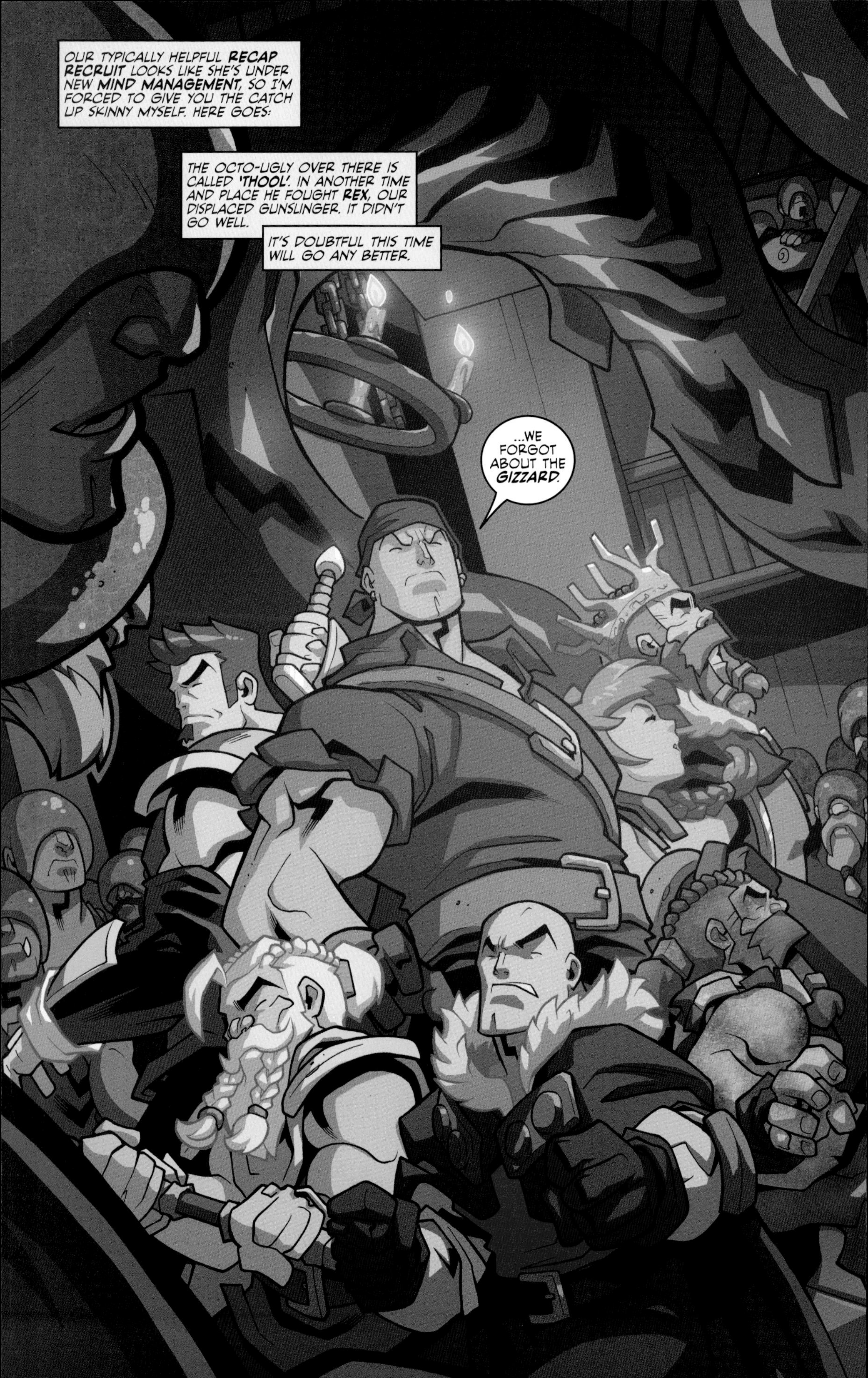
OUR TYPICALLY HELPFUL RECAP RECRUIT LOOKS LIKE SHE'S UNDER NEW MIND MANAGEMENT, SO I'M FORCED TO GIVE YOU THE CATCH UP SKINNY MYSELF. HERE GOES:
THE OCTO-UGLY OVER THERE IS CALLED 'THOOL'. IN ANOTHER TIME AND PLACE HE FOUGHT REX, OUR DISPLACED GUNSLINGER. IT DIDN'T GO WELL.
IT'S DOUBTFUL THIS TIME WILL GO ANY BETTER.
...WE FORGOT ABOUT THE GIZZARD.

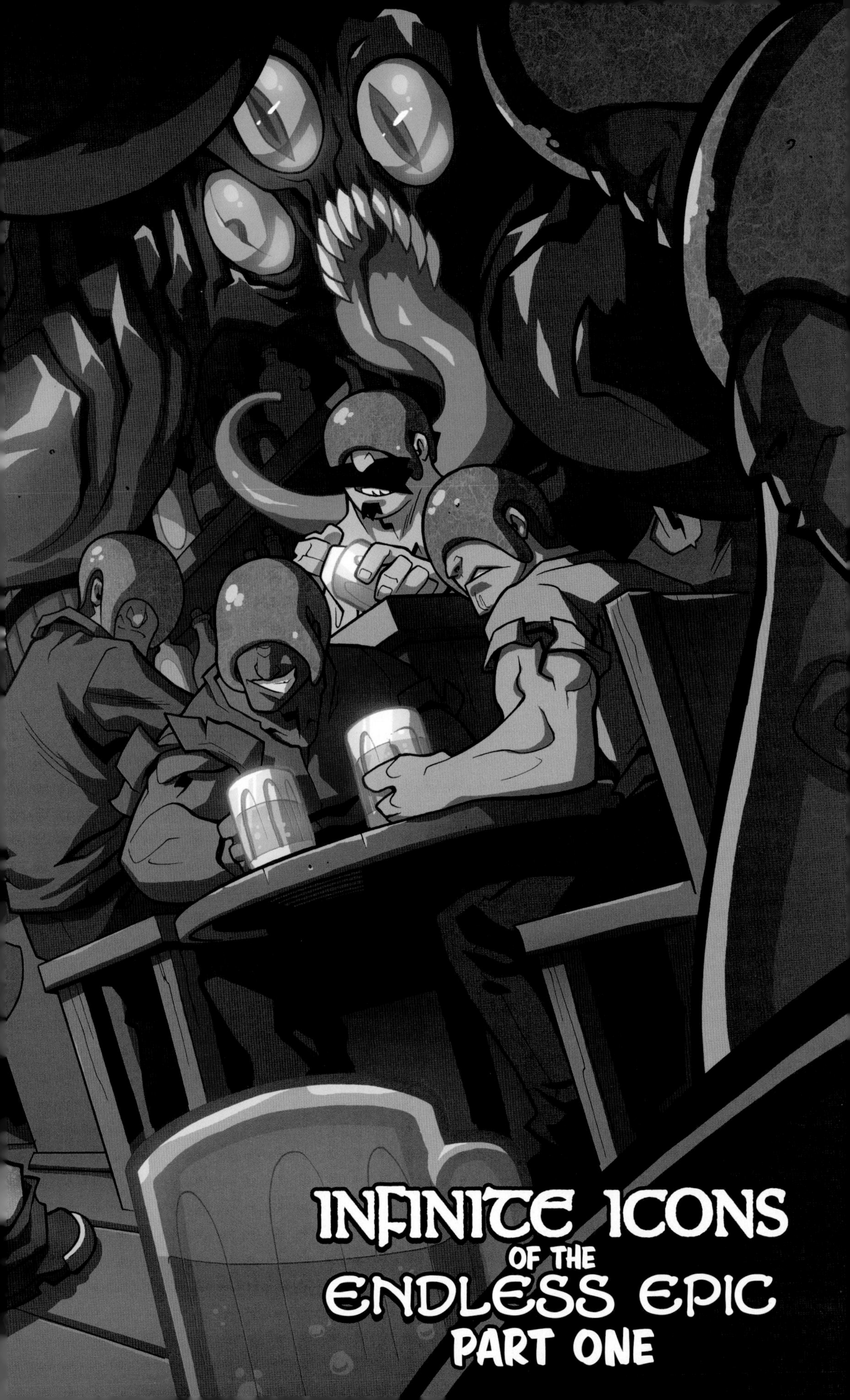
INFINITE ICONS
OF THE
ENDLESS EPIC
PART ONE

YOU MAY HAVE FORGOTTEN ABOUT *ME* BUT, LEMME TELL YA, I SURE AS $#@% *DIDN'T* FORGET ABOUT *YOU.*

NOPE!

Perfect Pour

THANKS TO *DIMENSIONAL TRAVEL DISTORTION* AND THE WEIRD AND WONDERFUL NATURE OF THIS *'NEXUS PUB',* I'VE BEEN WAITING HERE A LONG, LONG TIME.

"HOW LONG", YOU SAY?

LONG ENOUGH TO HATCH A *BABY THOOL* FOR EVERY BEER-SWIGGING *BUFFOON* IN THE BAR...

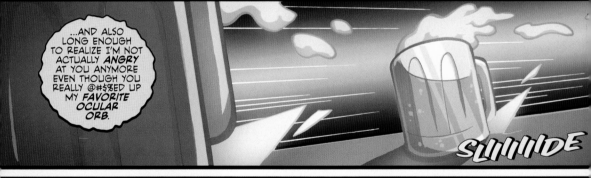

...AND ALSO LONG ENOUGH TO REALIZE I'M NOT ACTUALLY *ANGRY* AT YOU ANYMORE EVEN THOUGH YOU REALLY @#$%ED UP MY *FAVORITE OCULAR ORB.*

SLIIIIIIIDE

THIRSTY?

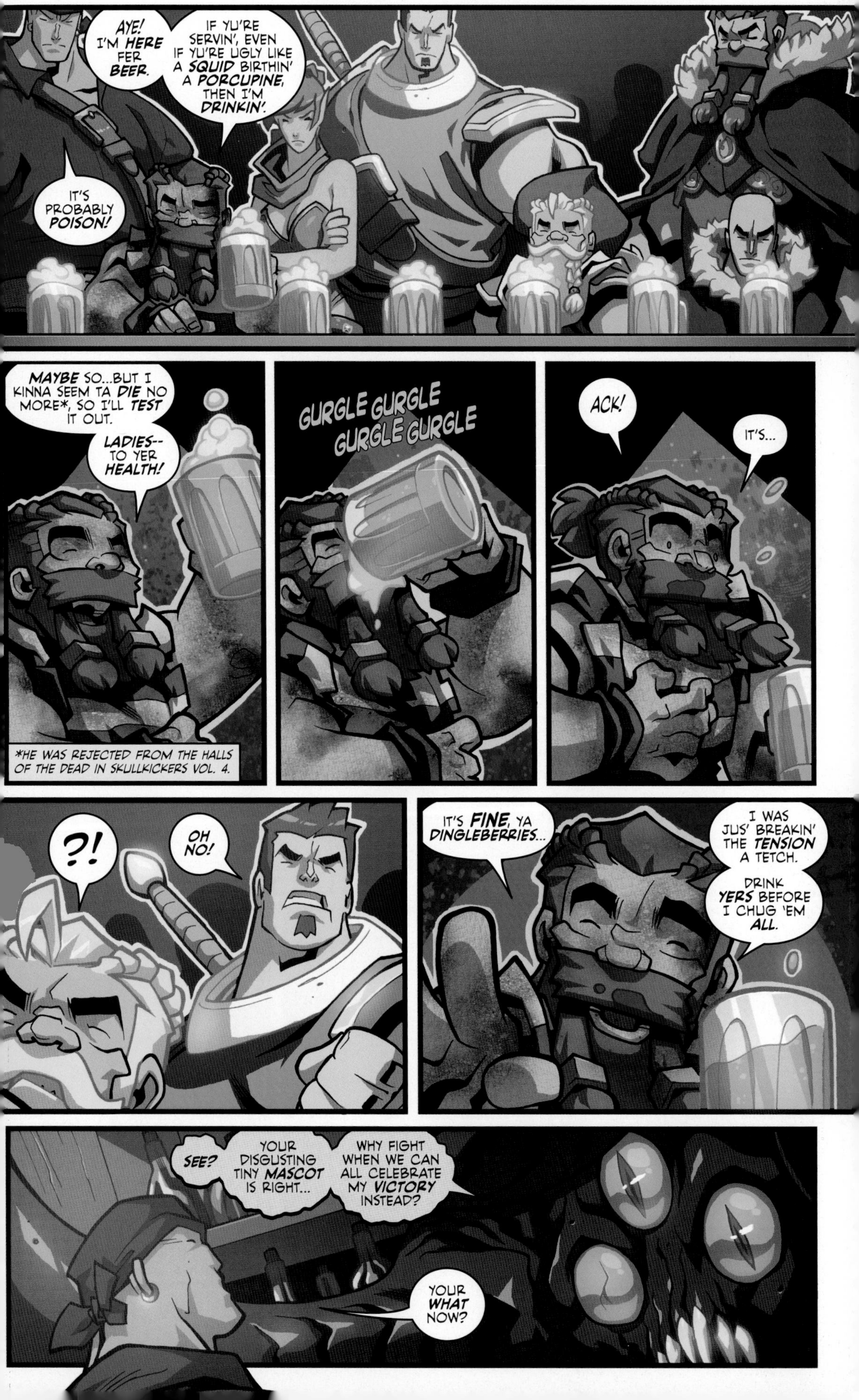
AYE! I'M HERE FER BEER.
IF YU'RE SERVIN', EVEN IF YU'RE UGLY LIKE A SQUID BIRTHIN' A PORCUPINE, THEN I'M DRINKIN'.
IT'S PROBABLY POISON!
MAYBE SO...BUT I KINNA SEEM TA DIE NO MORE*, SO I'LL TEST IT OUT.
LADIES-- TO YER HEALTH!
*HE WAS REJECTED FROM THE HALLS OF THE DEAD IN SKULLKICKERS VOL. 4.
GURGLE GURGLE GURGLE GURGLE
ACK!
IT'S...
?!
OH NO!
IT'S FINE, YA DINGLEBERRIES...
I WAS JUS' BREAKIN' THE TENSION A TETCH.
DRINK YERS BEFORE I CHUG 'EM ALL.
SEE?
YOUR DISGUSTING TINY MASCOT IS RIGHT...
WHY FIGHT WHEN WE CAN ALL CELEBRATE MY VICTORY INSTEAD?
YOUR WHAT NOW?

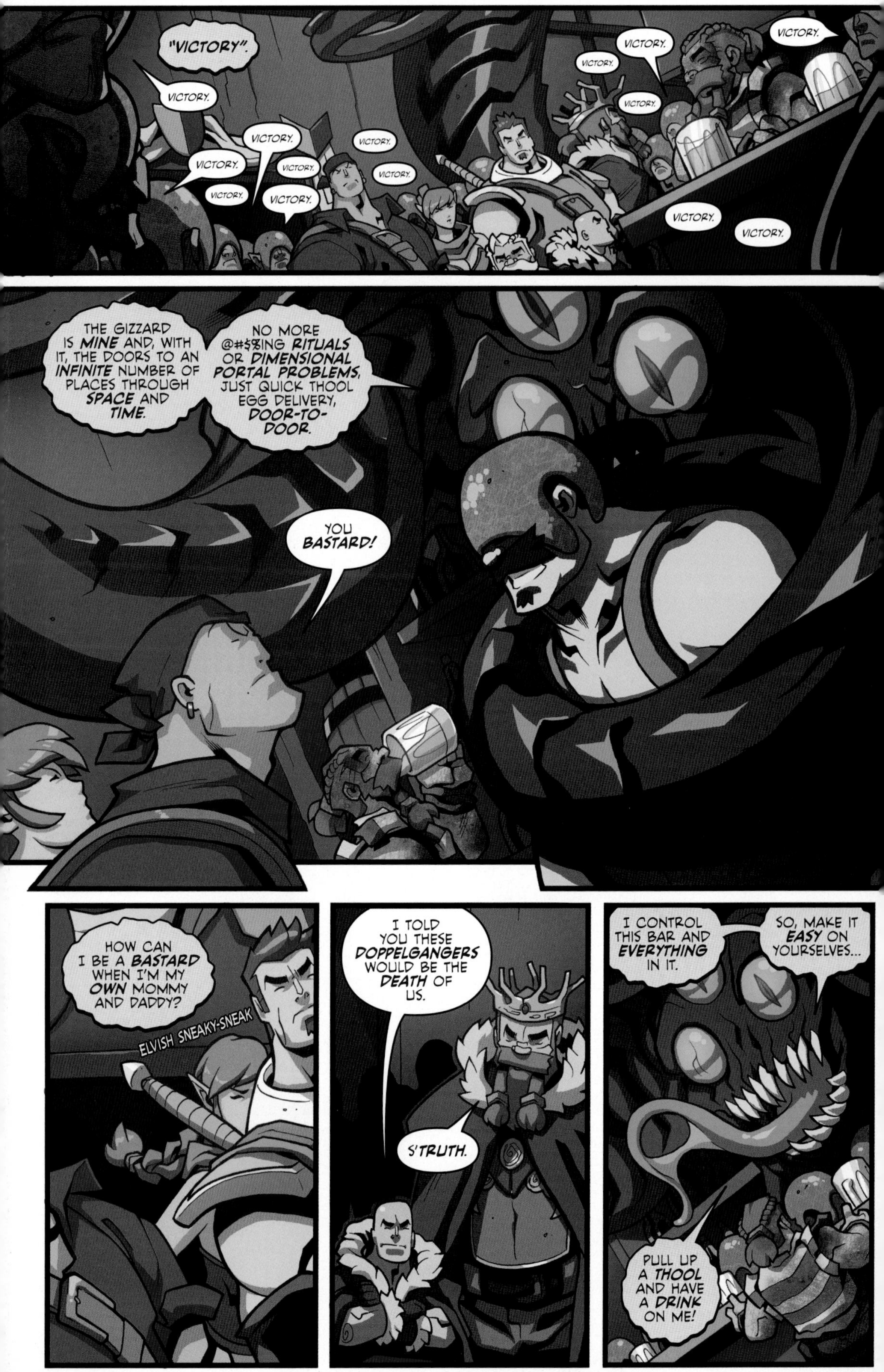
"VICTORY".
VICTORY.
VICTORY.
VICTORY.
VICTORY.
VICTORY.
VICTORY.
VICTORY.
VICTORY.
VICTORY.
VICTORY.
VICTORY.
VICTORY.
VICTORY.
VICTORY.
THE GIZZARD IS MINE AND, WITH IT, THE DOORS TO AN INFINITE NUMBER OF PLACES THROUGH SPACE AND TIME.
NO MORE @#$%ING RITUALS OR DIMENSIONAL PORTAL PROBLEMS. JUST QUICK THOOL EGG DELIVERY, DOOR-TO-DOOR.
YOU BASTARD!
HOW CAN I BE A BASTARD WHEN I'M MY OWN MOMMY AND DADDY?
ELVISH SNEAKY-SNEAK
I TOLD YOU THESE DOPPELGANGERS WOULD BE THE DEATH OF US.
S'TRUTH.
I CONTROL THIS BAR AND EVERYTHING IN IT.
SO, MAKE IT EASY ON YOURSELVES...
PULL UP A THOOL AND HAVE A DRINK ON ME!

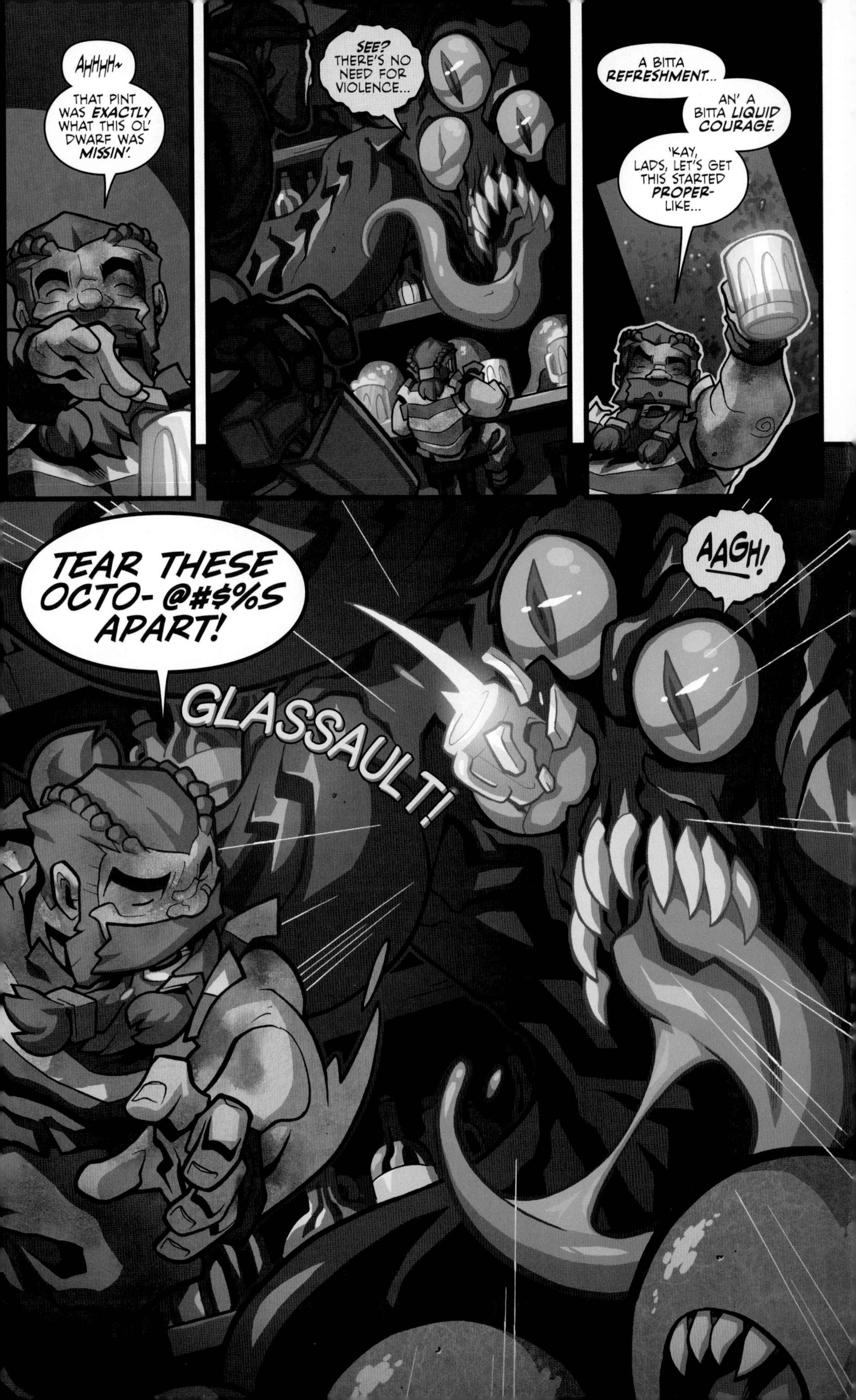
AHHHH~
THAT PINT WAS EXACTLY WHAT THIS OL' DWARF WAS MISSIN'.
SEE? THERE'S NO NEED FOR VIOLENCE...
A BITTA REFRESHMENT...
AN' A BITTA LIQUID COURAGE.
'KAY, LADS, LET'S GET THIS STARTED PROPER-LIKE...
TEAR THESE OCTO-@#$%S APART!
AAGH!
GLASSAULT!

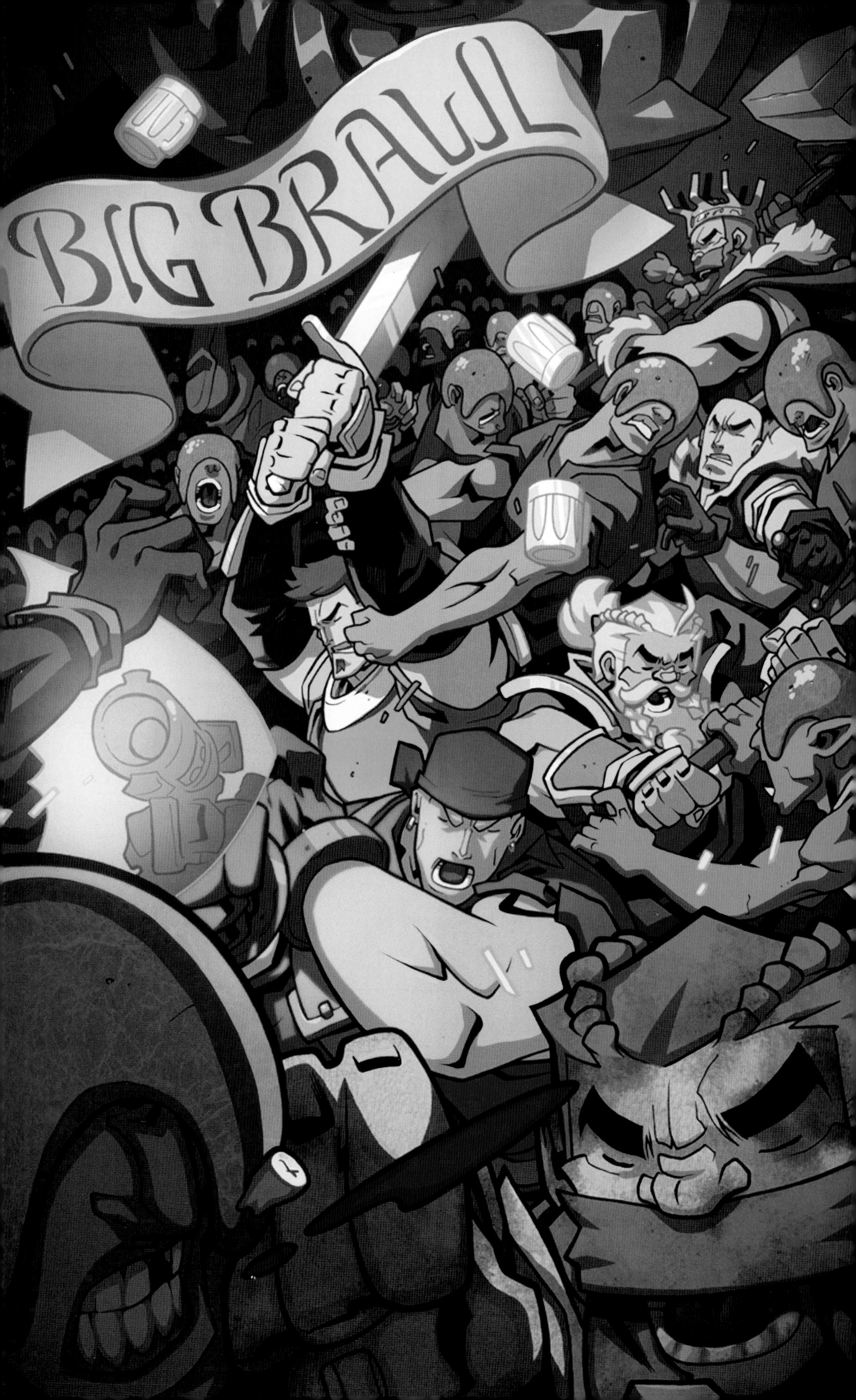
BIG BRAWL

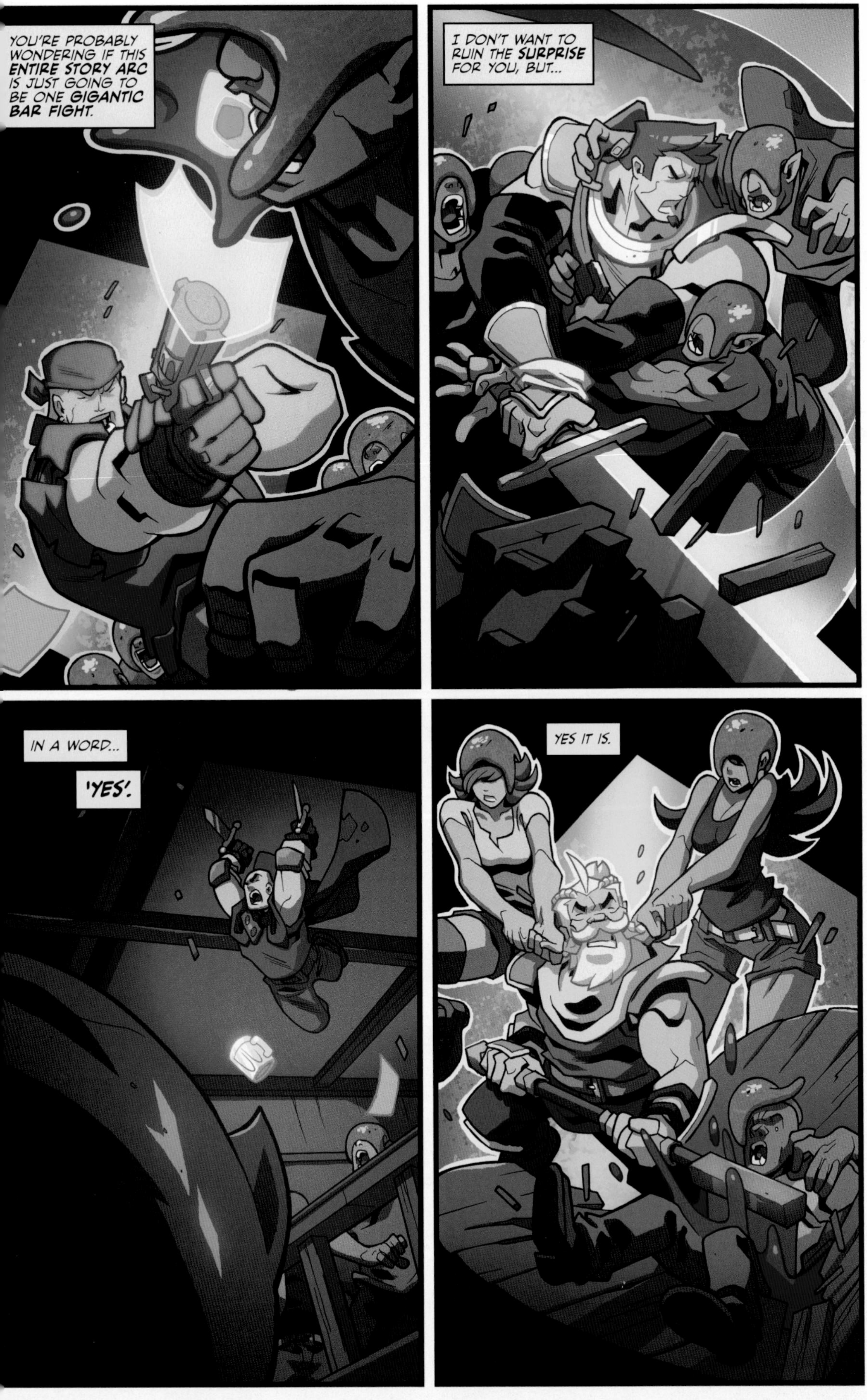
YOU'RE PROBABLY WONDERING IF THIS ENTIRE STORY ARC IS JUST GOING TO BE ONE GIGANTIC BAR FIGHT.
I DON'T WANT TO RUIN THE SURPRISE FOR YOU, BUT...
IN A WORD...
'YES'.
YES IT IS.

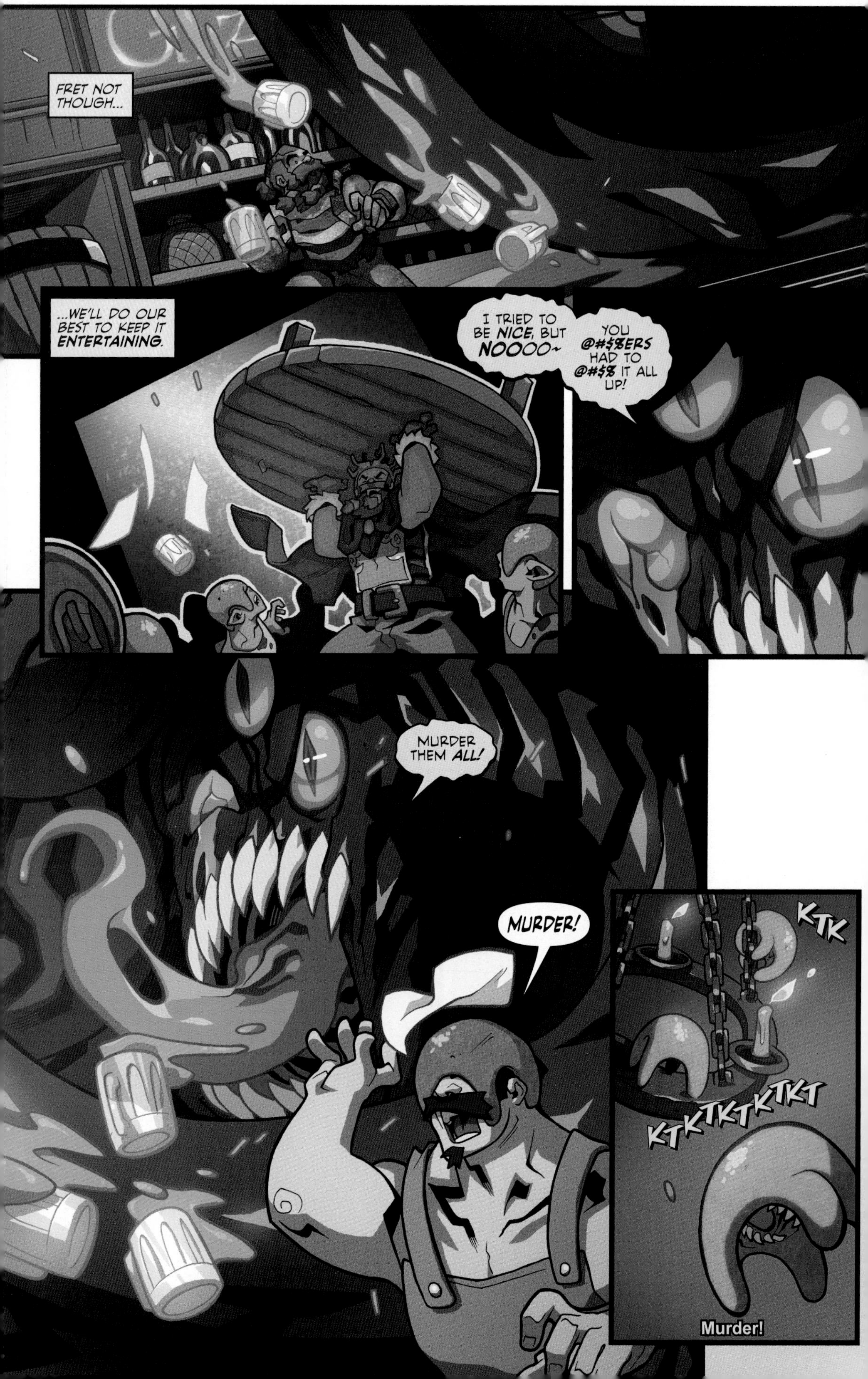
FRET NOT THOUGH...
...WE'LL DO OUR BEST TO KEEP IT ENTERTAINING.
I TRIED TO BE NICE, BUT NOOOO~
YOU @#$%ERS HAD TO @#$% IT ALL UP!
MURDER THEM ALL!
MURDER!
KTK
KTKTKTKTKT
Murder!

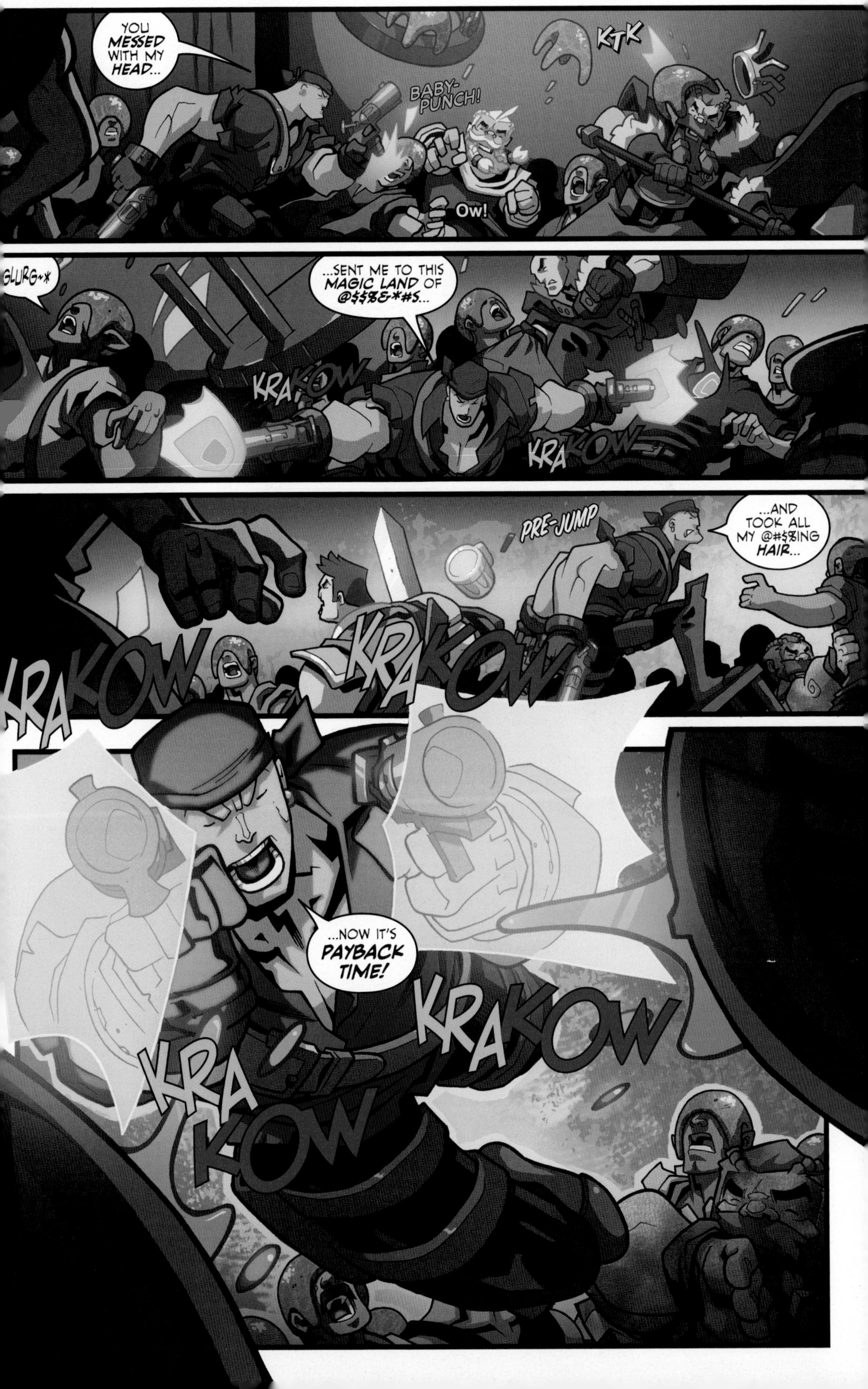
YOU MESSED WITH MY HEAD...
BABY-PUNCH!
KTK
OW!
GLURG~*
...SENT ME TO THIS MAGIC LAND OF @$$%&*#S...
KRAKOW
KRAKOW
PRE-JUMP
...AND TOOK ALL MY @#$%ING HAIR...
KRAKOW
KRAKOW
...NOW IT'S PAYBACK TIME!
KRAKOW
KRAKOW

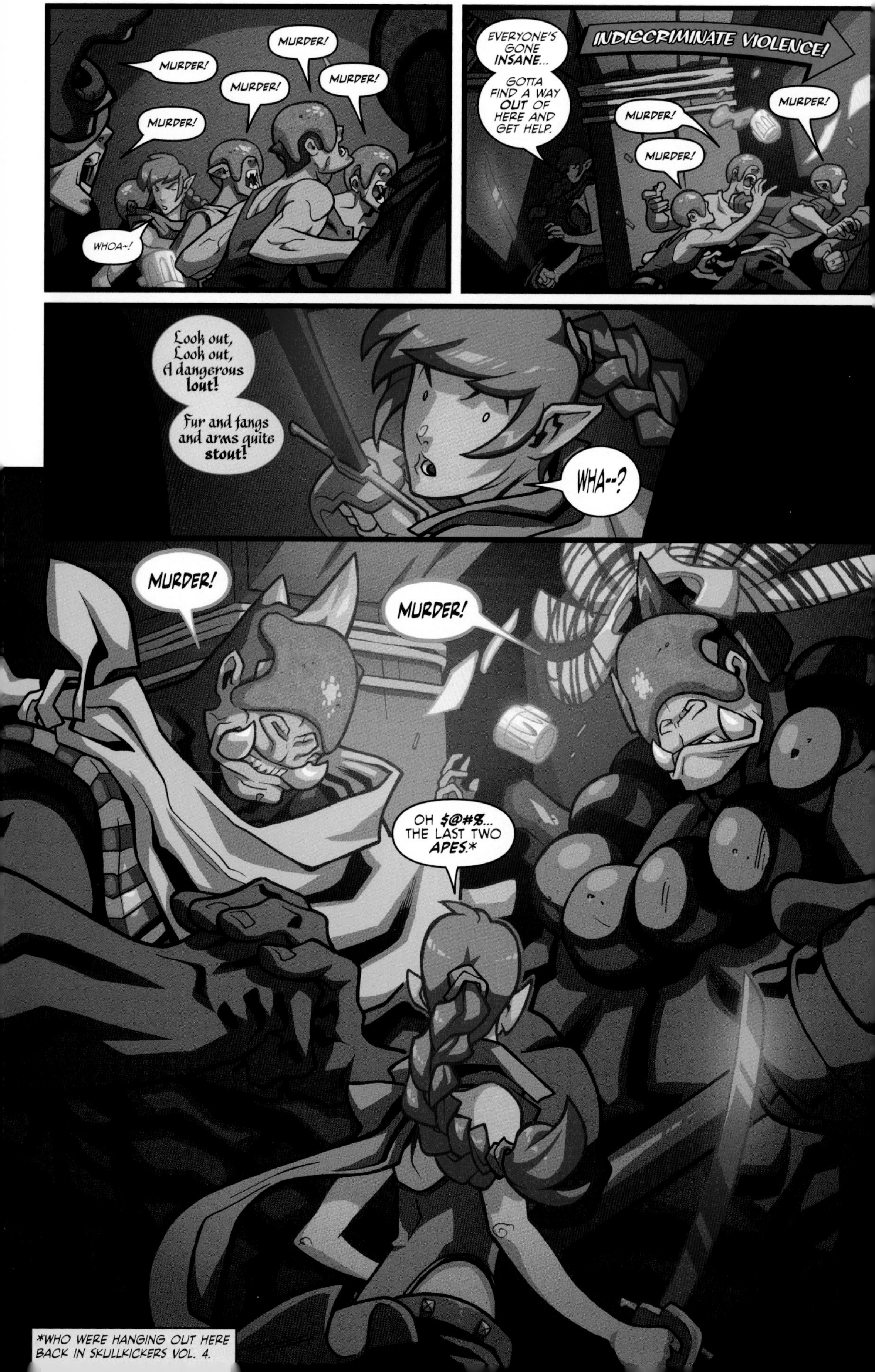
MURDER!
MURDER!
MURDER!
MURDER!
MURDER!
WHOA~!
EVERYONE'S GONE INSANE...
GOTTA FIND A WAY OUT OF HERE AND GET HELP.
INDISCRIMINATE VIOLENCE!
MURDER!
MURDER!
MURDER!
Look out, Look out, A dangerous lout!
Fur and fangs and arms quite stout!
WHA--?
MURDER!
MURDER!
OH $@#%... THE LAST TWO APES.*
*WHO WERE HANGING OUT HERE BACK IN SKULLKICKERS VOL. 4.

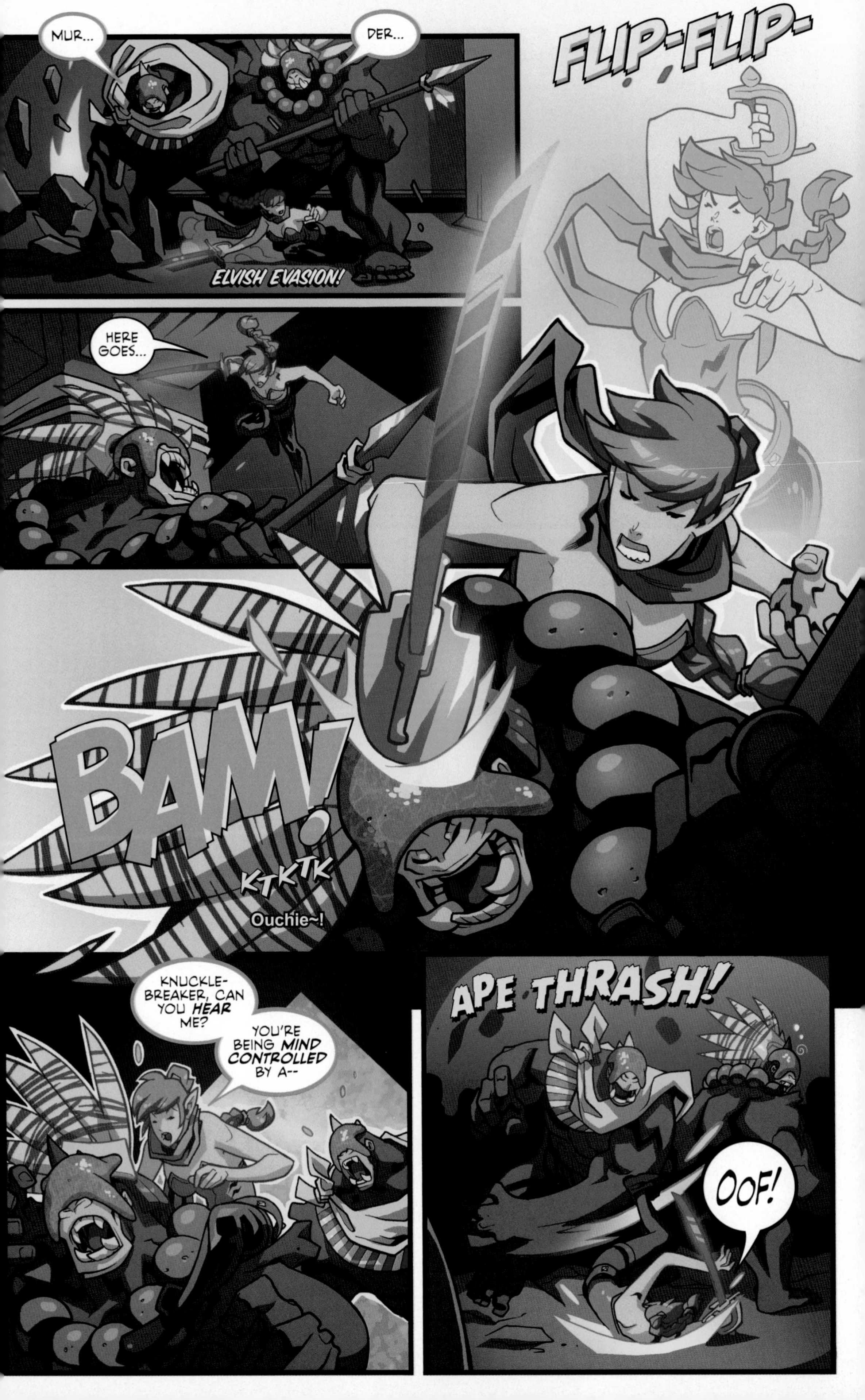
MUR...
DER...
FLIP-FLIP-
ELVISH EVASION!
HERE GOES...
BAM!
KTKTK
Ouchie~!
KNUCKLE-BREAKER, CAN YOU HEAR ME?
YOU'RE BEING MIND CONTROLLED BY A--
APE THRASH!
OOF!

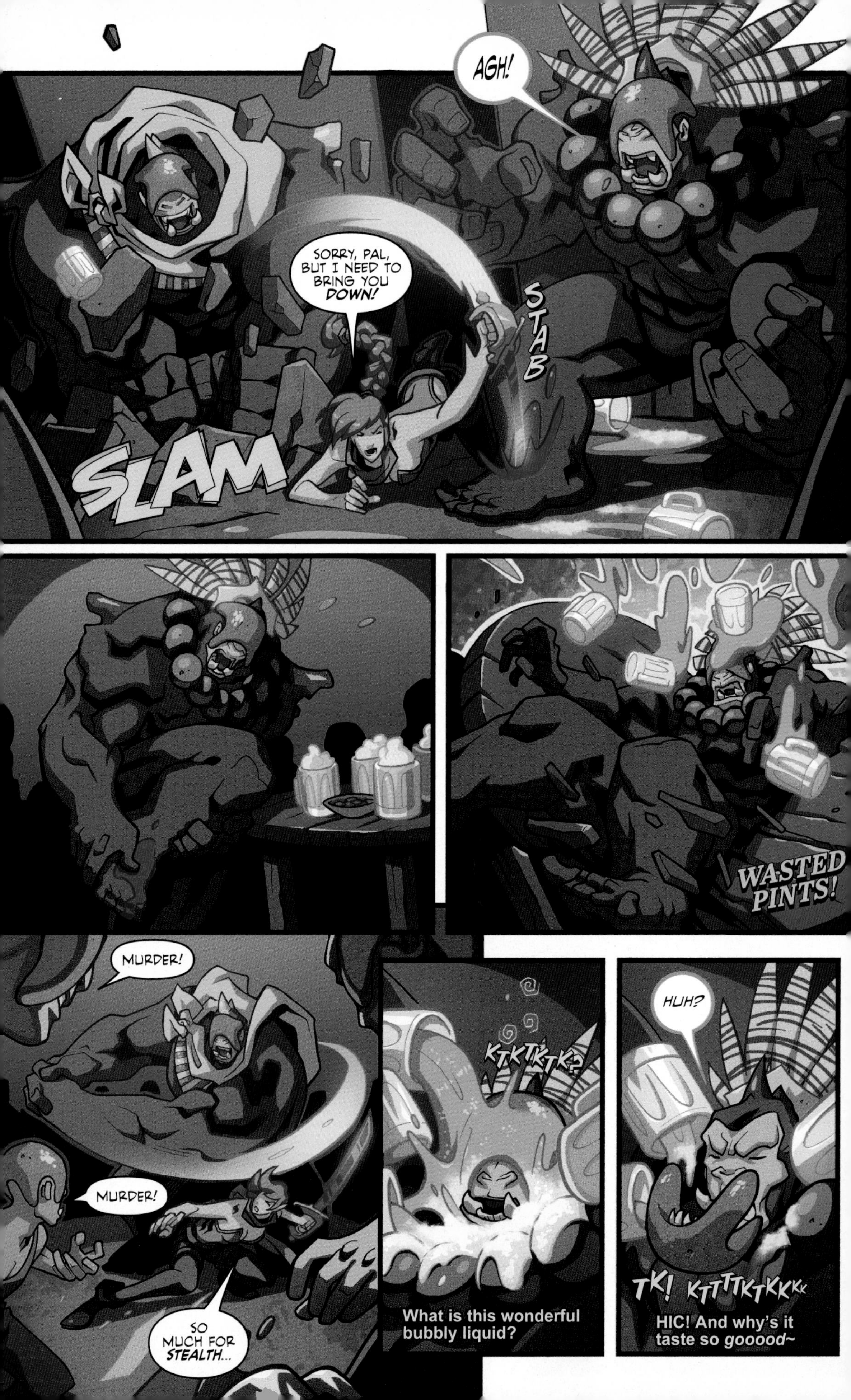
AGH!
SORRY, PAL, BUT I NEED TO BRING YOU DOWN!
STAB
SLAM
WASTED PINTS!
MURDER!
MURDER!
SO MUCH FOR STEALTH...
KTKTKTKTK?
What is this wonderful bubbly liquid?
HUH?
TK! KTTTTKTKKKK
HIC! And why's it taste so gooood~

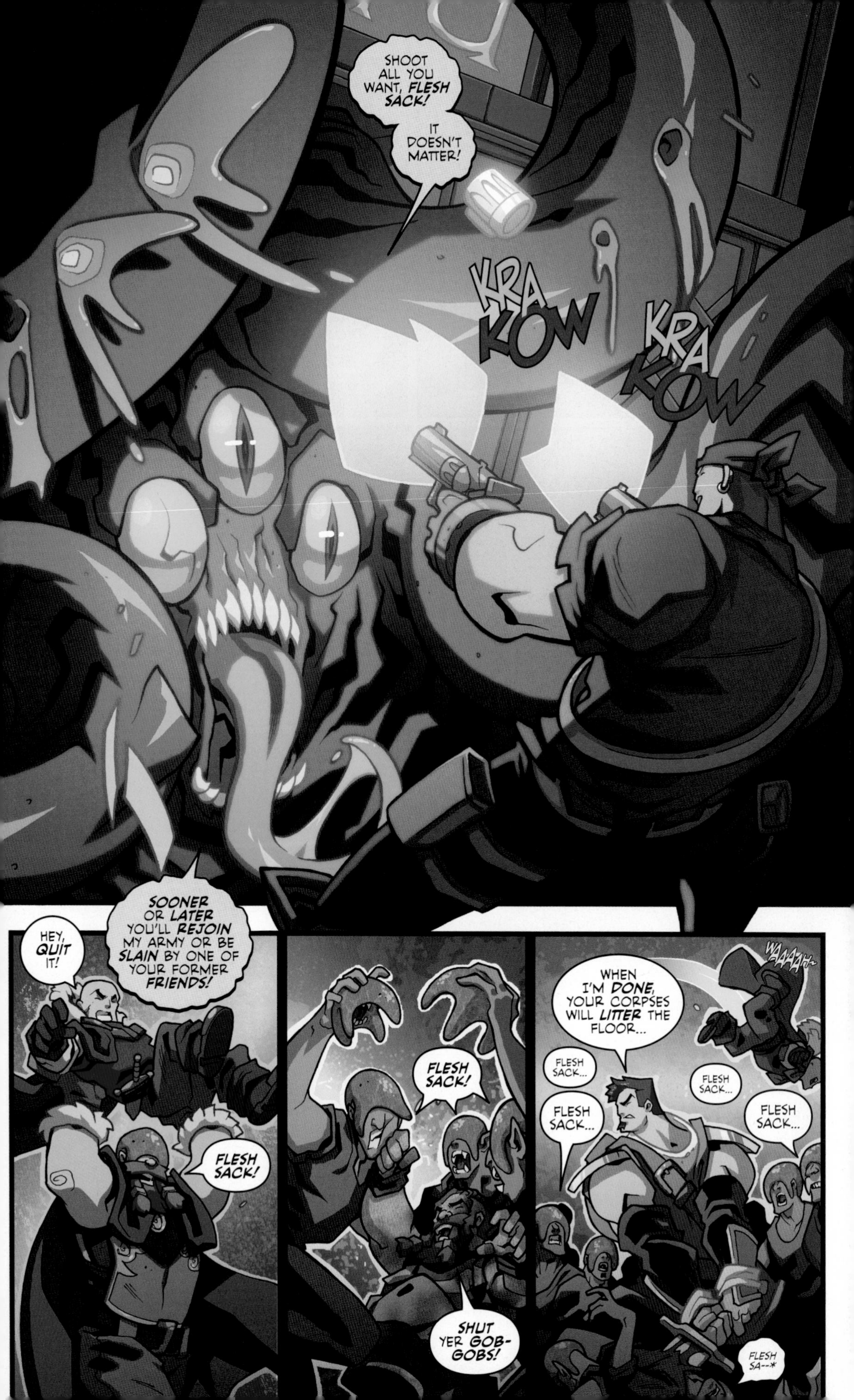
SHOOT ALL YOU WANT, FLESH SACK!
IT DOESN'T MATTER!
KRA KOW
KRA KOW
SOONER OR LATER YOU'LL REJOIN MY ARMY OR BE SLAIN BY ONE OF YOUR FORMER FRIENDS!
HEY, QUIT IT!
FLESH SACK!
FLESH SACK!
SHUT YER GOB-GOBS!
WAAAAH~
WHEN I'M DONE, YOUR CORPSES WILL LITTER THE FLOOR...
FLESH SACK...
FLESH SACK...
FLESH SACK...
FLESH SACK...
FLESH SA--*

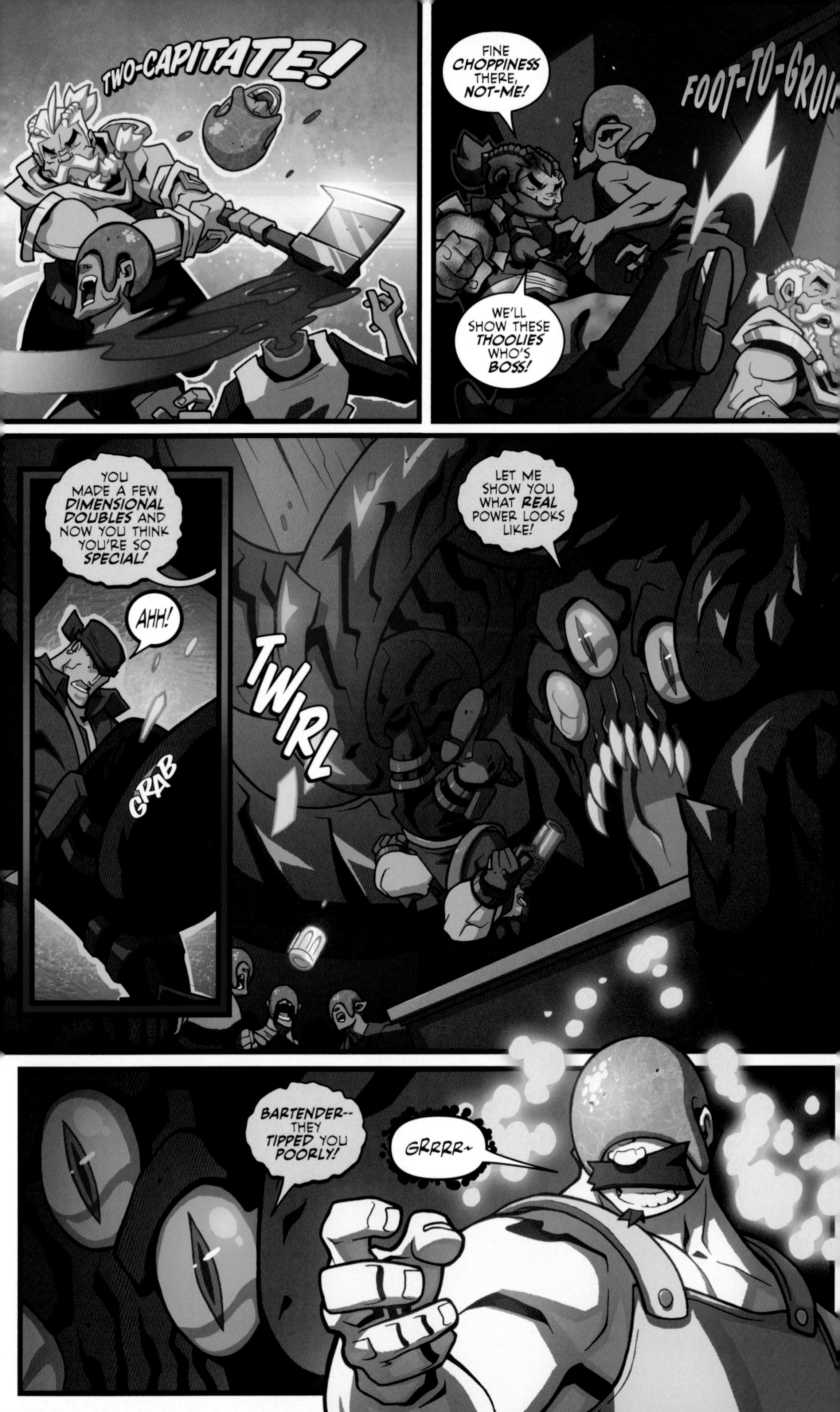
TWO-CAPITATE!
FINE CHOPPINESS THERE, NOT-ME!
FOOT-TO-GROI
WE'LL SHOW THESE THOOLIES WHO'S BOSS!
YOU MADE A FEW DIMENSIONAL DOUBLES AND NOW YOU THINK YOU'RE SO SPECIAL!
AHH!
GRAB
LET ME SHOW YOU WHAT REAL POWER LOOKS LIKE!
TWIRL
BARTENDER-- THEY TIPPED YOU POORLY!
GRRRR~

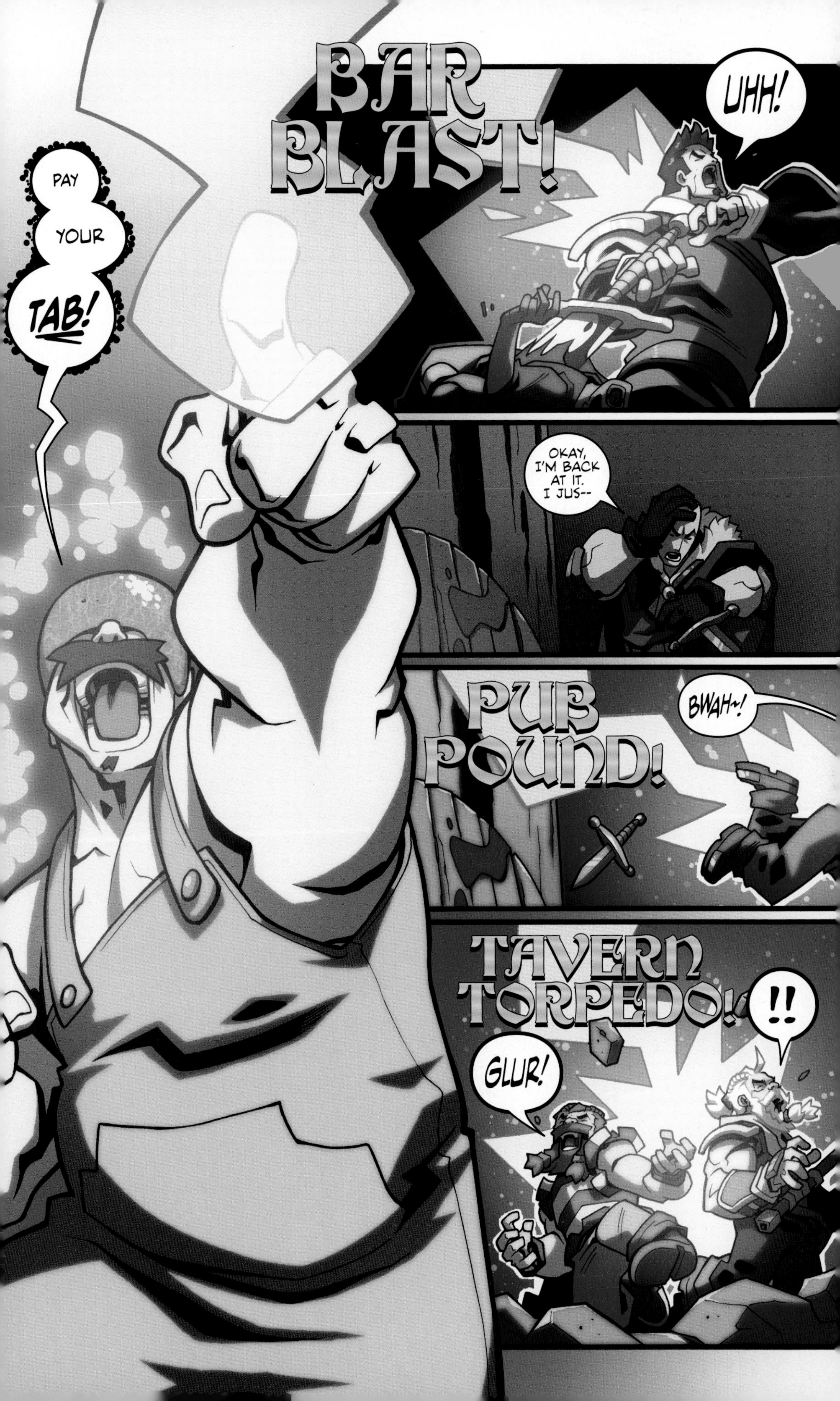

BAR BLAST!
UHH!
PAY YOUR TAB!
OKAY, I'M BACK AT IT. I JUS--
PUB POUND!
BWAH~!
TAVERN TORPEDO!
!!
GLUR!

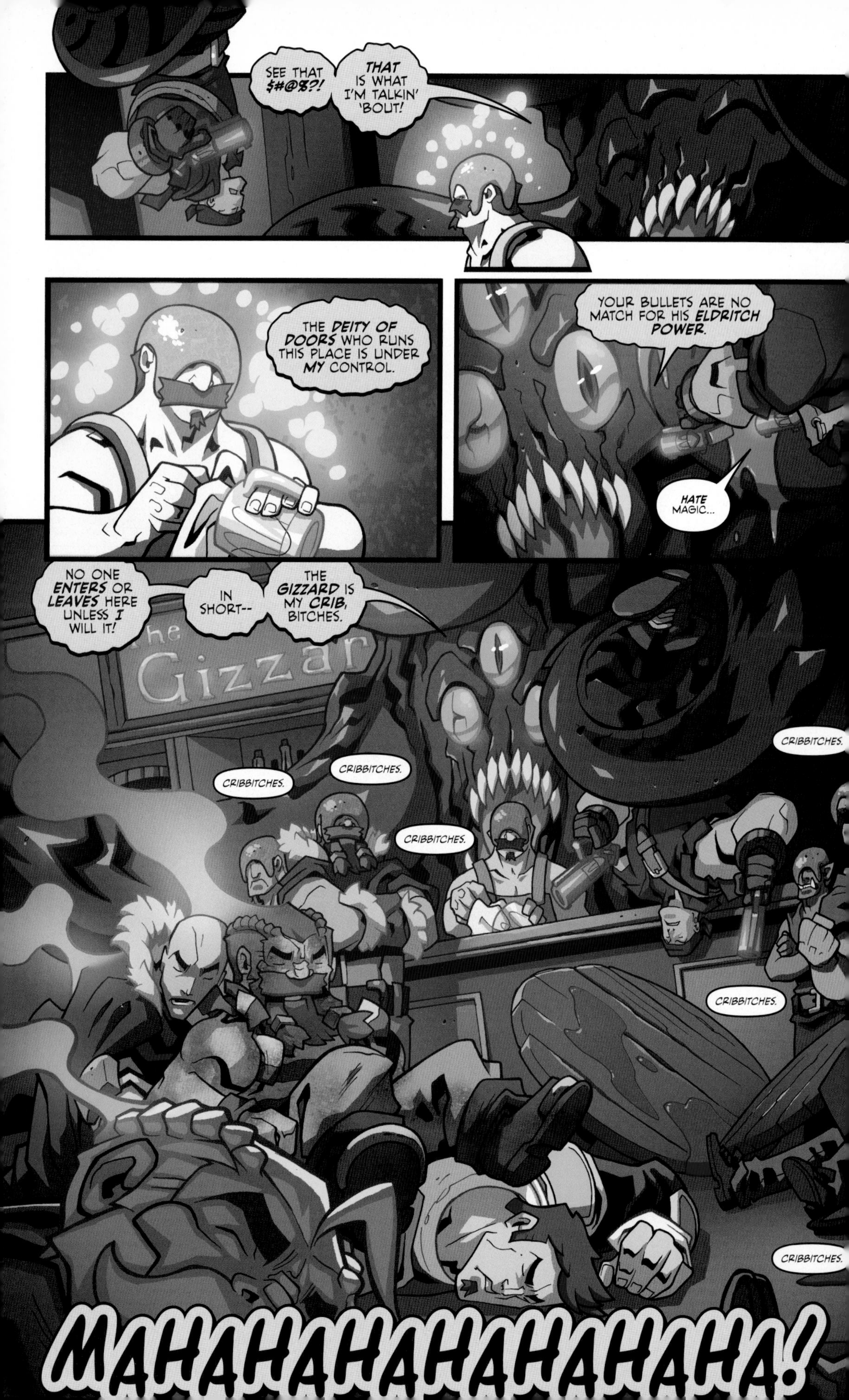

SEE THAT $#@%?!
THAT IS WHAT I'M TALKIN' 'BOUT!
THE DEITY OF DOORS WHO RUNS THIS PLACE IS UNDER MY CONTROL.
YOUR BULLETS ARE NO MATCH FOR HIS ELDRITCH POWER.
HATE MAGIC...
NO ONE ENTERS OR LEAVES HERE UNLESS I WILL IT!
IN SHORT--
THE GIZZARD IS MY CRIB, BITCHES.
The Gizzar
CRIBBITCHES.
CRIBBITCHES.
CRIBBITCHES.
CRIBBITCHES.
CRIBBITCHES.
CRIBBITCHES.
MAHAHAHAHAHAHAHAHA!

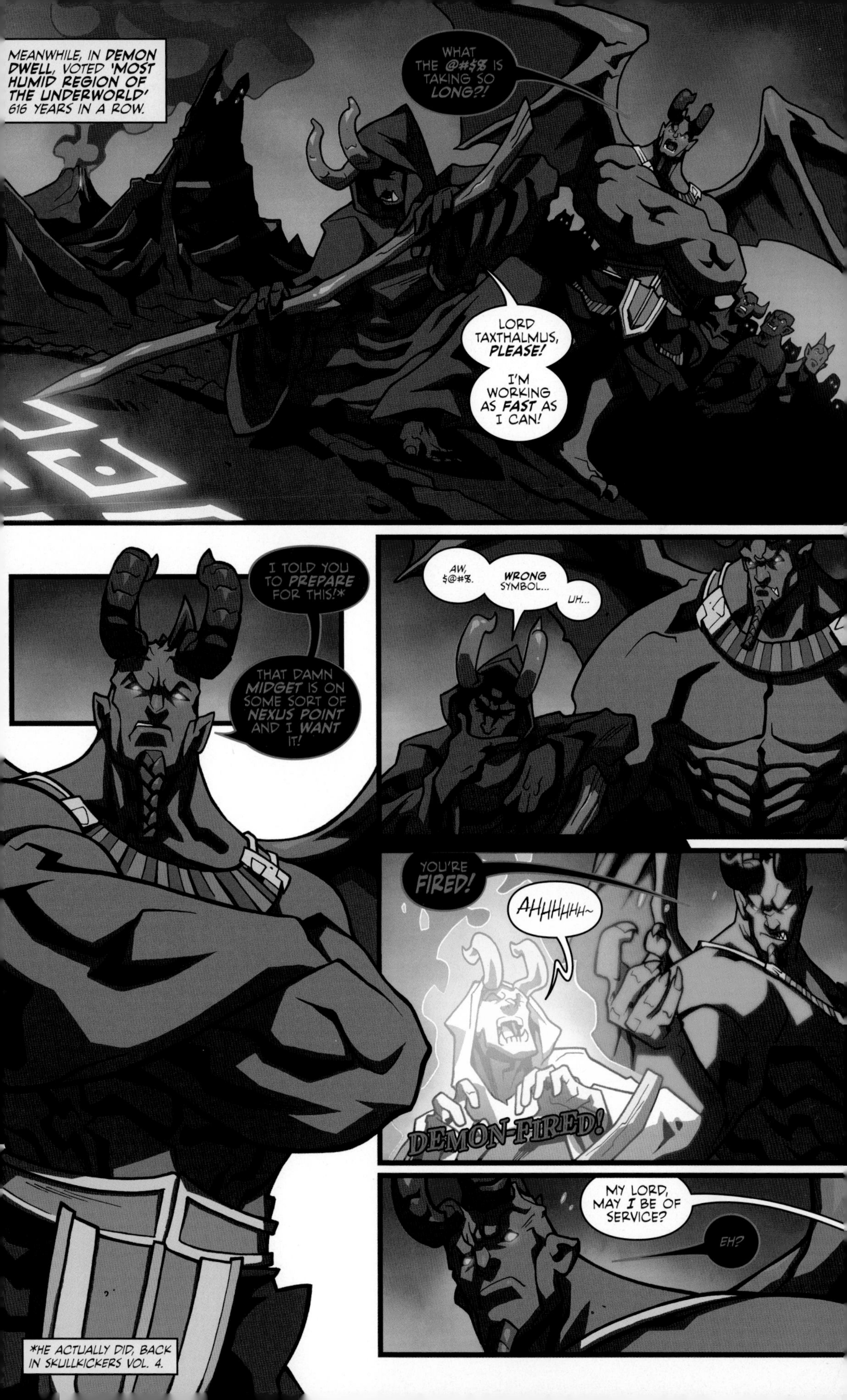
MEANWHILE, IN DEMON DWELL, VOTED 'MOST HUMID REGION OF THE UNDERWORLD' 616 YEARS IN A ROW.
WHAT THE @#$% IS TAKING SO LONG?!
LORD TAXTHALMUS, PLEASE!
I'M WORKING AS FAST AS I CAN!
I TOLD YOU TO PREPARE FOR THIS!*
THAT DAMN MIDGET IS ON SOME SORT OF NEXUS POINT AND I WANT IT!
AW, $@#%.
WRONG SYMBOL...
UH...
YOU'RE FIRED!
AHHHHHH~
DEMON-FIRED!
MY LORD, MAY I BE OF SERVICE?
EH?
*HE ACTUALLY DID, BACK IN SKULLKICKERS VOL. 4.

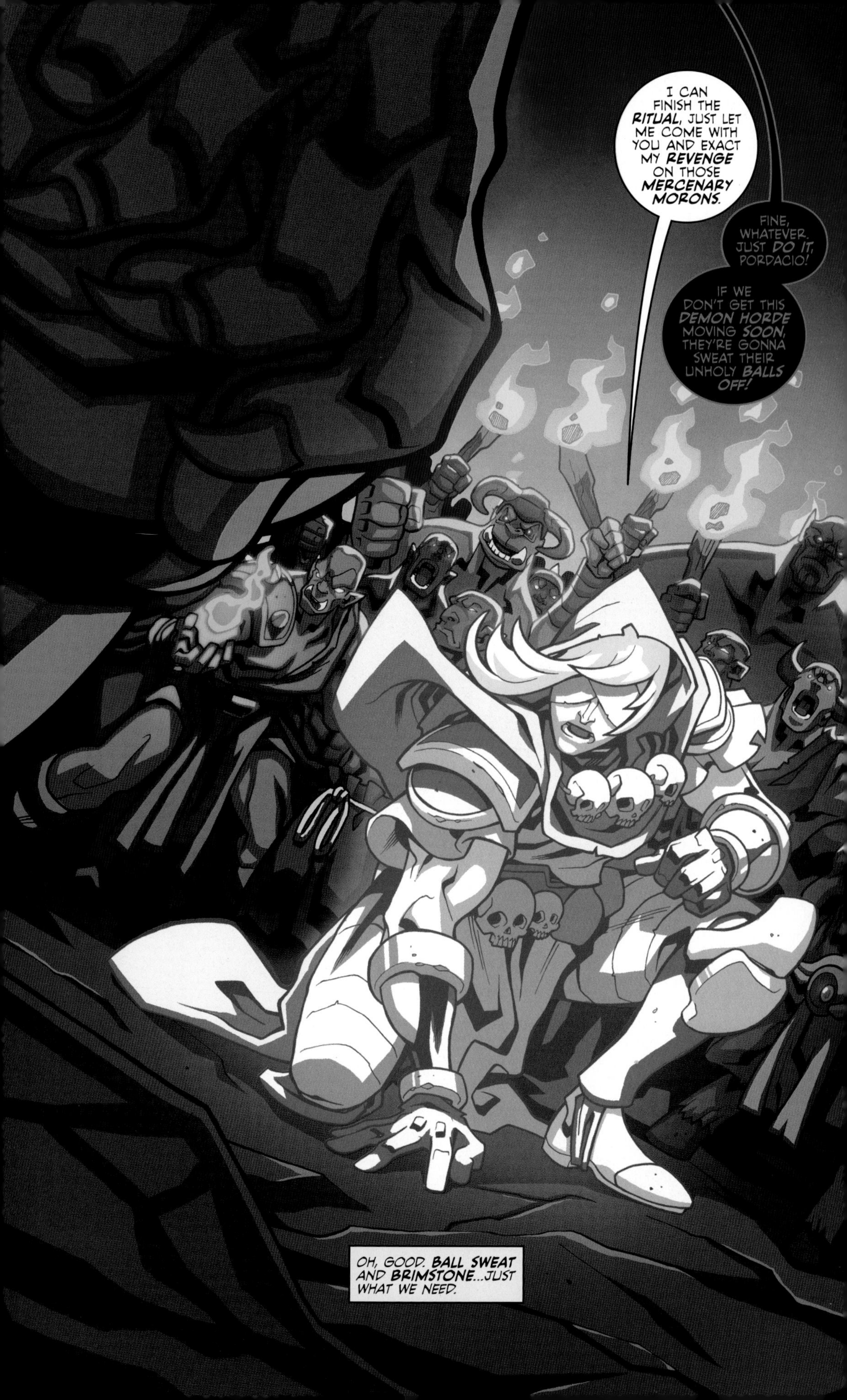
I CAN FINISH THE RITUAL, JUST LET ME COME WITH YOU AND EXACT MY REVENGE ON THOSE MERCENARY MORONS.
FINE, WHATEVER. JUST DO IT, PORDACIO!
IF WE DON'T GET THIS DEMON HORDE MOVING SOON, THEY'RE GONNA SWEAT THEIR UNHOLY BALLS OFF!
OH, GOOD. BALL SWEAT AND BRIMSTONE...JUST WHAT WE NEED.

CHAPTER TWO

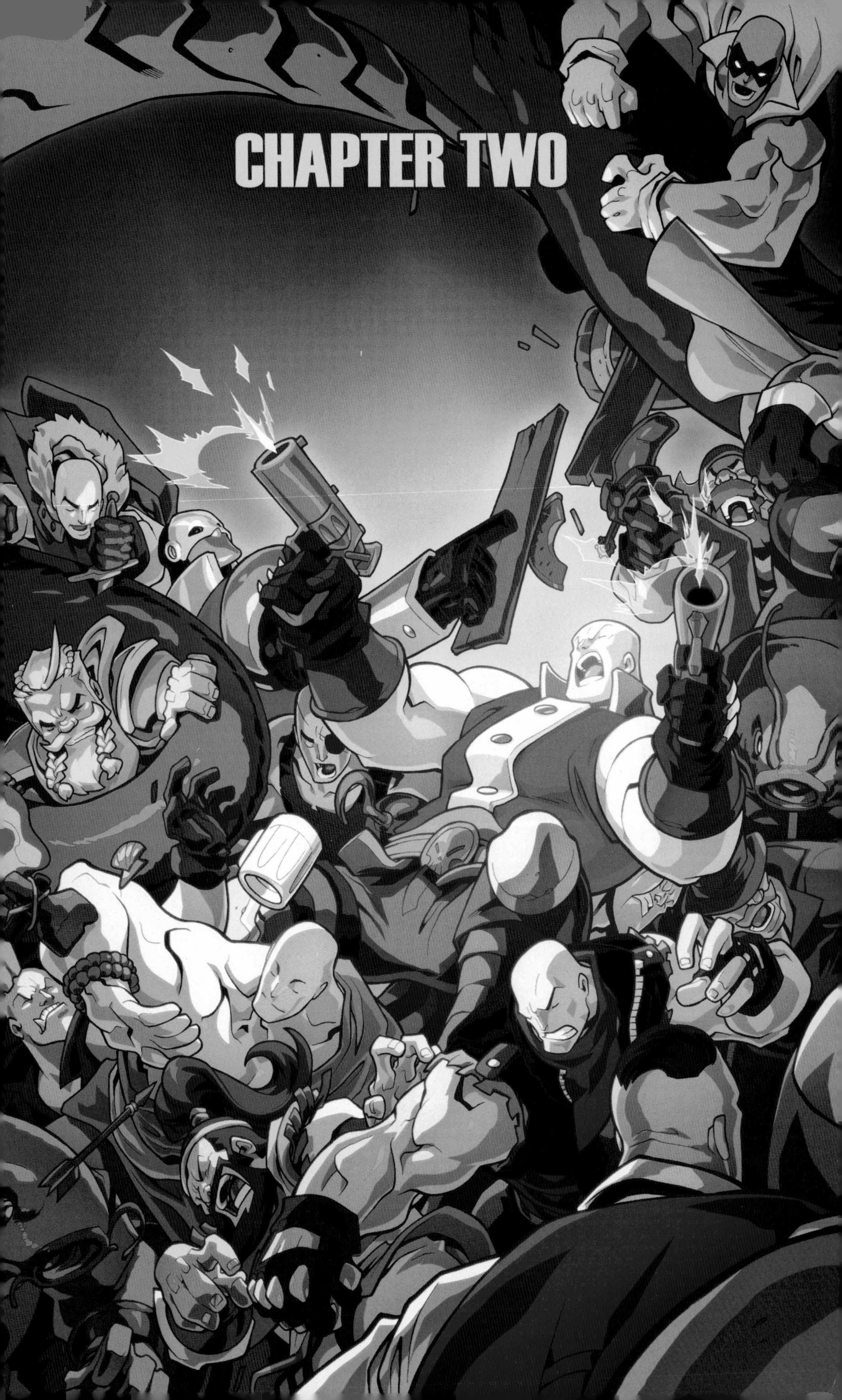

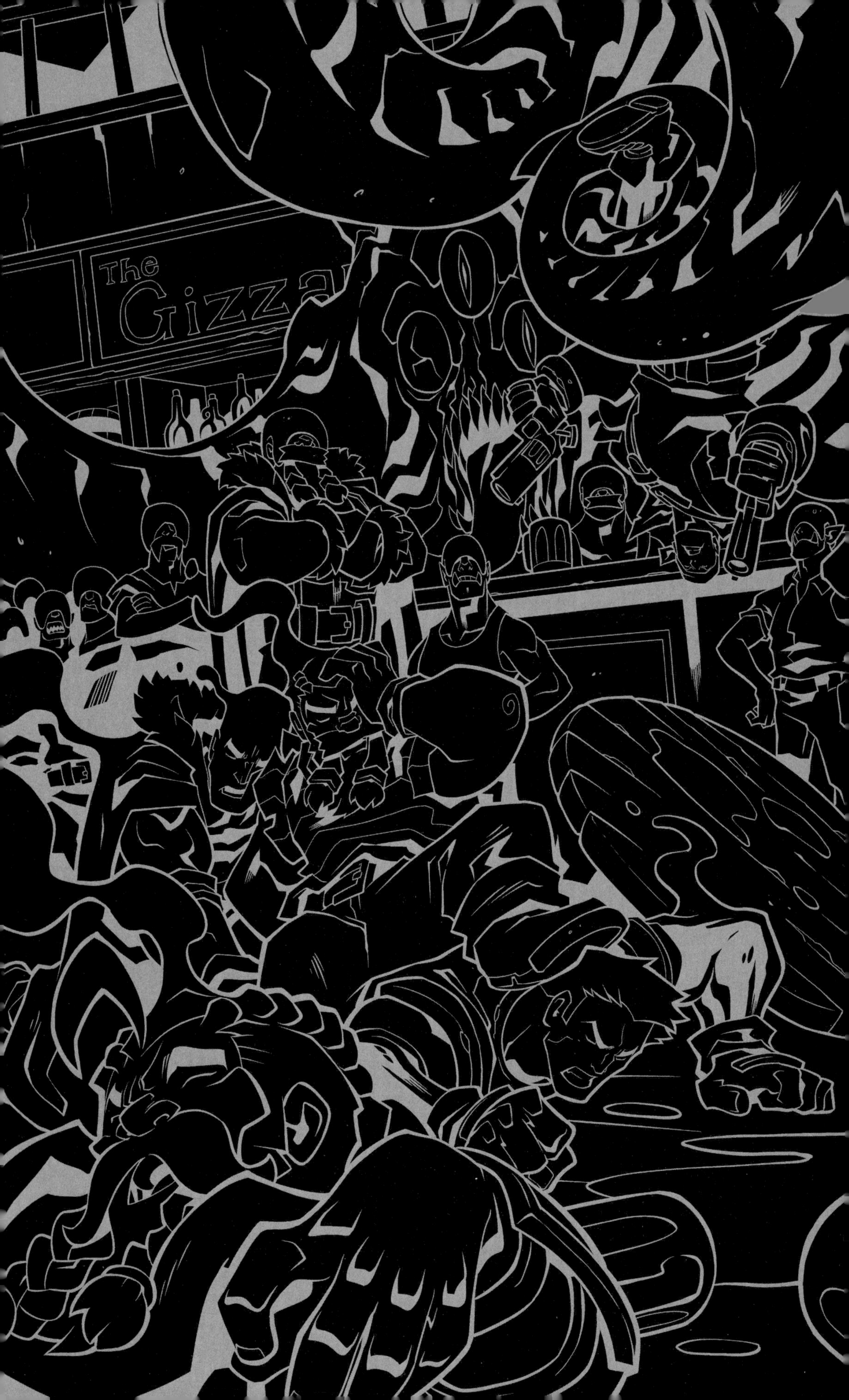
The
Gizz

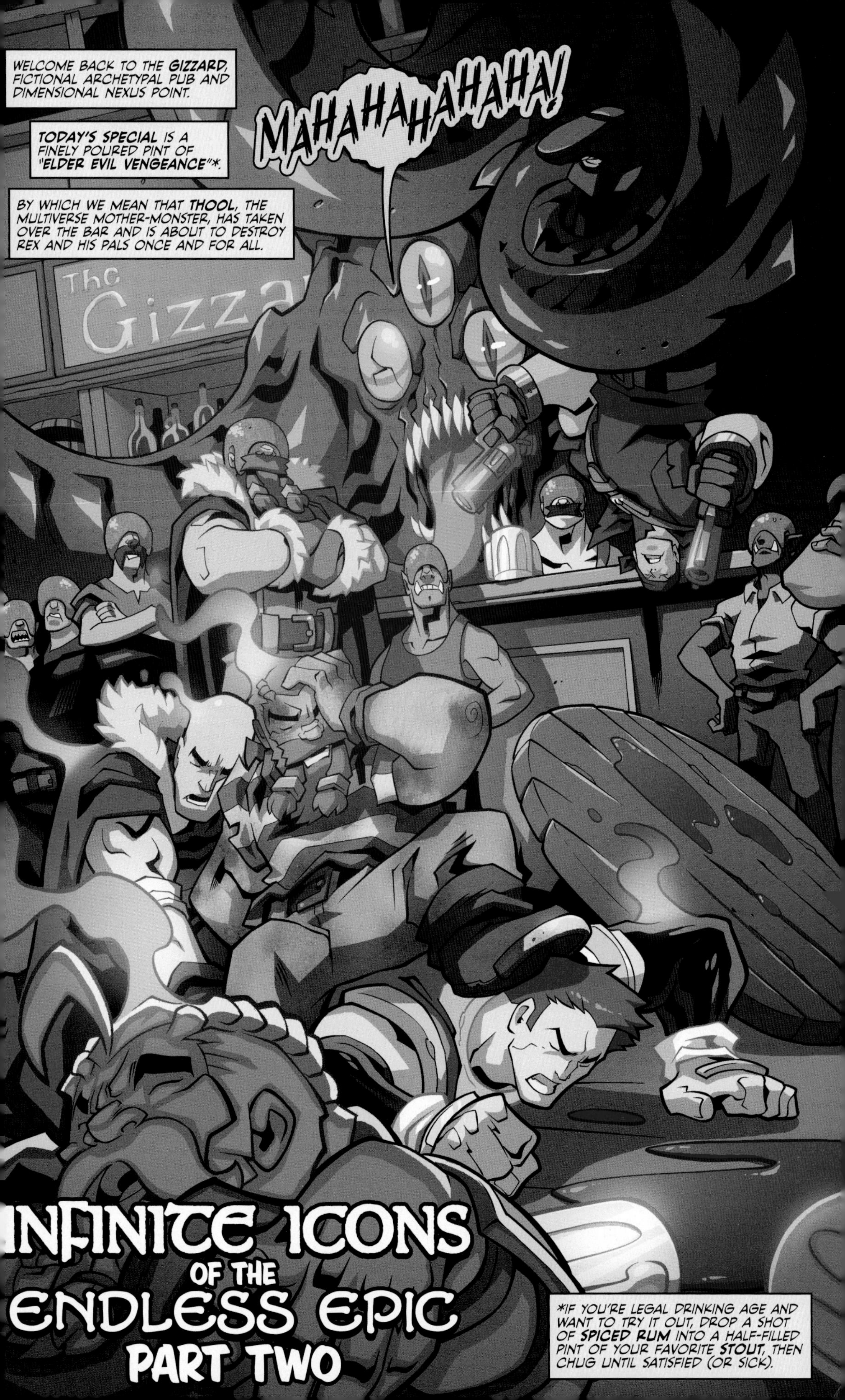
WELCOME BACK TO THE GIZZARD, FICTIONAL ARCHETYPAL PUB AND DIMENSIONAL NEXUS POINT.
TODAY'S SPECIAL IS A FINELY POURED PINT OF "ELDER EVIL VENGEANCE"*.
BY WHICH WE MEAN THAT THOOL, THE MULTIVERSE MOTHER-MONSTER, HAS TAKEN OVER THE BAR AND IS ABOUT TO DESTROY REX AND HIS PALS ONCE AND FOR ALL.
MAHAHAHAHAHAHA!
The Gizza
INFINITE ICONS OF THE ENDLESS EPIC PART TWO
*IF YOU'RE LEGAL DRINKING AGE AND WANT TO TRY IT OUT, DROP A SHOT OF SPICED RUM INTO A HALF-FILLED PINT OF YOUR FAVORITE STOUT, THEN CHUG UNTIL SATISFIED (OR SICK).

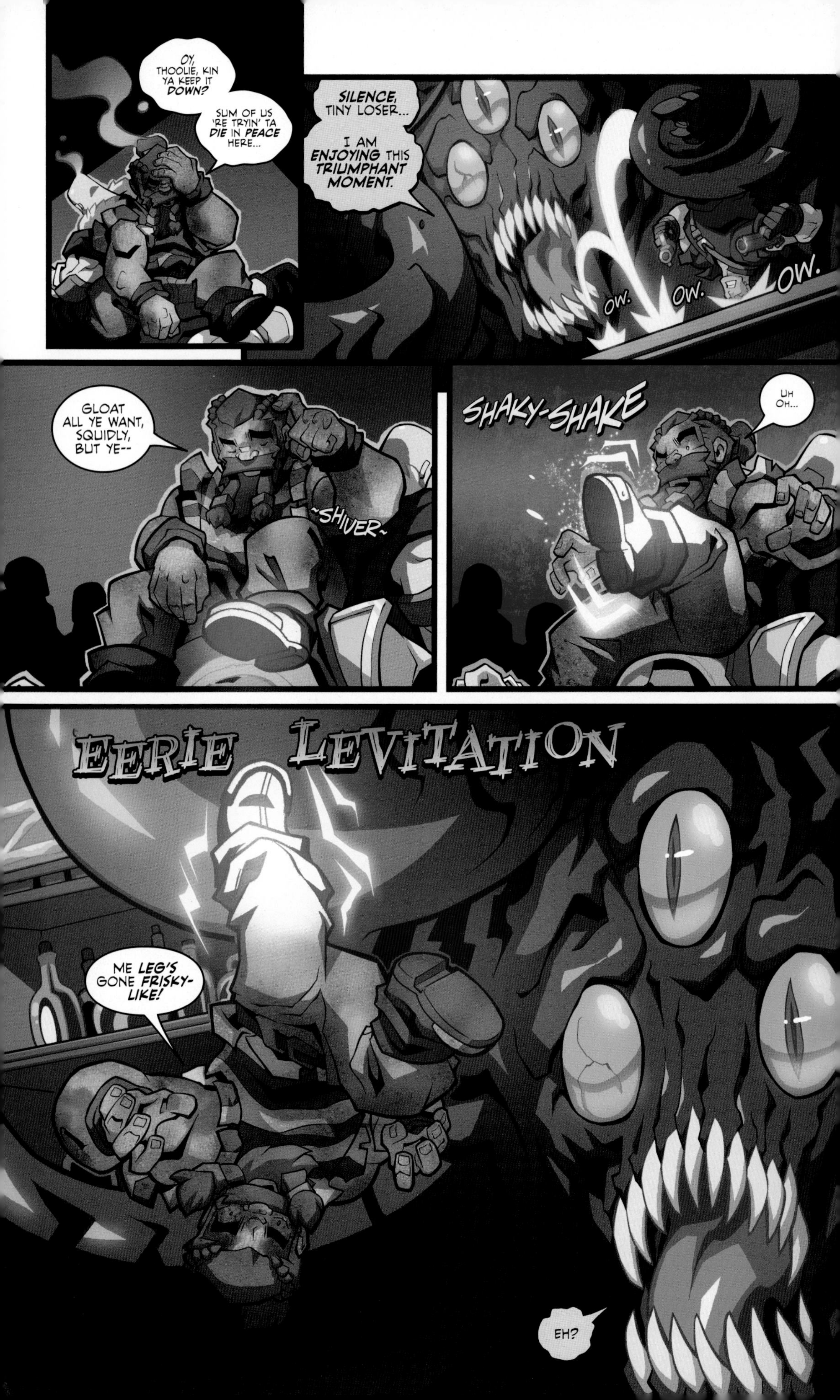

OY, THOOLIE, KIN YA KEEP IT DOWN?
SUM OF US 'RE TRYIN' TA DIE IN PEACE HERE...
SILENCE, TINY LOSER...
I AM ENJOYING THIS TRIUMPHANT MOMENT.
OW. OW. OW.
GLOAT ALL YE WANT, SQUIDLY, BUT YE--
~SHIVER~
SHAKY-SHAKE
UH OH...
EERIE LEVITATION
ME LEG'S GONE FRISKY-LIKE!
EH?

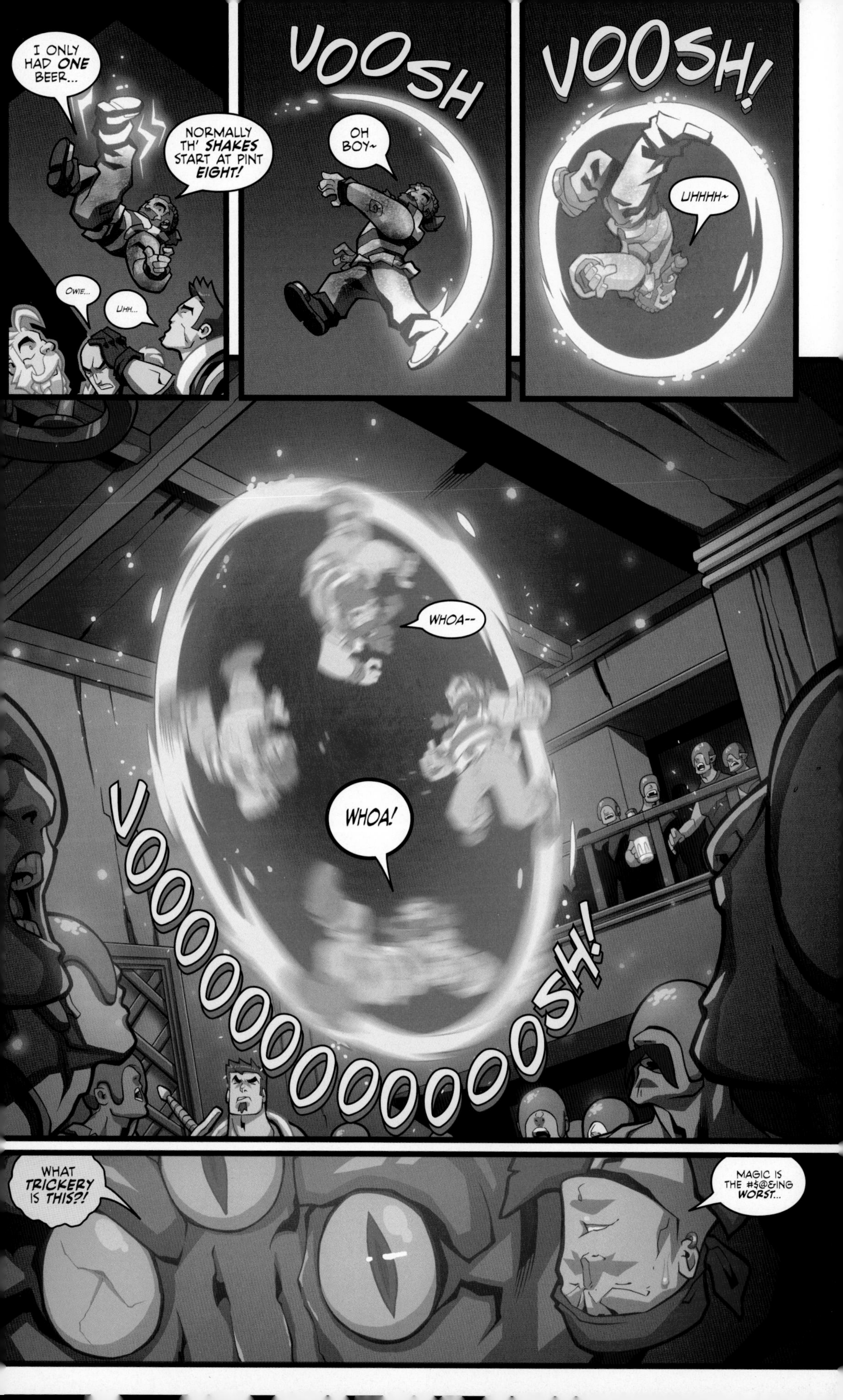
I ONLY HAD ONE BEER...
NORMALLY TH' SHAKES START AT PINT EIGHT!
OWIE...
UHH...
VOOSH
OH BOY~
VOOSH!
UHHHH~
WHOA--
WHOA!
VOOOOOOOOOOOOOSH!
WHAT TRICKERY IS THIS?!
MAGIC IS THE #$@&ING WORST...

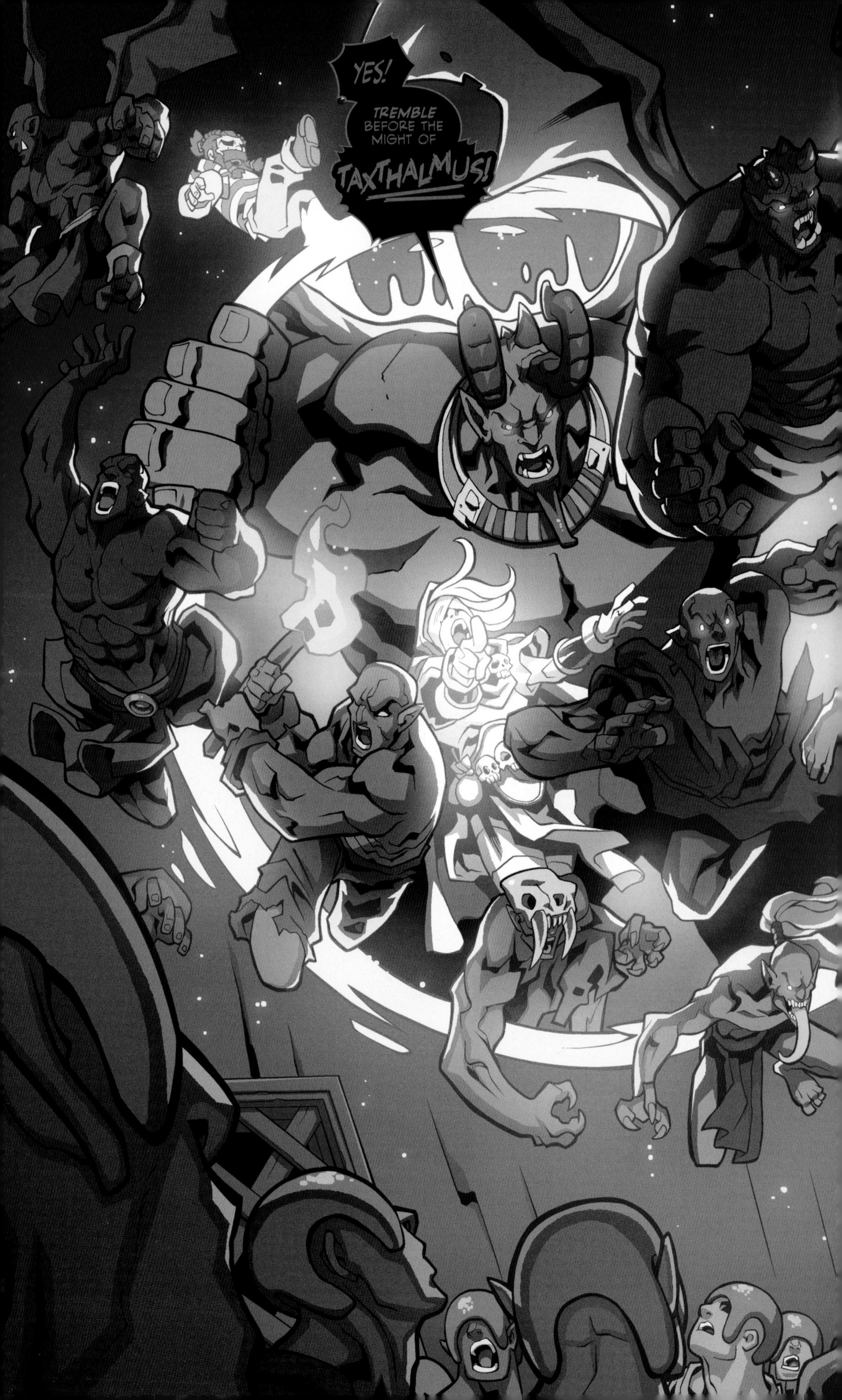
YES!
TREMBLE BEFORE THE MIGHT OF
TAXTHALMUS!

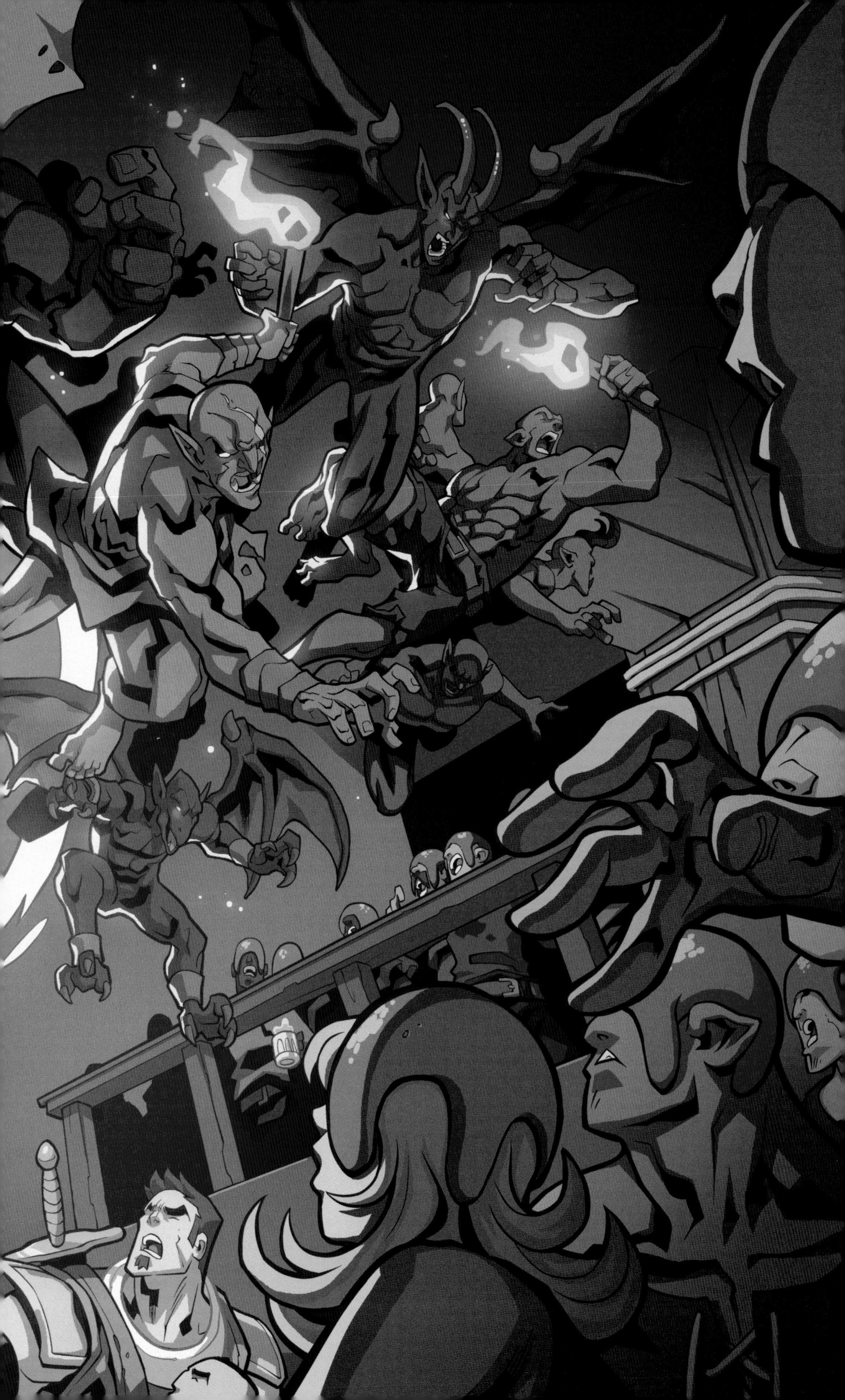

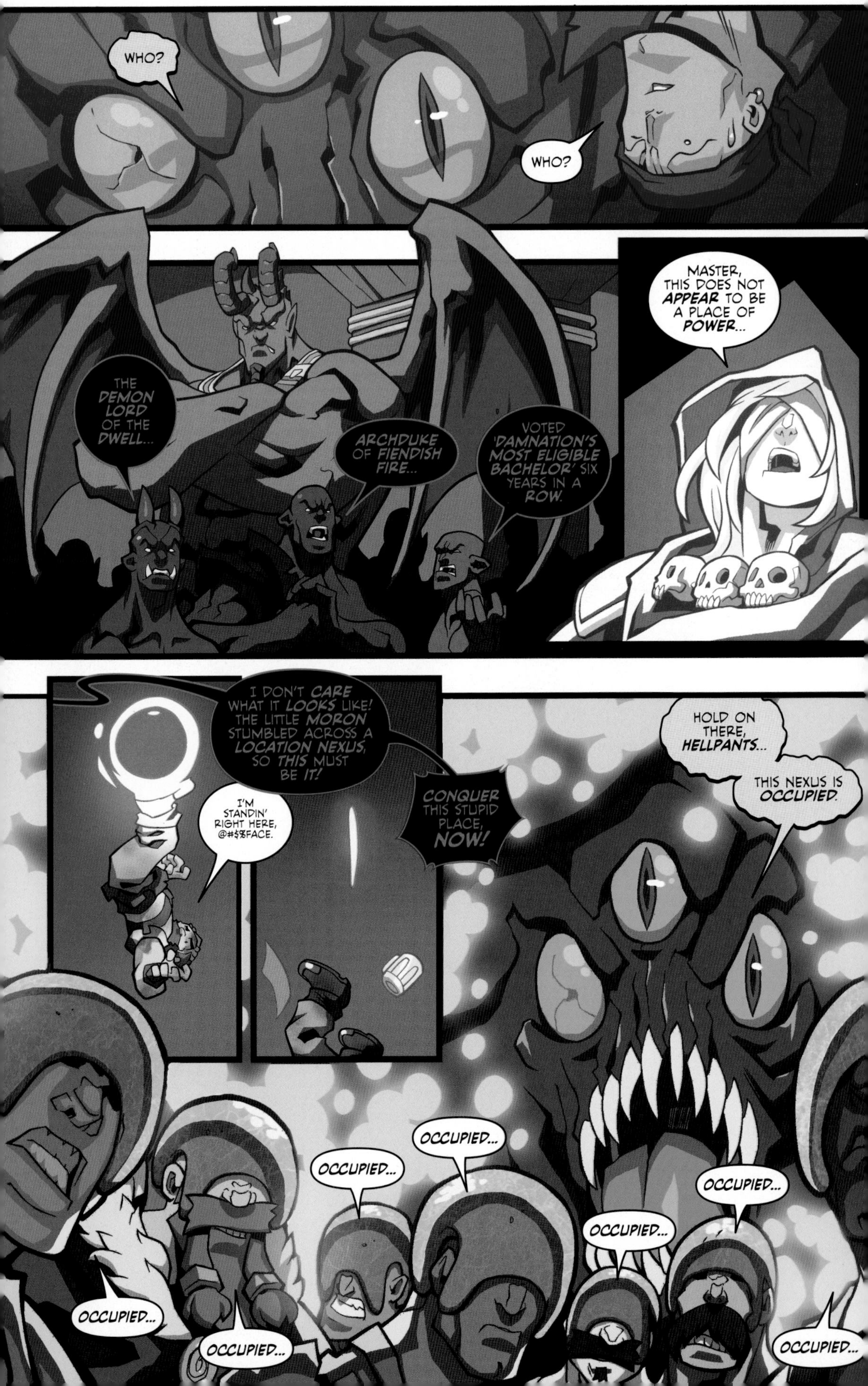
WHO?
WHO?
THE DEMON LORD OF THE DWELL...
ARCHDUKE OF FIENDISH FIRE...
VOTED 'DAMNATION'S MOST ELIGIBLE BACHELOR' SIX YEARS IN A ROW.
MASTER, THIS DOES NOT APPEAR TO BE A PLACE OF POWER...
I DON'T CARE WHAT IT LOOKS LIKE! THE LITTLE MORON STUMBLED ACROSS A LOCATION NEXUS, SO THIS MUST BE IT!
I'M STANDIN' RIGHT HERE, @#$%FACE.
CONQUER THIS STUPID PLACE, NOW!
HOLD ON THERE, HELLPANTS...
THIS NEXUS IS OCCUPIED.
OCCUPIED...
OCCUPIED...
OCCUPIED...
OCCUPIED...
OCCUPIED...
OCCUPIED...
OCCUPIED...

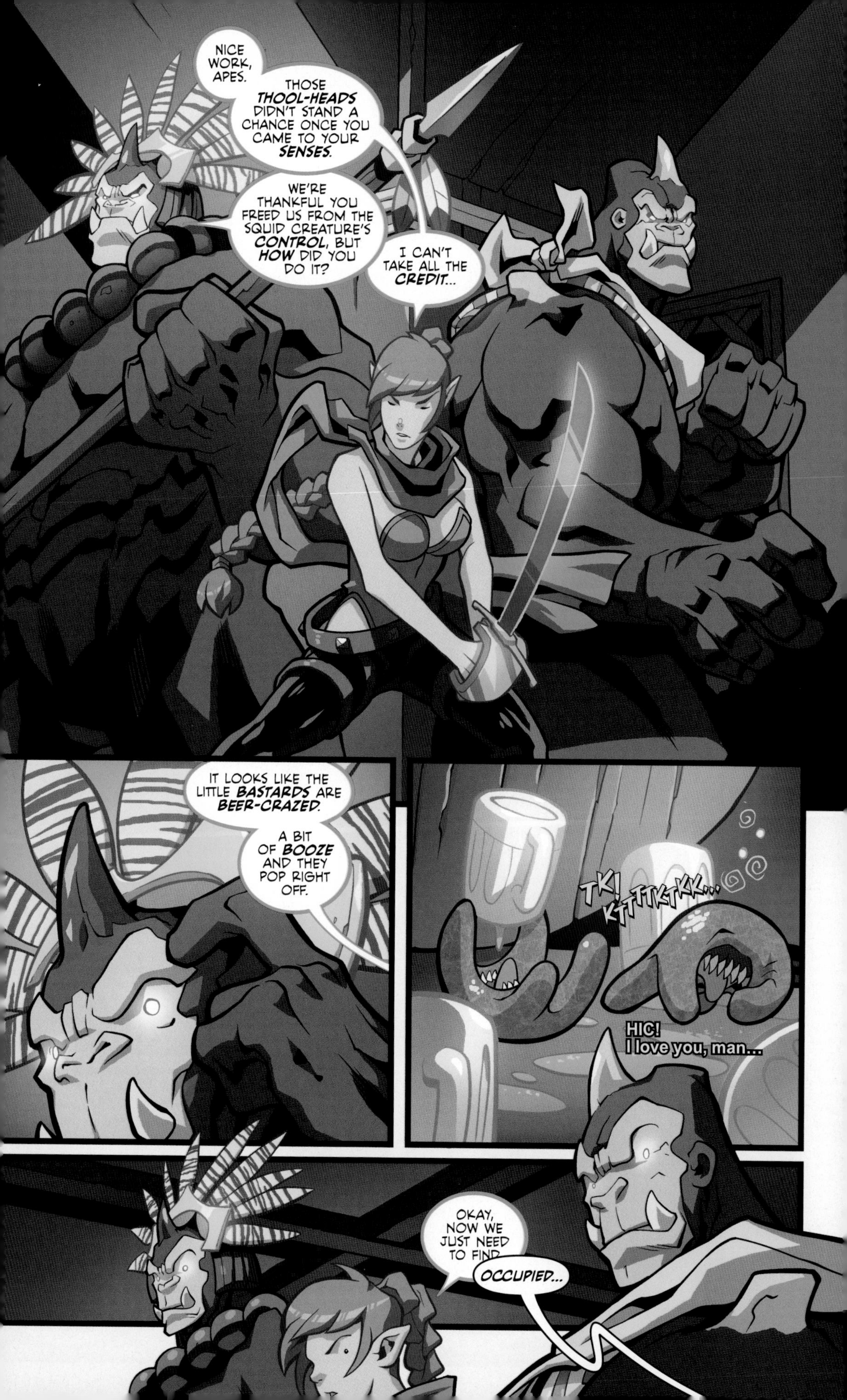
NICE WORK, APES.
THOSE THOOL-HEADS DIDN'T STAND A CHANCE ONCE YOU CAME TO YOUR SENSES.
WE'RE THANKFUL YOU FREED US FROM THE SQUID CREATURE'S CONTROL, BUT HOW DID YOU DO IT?
I CAN'T TAKE ALL THE CREDIT...
IT LOOKS LIKE THE LITTLE BASTARDS ARE BEER-CRAZED.
A BIT OF BOOZE AND THEY POP RIGHT OFF.
TK! KTTTTKTKK...
HIC! I love you, man...
OKAY, NOW WE JUST NEED TO FIND
OCCUPIED...

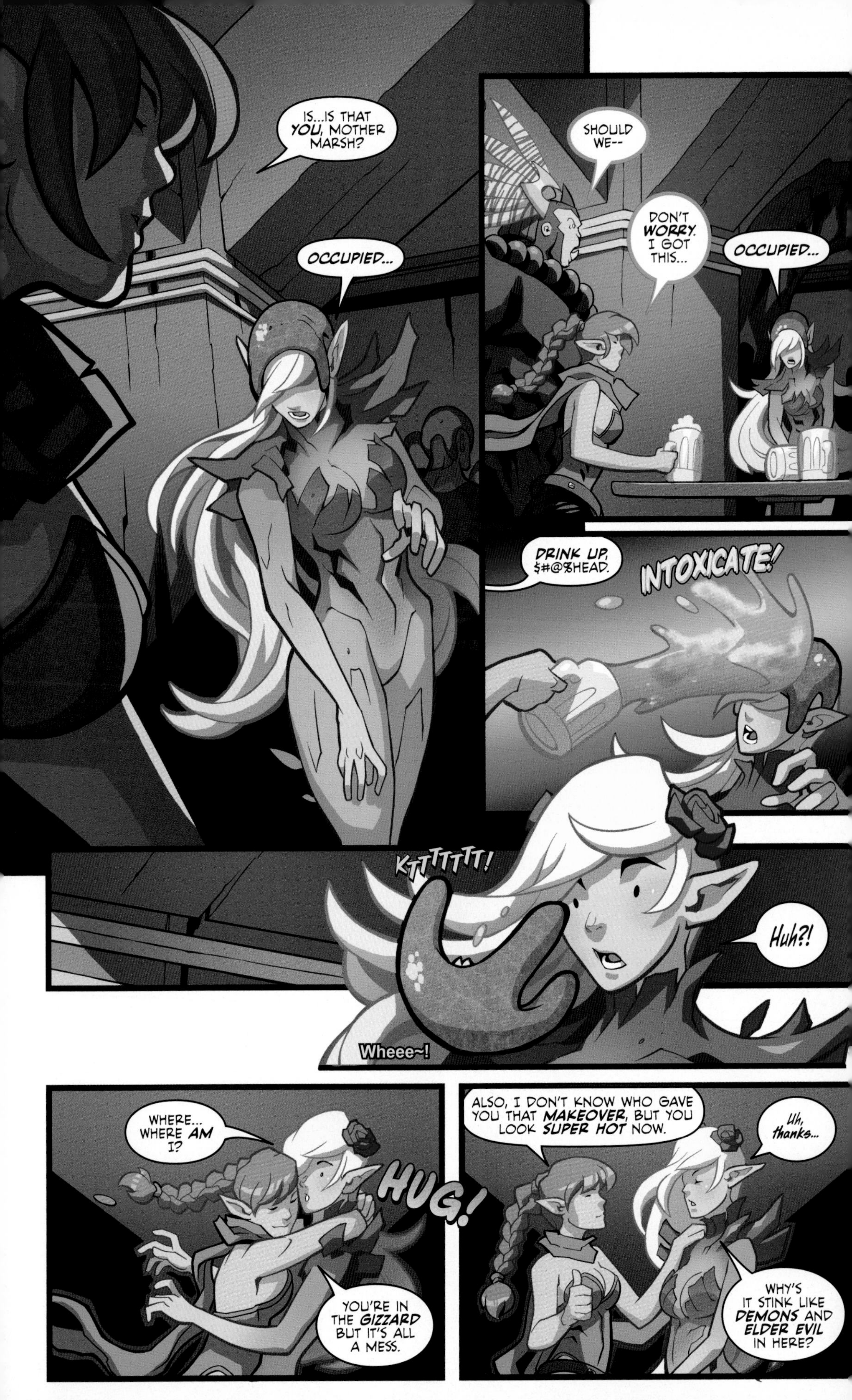
IS...IS THAT YOU, MOTHER MARSH?
OCCUPIED...
SHOULD WE--
DON'T WORRY. I GOT THIS...
OCCUPIED...
DRINK UP, $#@%HEAD.
INTOXICATE!
KTTTTTTT!
Huh?!
Wheee~!
WHERE... WHERE AM I?
HUG!
YOU'RE IN THE GIZZARD BUT IT'S ALL A MESS.
ALSO, I DON'T KNOW WHO GAVE YOU THAT MAKEOVER, BUT YOU LOOK SUPER HOT NOW.
Uh, thanks...
WHY'S IT STINK LIKE DEMONS AND ELDER EVIL IN HERE?

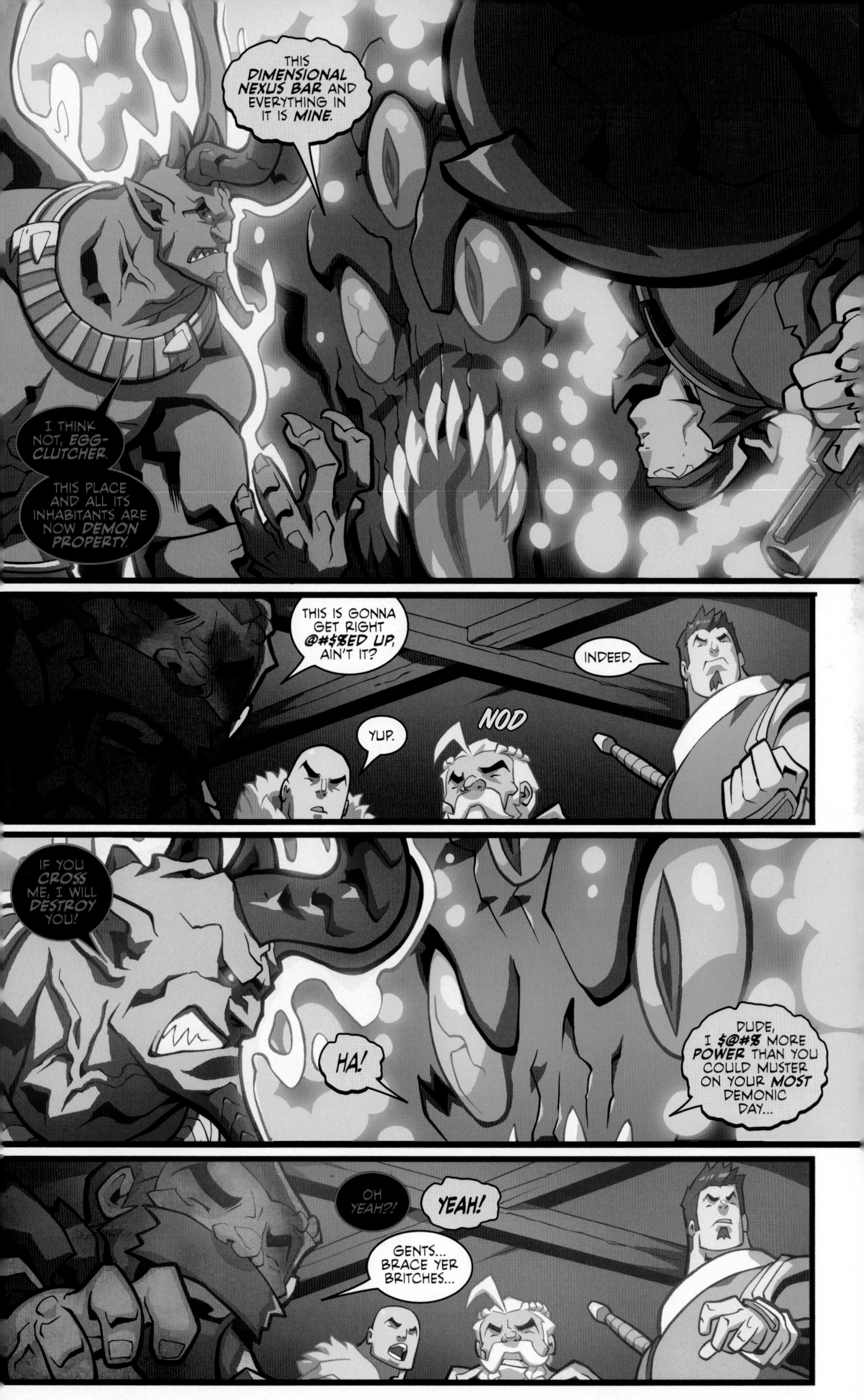
THIS DIMENSIONAL NEXUS BAR AND EVERYTHING IN IT IS MINE.
I THINK NOT, EGG-CLUTCHER.
THIS PLACE AND ALL ITS INHABITANTS ARE NOW DEMON PROPERTY.
THIS IS GONNA GET RIGHT @#$%ED UP, AIN'T IT?
INDEED.
YUP.
NOD
IF YOU CROSS ME, I WILL DESTROY YOU!
HA!
DUDE, I $@#% MORE POWER THAN YOU COULD MUSTER ON YOUR MOST DEMONIC DAY...
OH YEAH?!
YEAH!
GENTS... BRACE YER BRITCHES...

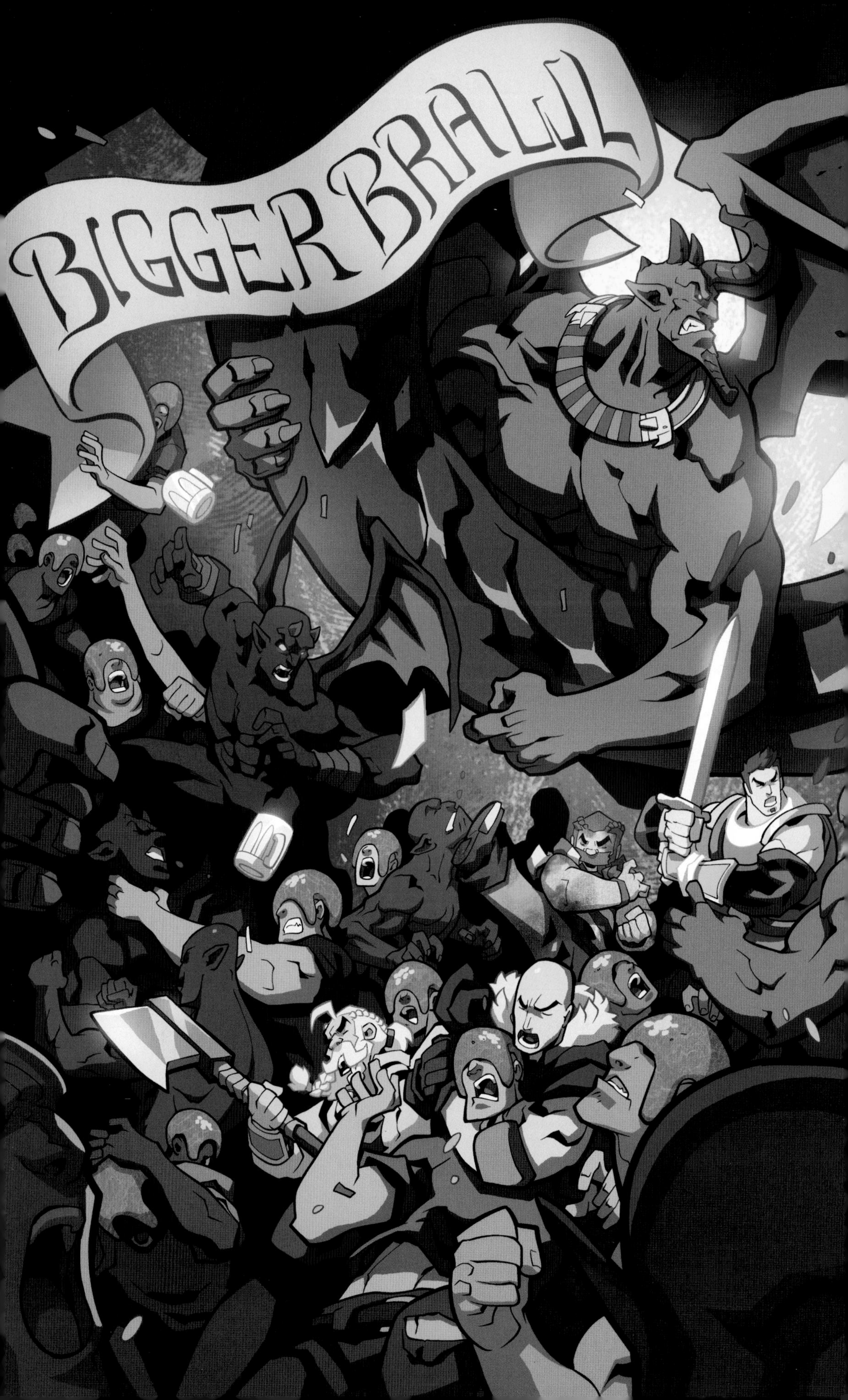
BIGGER BRAWL

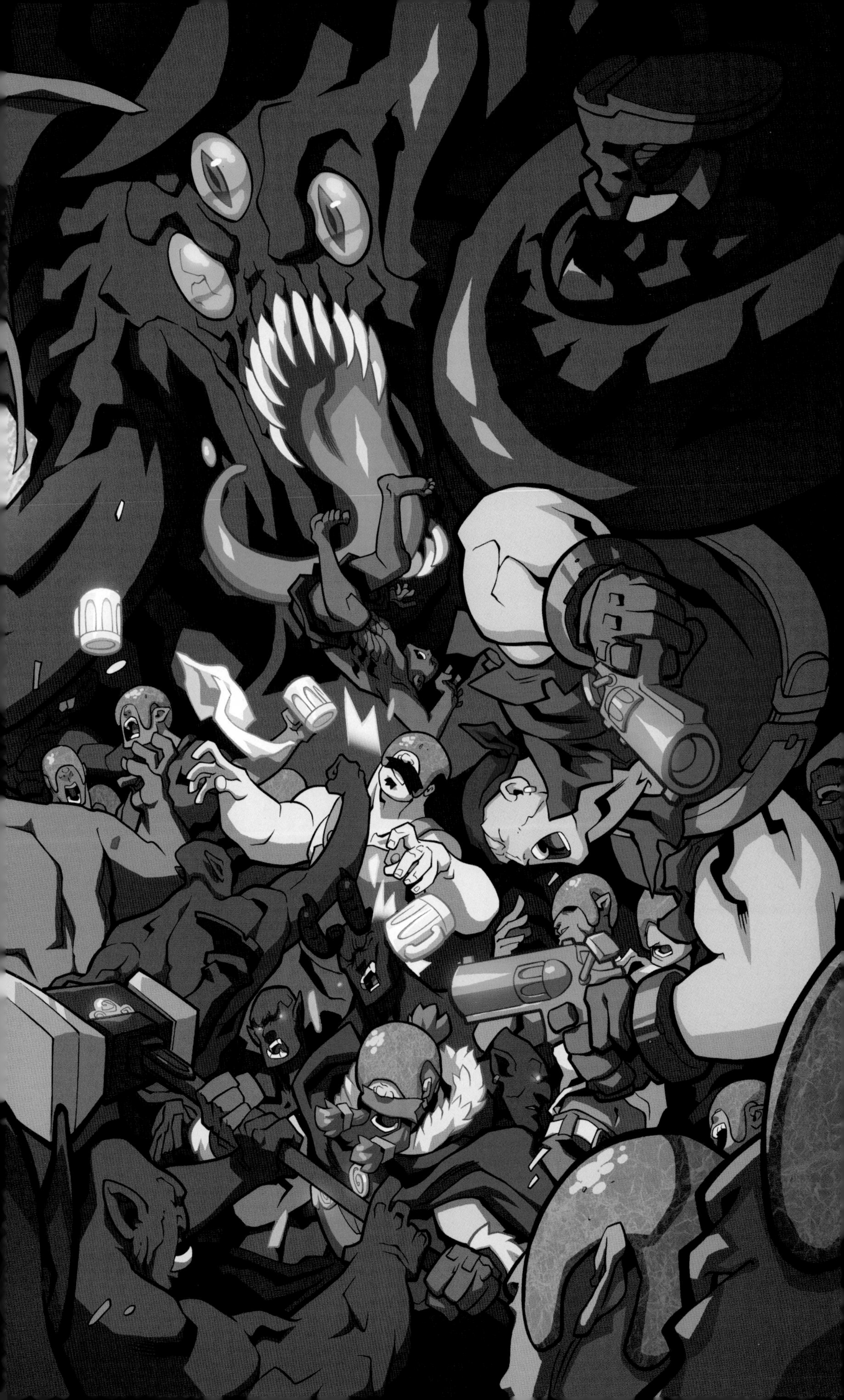

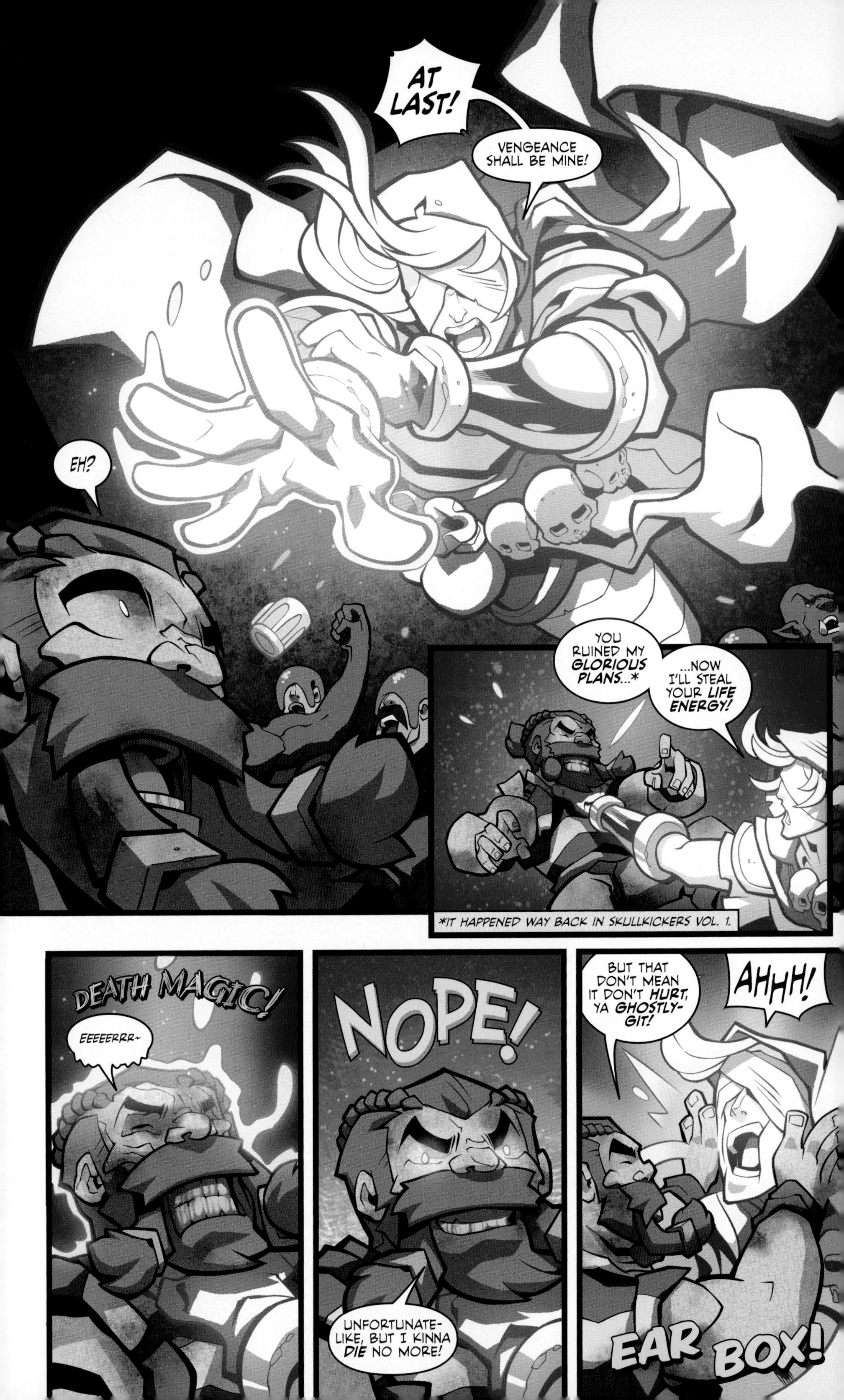
AT LAST!
VENGEANCE SHALL BE MINE!
EH?
YOU RUINED MY GLORIOUS PLANS...*
...NOW I'LL STEAL YOUR LIFE ENERGY!
*IT HAPPENED WAY BACK IN SKULLKICKERS VOL. 1.
DEATH MAGIC!
EEEEERRR~
NOPE!
UNFORTUNATE-LIKE, BUT I KINNA DIE NO MORE!
BUT THAT DON'T MEAN IT DON'T HURT, YA GHOSTLY-GIT!
AHHH!
EAR BOX!

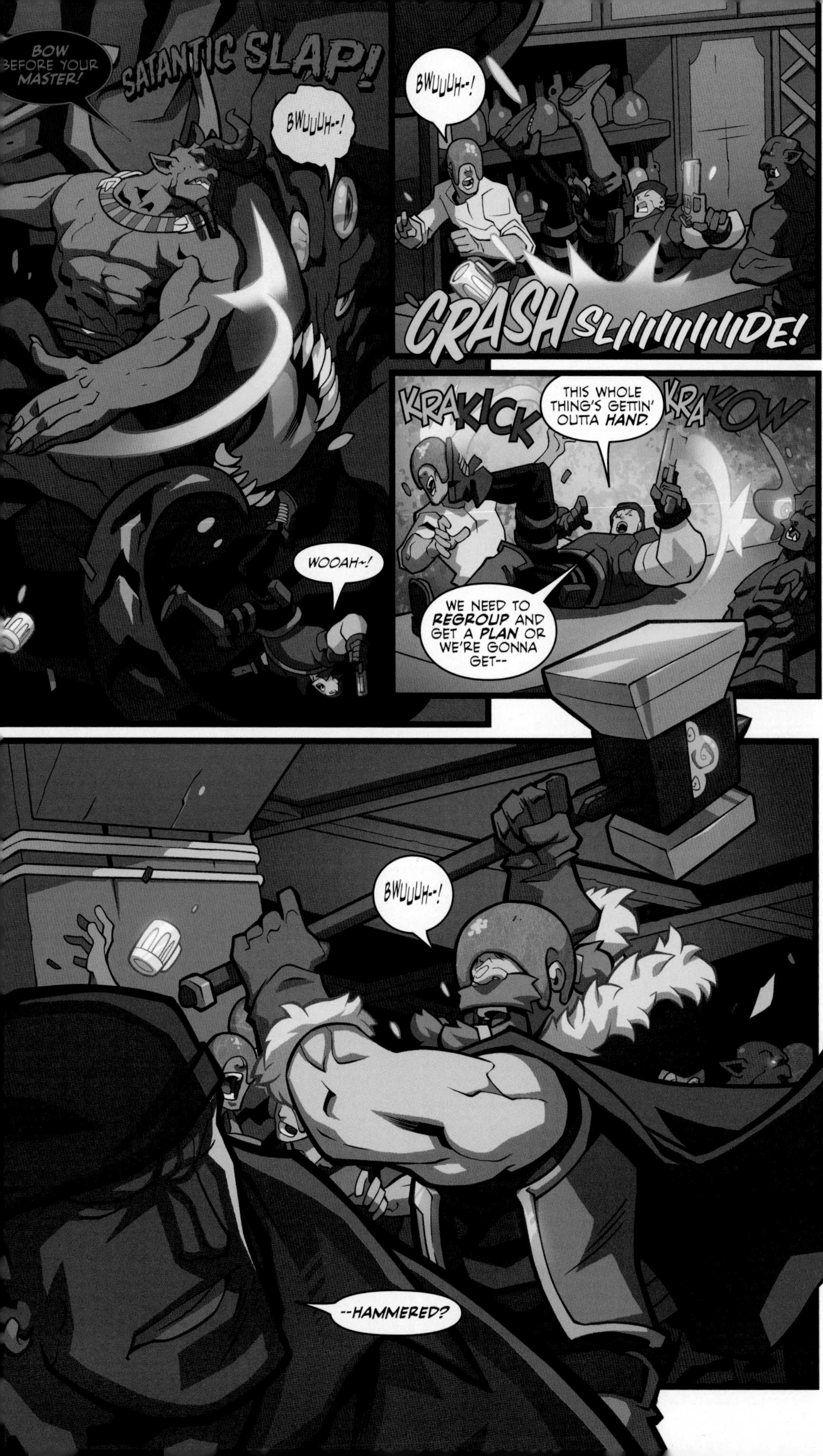
BOW BEFORE YOUR MASTER!
SATANTIC SLAP!
BWUUUH--!
WOOAH~!
BWUUUH--!
CRASH
SLIIIIIIIIIDE!
KRAKICK
THIS WHOLE THING'S GETTIN' OUTTA HAND.
KRAKOW
WE NEED TO REGROUP AND GET A PLAN OR WE'RE GONNA GET--
BWUUUH--!
--HAMMERED?

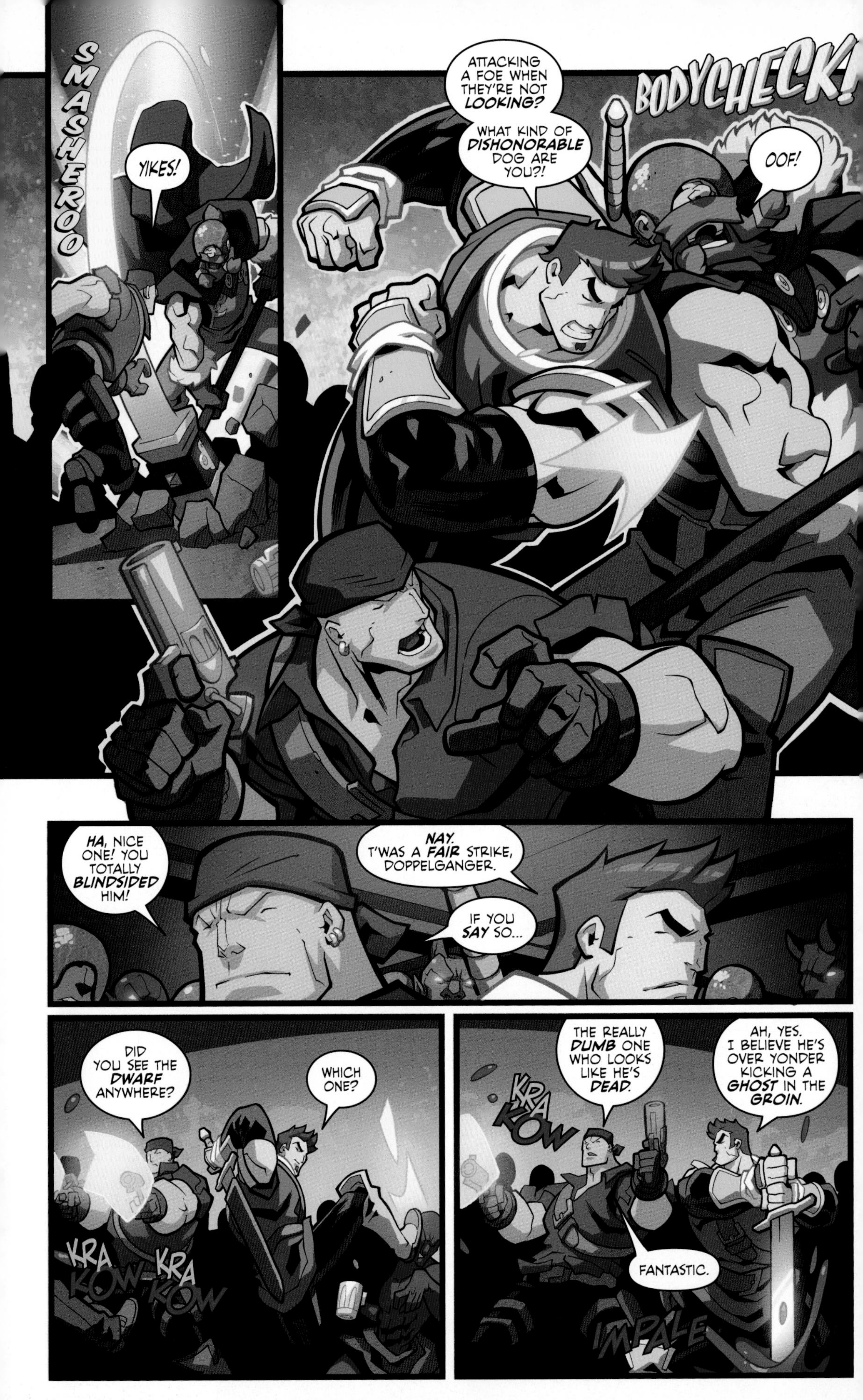
SMASHEROO
YIKES!
ATTACKING A FOE WHEN THEY'RE NOT LOOKING?
WHAT KIND OF DISHONORABLE DOG ARE YOU?!
BODYCHECK!
OOF!
HA, NICE ONE! YOU TOTALLY BLINDSIDED HIM!
NAY. T'WAS A FAIR STRIKE, DOPPELGANGER.
IF YOU SAY SO...
DID YOU SEE THE DWARF ANYWHERE?
WHICH ONE?
KRA KOW KRA KOW
THE REALLY DUMB ONE WHO LOOKS LIKE HE'S DEAD.
KRA KOW
AH, YES. I BELIEVE HE'S OVER YONDER KICKING A GHOST IN THE GROIN.
FANTASTIC.
IMPALE

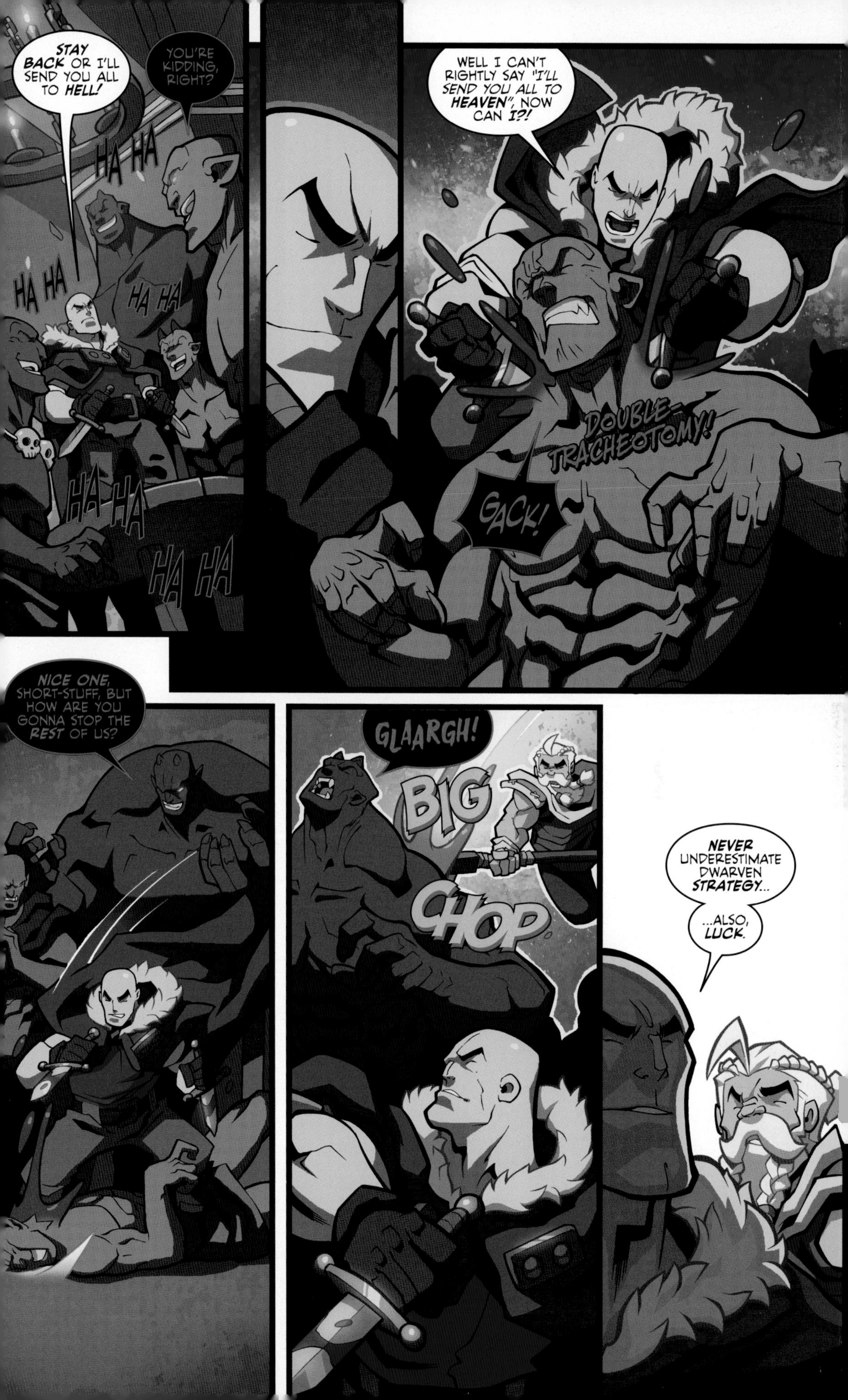
STAY BACK OR I'LL SEND YOU ALL TO HELL!
YOU'RE KIDDING, RIGHT?
HA HA
HA HA
HA HA
HA HA
HA HA
WELL I CAN'T RIGHTLY SAY "I'LL SEND YOU ALL TO HEAVEN", NOW CAN I?!
DOUBLE-TRACHEOTOMY!
GACK!
NICE ONE, SHORT-STUFF, BUT HOW ARE YOU GONNA STOP THE REST OF US?
GLAARGH!
BIG
CHOP
NEVER UNDERESTIMATE DWARVEN STRATEGY...
...ALSO, LUCK.

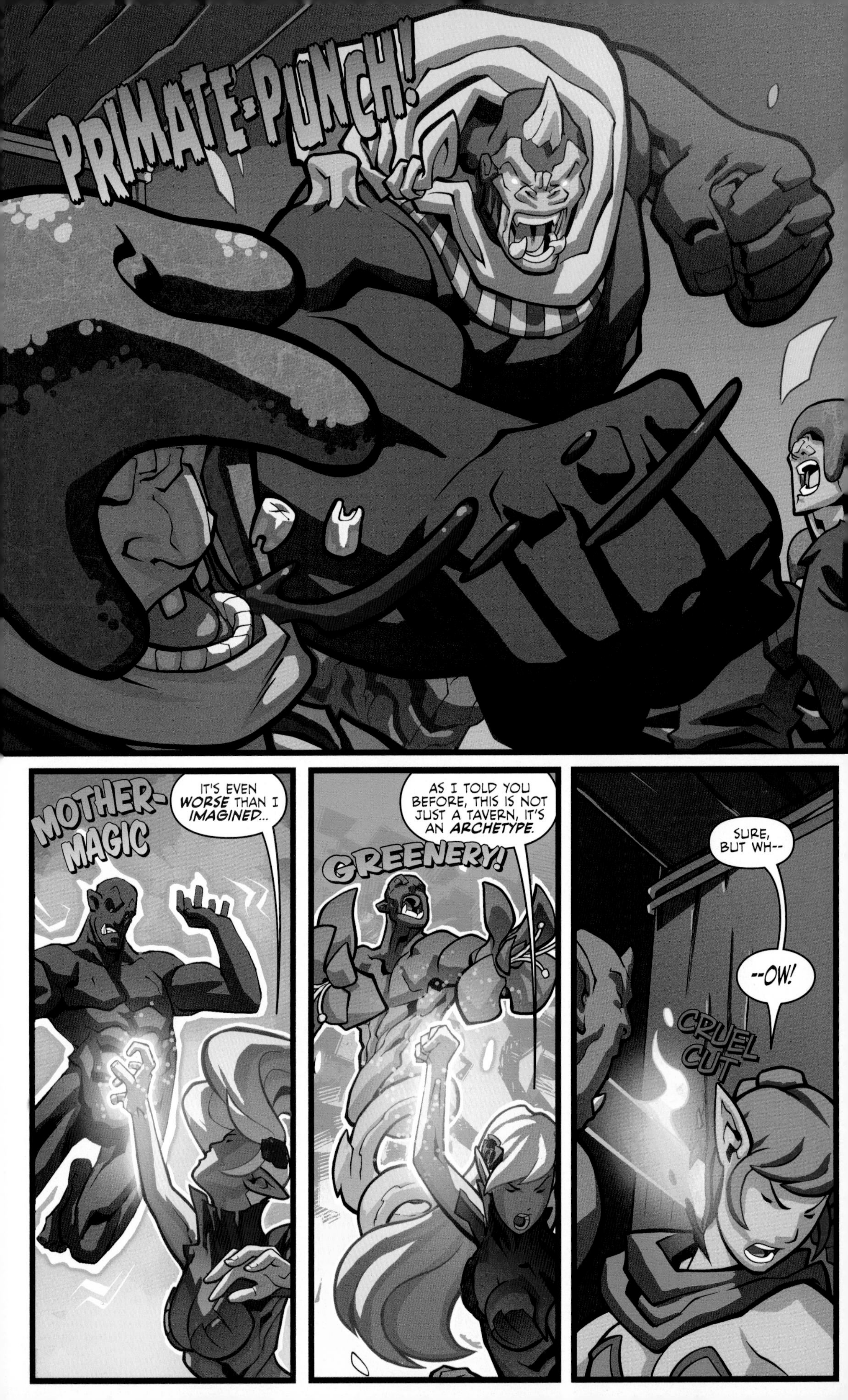
PRIMATE-PUNCH!
MOTHER-MAGIC
IT'S EVEN WORSE THAN I IMAGINED...
AS I TOLD YOU BEFORE, THIS IS NOT JUST A TAVERN, IT'S AN ARCHETYPE.
GREENERY!
SURE, BUT WH--
--OW!
CRUEL CUT

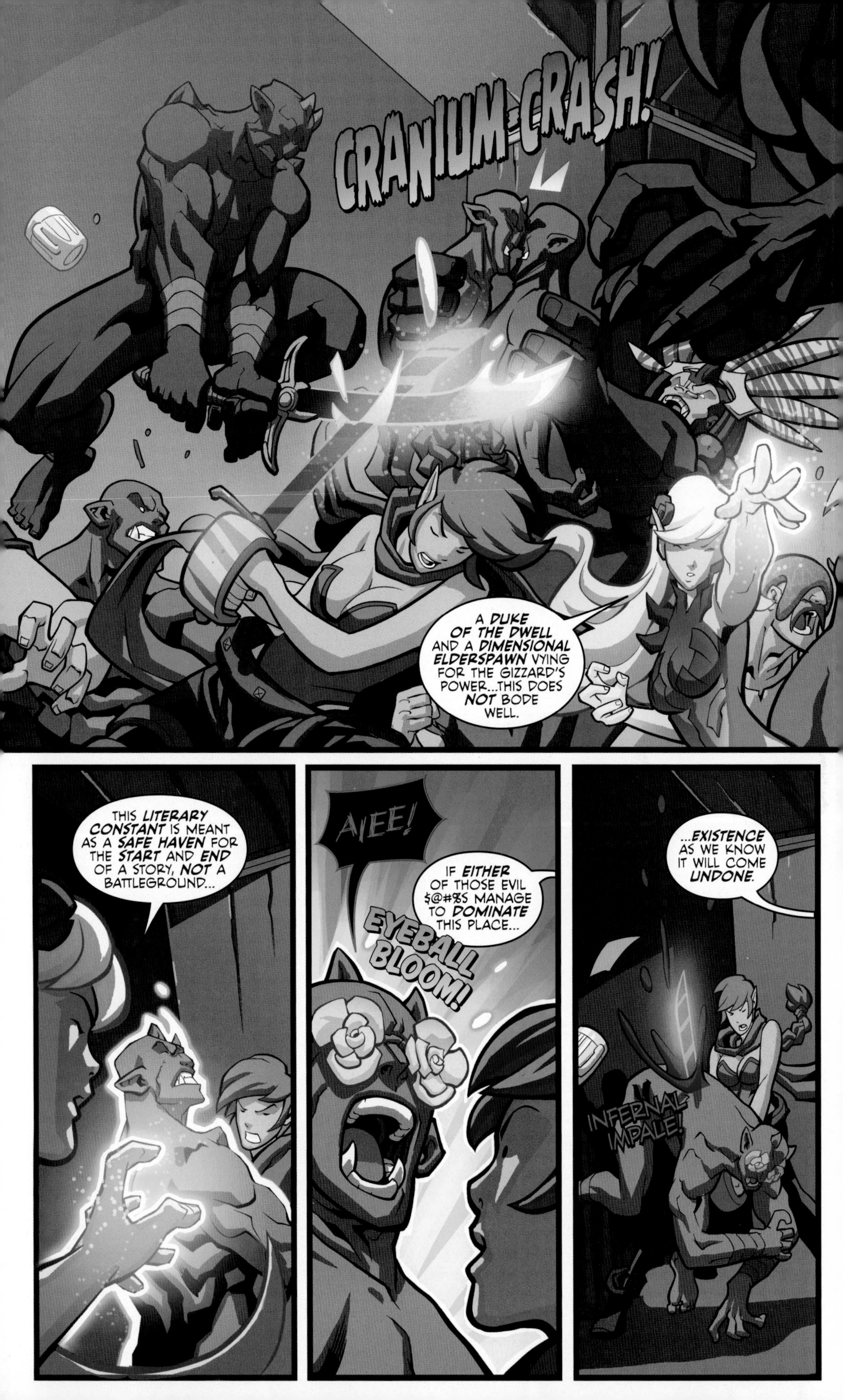
CRANIUM-CRASH!
A DUKE OF THE DWELL AND A DIMENSIONAL ELDERSPAWN VYING FOR THE GIZZARD'S POWER...THIS DOES NOT BODE WELL.
THIS LITERARY CONSTANT IS MEANT AS A SAFE HAVEN FOR THE START AND END OF A STORY, NOT A BATTLEGROUND...
AIEE!
IF EITHER OF THOSE EVIL $@#%S MANAGE TO DOMINATE THIS PLACE...
EYEBALL BLOOM!
...EXISTENCE AS WE KNOW IT WILL COME UNDONE.
INFERNAL IMPALE!

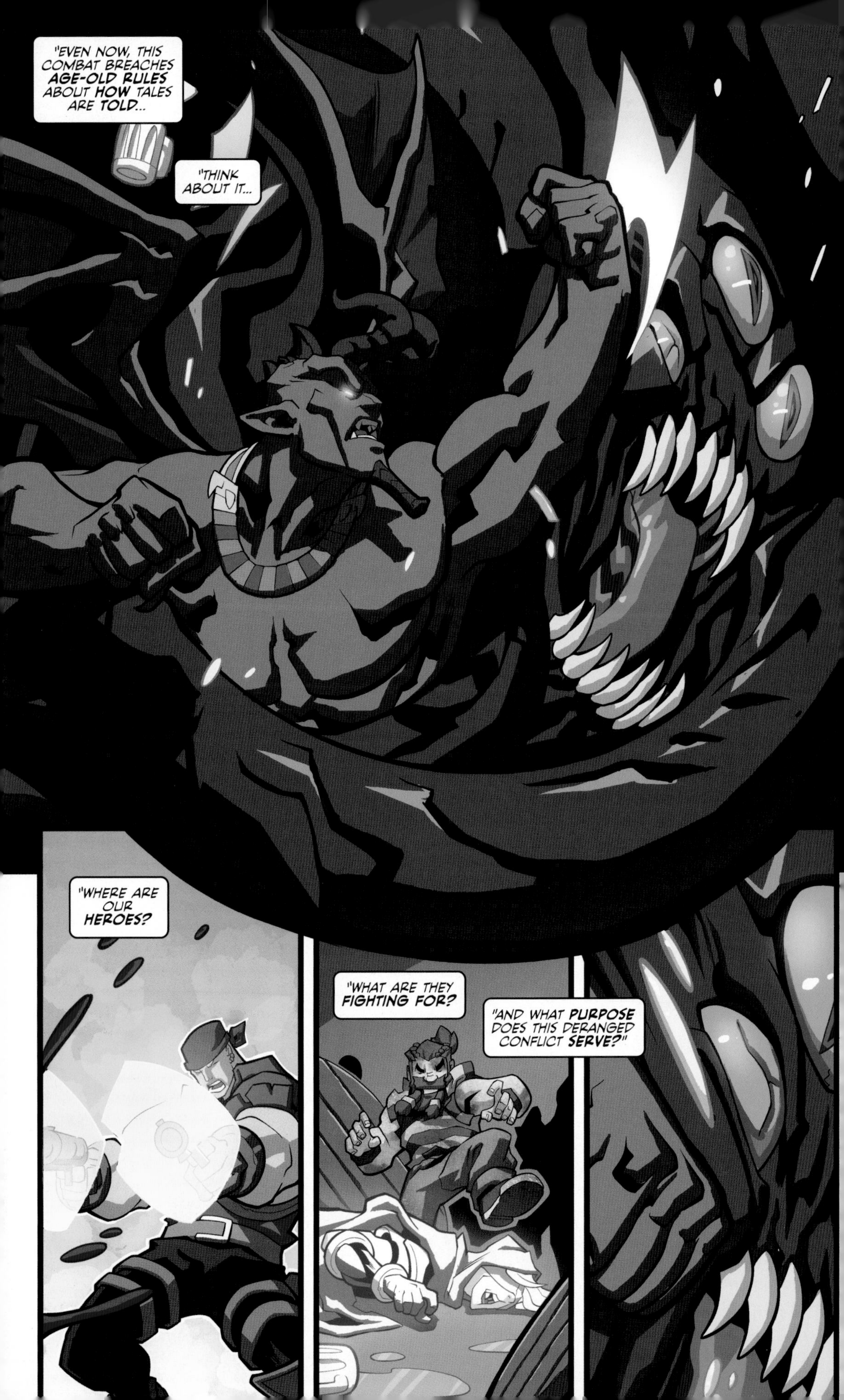
"EVEN NOW, THIS COMBAT BREACHES AGE-OLD RULES ABOUT HOW TALES ARE TOLD...
"THINK ABOUT IT...
"WHERE ARE OUR HEROES?
"WHAT ARE THEY FIGHTING FOR?
"AND WHAT PURPOSE DOES THIS DERANGED CONFLICT SERVE?"

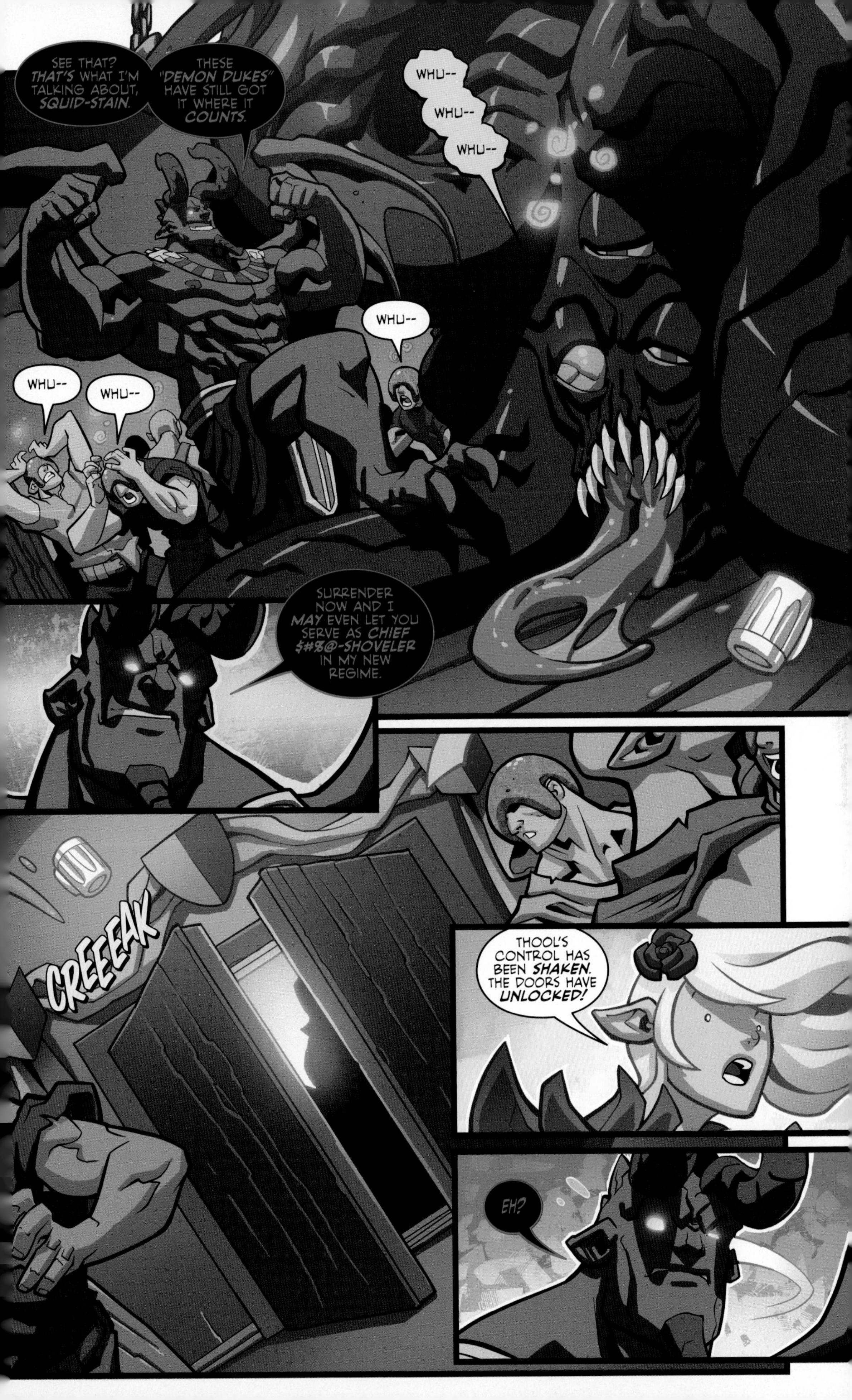
SEE THAT? THAT'S WHAT I'M TALKING ABOUT, SQUID-STAIN.
THESE "DEMON DUKES" HAVE STILL GOT IT WHERE IT COUNTS.
WHU--
WHU--
WHU--
WHU--
WHU--
WHU--
SURRENDER NOW AND I MAY EVEN LET YOU SERVE AS CHIEF $#%@-SHOVELER IN MY NEW REGIME.
CREEEAK
THOOL'S CONTROL HAS BEEN SHAKEN. THE DOORS HAVE UNLOCKED!
EH?

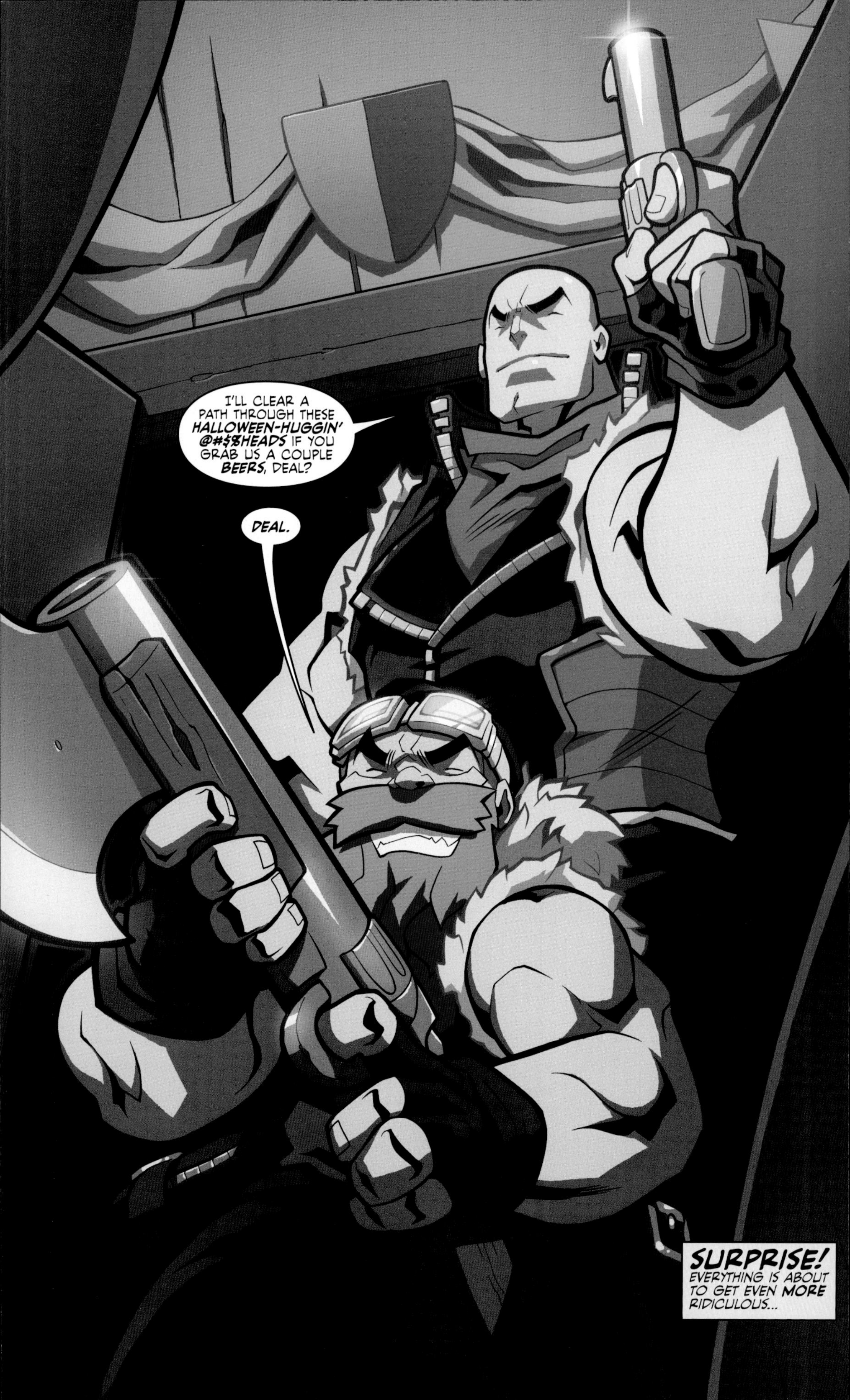
I'LL CLEAR A PATH THROUGH THESE HALLOWEEN-HUGGIN' @#$%HEADS IF YOU GRAB US A COUPLE BEERS, DEAL?
DEAL.
SURPRISE! EVERYTHING IS ABOUT TO GET EVEN MORE RIDICULOUS...

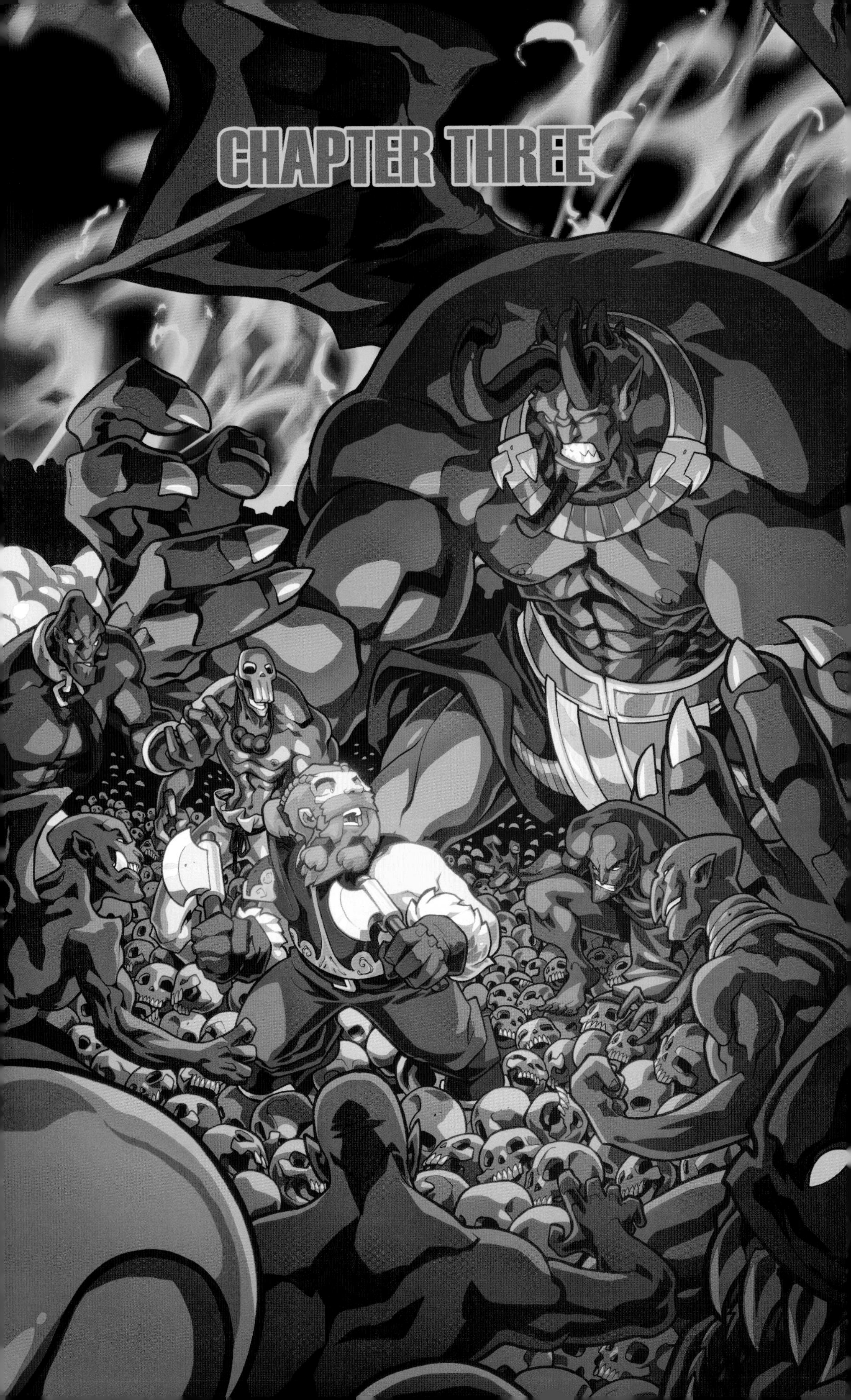
CHAPTER THREE

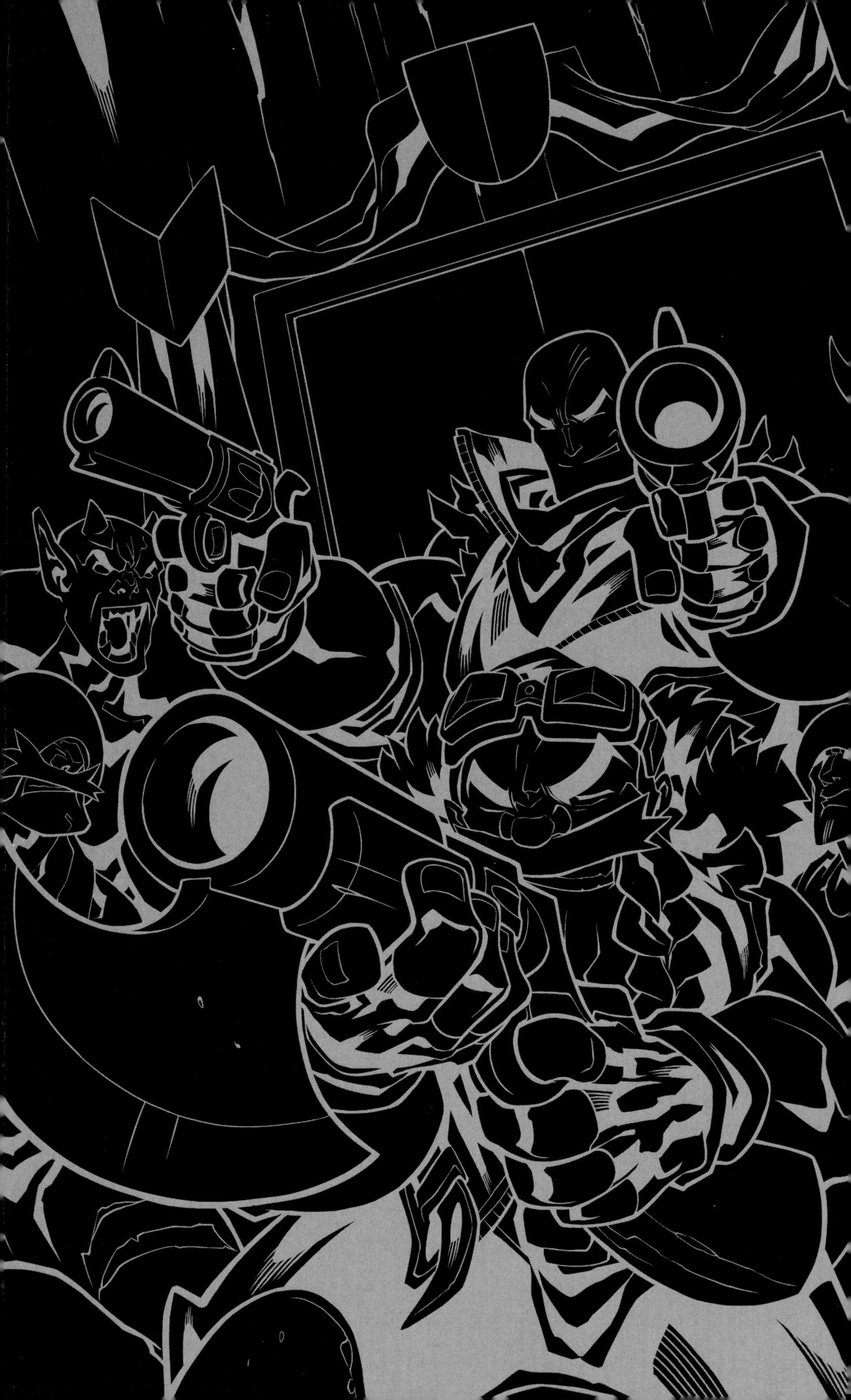

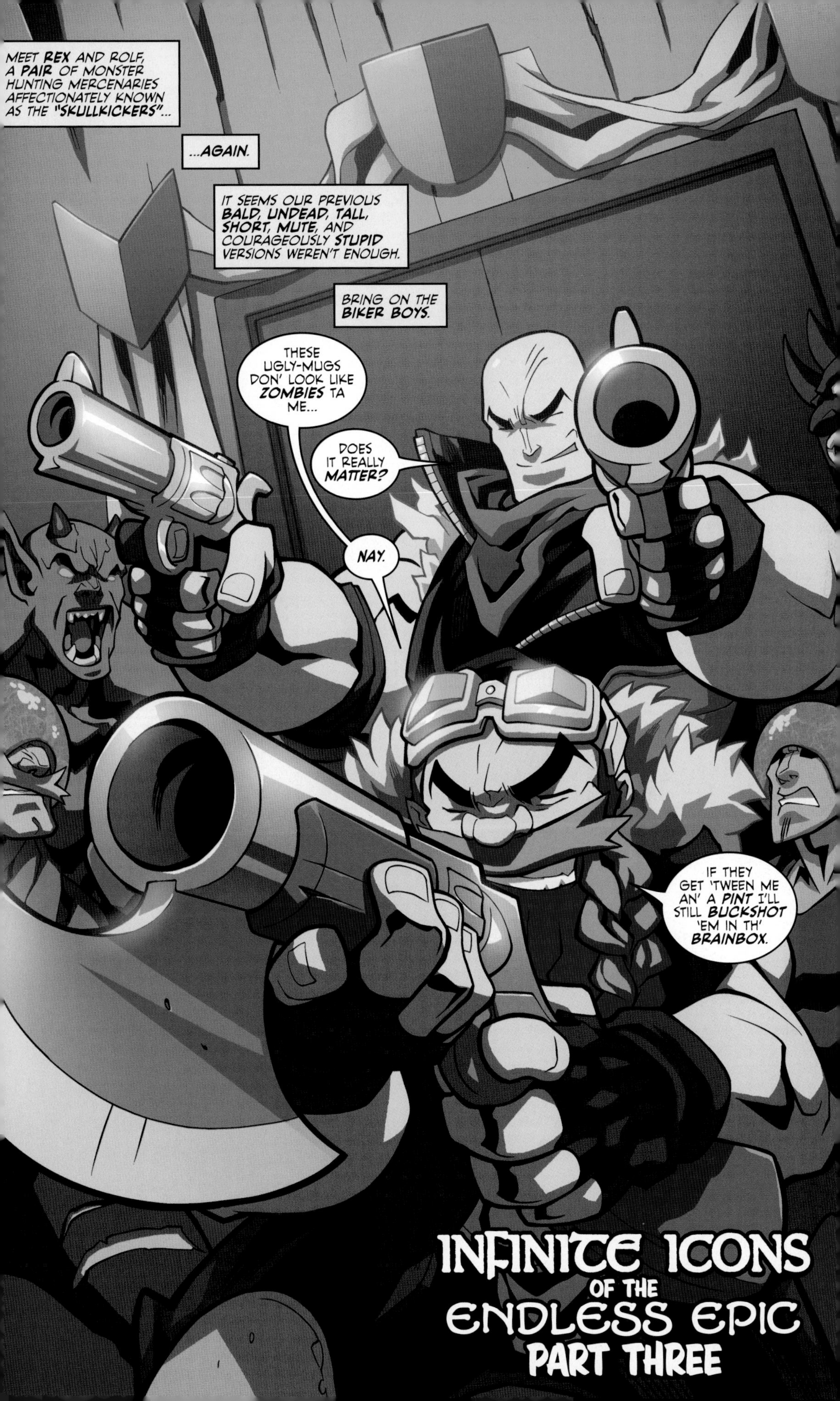

MEET REX AND ROLF, A PAIR OF MONSTER HUNTING MERCENARIES AFFECTIONATELY KNOWN AS THE "SKULLKICKERS"...
...AGAIN.
IT SEEMS OUR PREVIOUS BALD, UNDEAD, TALL, SHORT, MUTE, AND COURAGEOUSLY STUPID VERSIONS WEREN'T ENOUGH.
BRING ON THE BIKER BOYS.
THESE UGLY-MUGS DON' LOOK LIKE ZOMBIES TA ME...
DOES IT REALLY MATTER?
NAY.
IF THEY GET 'TWEEN ME AN' A PINT I'LL STILL BUCKSHOT 'EM IN TH' BRAINBOX.
INFINITE ICONS OF THE ENDLESS EPIC PART THREE

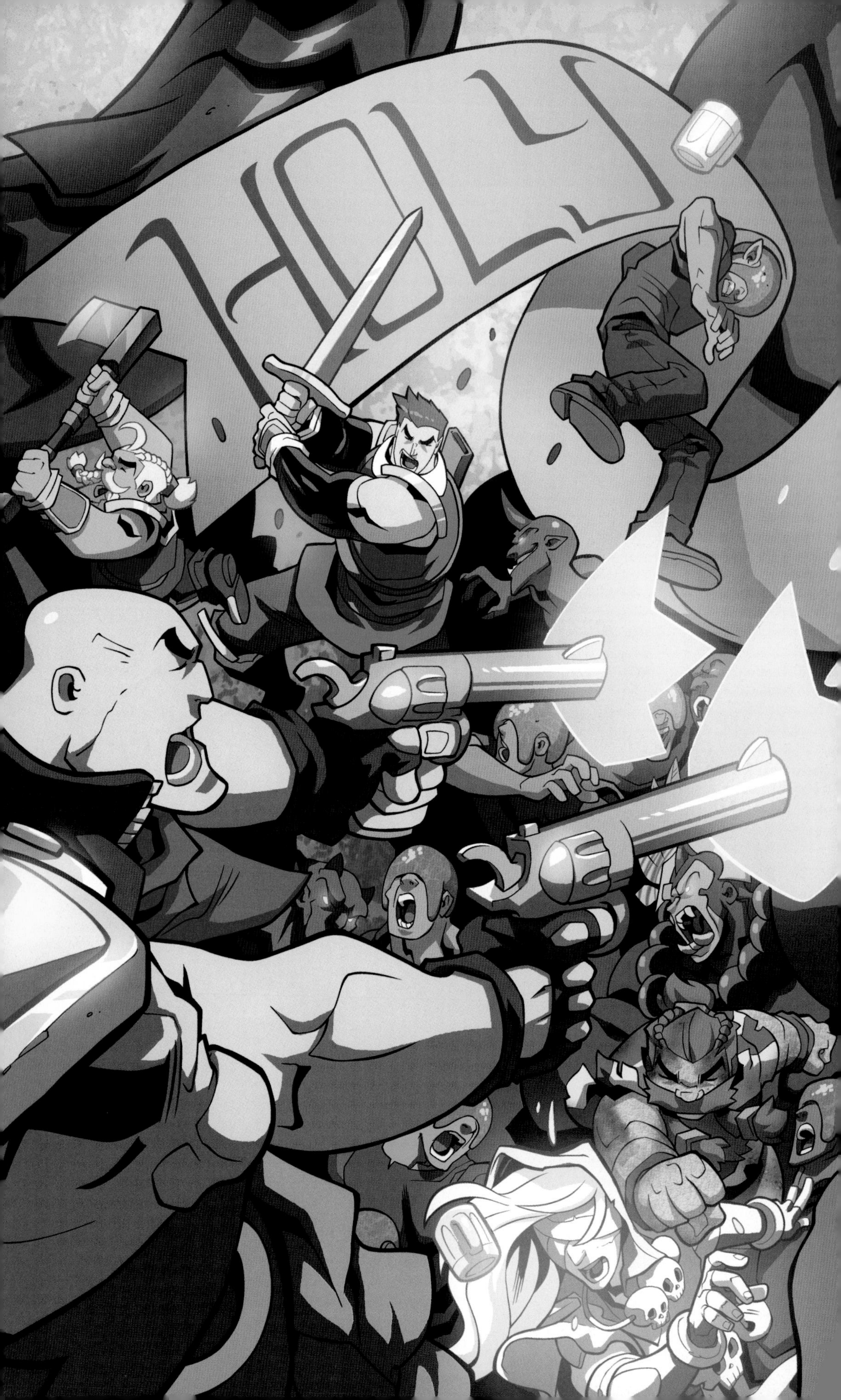

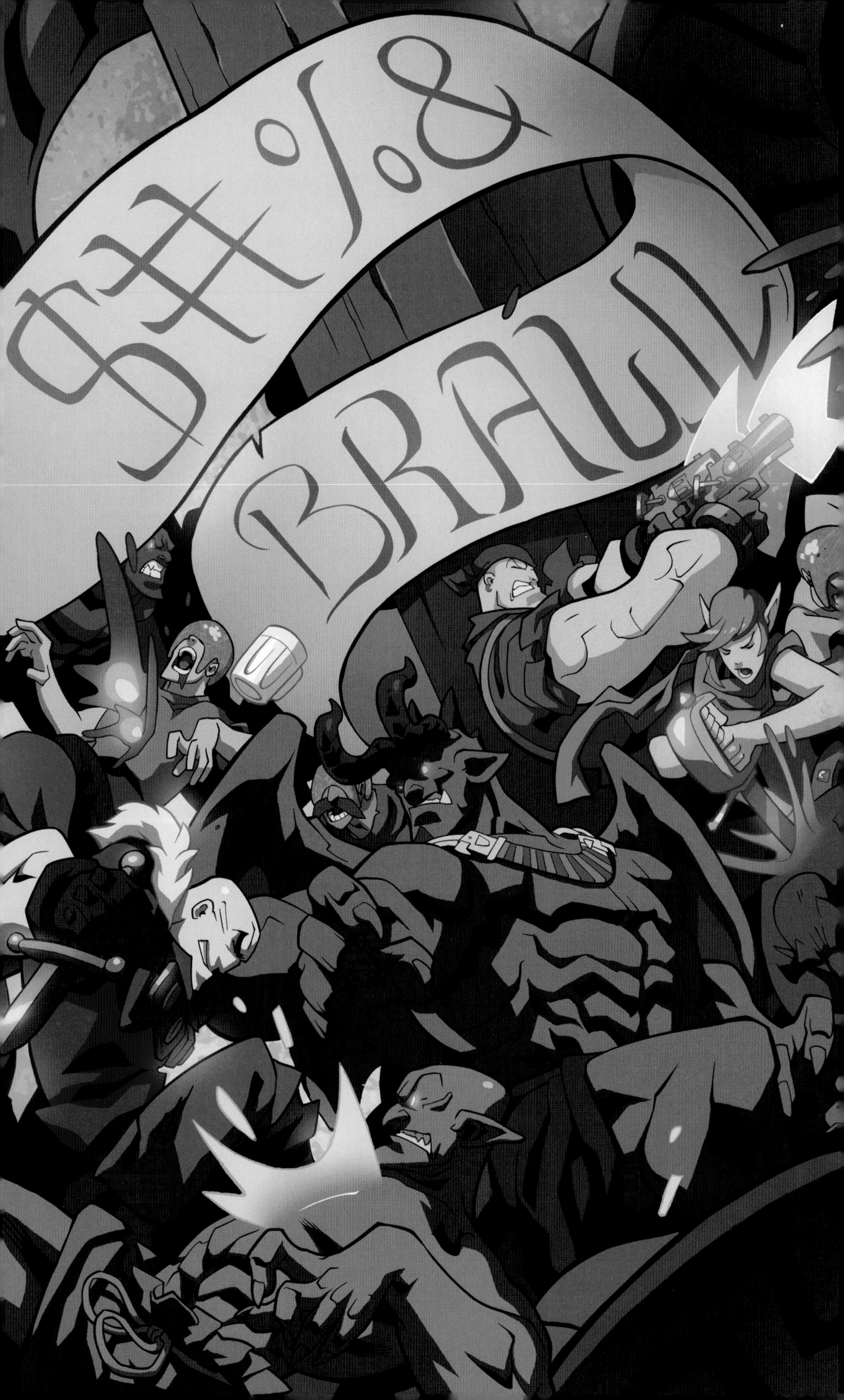
$#%&
BRAWL

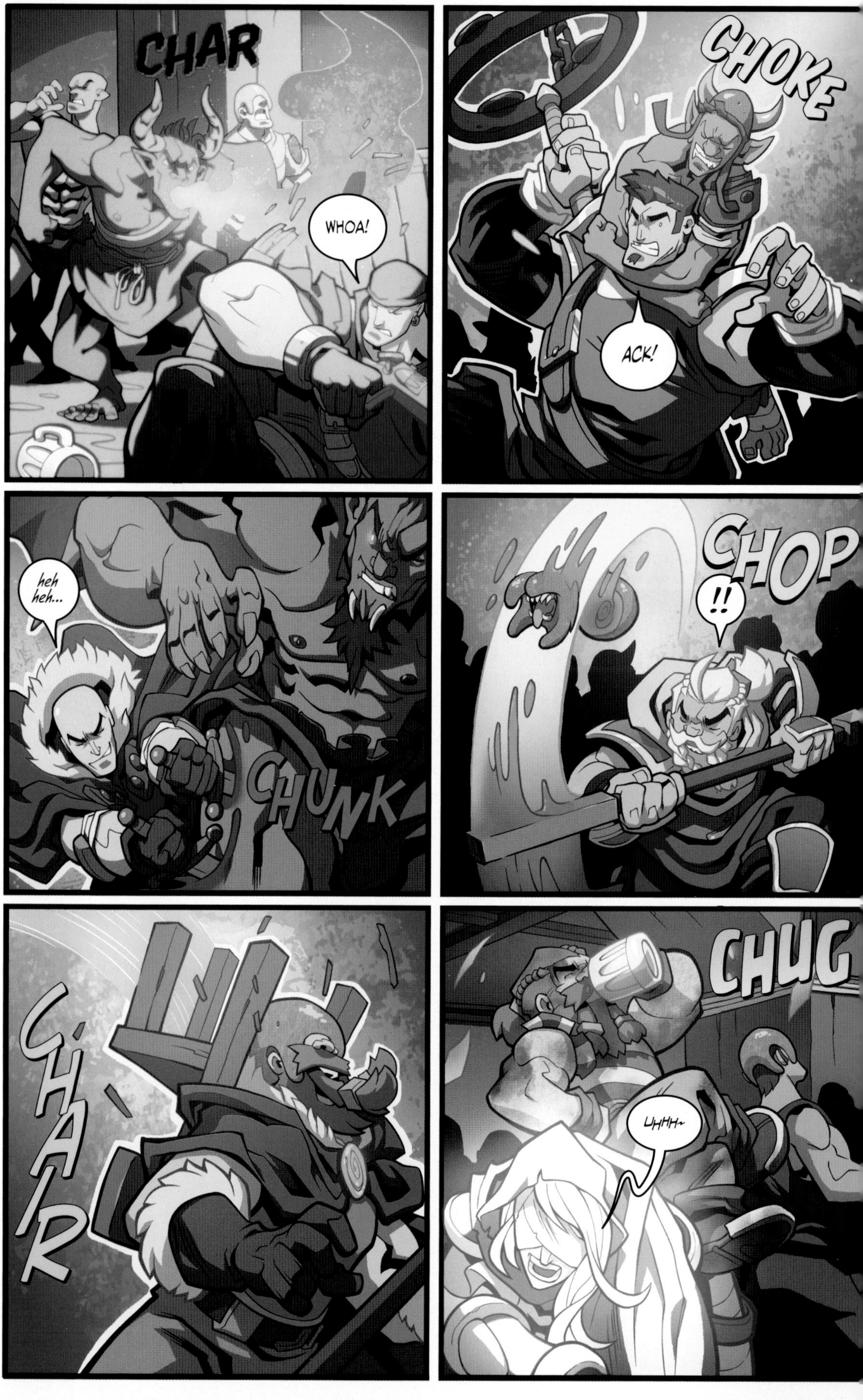
CHAR
WHOA!
CHOKE
ACK!
heh heh...
CHUNK
CHOP
!!
CHAIR
CHUG
UHHH

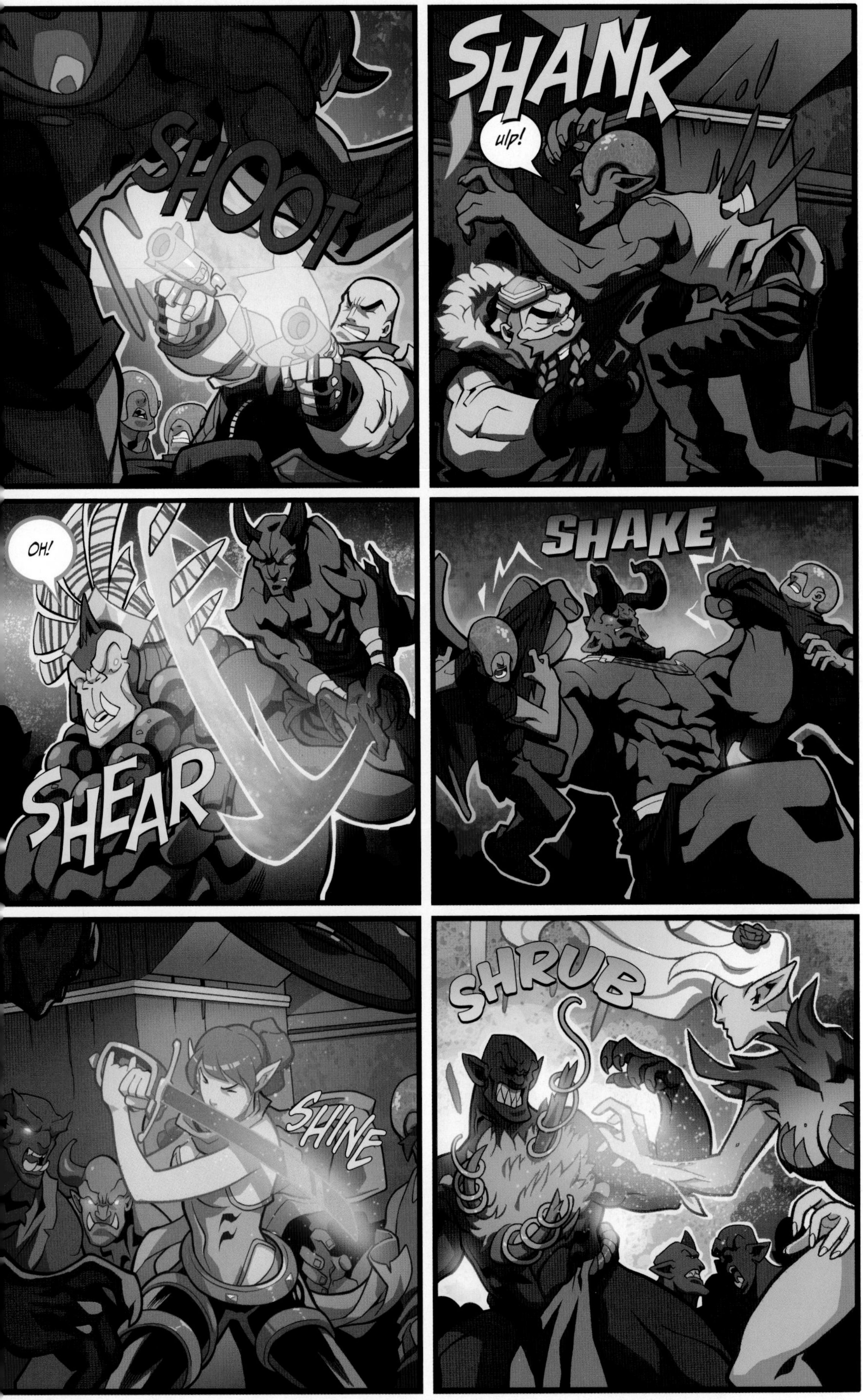
SHOOT
SHANK
ulp!
OH!
SHEAR
SHAKE
SHINE
SHRUB

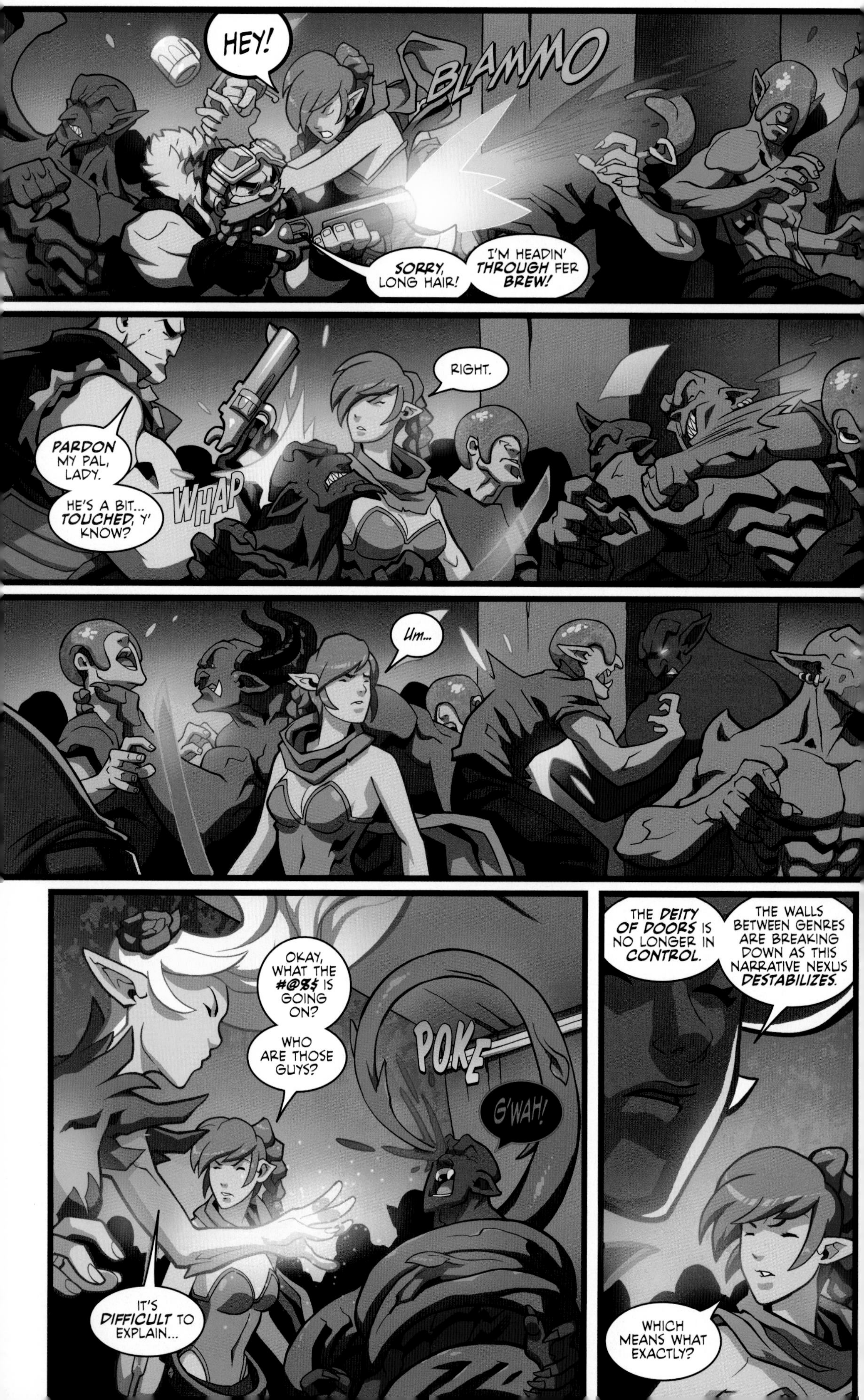
HEY!
BLAMMO
SORRY, LONG HAIR!
I'M HEADIN' THROUGH FER BREW!
PARDON MY PAL, LADY.
HE'S A BIT... TOUCHED, Y' KNOW?
WHAP
RIGHT.
Um...
OKAY, WHAT THE #@%$ IS GOING ON?
WHO ARE THOSE GUYS?
POKE
G'WAH!
IT'S DIFFICULT TO EXPLAIN...
THE DEITY OF DOORS IS NO LONGER IN CONTROL.
THE WALLS BETWEEN GENRES ARE BREAKING DOWN AS THIS NARRATIVE NEXUS DESTABILIZES.
WHICH MEANS WHAT EXACTLY?

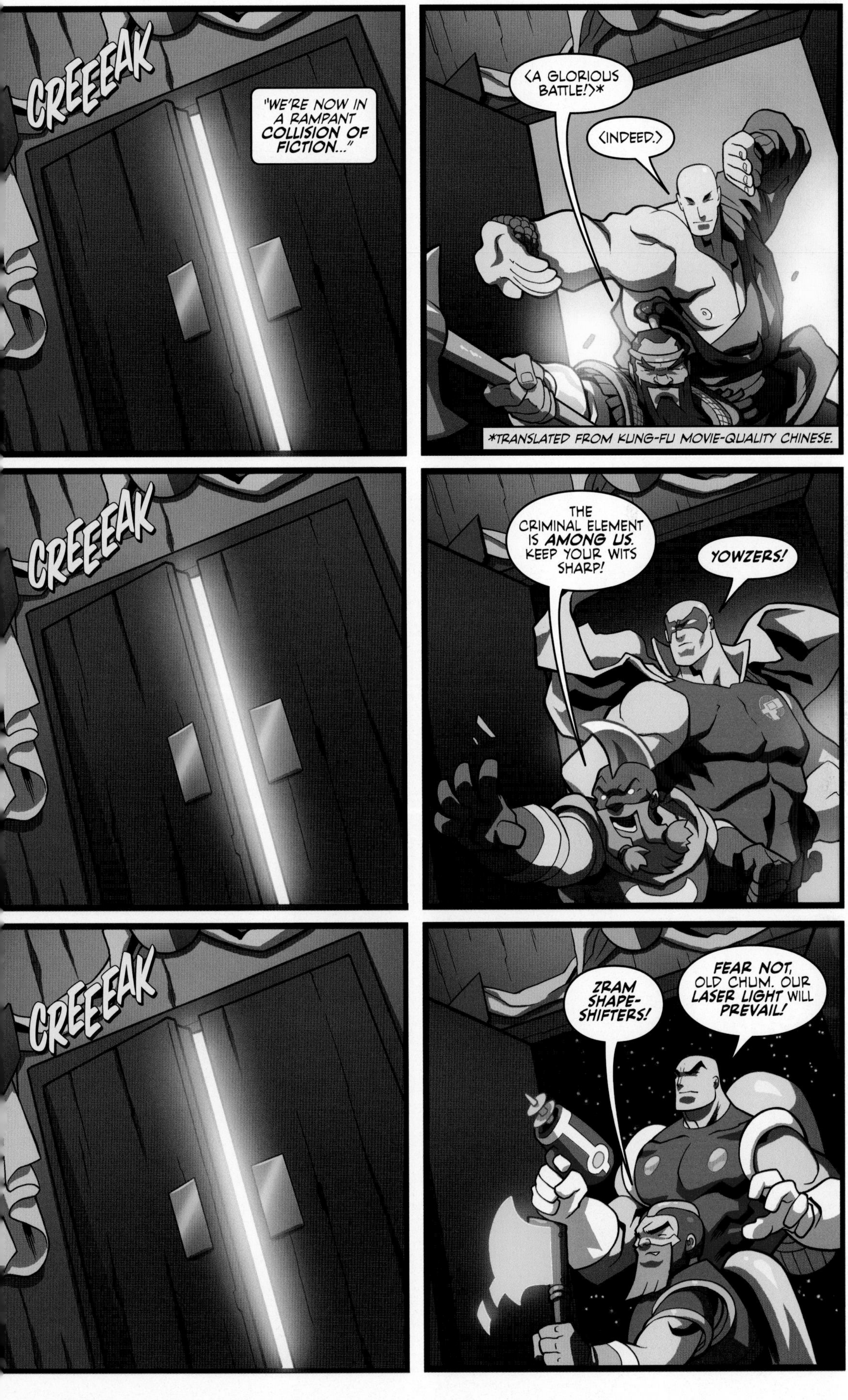
CREEEAK
"WE'RE NOW IN A RAMPANT COLLISION OF FICTION..."
<A GLORIOUS BATTLE!>*
<INDEED.>
*TRANSLATED FROM KUNG-FU MOVIE-QUALITY CHINESE.
CREEEAK
THE CRIMINAL ELEMENT IS AMONG US. KEEP YOUR WITS SHARP!
YOWZERS!
CREEEAK
ZRAM SHAPE-SHIFTERS!
FEAR NOT, OLD CHUM. OUR LASER LIGHT WILL PREVAIL!

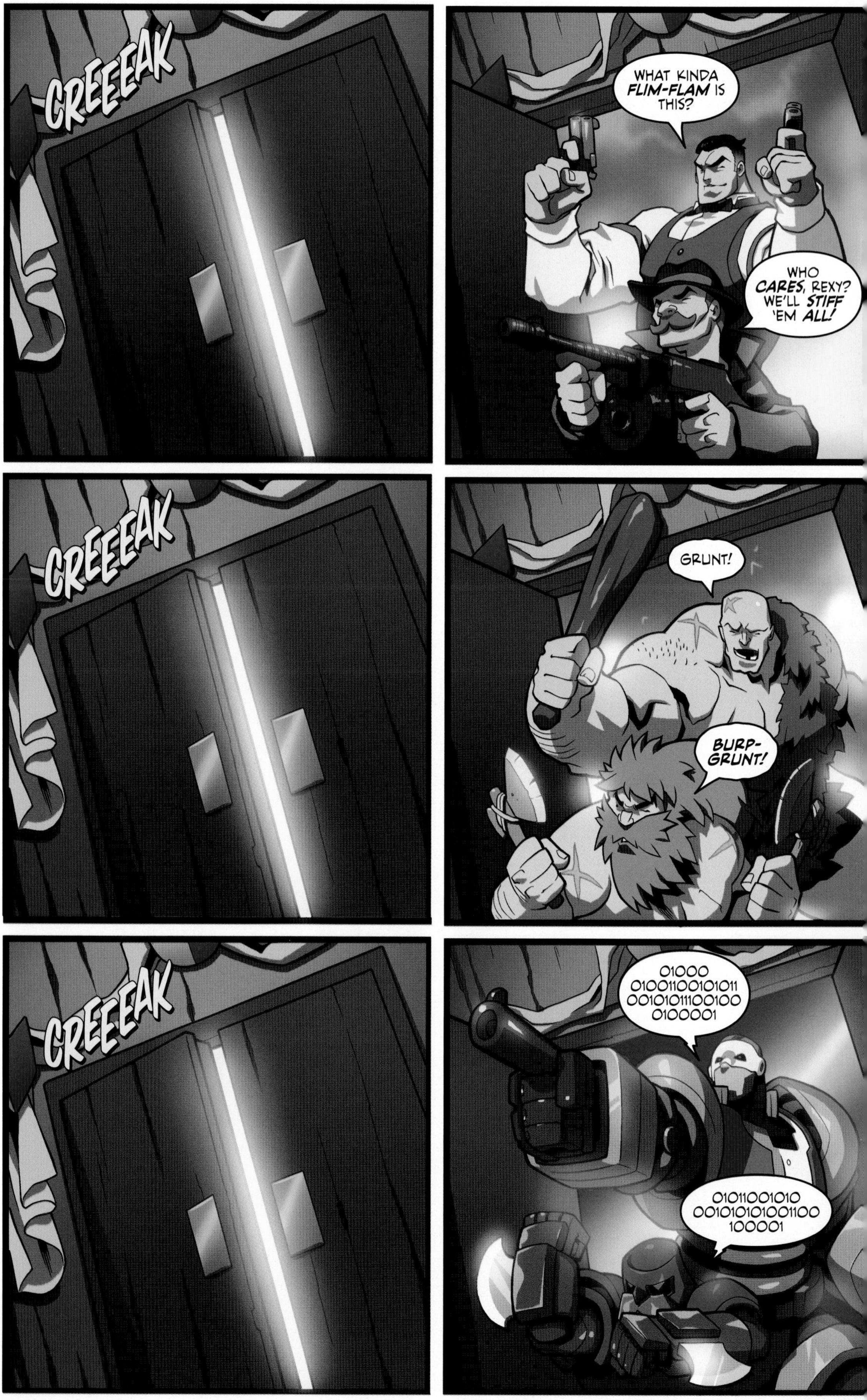
CREEEAK
WHAT KINDA FLIM-FLAM IS THIS?
WHO CARES, REXY? WE'LL STIFF 'EM ALL!
CREEEAK
GRUNT!
BURP-GRUNT!
CREEEAK
01000 01001100101011 00101011100100 0100001
01011001010 001010101001100 100001

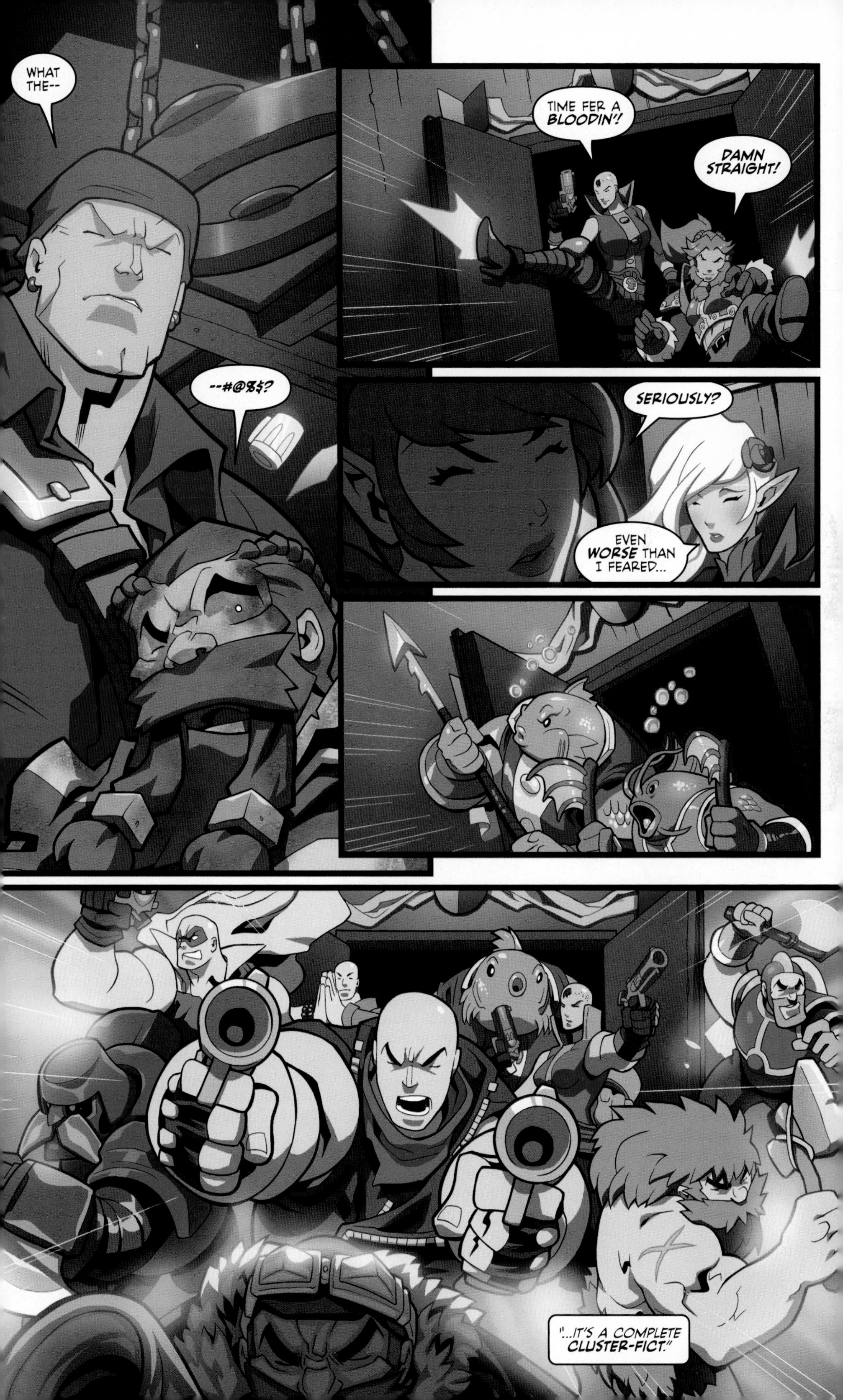

WHAT THE--
--#@%$?
TIME FER A BLOODIN'!
DAMN STRAIGHT!
SERIOUSLY?
EVEN WORSE THAN I FEARED...
"...IT'S A COMPLETE CLUSTER-FICT."

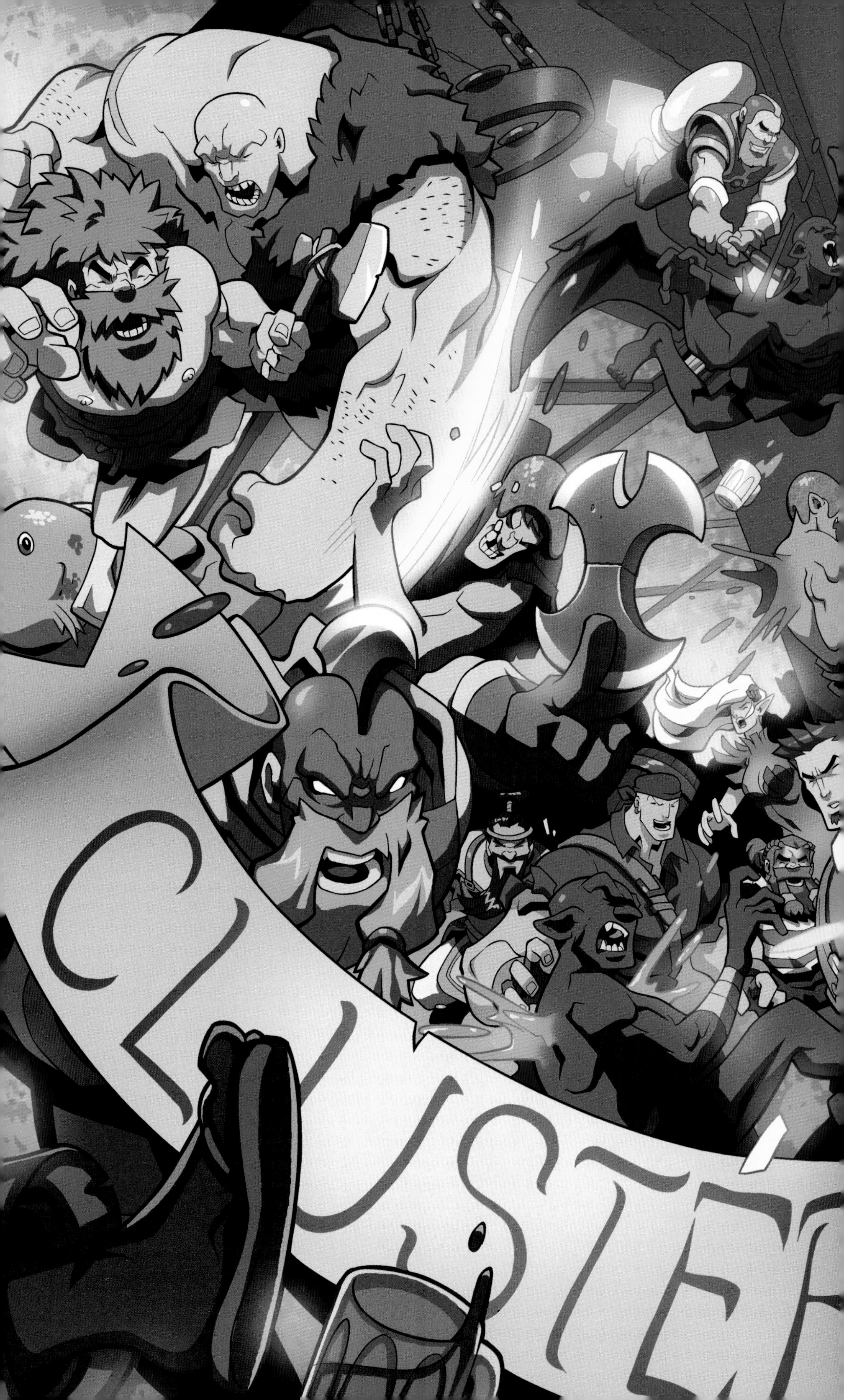

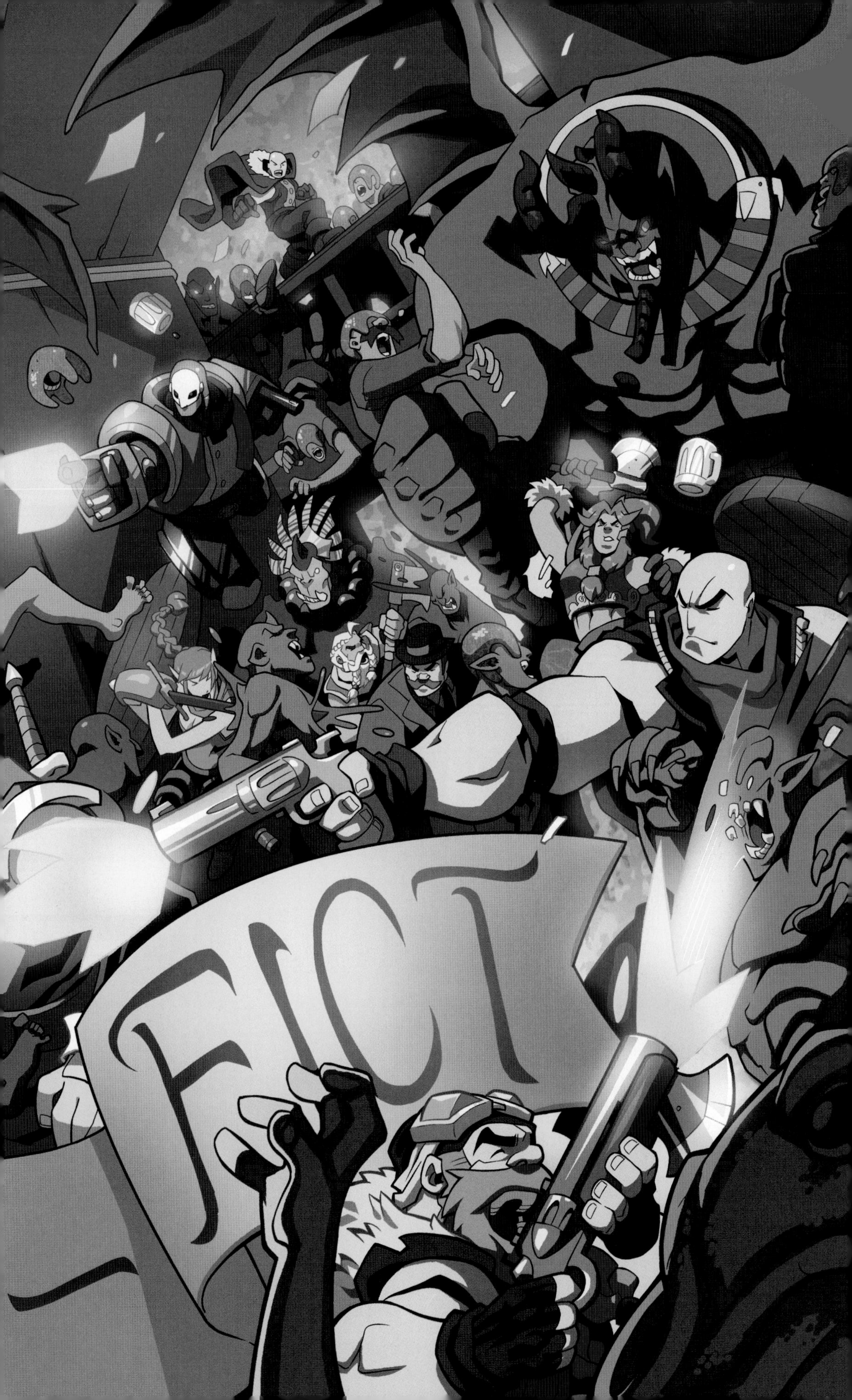
FICT

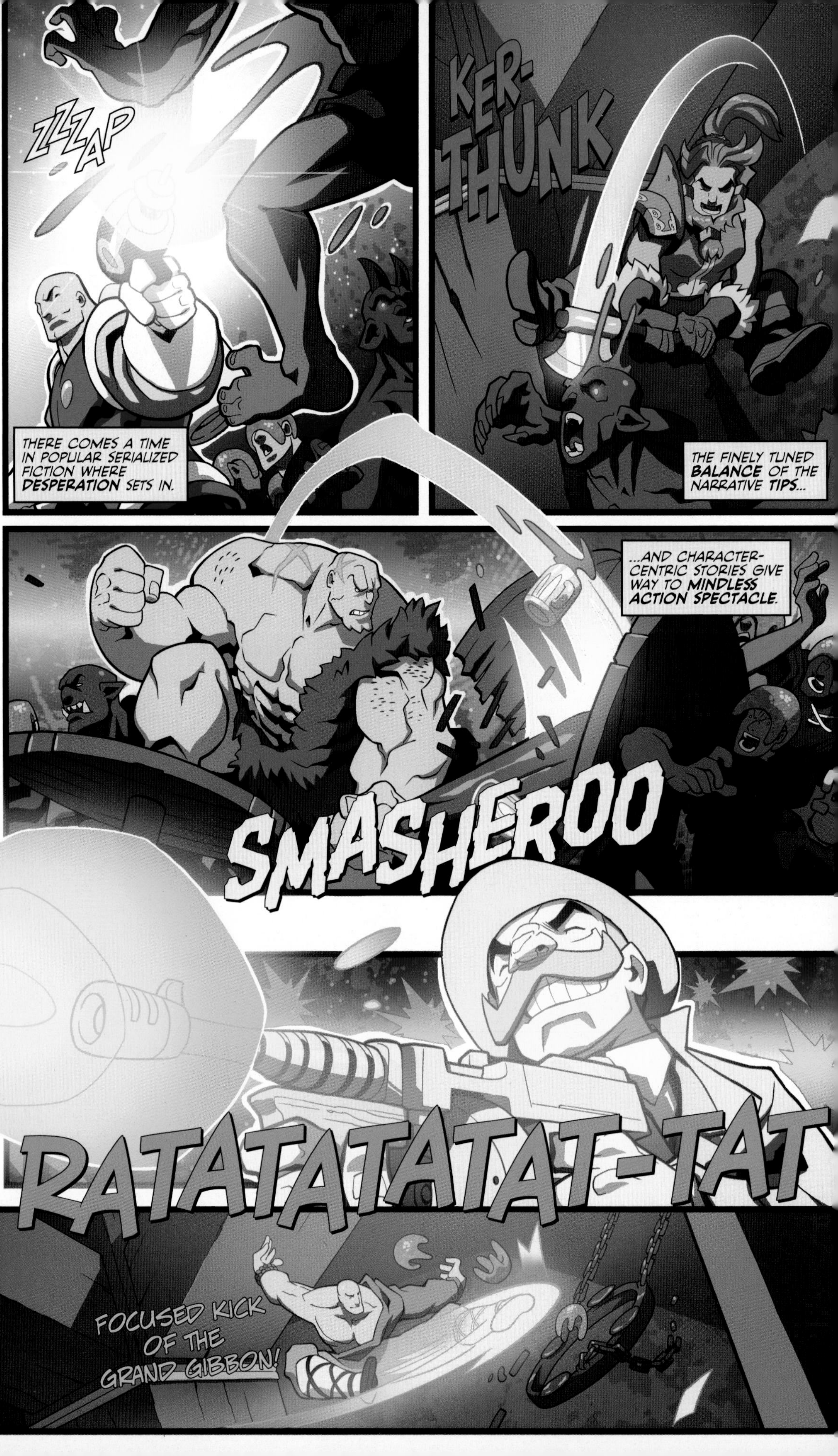

ZZZAP
THERE COMES A TIME IN POPULAR SERIALIZED FICTION WHERE DESPERATION SETS IN.
KER-THUNK
THE FINELY TUNED BALANCE OF THE NARRATIVE TIPS...
...AND CHARACTER-CENTRIC STORIES GIVE WAY TO MINDLESS ACTION SPECTACLE.
SMASHEROO
RATATATATAT-TAT
FOCUSED KICK OF THE GRAND GIBBON!

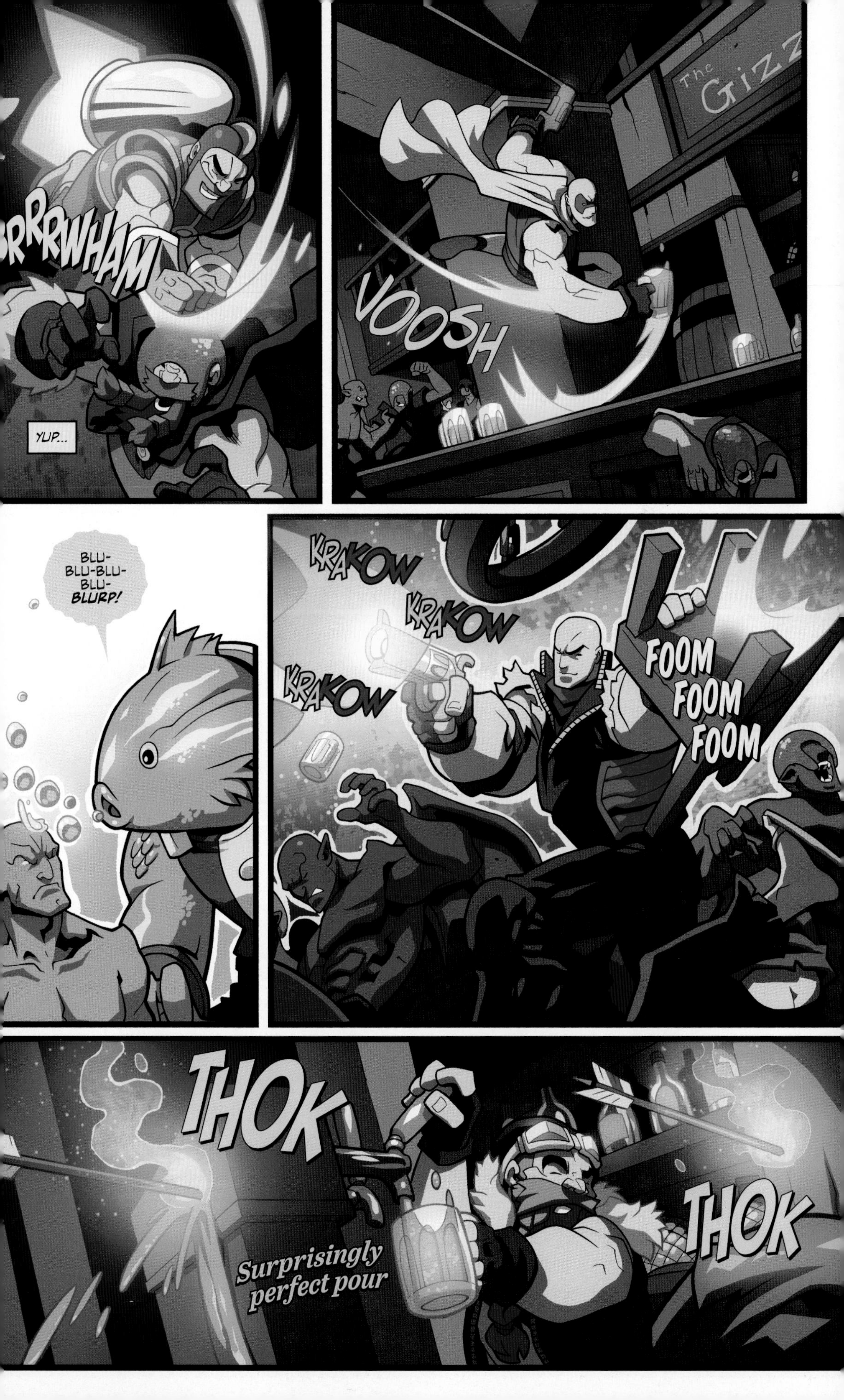
BRRRWHAM
YUP...
VOOSH
The GIZZ
BLU-
BLU-BLU-
BLU-
BLURP!
KRAKOW
KRAKOW
KRAKOW
FOOM
FOOM
FOOM
THOK
THOK
Surprisingly perfect pour

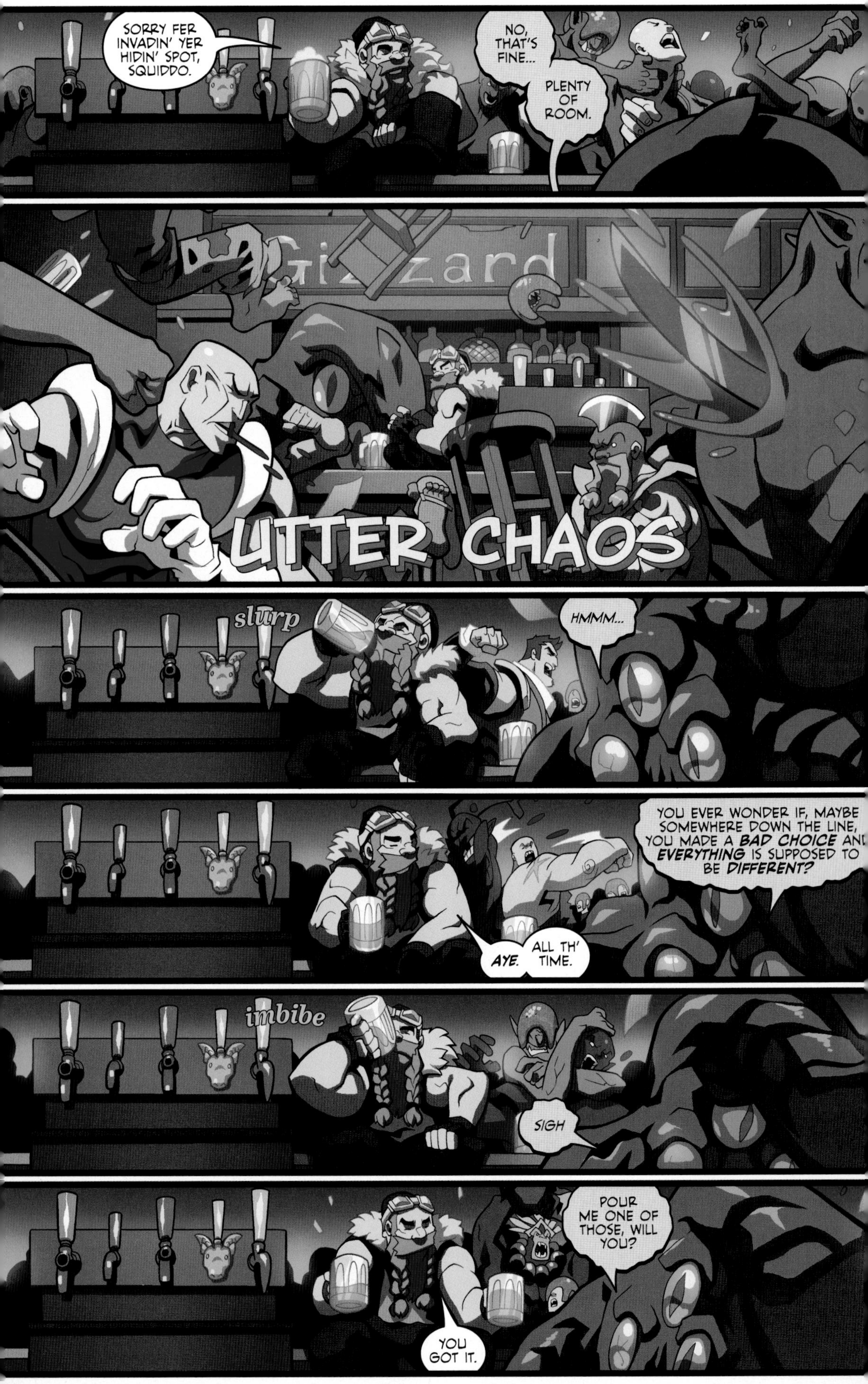
SORRY FER INVADIN' YER HIDIN' SPOT, SQUIDDO.
NO, THAT'S FINE...
PLENTY OF ROOM.
Gizzard
UTTER CHAOS
slurp
HMMM...
YOU EVER WONDER IF, MAYBE SOMEWHERE DOWN THE LINE, YOU MADE A BAD CHOICE AND EVERYTHING IS SUPPOSED TO BE DIFFERENT?
AYE.
ALL TH' TIME.
imbibe
SIGH
POUR ME ONE OF THOSE, WILL YOU?
YOU GOT IT.

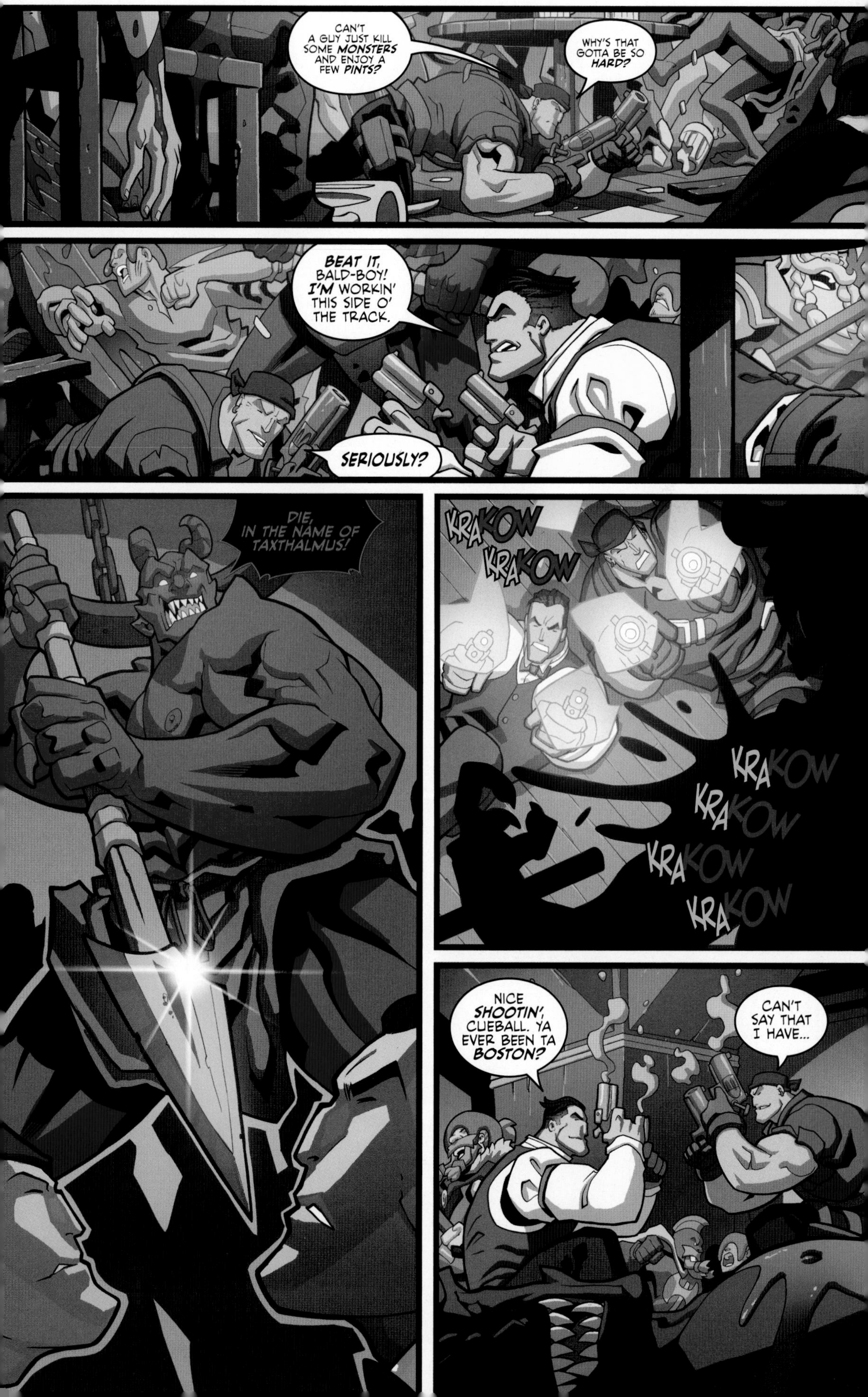
CAN'T A GUY JUST KILL SOME MONSTERS AND ENJOY A FEW PINTS?
WHY'S THAT GOTTA BE SO HARD?
BEAT IT, BALD-BOY! I'M WORKIN' THIS SIDE O' THE TRACK.
SERIOUSLY?
DIE, IN THE NAME OF TAXTHALMUS!
KRAKOW
KRAKOW
KRAKOW
KRAKOW
KRAKOW
KRAKOW
NICE SHOOTIN', CUEBALL. YA EVER BEEN TA BOSTON?
CAN'T SAY THAT I HAVE...

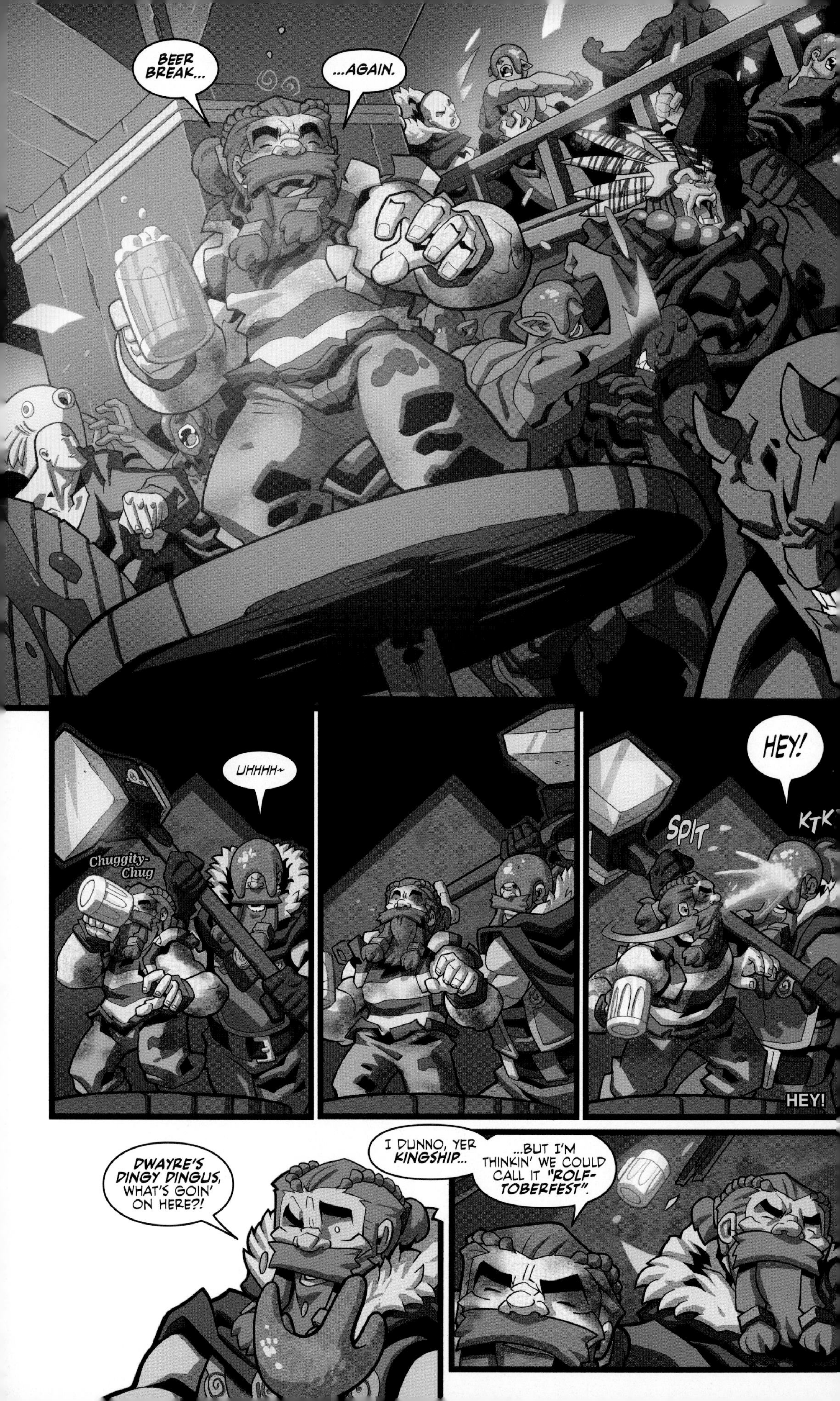
BEER BREAK...
...AGAIN.
UHHHH~
Chuggity-Chug
HEY!
SPIT
KTK
HEY!
DWAYRE'S DINGY DINGUS, WHAT'S GOIN' ON HERE?!
I DUNNO, YER KINGSHIP...
...BUT I'M THINKIN' WE COULD CALL IT "ROLF-TOBERFEST".

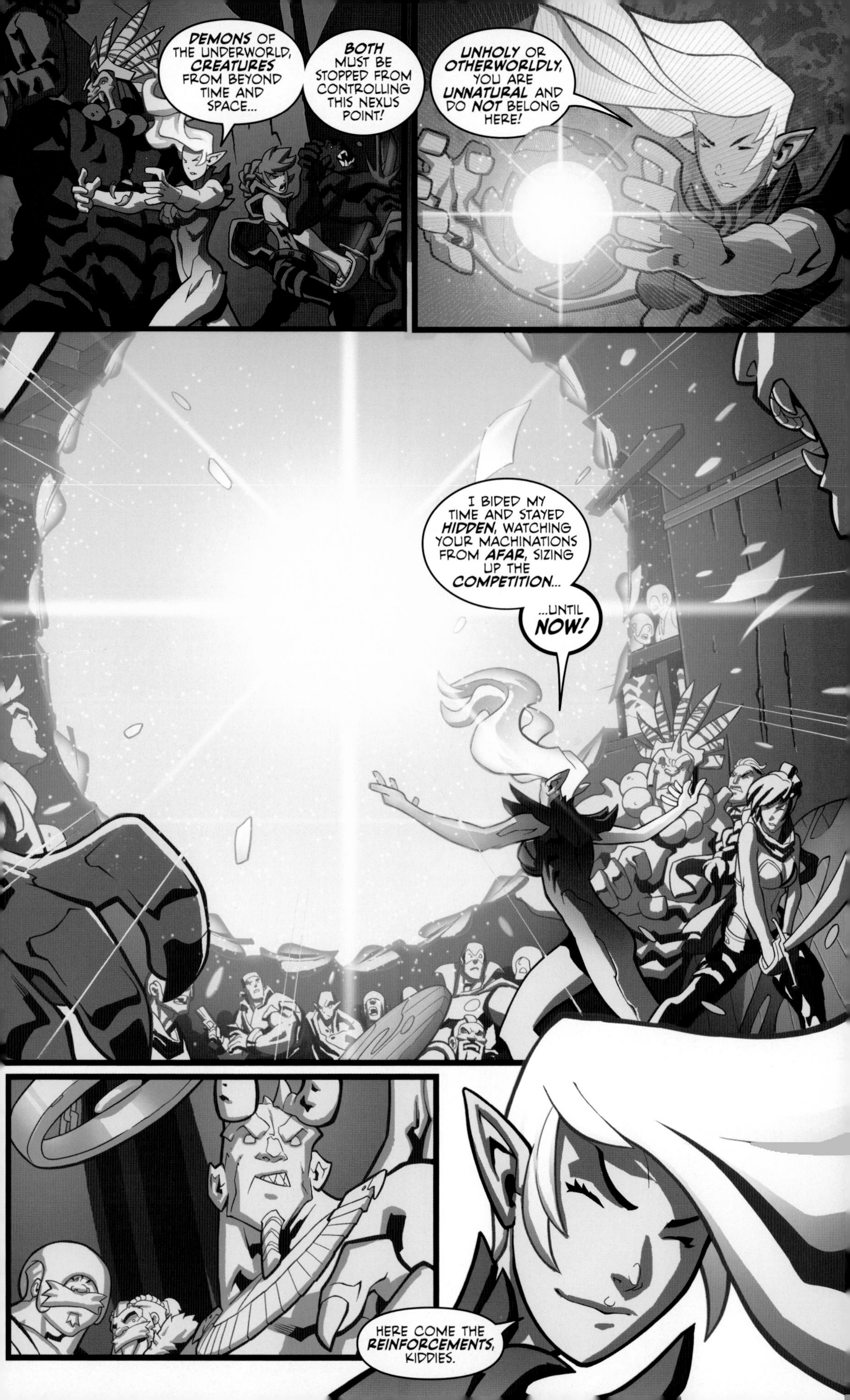
DEMONS OF THE UNDERWORLD, CREATURES FROM BEYOND TIME AND SPACE...
BOTH MUST BE STOPPED FROM CONTROLLING THIS NEXUS POINT!
UNHOLY OR OTHERWORLDLY, YOU ARE UNNATURAL AND DO NOT BELONG HERE!
I BIDED MY TIME AND STAYED HIDDEN, WATCHING YOUR MACHINATIONS FROM AFAR, SIZING UP THE COMPETITION...
...UNTIL NOW!
HERE COME THE REINFORCEMENTS, KIDDIES.

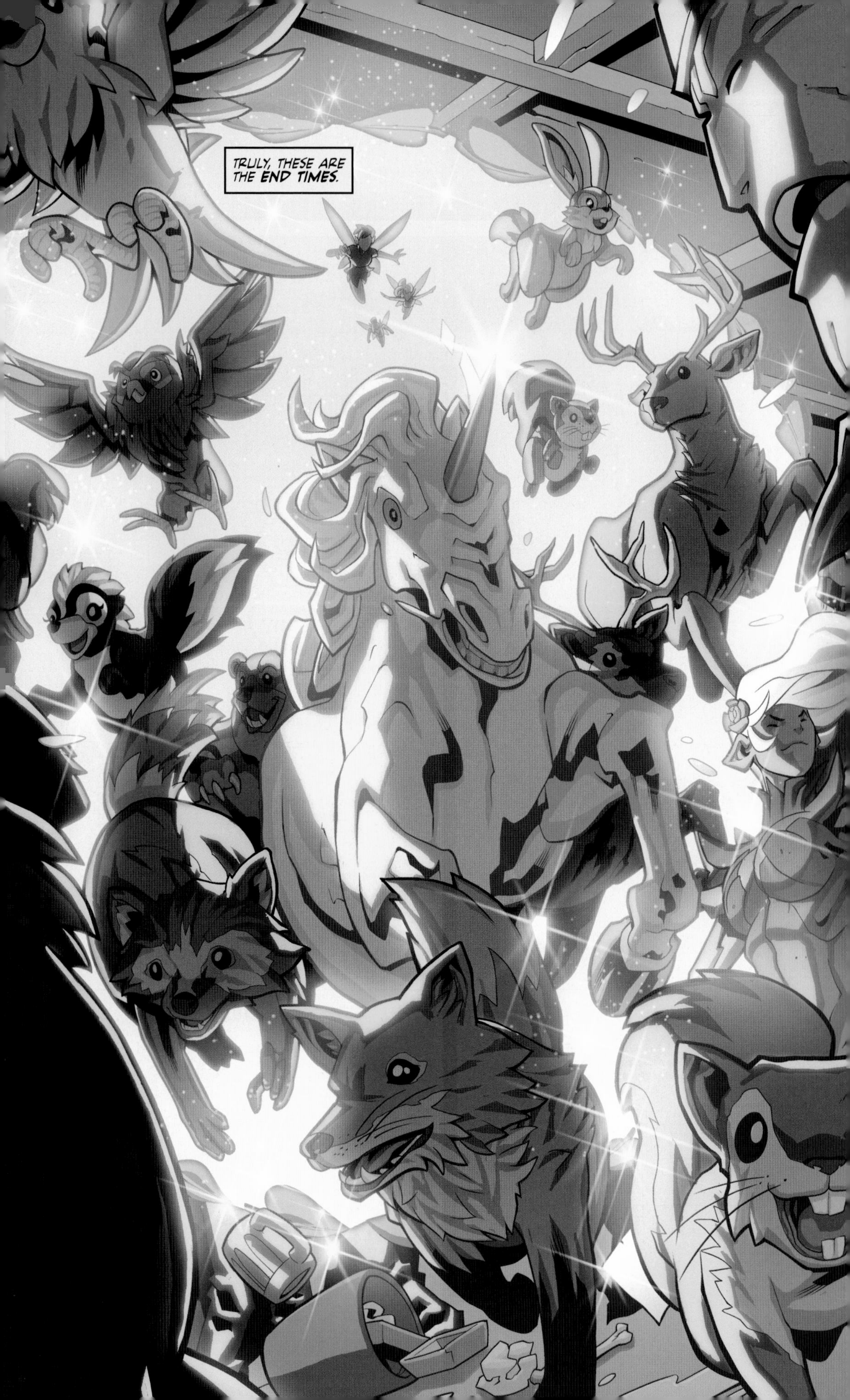
TRULY, THESE ARE THE END TIMES.

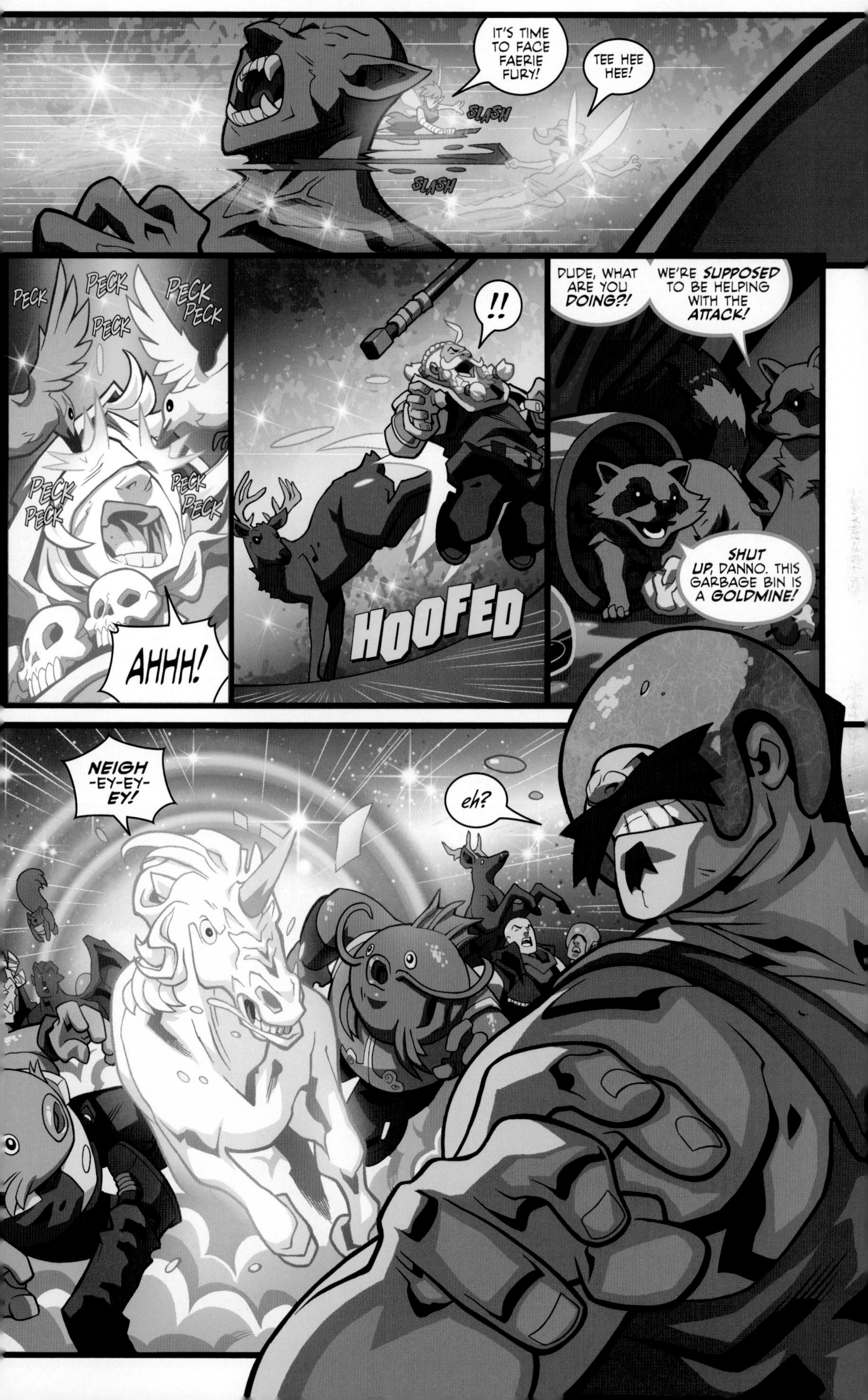

IT'S TIME TO FACE FAERIE FURY!
TEE HEE HEE!
SLASH
SLASH
PECK
PECK
PECK
PECK PECK
PECK PECK
PECK PECK
AHHH!
!!
HOOFED
DUDE, WHAT ARE YOU DOING?!
WE'RE SUPPOSED TO BE HELPING WITH THE ATTACK!
SHUT UP, DANNO. THIS GARBAGE BIN IS A GOLDMINE!
NEIGH -EY-EY-EY!
eh?

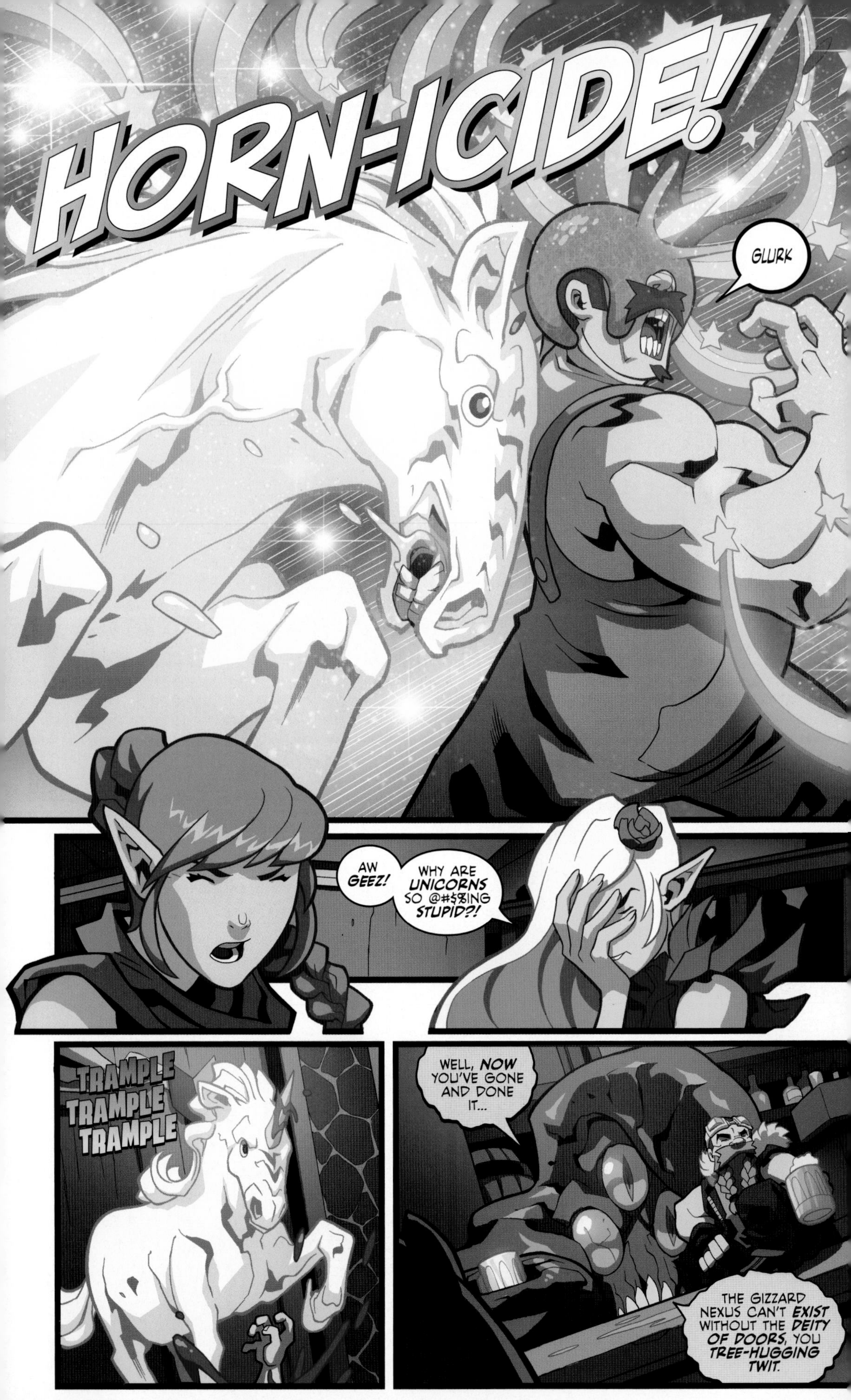
HORN-ICIDE!
GLURK
AW GEEZ!
WHY ARE UNICORNS SO @#$%ING STUPID?!
TRAMPLE TRAMPLE TRAMPLE
WELL, NOW YOU'VE GONE AND DONE IT...
THE GIZZARD NEXUS CAN'T EXIST WITHOUT THE DEITY OF DOORS, YOU TREE-HUGGING TWIT.

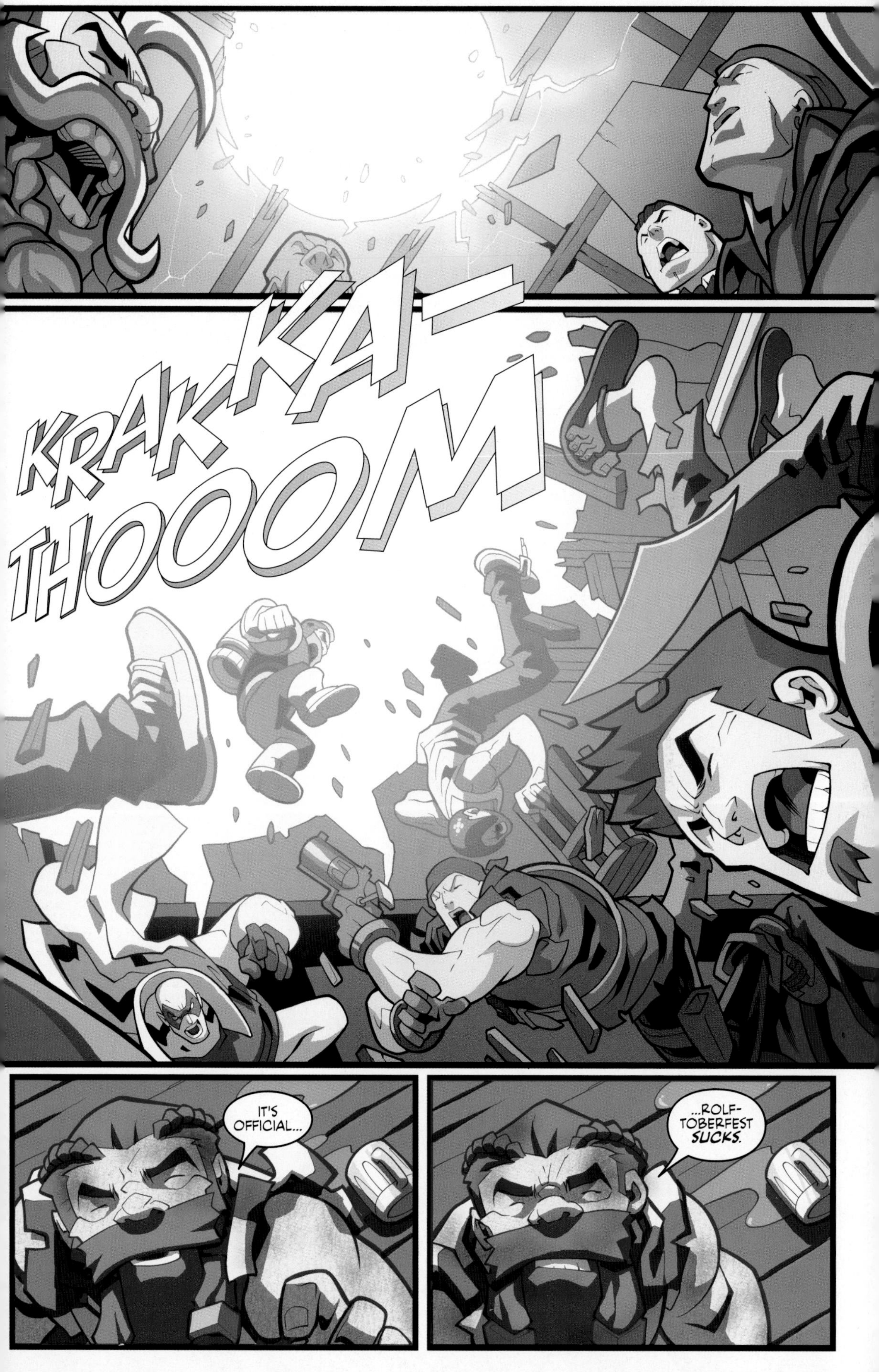
KRAK-KA-THOOOM
IT'S OFFICIAL...
...ROLF-TOBERFEST SUCKS.

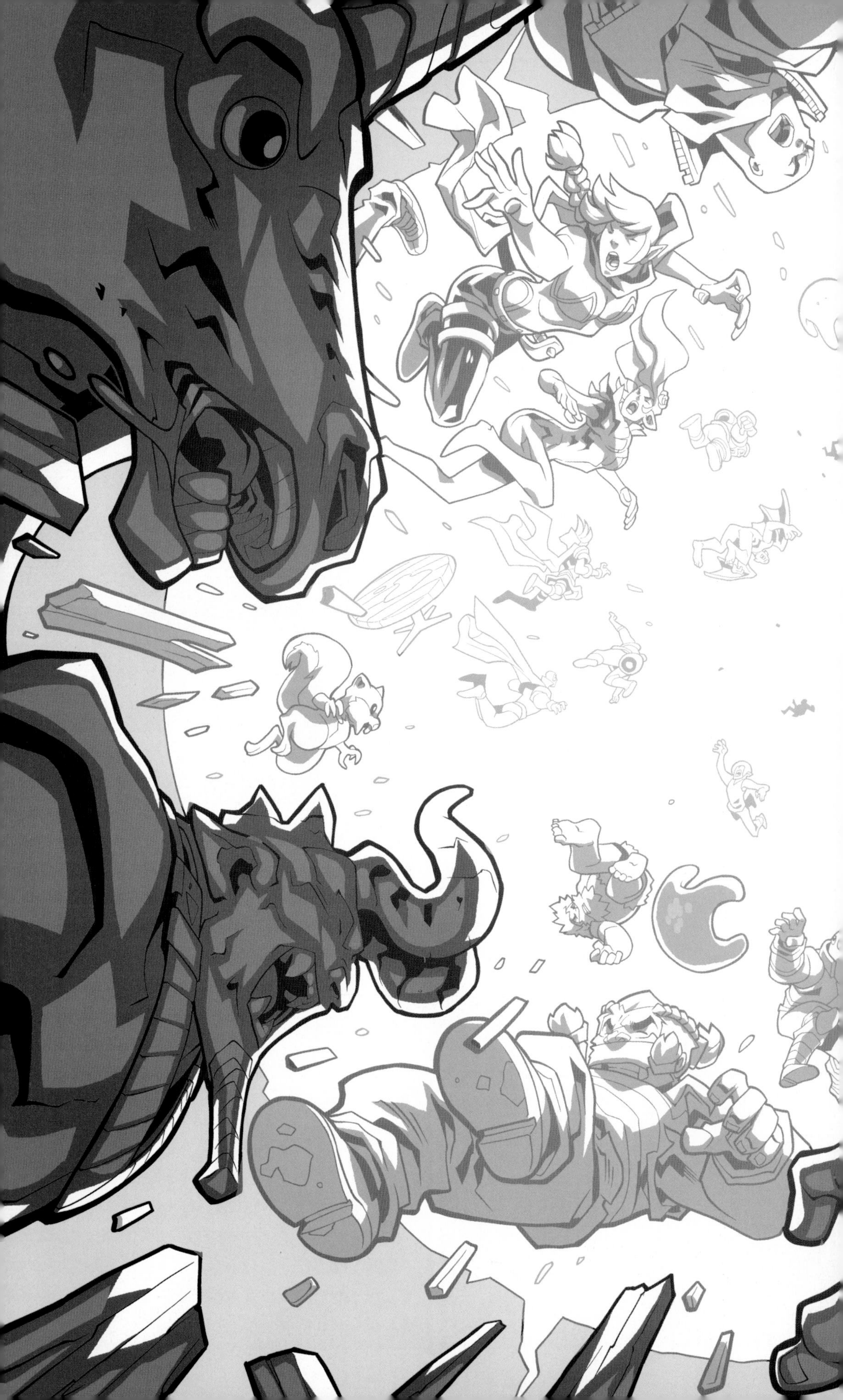

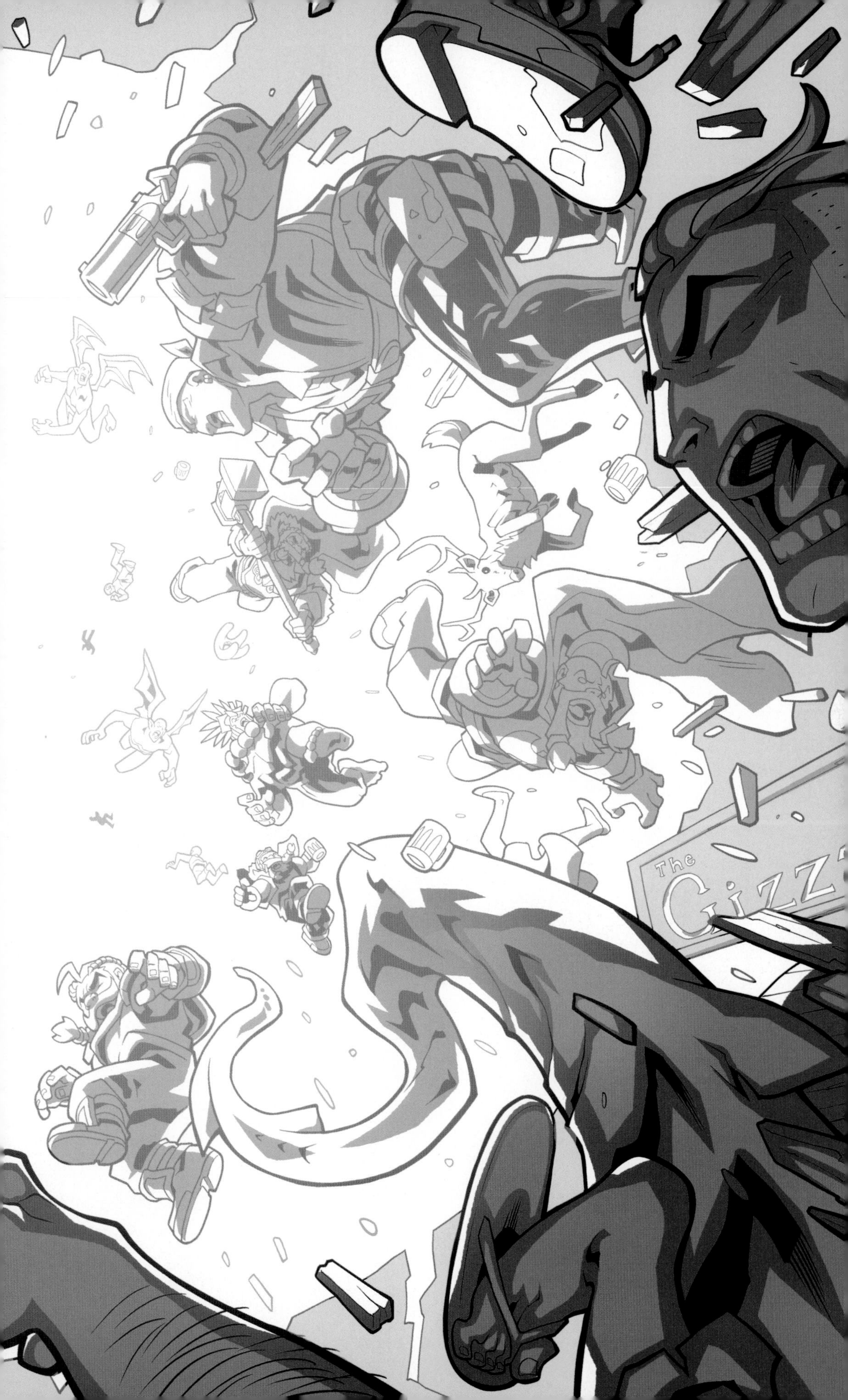
The
GIZZ

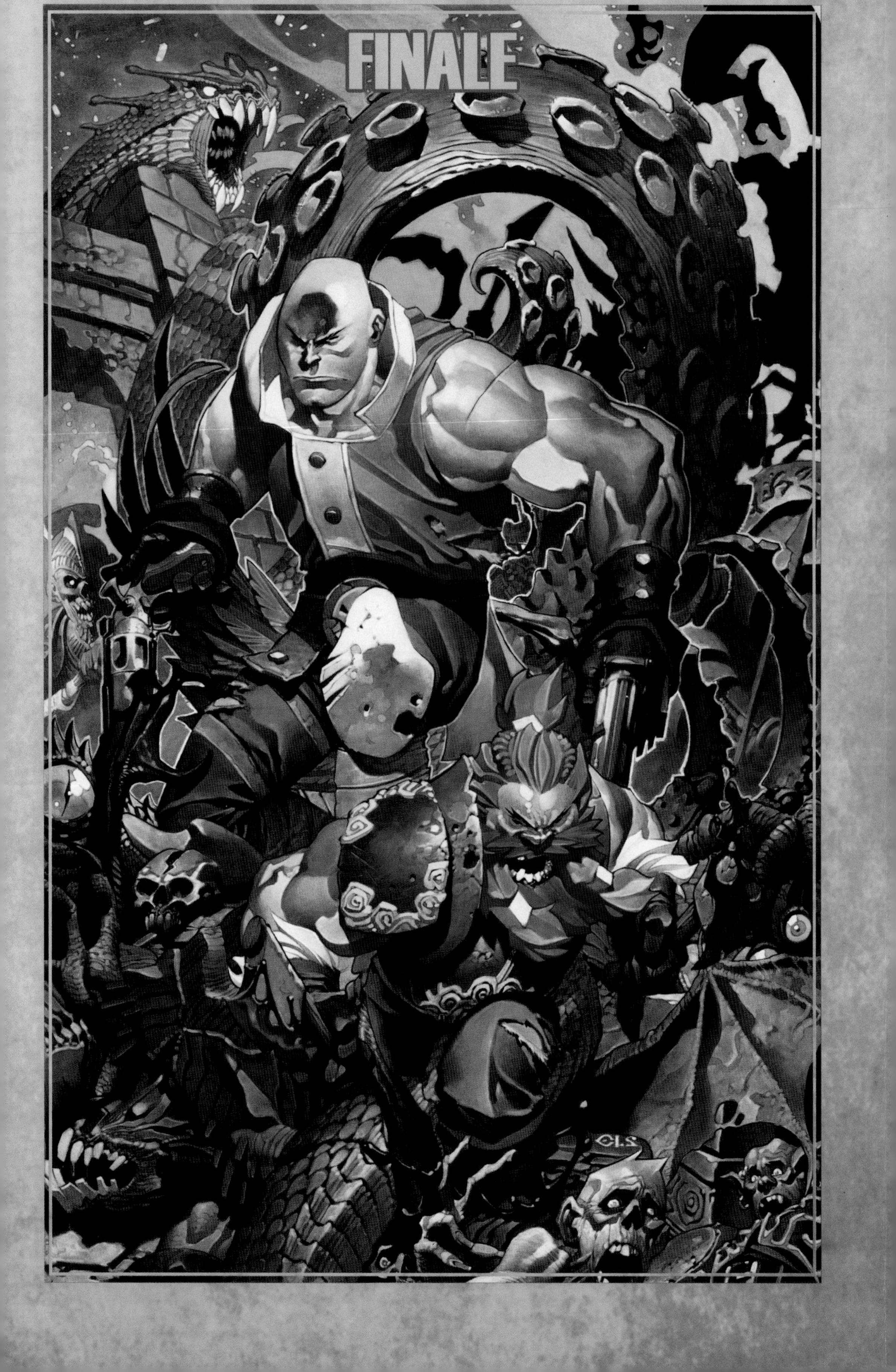
FINALE

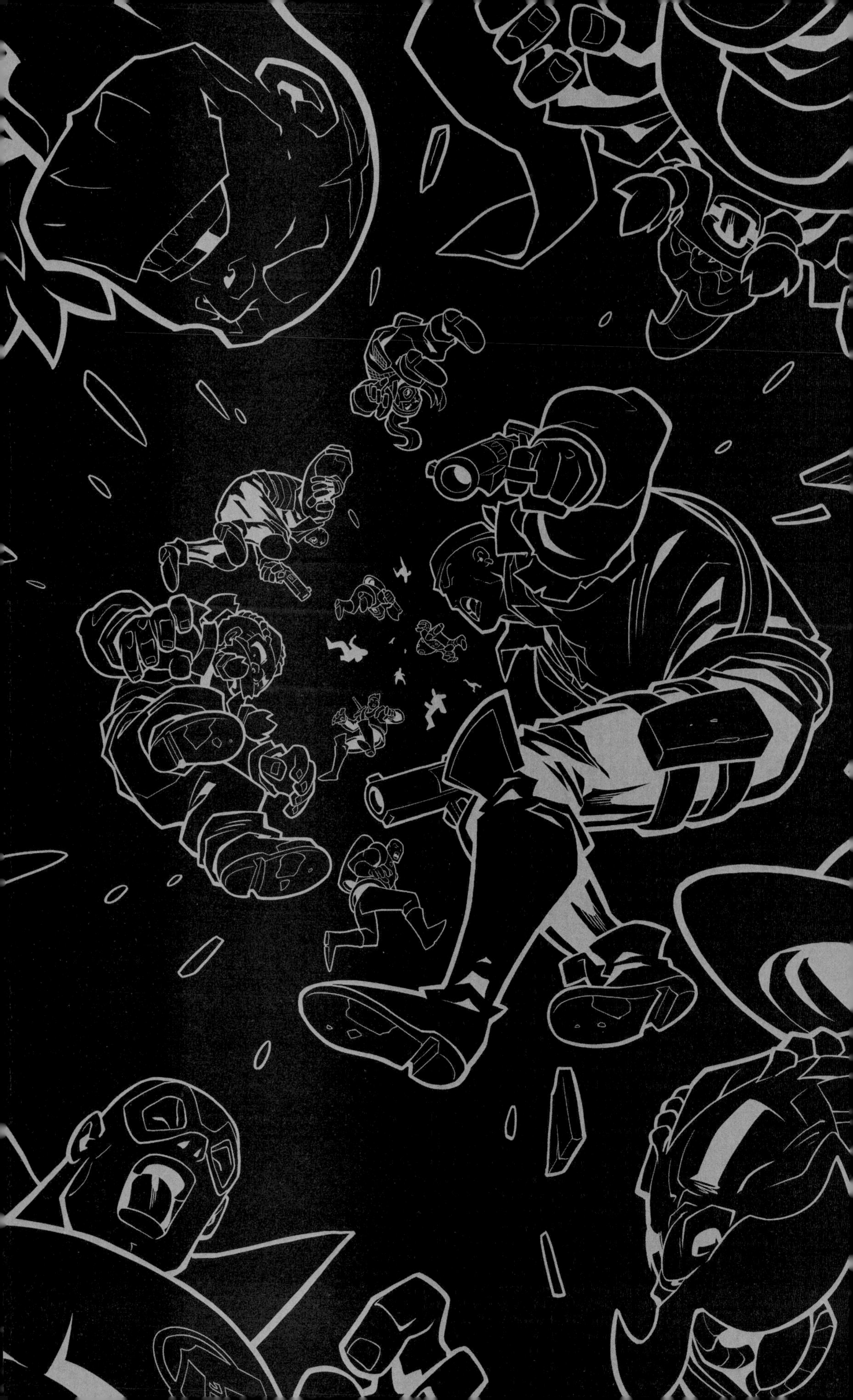

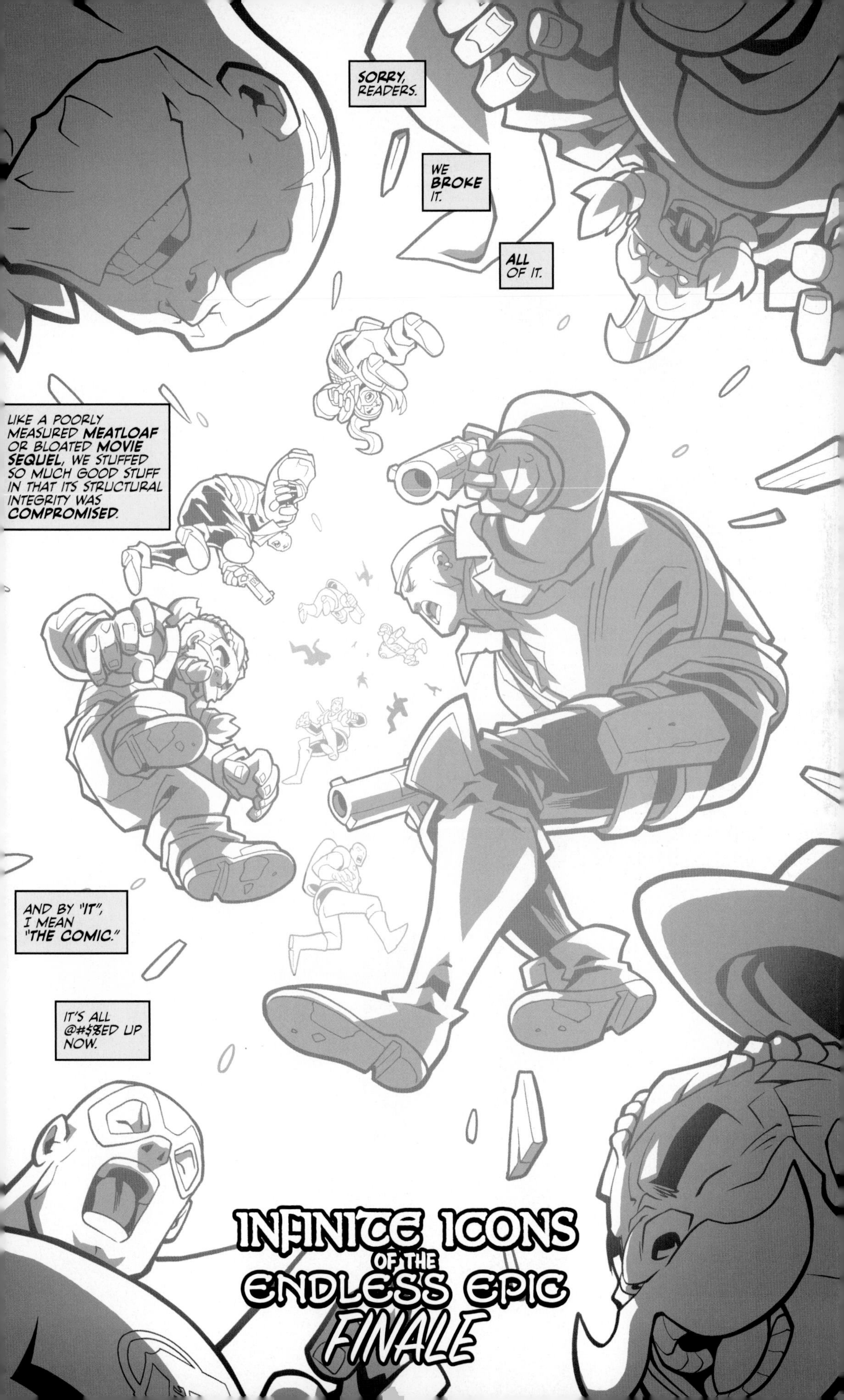
SORRY, READERS.
WE BROKE IT.
ALL OF IT.
LIKE A POORLY MEASURED MEATLOAF OR BLOATED MOVIE SEQUEL, WE STUFFED SO MUCH GOOD STUFF IN THAT ITS STRUCTURAL INTEGRITY WAS COMPROMISED.
AND BY "IT", I MEAN "THE COMIC."
IT'S ALL @#$%ED UP NOW.
INFINITE ICONS OF THE ENDLESS EPIC
FINALE

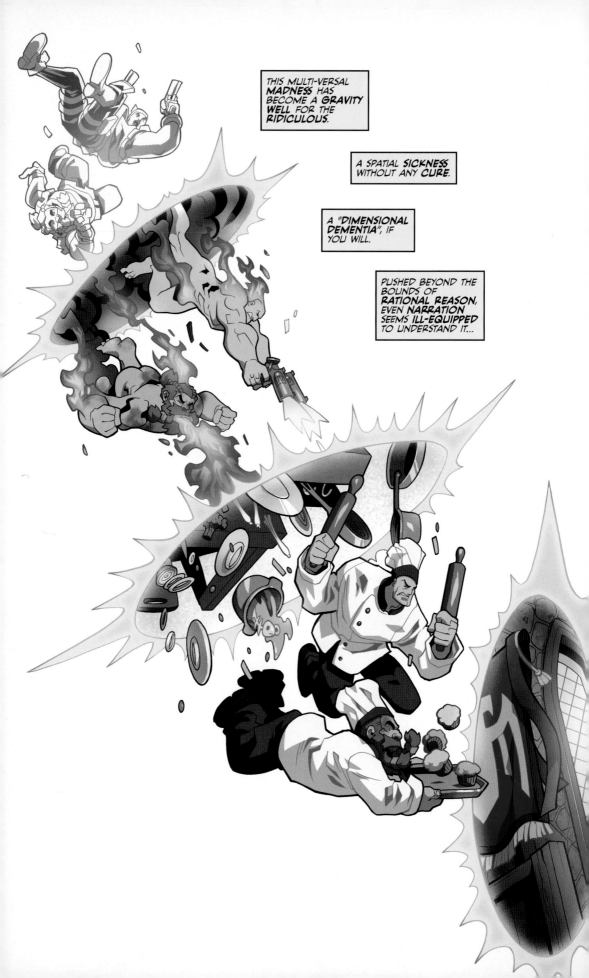

THIS MULTI-VERSAL **MADNESS** HAS BECOME A **GRAVITY WELL** FOR THE **RIDICULOUS.**

A SPATIAL **SICKNESS** WITHOUT ANY **CURE.**

A "DIMENSIONAL **DEMENTIA**", IF YOU WILL.

PUSHED BEYOND THE BOUNDS OF **RATIONAL REASON,** EVEN **NARRATION** SEEMS ILL-EQUIPPED TO UNDERSTAND IT...

EH? ...WHAT'S THAT?
DUDE, I'VE STILL GOT FOUR PAYMENTS TO MAKE ON MY NEW STOVE!
AW, COME ON!
YOU DON'T NEED ME ANYMORE?

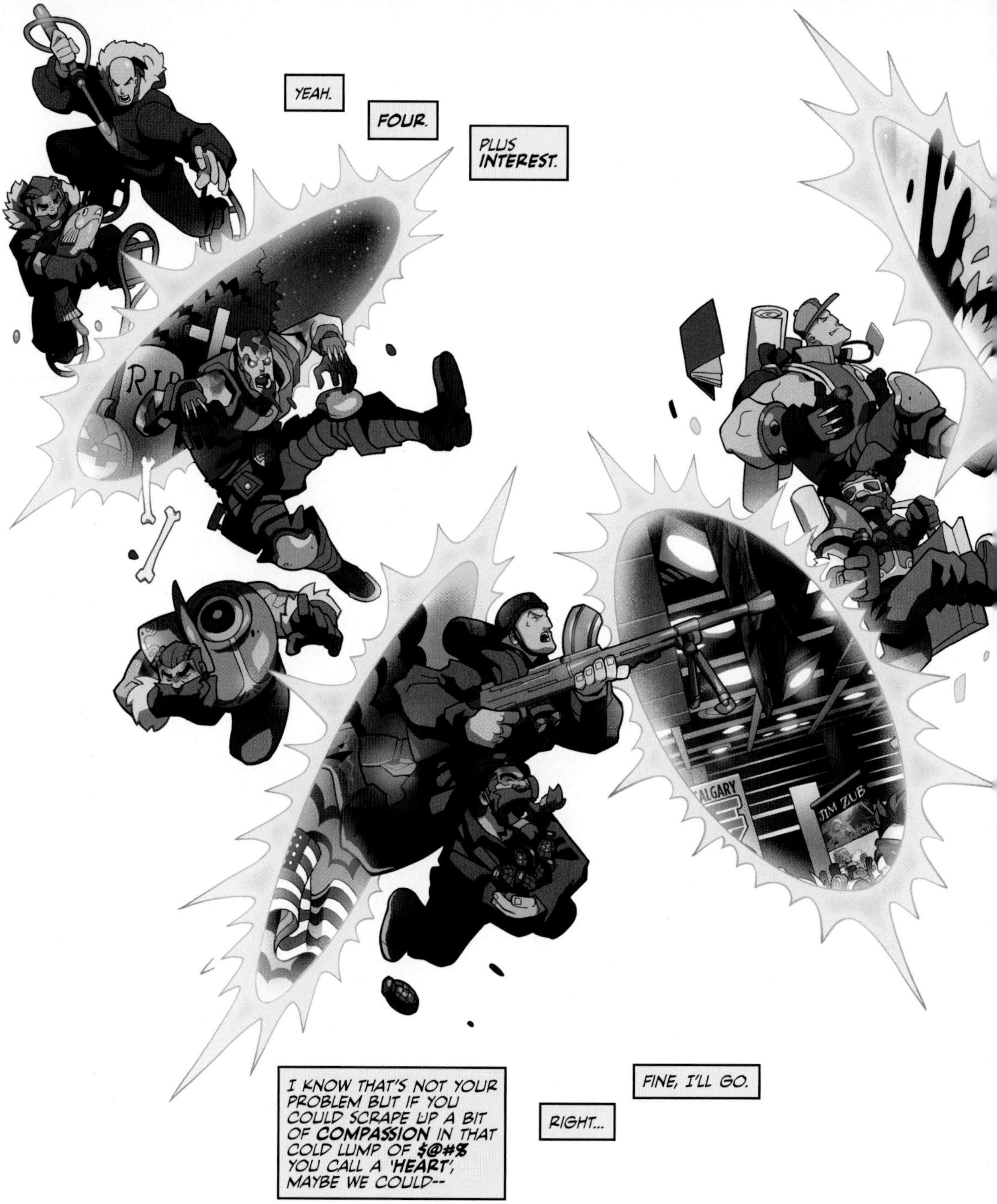
YEAH.
FOUR.
PLUS INTEREST.
JIM ZUB
I KNOW THAT'S NOT YOUR PROBLEM BUT IF YOU COULD SCRAPE UP A BIT OF COMPASSION IN THAT COLD LUMP OF $@#% YOU CALL A 'HEART', MAYBE WE COULD--
RIGHT...
FINE, I'LL GO.

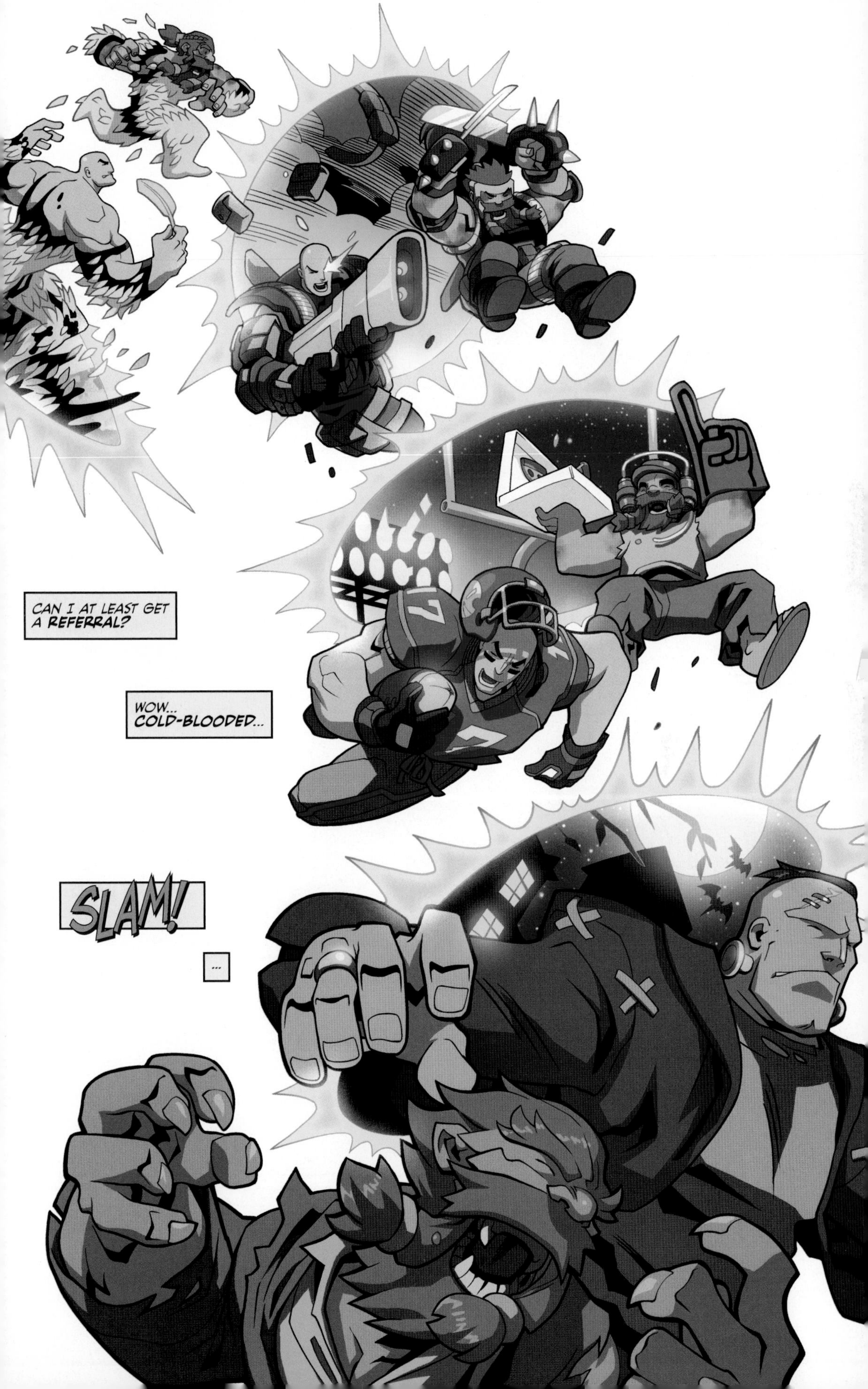
CAN I AT LEAST GET A REFERRAL?
WOW... COLD-BLOODED...
SLAM!
...

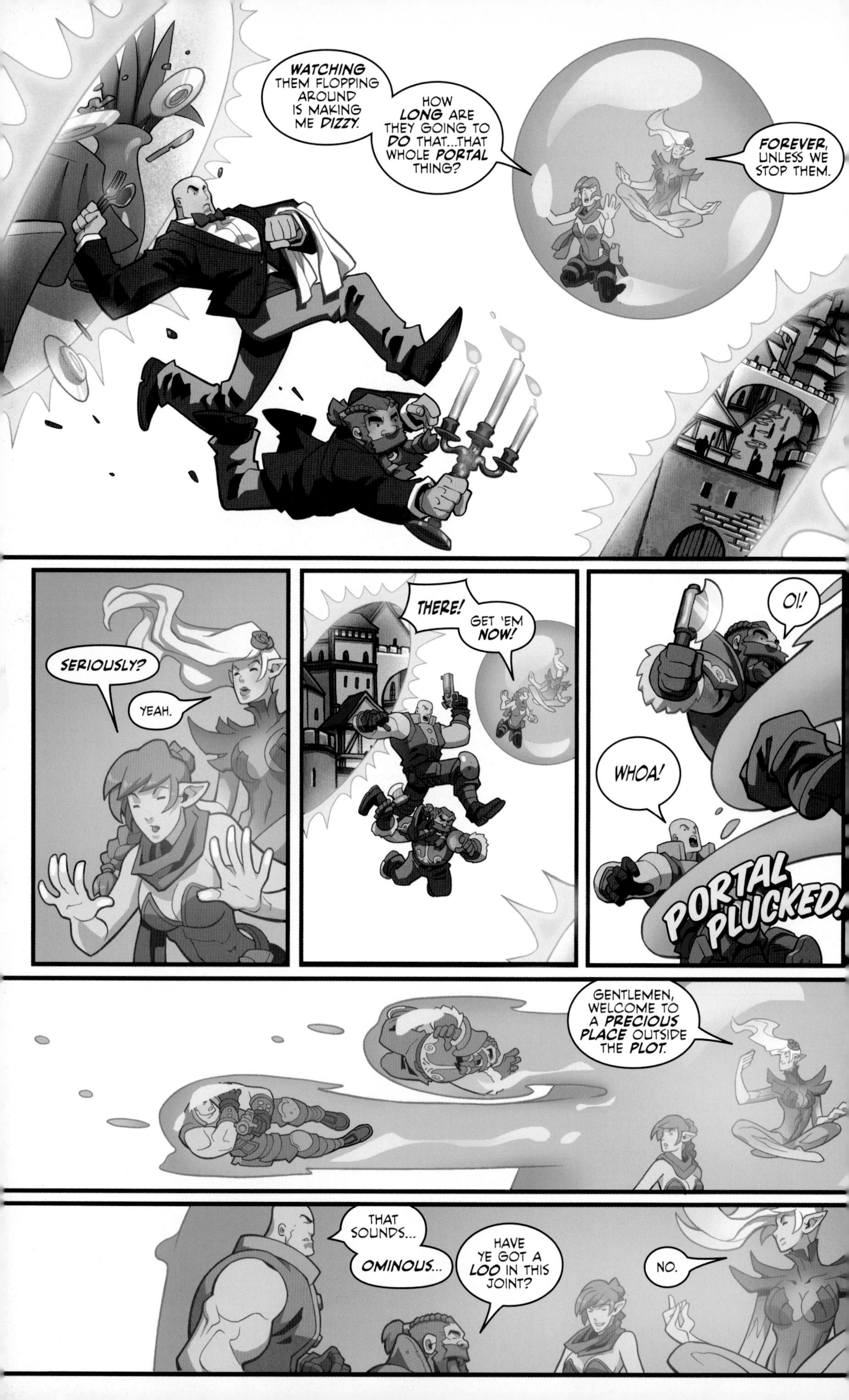
WATCHING THEM FLOPPING AROUND IS MAKING ME DIZZY.
HOW LONG ARE THEY GOING TO DO THAT...THAT WHOLE PORTAL THING?
FOREVER, UNLESS WE STOP THEM.
SERIOUSLY?
YEAH.
THERE!
GET 'EM NOW!
OI!
WHOA!
PORTAL PLUCKED!
GENTLEMEN, WELCOME TO A PRECIOUS PLACE OUTSIDE THE PLOT.
THAT SOUNDS...
OMINOUS...
HAVE YE GOT A LOO IN THIS JOINT?
NO.

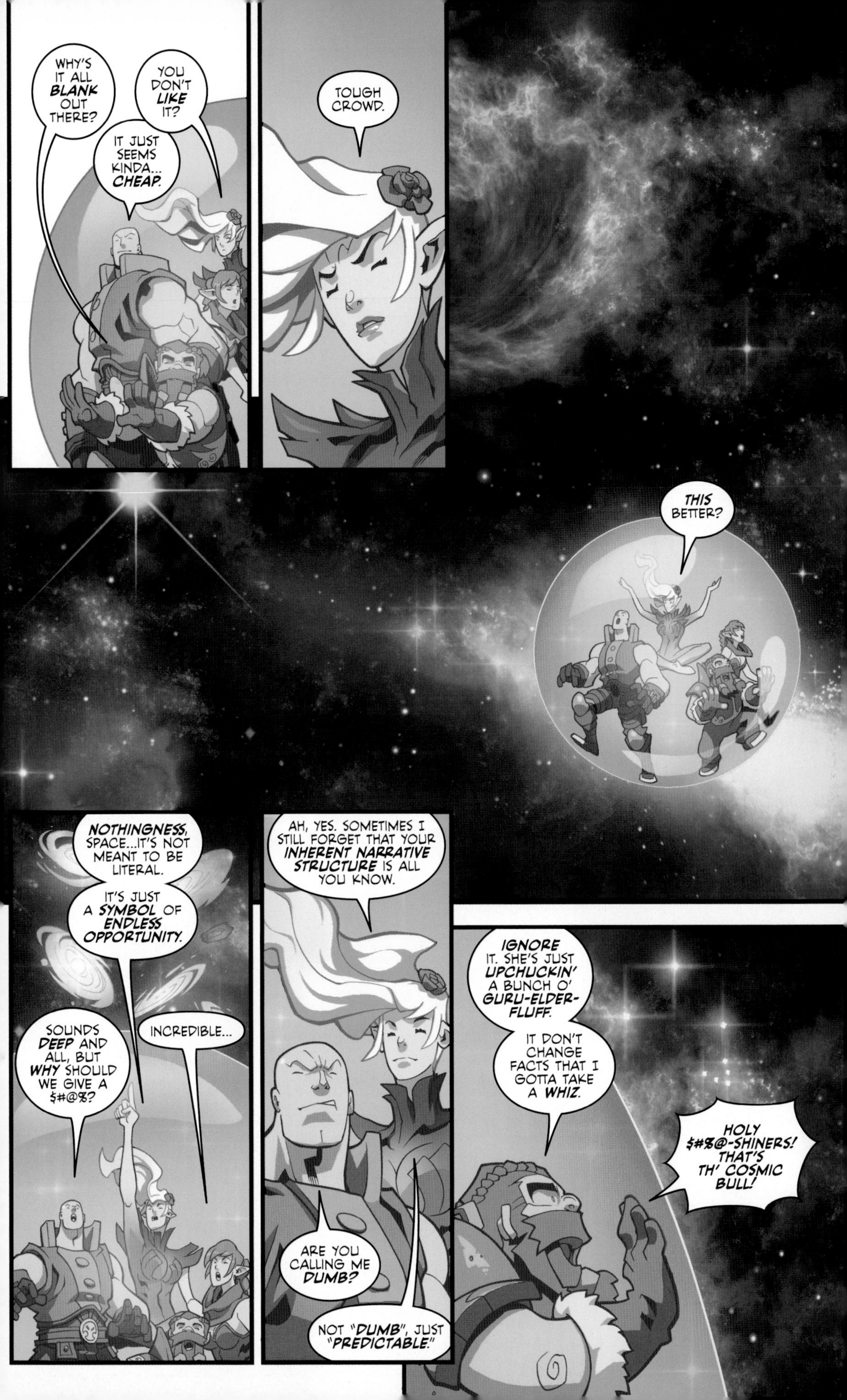

WHY'S IT ALL BLANK OUT THERE?
YOU DON'T LIKE IT?
IT JUST SEEMS KINDA... CHEAP.
TOUGH CROWD.
THIS BETTER?
NOTHINGNESS, SPACE...IT'S NOT MEANT TO BE LITERAL.
IT'S JUST A SYMBOL OF ENDLESS OPPORTUNITY.
SOUNDS DEEP AND ALL, BUT WHY SHOULD WE GIVE A $#@%?
INCREDIBLE...
AH, YES. SOMETIMES I STILL FORGET THAT YOUR INHERENT NARRATIVE STRUCTURE IS ALL YOU KNOW.
ARE YOU CALLING ME DUMB?
NOT "DUMB", JUST "PREDICTABLE."
IGNORE IT. SHE'S JUST UPCHUCKIN' A BUNCH O' GURU-ELDER-FLUFF.
IT DON'T CHANGE FACTS THAT I GOTTA TAKE A WHIZ.
HOLY $#%@-SHINERS! THAT'S TH' COSMIC BULL!

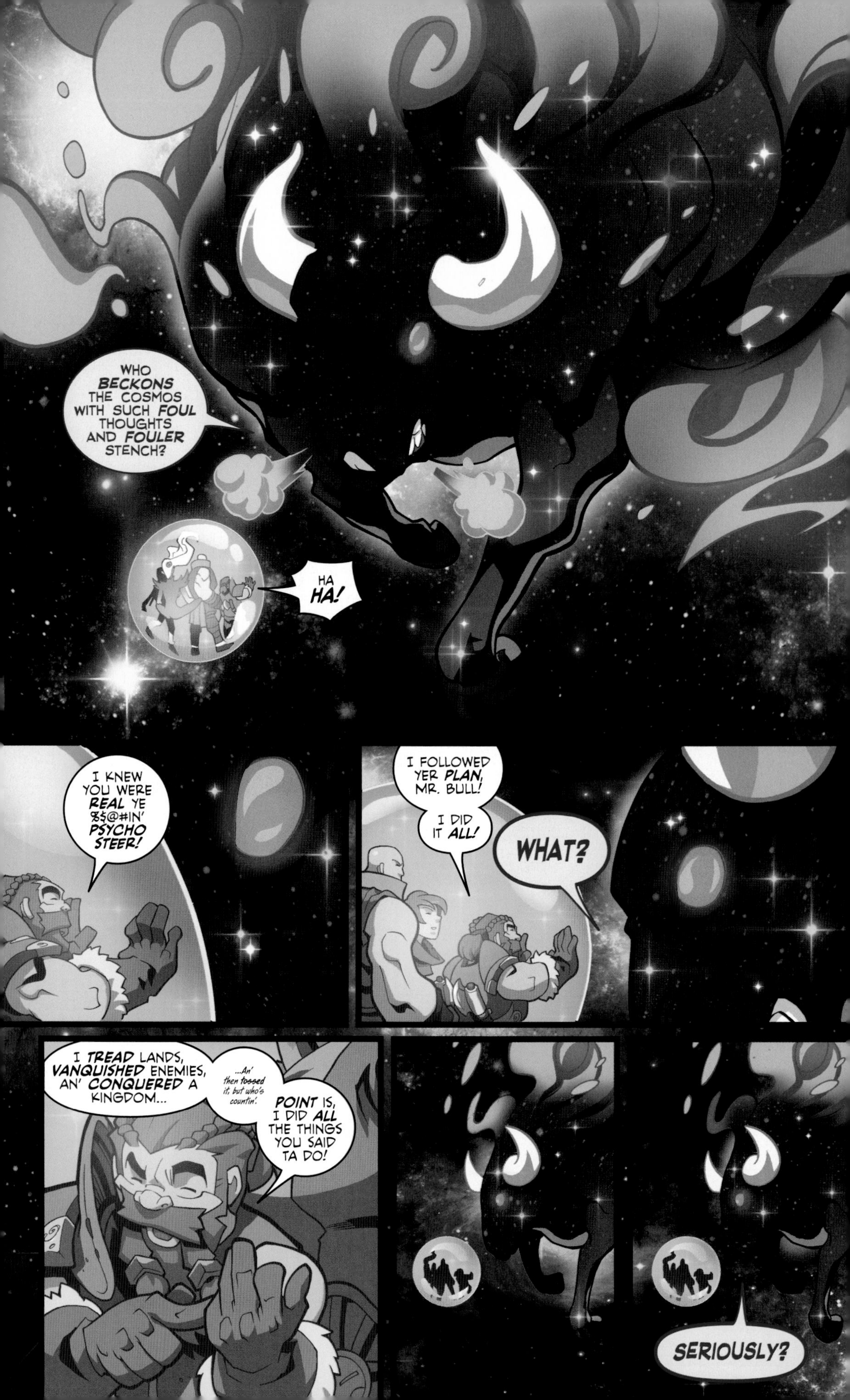
WHO BECKONS THE COSMOS WITH SUCH FOUL THOUGHTS AND FOULER STENCH?
HA HA!
I KNEW YOU WERE REAL YE %$@#IN' PSYCHO STEER!
I FOLLOWED YER PLAN, MR. BULL!
I DID IT ALL!
WHAT?
I TREAD LANDS, VANQUISHED ENEMIES, AN' CONQUERED A KINGDOM...
...An' then tossed it, but who's countin'.
POINT IS, I DID ALL THE THINGS YOU SAID TA DO!
SERIOUSLY?

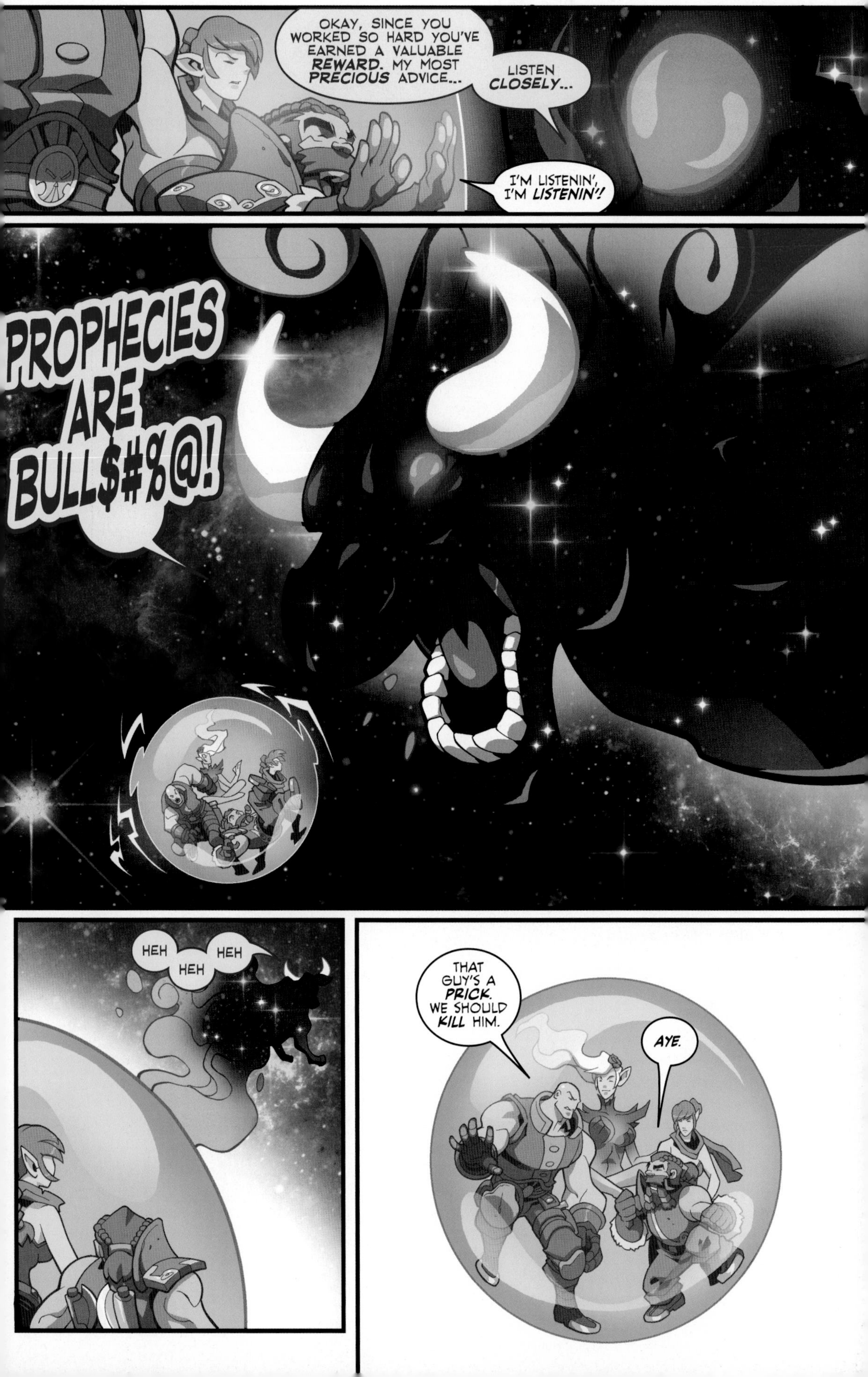

OKAY, SINCE YOU WORKED SO HARD YOU'VE EARNED A VALUABLE REWARD. MY MOST PRECIOUS ADVICE...
LISTEN CLOSELY...
I'M LISTENIN', I'M LISTENIN'!
PROPHECIES ARE BULL$#%@!
HEH
HEH
HEH
THAT GUY'S A PRICK. WE SHOULD KILL HIM.
AYE.

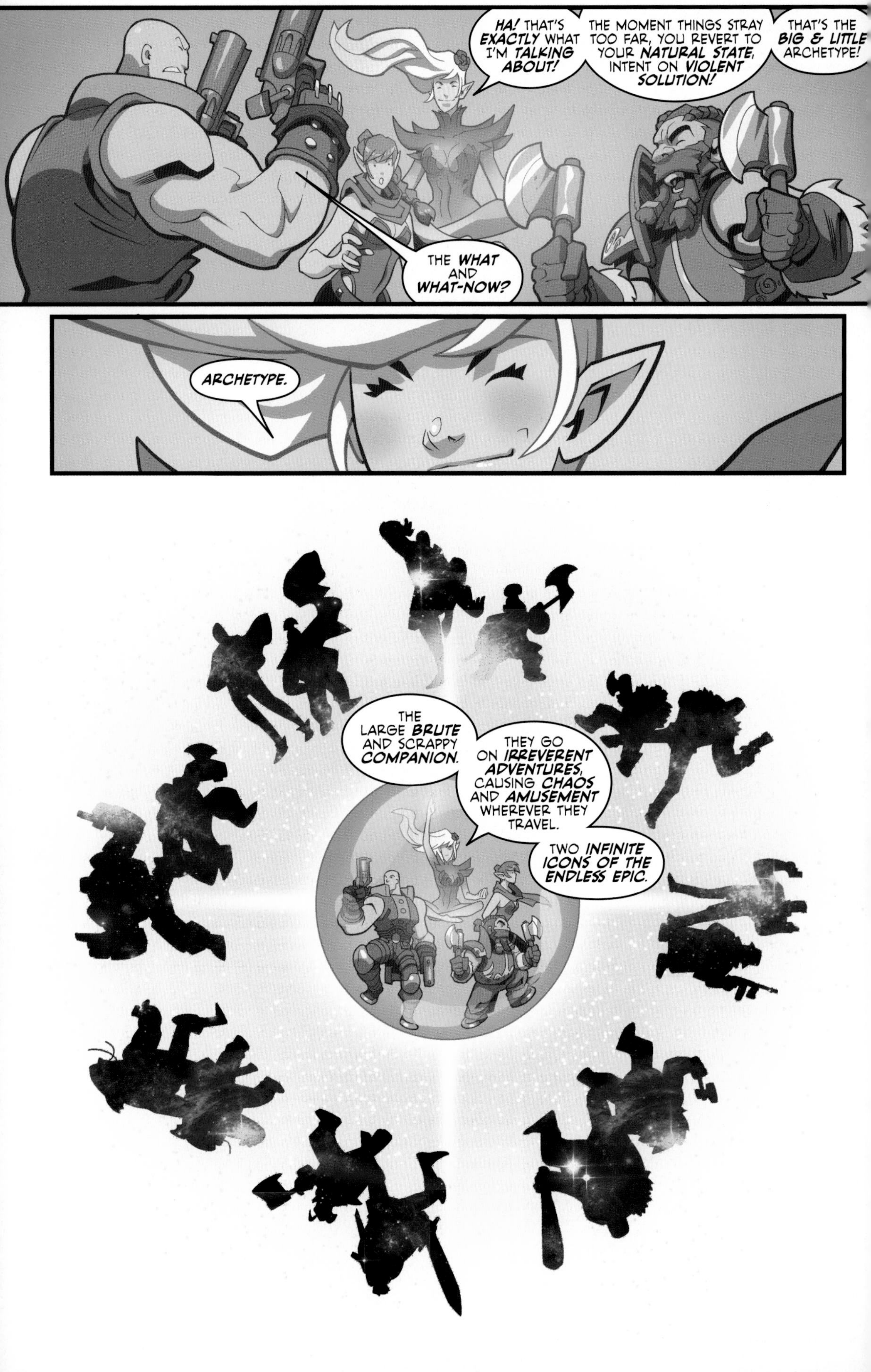
HA! THAT'S EXACTLY WHAT I'M TALKING ABOUT!
THE MOMENT THINGS STRAY TOO FAR, YOU REVERT TO YOUR NATURAL STATE, INTENT ON VIOLENT SOLUTION!
THAT'S THE BIG & LITTLE ARCHETYPE!
THE WHAT AND WHAT-NOW?
ARCHETYPE.
THE LARGE BRUTE AND SCRAPPY COMPANION.
THEY GO ON IRREVERENT ADVENTURES, CAUSING CHAOS AND AMUSEMENT WHEREVER THEY TRAVEL.
TWO INFINITE ICONS OF THE ENDLESS EPIC.

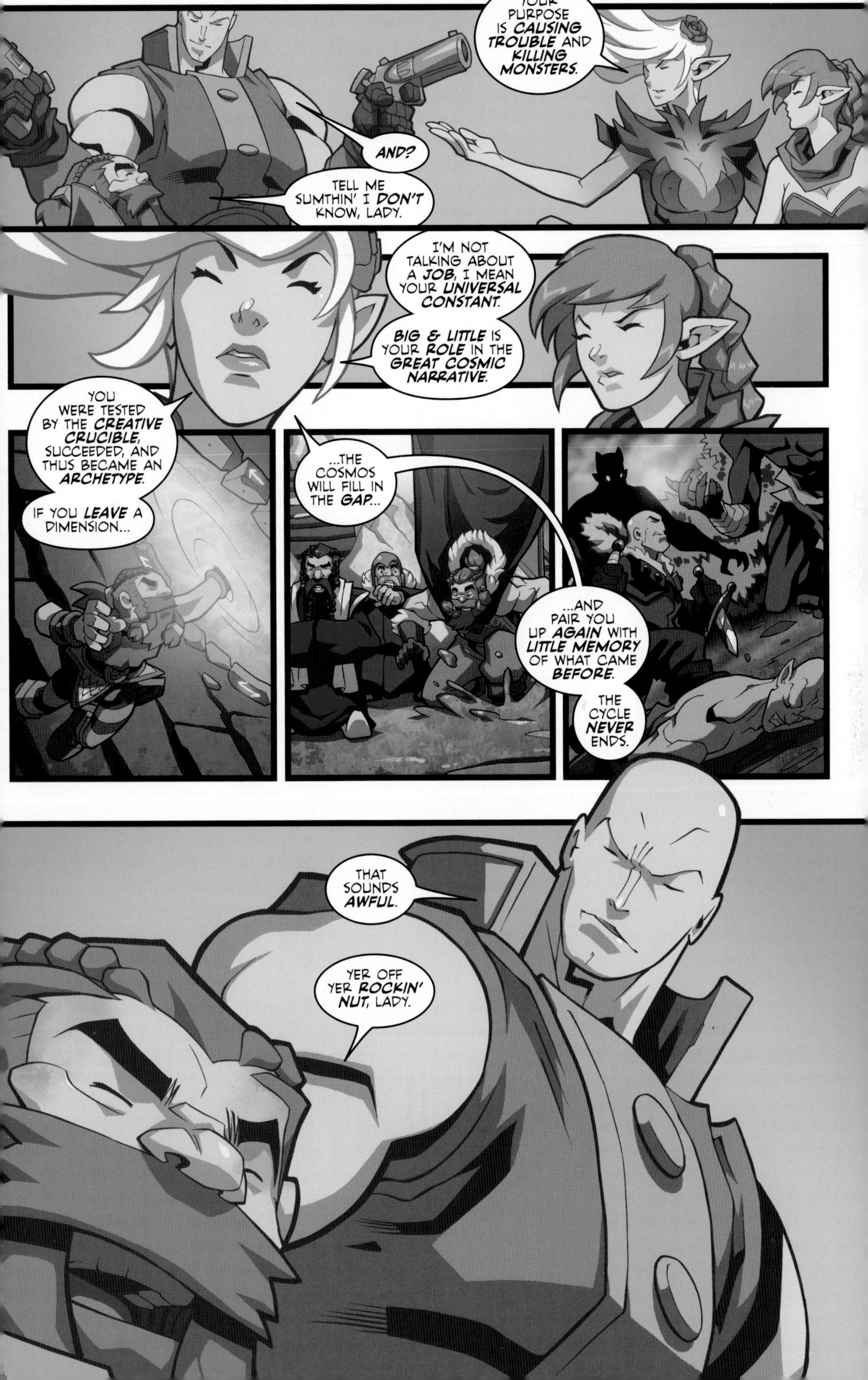
YOUR PURPOSE IS CAUSING TROUBLE AND KILLING MONSTERS.
AND?
TELL ME SUMTHIN' I DON'T KNOW, LADY.
I'M NOT TALKING ABOUT A JOB, I MEAN YOUR UNIVERSAL CONSTANT.
BIG & LITTLE IS YOUR ROLE IN THE GREAT COSMIC NARRATIVE.
YOU WERE TESTED BY THE CREATIVE CRUCIBLE, SUCCEEDED, AND THUS BECAME AN ARCHETYPE.
IF YOU LEAVE A DIMENSION...
...THE COSMOS WILL FILL IN THE GAP...
...AND PAIR YOU UP AGAIN WITH LITTLE MEMORY OF WHAT CAME BEFORE.
THE CYCLE NEVER ENDS.
THAT SOUNDS AWFUL.
YER OFF YER ROCKIN' NUT, LADY.

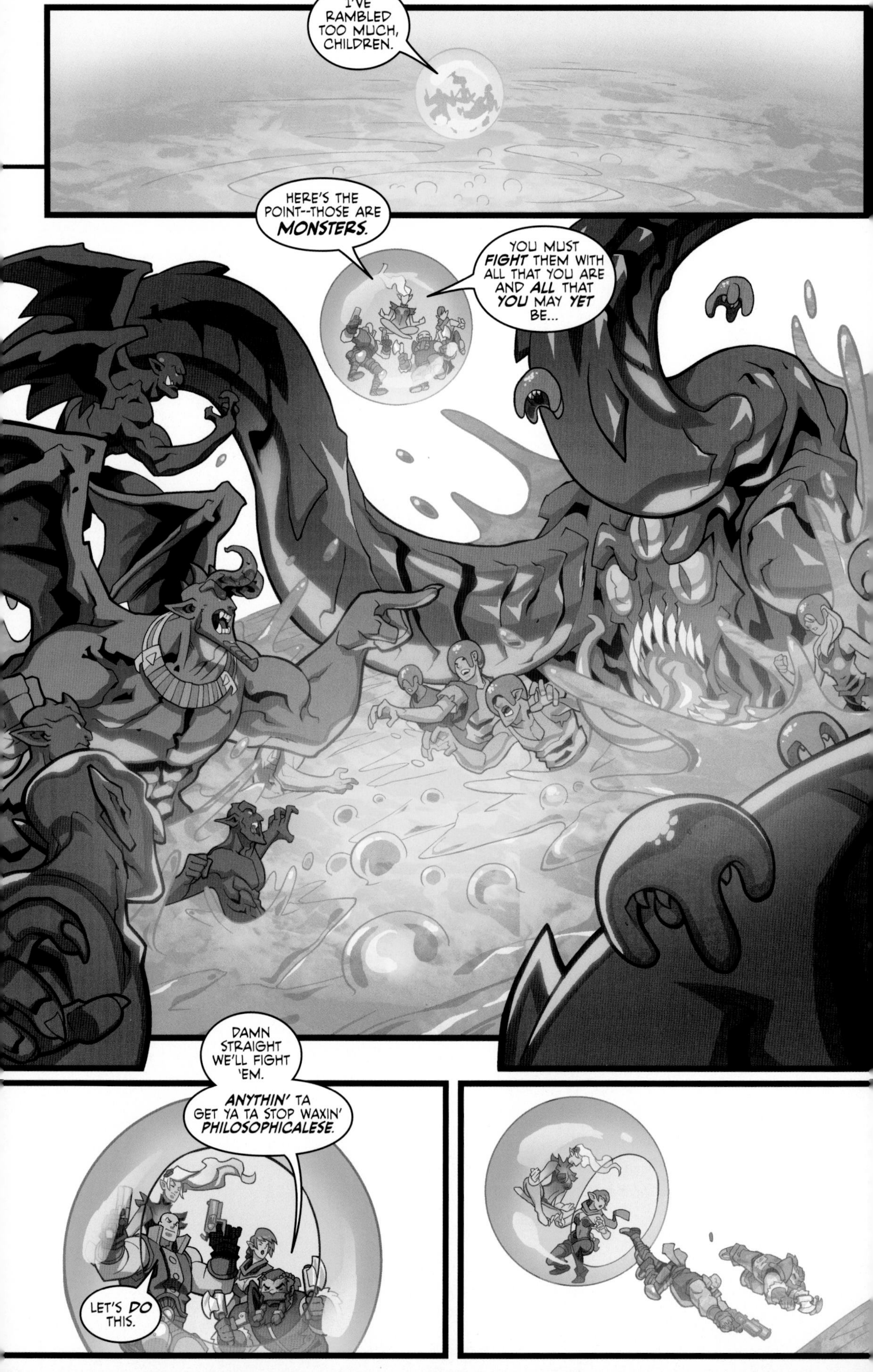
I'VE RAMBLED TOO MUCH, CHILDREN.
HERE'S THE POINT--THOSE ARE *MONSTERS*.
YOU MUST *FIGHT* THEM WITH ALL THAT YOU ARE AND *ALL* THAT *YOU* MAY *YET* BE...
DAMN STRAIGHT WE'LL FIGHT 'EM.
ANYTHIN' TA GET YA TA STOP WAXIN' *PHILOSOPHICALESE*.
LET'S *DO* THIS.

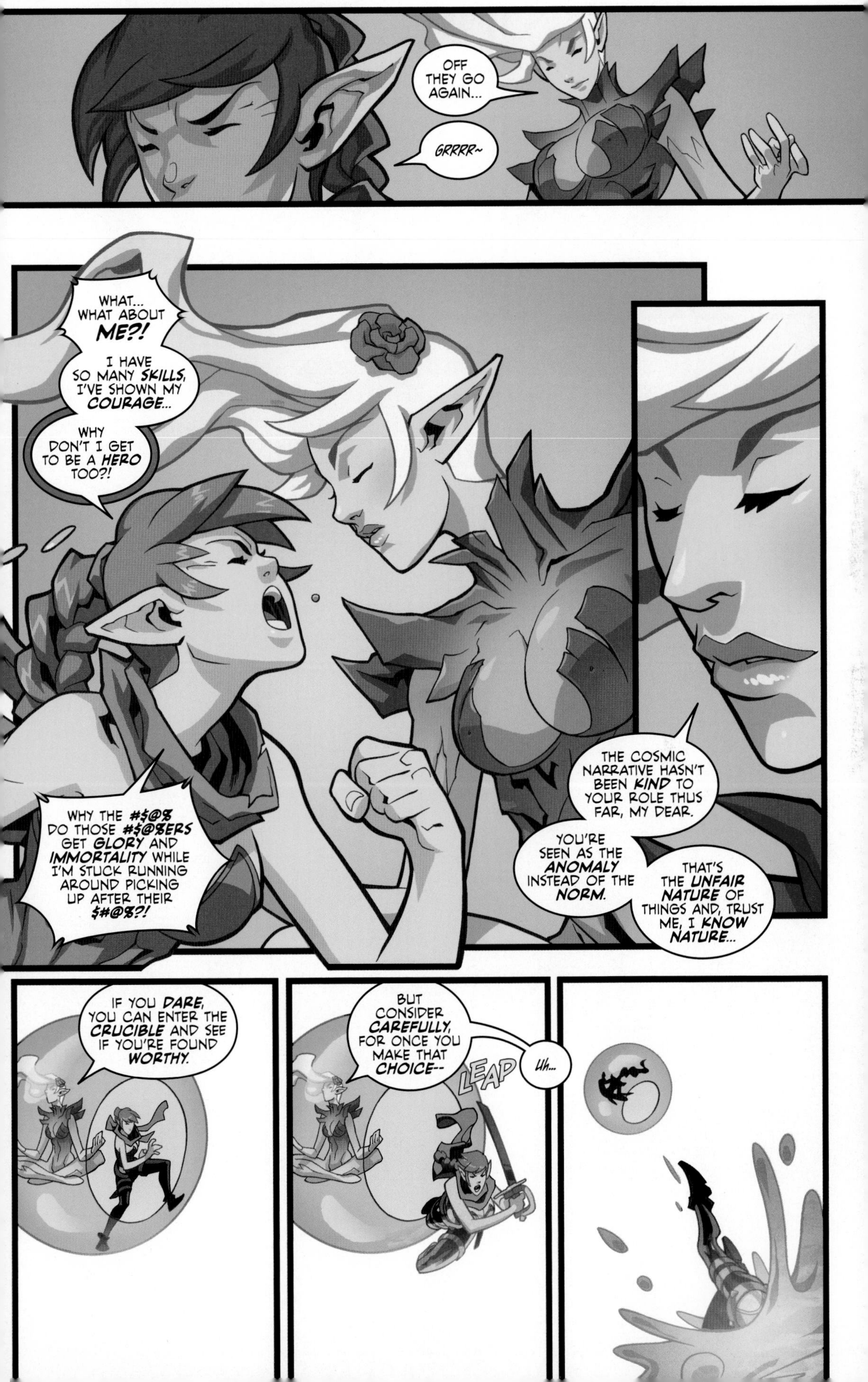

OFF THEY GO AGAIN...
GRRRR~
WHAT... WHAT ABOUT ME?!
I HAVE SO MANY SKILLS, I'VE SHOWN MY COURAGE...
WHY DON'T I GET TO BE A HERO TOO?!
WHY THE #$@% DO THOSE #$@%ERS GET GLORY AND IMMORTALITY WHILE I'M STUCK RUNNING AROUND PICKING UP AFTER THEIR $#@%?!
THE COSMIC NARRATIVE HASN'T BEEN KIND TO YOUR ROLE THUS FAR, MY DEAR.
YOU'RE SEEN AS THE ANOMALY INSTEAD OF THE NORM.
THAT'S THE UNFAIR NATURE OF THINGS AND, TRUST ME, I KNOW NATURE...
IF YOU DARE, YOU CAN ENTER THE CRUCIBLE AND SEE IF YOU'RE FOUND WORTHY.
BUT CONSIDER CAREFULLY, FOR ONCE YOU MAKE THAT CHOICE--
LEAP
Uh...

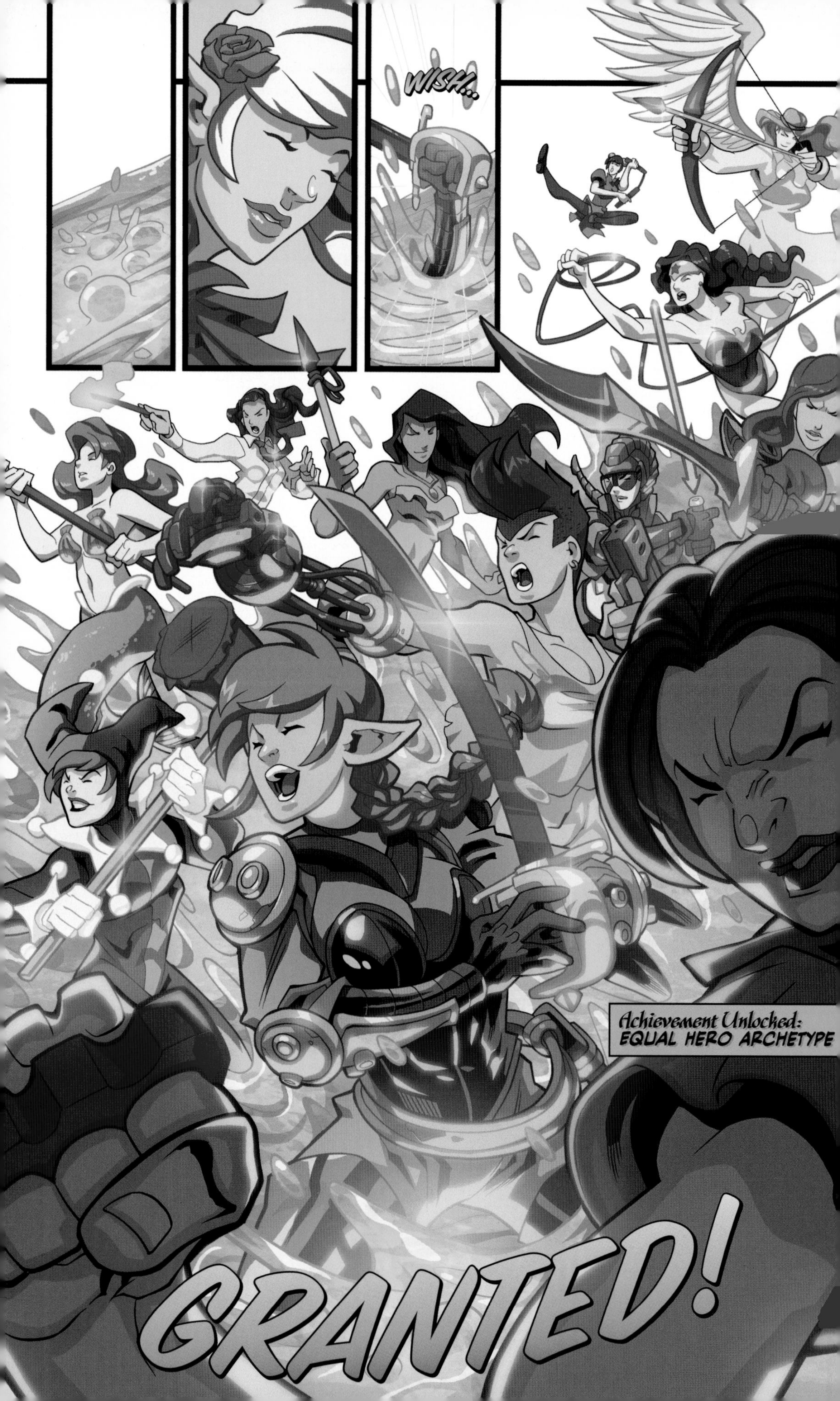
WISH...
Achievement Unlocked:
EQUAL HERO ARCHETYPE
GRANTED!

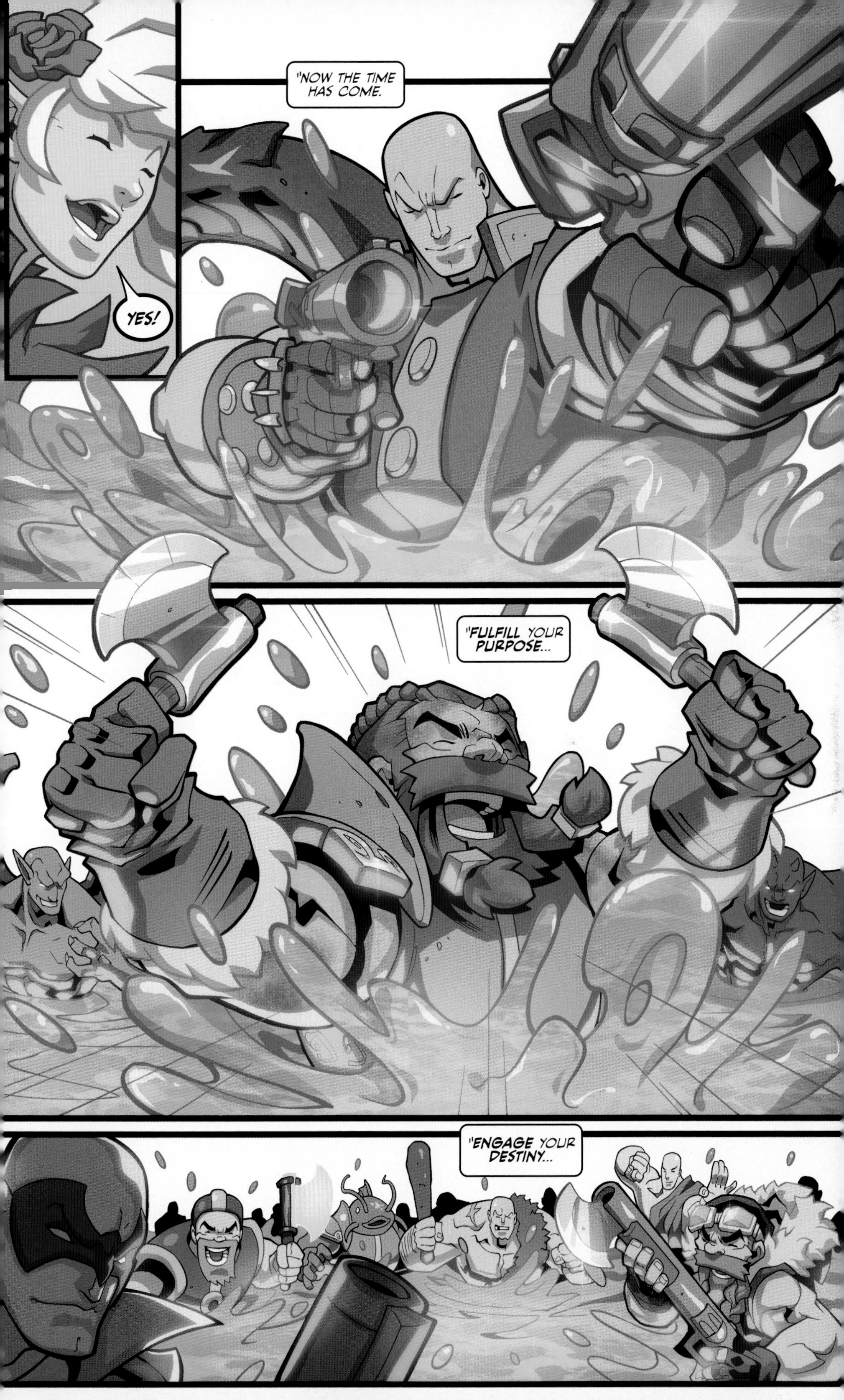

"NOW THE TIME HAS COME.
YES!
"FULFILL YOUR PURPOSE...
"ENGAGE YOUR DESTINY...

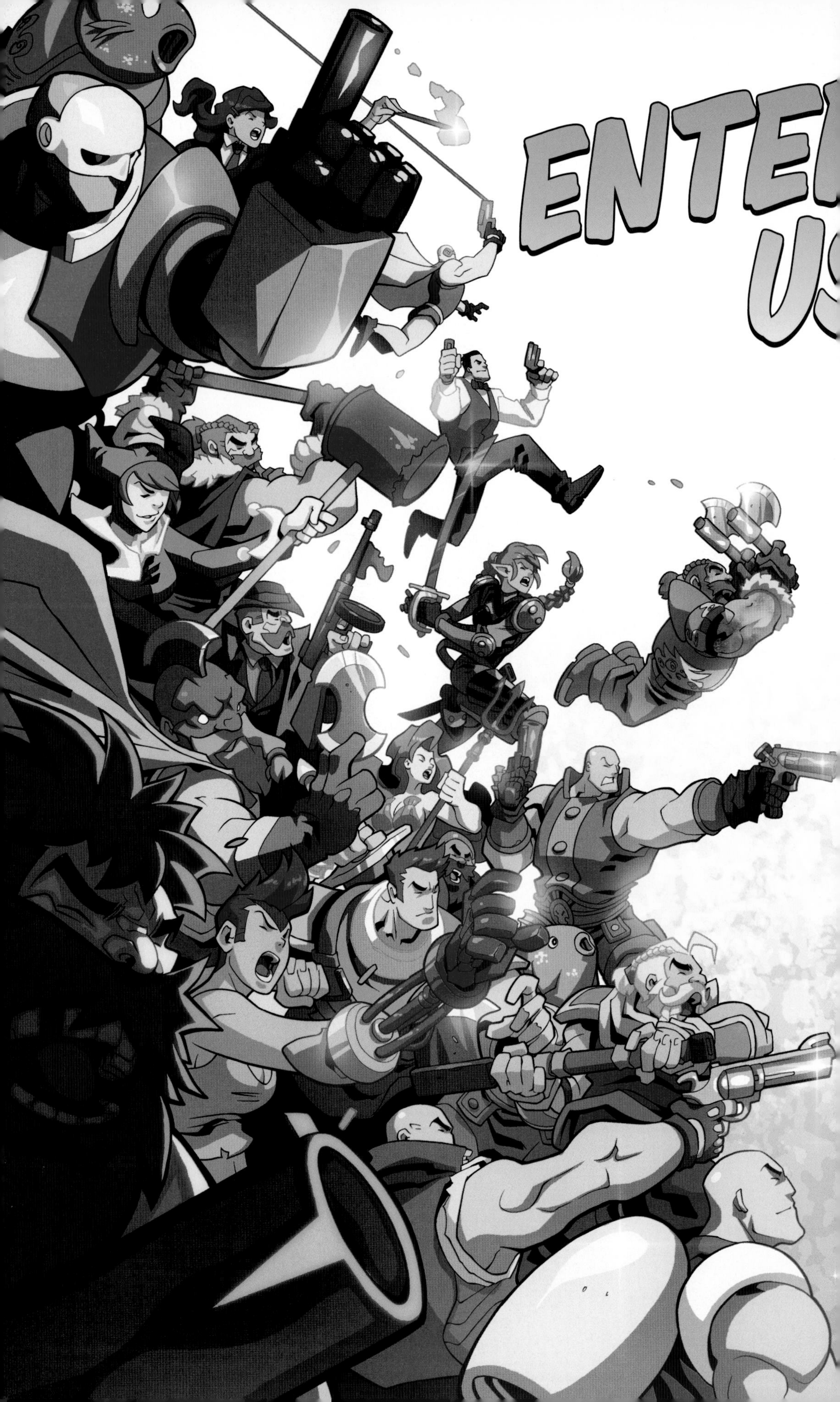
ENTE
US

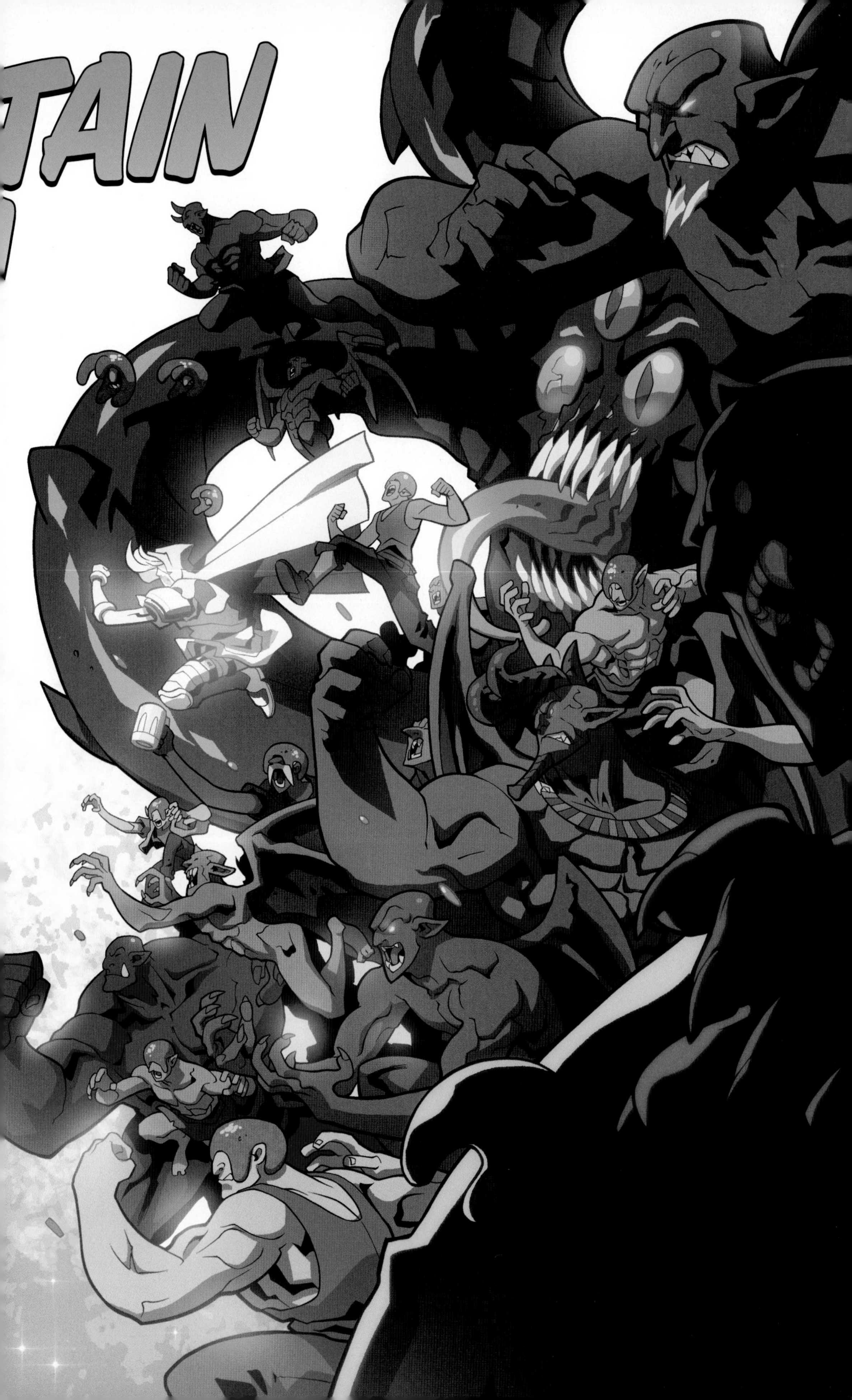
TAIN

SLASH

CHOP

STAB

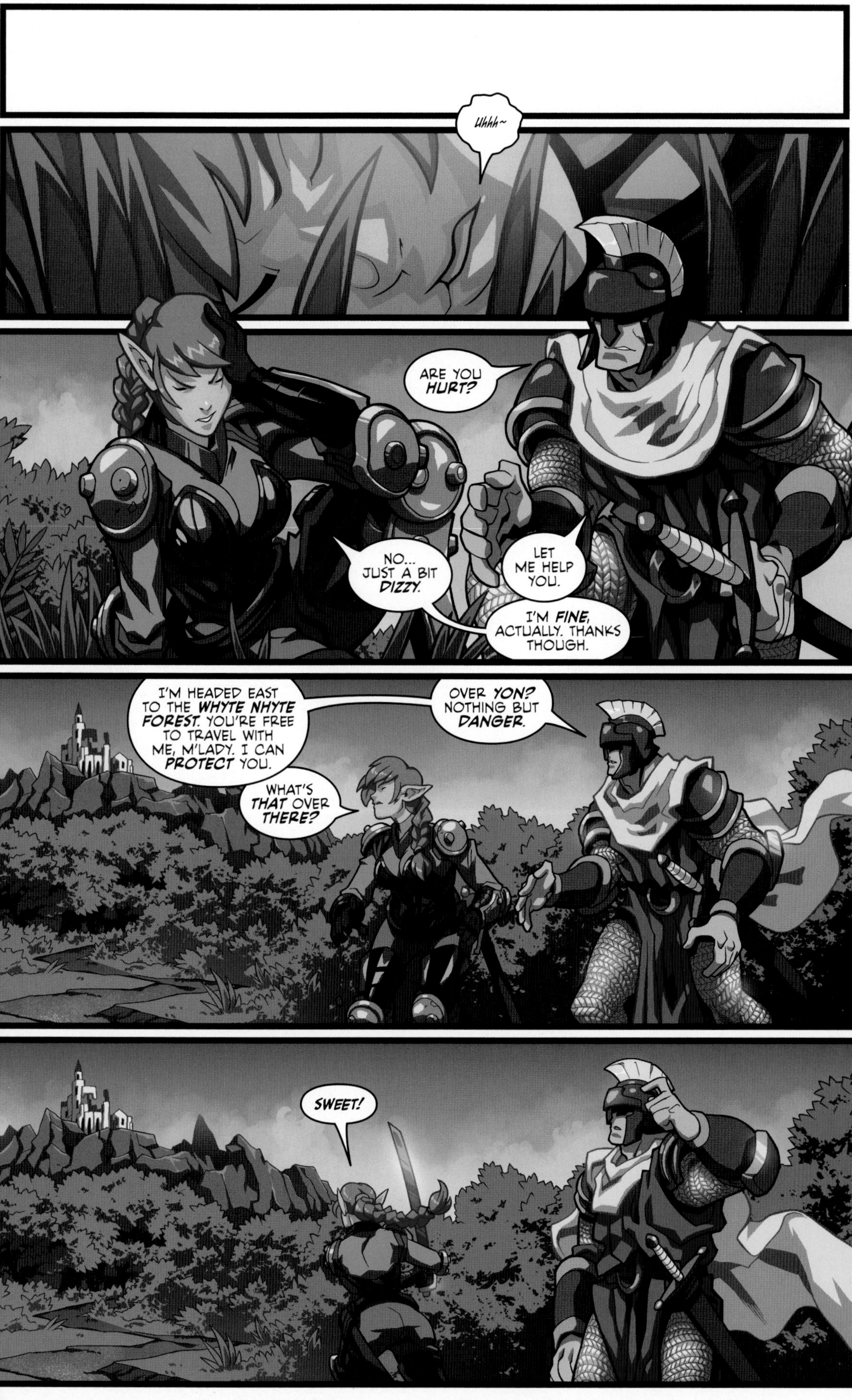
Uhhh~
ARE YOU HURT?
NO... JUST A BIT DIZZY.
LET ME HELP YOU.
I'M FINE, ACTUALLY. THANKS THOUGH.
I'M HEADED EAST TO THE WHYTE NHYTE FOREST. YOU'RE FREE TO TRAVEL WITH ME, M'LADY. I CAN PROTECT YOU.
WHAT'S THAT OVER THERE?
OVER YON? NOTHING BUT DANGER.
SWEET!

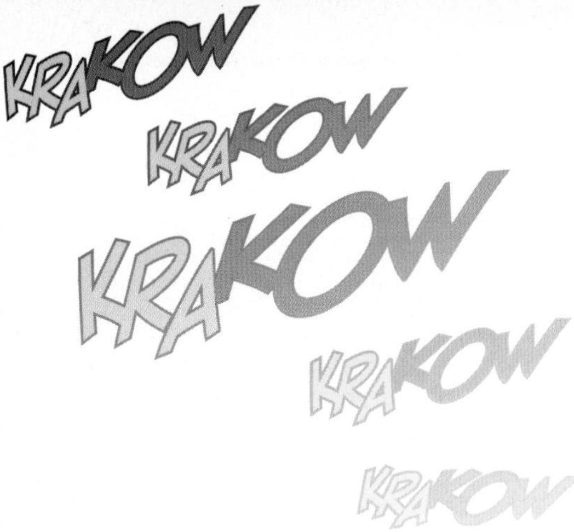
KRAKOW
KRAKOW
KRAKOW
KRAKOW
KRAKOW

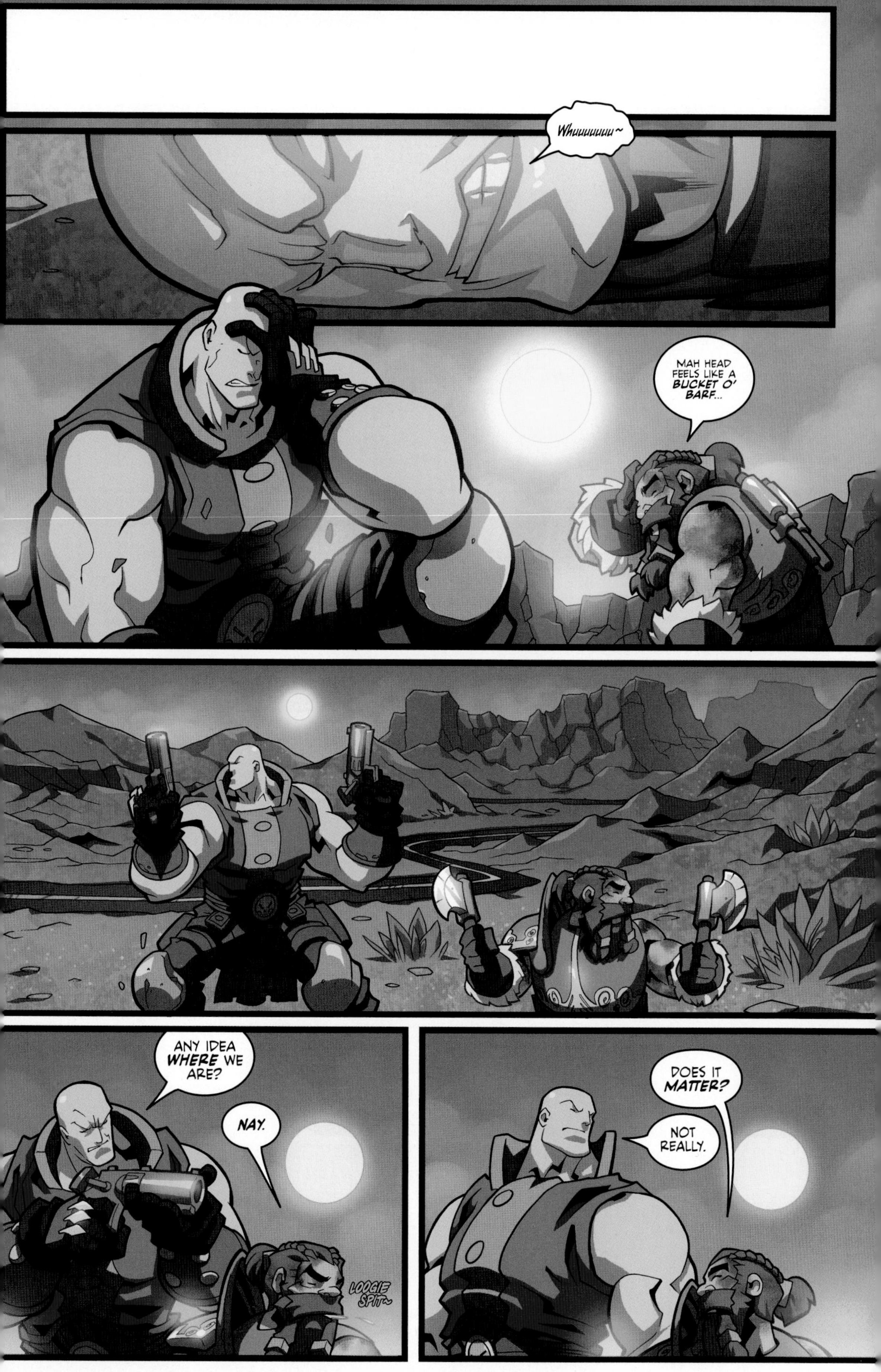
Whuuuuuuu~
MAH HEAD FEELS LIKE A BUCKET O' BARF...
ANY IDEA WHERE WE ARE?
NAY.
LOOGIE SPIT~
DOES IT MATTER?
NOT REALLY.

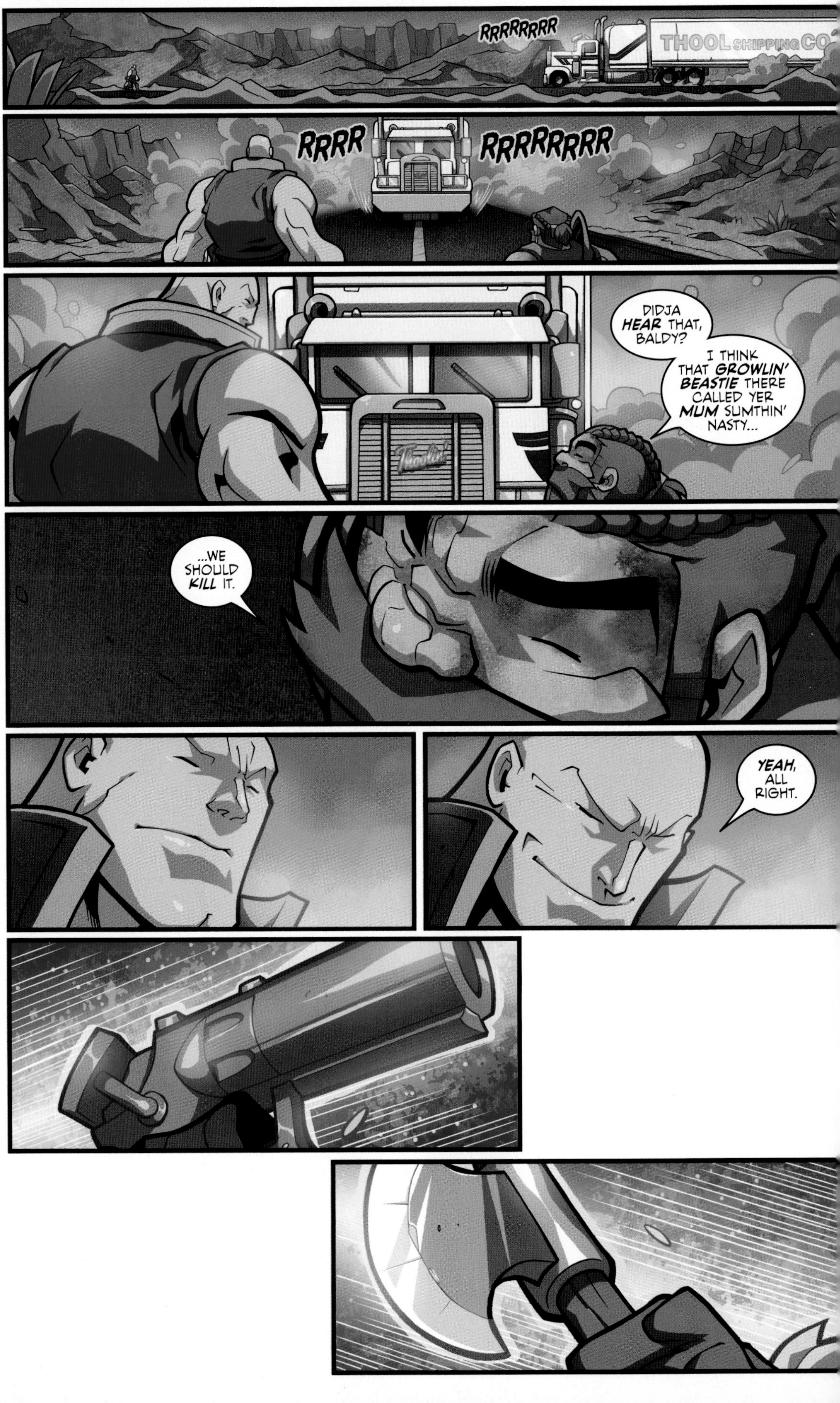
RRRRRRRR
THOOL SHIPPING CO
RRRR
RRRRRRRR
DIDJA HEAR THAT, BALDY?
I THINK THAT GROWLIN' BEASTIE THERE CALLED YER MUM SUMTHIN' NASTY...
...WE SHOULD KILL IT.
YEAH, ALL RIGHT.

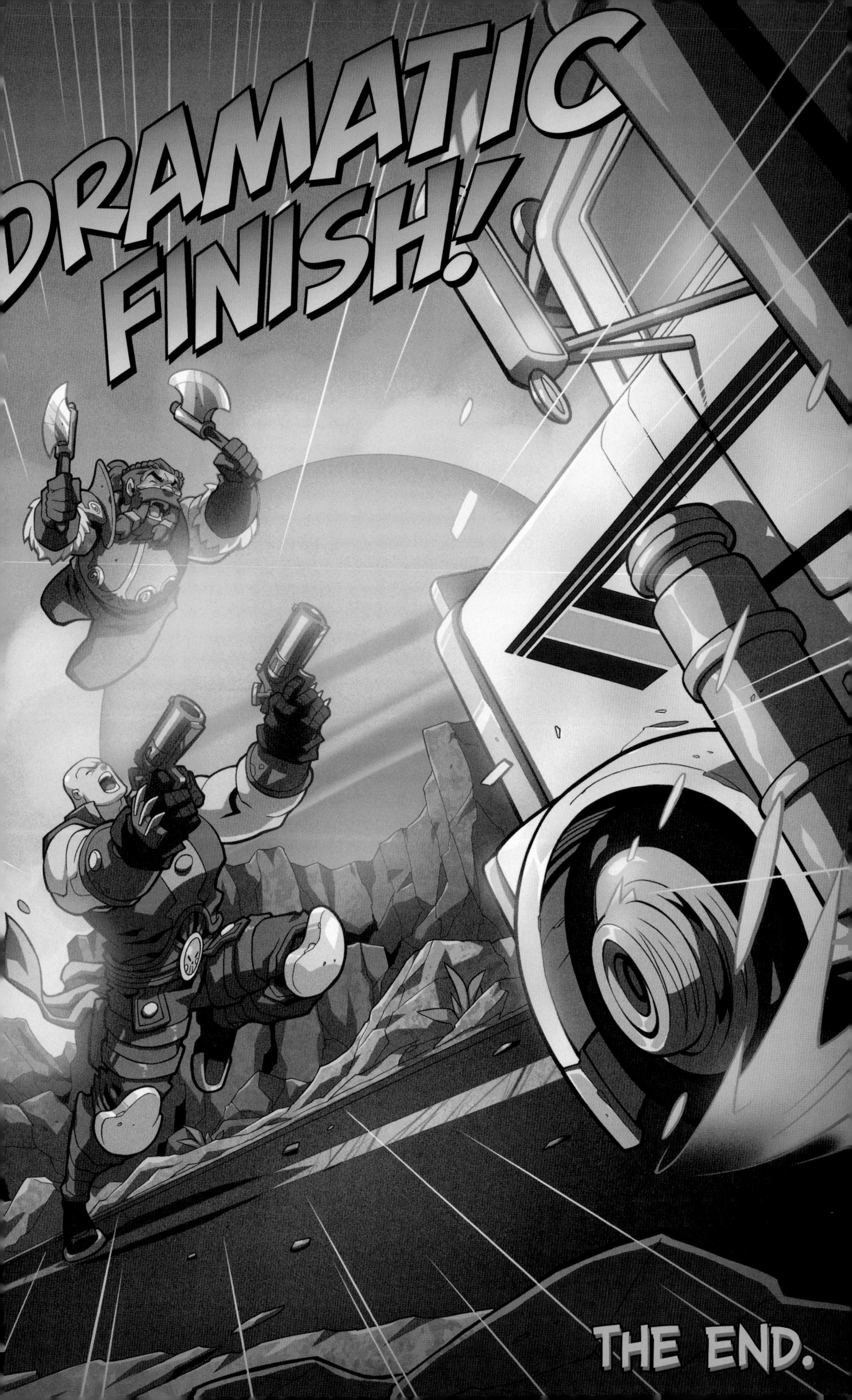
DRAMATIC FINISH!
THE END.

FAREWELL TO

Fellow kickers of skulls,

What a wild ride it's been, eh? I'm so glad to have been a part of this journey, and even more so that you all have saddled up along with us for it. As Rex and Rolf (or, forever Baldy and Shorty to me) ride off into the high-octane sunset, I just wanted to thank you all for your support and to bid you a fond farewell!

I couldn't have worked with a better group of talented people on this comic. Thank you, Jim, for allowing me to be a part of this epic adventure! The story you put together has been a blast from issue to issue and I'm glad I got to see it unfold. Getting to color Edwin's fantastic art was such a privilege and I couldn't be more proud of what we were able to accomplish together with our wonder twin powers! Marshall's lettering was always top notch and really tied everything together in a nice, neat little face smashing package. Also, thanks to Ross and Mike for their tag team assistance with colors, which kept my sanity in check during some of the more pressing deadlines.

It's sad to see this tale end, but I'm so very proud of the work that everyone has done on it. I hope you all enjoyed reading as much as I enjoyed coloring for this comic.

To many more adventures and skullkicking!

-Misty Coats

Thanks to Jim and Edwin for letting me play in their sandbox, what a ride it's been! Thanks to Misty and the rest of the coloring crew for some of the best color work I've had the privilege of working on. Thanks to my wife Gina for understanding that Skullkickers is a labor of love.

- Marshall Dillon

I'd like to dedicate this last issue to the fans.

Thank you for the overwhelming support of the book throughout the years.

Next round is on me! Cheers!

- **Edwin Huang**

SKULL✦KICKERS

Done.

Yeah, it feels really weird even typing that.

Five years ago Edwin, Misty, Marshall, Chris, and I launched SKULLKICKERS. Since then it feels like the entire world has changed and, at least for me, it really has. Back then I wanted to prove that I could write a professional-quality comic and show people my storytelling skills. That unleashed hundreds of pages of comics for Image and a host of other publishers, meeting readers, peers, and lifelong heroes, travelling the convention circuit in North America and abroad and a whole new career as a comic writer.

"Comic writer."

Even just seeing that in front of me on the page, it seems impossible and surreal. People ask me what I do for a living and I tell them I'm a "comic writer." For real.

It sounds dramatic, but Skullkickers has changed my life. It became my own creative Crucible where I learned how to open myself up to new ideas, push through my fears, and carry through on my professional commitments. It's a rambling and childish yarn inspired by tabletop RPGs and the fantasy stories I grew up on but it's also a representation of me in the here and now as a creator. My creative journey doesn't end here, but this milestone is incredibly important to who I am as I look ahead to challenges still to come. Saying "thank you" for that kind of thing doesn't seem adequate, but I'll try.

Edwin Huang is one of the most professional and hard-working artists I know. His eagerness, energy, and dedication to this book that didn't even start off as his is staggering. No matter what ridiculous visuals I asked for, Edwin hunkered down and found a way to deliver it. Watching his art grow issue by issue, arc by arc has been one of the most rewarding aspects of working on the series. Whatever he works on next, it's going to be something special.

Misty Coats took Edwin's line art and made it explode on the page. Her animated color sense was always on target and she delivered her best right up until the very last page. We couldn't have done the book without her taking it to the next level each and every time.

Marshall Dillon is a rock. Solid, dependable, unflappable. His lettering took a whirlwind of disparate ideas and brought them together in a way that made even the most ludicrous things I wrote flow across each page. They say good lettering feels invisible because you're too busy enjoying the story to realize how effortlessly the captions and balloons guide you across the page and that's exactly what Marshall did. Great flow, unforgettable onomatopoeia.

The rest of the pitch hitters: Kevin, Ross, Mike, Espen, Chamba, Royce, and all the wonderful writers and artists who lent their talents to our Tavern Tales short stories – you rock. You made something fun even better and helped forge lasting friendships.

Thank you to Eric Stephenson and the rest of the Image Comics crew. Your unshakable support for this book has been wonderful. I can't believe we were able to take it this far. Thank you for your expertise, your guidance, and good humor. I should probably also thank all the far-more profitable Image creators whose successes helped create Image's stalwart cash flow reserves for printing and distribution.

The readers who stuck with us, the retailers who helped push the book, convention promoters who brought us out to shows, the people who have shared the book with their friends... There are too many people to thank and I wish I could high-five you all right now.

Chris Stevens asked me if I wanted to make a short comic story with him back in 2007. Eight years later it's become the foundation of my creative career. Thank you, Chris. Your stunning artwork put this series on the map and I'm thrilled you were able to contribute the final cover to wrap it all up.

I hope that if you've all learned anything by reading this, it's that stories are eternal. We're closing this particular book but I'd optimistically like to think that out across the infinite these characters and their foolishness will live on.

-**Jim Zub**

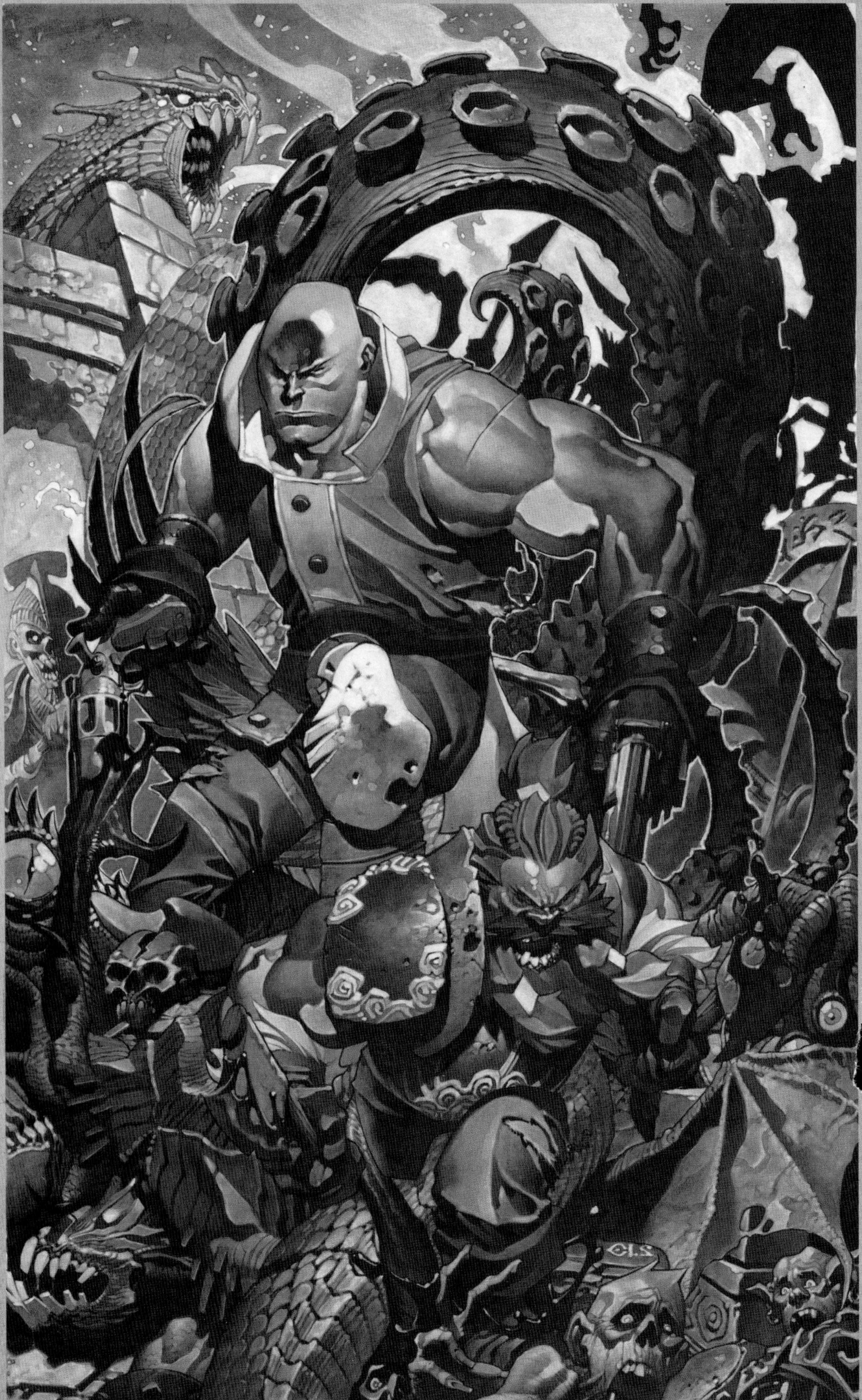